Dreams and Baseball

(All Nine Innings)

Reagan Rothe

Black Rose Writing

www.blackrosewriting.com

The final approval for this literary material is granted by the author.

First printing

ISBN: 978-1-61296-106-4

PUBLISHED BY BLACK ROSE WRITING

www.blackrosewriting.com

Printed in the United States of America

Dreams and Baseball is printed in Book Antiqua

Other Books by Reagan Rothe

Misanthropy: Book I: The Tower

Misanthropy: Book II: The Cellar Door

Give Wings to My Triumph

blacke

Dreams and Baseball
Is dedicated to...

My grandfather, Leslie "Tex" Aulds
—Boston Red Sox (Ted Williams' roommate)
—Scranton Red Sox (Top 100 minor league teams of all-time)
—Louisville Colonels (Severely spiked in hand, 27 stitches)
—Plymouth Oilers (Won the NBC Texas Championship)

My father, Walt Rothe
—Jamestown Expos (Signed by Montreal Expos after college)
—Univ. of Texas Longhorns (1-Time SWC Player of the Year)

And my brother, Ryan Rothe
—Alexandria Aces (2-Time TLL Champions, 3-Time All-Star)
—Shreveport Sports (Deemed one of the best defensive CF's)
—Univ. of Texas Longhorns (Traveled to CWS in Omaha)

(Three generations of great baseball!)

In loving memory,

Leslie "Tex" Aulds & Bonnard Rothe

AUTHOR'S NOTE

Dreams and Baseball, the complete works at last. This project has taken me over eleven years to complete. I cannot think of anything that I have started at one time in my life, and then finished it after a decade of on and off bold efforts.

This wasn't like the *Misanthropy series* or *blacke.* True, *Dreams and Baseball* is also fiction, like the others, but there was so much authenticity I wanted to portray through the fictional baseball season: the stats, the boxscores, the numbers and the legitimacy they derived from, it was all real. Every batting average and earned run average to every homer and every run scored, no number was just "inserted" because it looked right; no, my dear reader, that number was real, simulated and pulled from within me.

So grab some peanuts or crackerjack and enjoy, whether you are watching the Yankees-Red Sox, or Dodgers-Giants, or Cardinals-Cubs before you pick up this book for another reading session.

I want to thank my wife, Minna, for her love and support as always. I would also like to thank my editor, Morten Rand; my sister, Robin Simmons, for a second look; and Tommy Wilson, for giving me the final motivational speech that I needed to finish.

At the end of the book, I have inserted some of the actual notes and handwritten boxes; hopefully this will also add to the overall feel and true impression. This was part of me, something I was eager yet scared to finish. Yet now it's complete, and I feel relieved.

A baseball story.

Dreams and Baseball

(All Nine Innings)

(Top of the Inning)

WELCOMING THE DREAMS

I

"High fly ball hit by Allen to centerfield. Lewis takes a few steps back, and makes the catch. That ends the fifth, Demons one, Knights nothing. Due up for Los Angeles in the sixth, Parks, Hicks, and Gunn," Darrell Marinville announces to the Demon faithful.

Jogging in from second, I wonder how in the hell I can hear Marinville doing the radio broadcast. After all, Marinville is in the booth, I am standing on the field. The announcer is glassed in and speaking over the radio, I am entering the dugout via the infield. Kyle Queen's voice is the one spilling through the loudspeakers throughout Diego Field, not Marinville's. Queen's the one I should be hearing, along with the fans.

So let me say it again, because it's worth repeating. I can hear Darrell "The Duke" Marinville's broadcast, along with Kyle Queen's announcing over the loudspeakers, and finally, the buzzing of the crowd altogether.

I sit in the left side corner of the always-rectangular bench. I can smell sweat in the air, tasting the cool, refreshing breeze turned sour. The smell reminds me of going to Dodgers games in the early 90s. Me and pops, having the time of our lives while rooting for one of the greatest coaches of my youth, Mr. Lasorda. *But who other than Tommy Lasorda?* And his extremely vocal, and sometimes outrageous, rants —

I remember I always ordered the same things around

the same innings. Right before the fourth or fifth, Dad would make a run to the concession stand and grab a couple of hotdogs and a Dr. Pepper, along with a beer for himself. We would heckle the opposing team's rightfielder from our second row outfield seats, and hope to God that Pedro Guerrero would hit one out in our section. Man, I wanted a homerun ball bad... I never got one. But this jerkoff next to us caught several homers throughout the season. But that's beside the point.

Actually, the point isn't very clear. I lean back into the wall, befuddled by the fact that I couldn't stop hearing the Duke. I mean come on, is this possible? I am literally sitting here in the dugout listening to the man who is supposed to be the Demons' radio guy call the game in my ears—in my head. Not possible, is it?

The brash, yet smooth-flowing announcer's voice rattles on, "Here's a recap for the fans who may have missed one of the earlier games in this dazzling series. The Demons took game one in San Diego five-to-three, but San Diego's offense came alive in game two to get the split. The final was San Diego nine, L.A. two. They headed to Los Angeles for games three and four, where the Knights got a great performance from Erwin Hammel, who threw eight shutout innings and helped San Diego blank L.A. three-to-nothing.

Once again, though, like the Demons have done all year long, they battled back. This L.A. team left the yard three times, with homers from Jason Hicks, Bobby Parks, and Nathan Willis (hearing the name stings my side; it aches my heart for reasons unknown), leading the home team to a six-four victory and a trip back to San Diego. Jacques Martin injured his knee in that game on a bang-bang play at first, and it sure looks as though San Diego is missing his bat in the lineup right now."

The sounds are getting unbearable. The crowd's constant static (chit-chatter and cheering — continuous level of noise throughout the game) enter into my mind through one ear, while the Duke's broadcast in the other ear, and the dugout conversation enters my auditory system from God knows where. I can't take anymore, *the noise, the freaking noise.* I try to focus my attention elsewhere, gazing into the sky. The moon is full (the man is smiling at me as if to say 'nothing you can do Hartes, don't fight the noise') and the stars shine bright. *The noise, the noise,* blaring from every direction.

I turn my attention southward into the stands. People visiting, yelling, kids eating popcorn, hotdogs, drinking sodas. But as I roam the San Diego crowd, one girl (she appears to be glowing) catches my eye as she makes her way down the stairs. Still, *the noise,* coming from everywhere.

Coming from inside my mind... coming from outside my skull...

The noise, the noise —

"Jeff... Jeff, wake up!" Shae's voice filled the room, the sound seeming to be coming from a mile away. "Jeff! Stop saying that!"

"What? Saying what?" he asked her, waking up and trying to lift his heavy eyelids off of his drowsy eyes.

"Quit saying, 'I wish the noise from everywhere would just stop.'" Jeff looked at Shae with a confused face. "You said it like ten times, hun'."

"Sorry... damn. Bad dream, I guess." A slight pause, then the look on her face transformed from frustration to one of concern. Her eyebrows rose, and then lowered. "Not a bad dream, a weird dream."

"About what?" Shae asked, now calm, eager to listen. That was one of her most brilliant traits. No matter how her own day went, or how much she had on her mind, Shae always seemed prepared to listen—and listen intently. She made the person speaking to her feel as though they were the only person in the world worth receiving her undivided attention. To Jeff, it was mere magic. Simply because he typically didn't give a damn about hearing what most people had to say.

"I can't remember," Jeff replied, changing the subject whether he tried to or not. "I really can't remember." He said the last part of his answer with some doubt, but could he remember? It felt like a word that is on the tip of your tongue and once the situation is over... you remember it. But he couldn't remember anything at this moment.

Maybe it will come back to me—

Jeff closed his eyes and tried to focus on whatever Shae might have been talking about. Nothing came to his mind that might have helped, only an image of Shae and him making love as they did almost every night. Except on the occasional hot streaks or drastic slumps, where Jeff needed a change. He began to caress Shae's back while kissing her neck. His hands reached downward towards—

Shae pushed him, realizing his thoughts had diverted from the bad dream to something that had drawn a harmless, yet deviant smile on his face.

"What was that for?" he asked, feeling his excitement disappear as quickly as it had come, showing signs of sexual simplicity much like a light switch turning a room from bright to dark.

"Never mind, baby, let's go get some breakfast." Shae hopped up, grabbed Jeff's hands, and pulled him out of the bed. Jeff realized he wasn't going to get what he wanted this morning, so he went along without resisting.

II

That's when the dreams first started, early April. They halted as quickly as they came, within a year of my life's time on this Earth. It was the most memorable and forever lasting thing that ever occurred to me, and I'm positive nothing will surpass it now. I never had another season similar to the one in 1999 with the Demons. I've also never had a year similar to that one. I've never experienced anything like it... period. It was the greatest season, the scariest season, and the only season of its kind balled into one very small frame of time.

My loneliness continues to grow like the swelling of a sponge when it comes in contact with water. All I have now are my memories and my recollection—not always accurate, I may add—of the way things were. I lost my best friend a long, long time ago during the season with the Demons. My little brother died of the Big 'C' in 2030. Another short-lived, yet accomplished life that cancer destroyed. I tried to run away and hide from my feelings, but Shae wouldn't let me then, as she wouldn't have let me when my son, Jeffrey Jr., died in a car accident at the age of 35 (with one divorce and no kids to show for it). But I had Shae to cry on and keep everything together. She was always the stronger one between us, never showing defeat or remorse, but continuing on, as she believed God had meant her to do. But now when something goes wrong, I just want to travel to that great "Field of Dreams" in the sky. Maybe meet up with "Shoeless" Joe Jackson and get his side of the White Sox 1919 scandal. Or try and hit a couple of Bob Gibson's sliders out to deep rightfield. Or possibly look through Teddy Ballgame's eyes, picking up the seam's rotation on a hanging "Charlie." Or even just sit back in the dugout, watching the greatest team, the '27 Yankees, play on their way to another unprecedented World Series title. Who knows? Just who goddamn knows?

Now, I just wish it would end soon, living my life without my son and without Shae is unbearable. If it wasn't for Leslie, I'd have done myself in by now. I'd have pulled the trigger and ended this arthritic misery—a banged up ex-major leaguer with bad knees, stiff wrists and a limp pecker. What did Leslie say the difference between a young golfer and an old golfer was? Something like an old golfer has stiff wrists and a limp pecker, and a young one has limp wrist and a stiff... forget it.

Shae passed away exactly one year ago today, April 1st, 2051. The "Best" April fool's joke I've ever been hit with, I just couldn't believe it. The doctors did everything they could, but her body just couldn't press on any longer. Pressing on was all her body ever did; it always seemed to be telling her 'next challenge, please.' She never looked back the way I did—I, always wishing to repeat 1999 over and over again no matter the circumstance—she, always looking forward to the next year and what it brought. She always did her best to enhance her life as well as everyone's around her.

With her unbelievable patience... with her untiring dedication to those she loved. Sometimes, it made me sick (in a good way if that's possible). It made me feel less of a man as she continued to put this same demeanor, same attitude, across her beautiful face day after day. If it were me doing the same, everyone would have seen through my charade. But Shae's concerning manner was no fallacy.

I spent exactly 2 months and 12 days in the "Big's" (Major League Baseball) with the Minnesota Twins. I won't lie and say that it wasn't a boyhood dream of mine, but it wasn't a defining moment. Meeting Shae, the love of my life, the greatest thing that ever happened to me, wasn't a defining moment either. Nothing was, nothing is, and nothing ever will be, compared to the dreams. Nothing but the dreams... they defined my life and changed it forever. The dreams are the one thing (the dreams and them alone) I can remember, in spite of everything that has happened to me, just fine.

"I remember those days, nineteen ninety-nine especially, when I was six feet tall with light brown hair gelled perfectly in place. I remember the handsome face I once had that only needed a fresh shave once a week. I remember the young man who would flex shirtless in the mirror, admiring his build. A body that wasn't utterly muscle-bounded, but cut enough to cause the ladies to go wild. It didn't matter what food I ate, or how late I ate out, or whether or not I even touched the weights, I had a naturally toned body that made others jealous because of my ease in maintaining it.

And I remember my beautiful wife, Shae. Not my wife during the dreams, during the ninety-nine season, but my wife to be. The long, straight brown hair that lightly fell down her back. Her always intriguing and thoughtful blue eyes, never leaving me when I had something to say to her and always aware of everything around her. Her breasts, her legs, her body, her smile, all perfect in 'Jeff Hartes' book of women,' nothing more satisfying than caressing a woman's body that maintained its softness and smoothness each and every time.

Finally, Shae's face... blue eyes, subtle and definitive features, and a short, pointed nose comparative to the girl on the old television series "Buffy The Vampire Slayer." The girl's name, Sarah Michelle Gellar, never entered my thoughts, as I immediately pushed my mind back to 1999. I remember... leaving Shae after breakfast. She had to go to work at around noon. I remember traveling back home, taking a nap, and then heading out to pick up my order at L.A. Sports. Shae always seemed to know I was going to make the Demons' team, despite my own confidence, I wasn't saying it was a guarantee. I arrived at the local Los Angeles sporting goods store and—"

Chapter One
Demon Baseball

I

Jeff gathered his order; it consisted of a couple of bats, several batting gloves, and some Hawken's, the traditional baseball tobacco. Just in case one might need a 'rally dip.' The teenage girl at the counter smiled and asked if that was all he needed. He returned the smile, trying not to flirt too openly in the process. He said yes and carried everything to his truck, stopping to hold the door open for a middle-aged woman and her son. Tomorrow was his first tryout for a professional team.

Jeff played baseball at the University of California, but dropped out due to grades... or lack thereof. He recalled the day when he was supposed to be a star second baseman on full scholarship at Cal, driving in runs and playing stellar 'D' for the Golden Bears, but it didn't happen that way. The change from growing up in a small town outside of Los Angeles to the big city was too much. He enjoyed the night crowd and partying too often, and hardly ever hit the books.

Now he was settled in as a banker's assistant who makes just enough to get by. Damn shitty job if you'd ask him. He wanted to get back into baseball and get a second crack at things, but if it hadn't been for Shae's persistence, he wouldn't have had this opportunity. Shae's voice was always ringing in his head, saying 'Jeff Anthony Hartes, are you going to wake up and make something of yourself today or be content with your life at the age of twenty-one?'

He arrived home around 8:30 in the evening and flipped through some cable channels before landing on *Cheers*. Usually, the television settled on *Sportscenter*, but tonight, with baseball on his mind, comedy appeared to be the answer. Jeff slid on a pair of orange Coca-Cola boxers, and collapsed into the blue air mattress camped out in his living room. One of his old college buddies (one of those friends that aren't really your 'best' or 'true' friends, but are fun to see every so often) crashed at his apartment a few nights earlier, and Jeff hadn't gotten around to putting the aired-up bed back in the closet.

As he tried to drift off to sleep, all he could think about was whether he was good enough to make the Demons' team. Hell... Shae thought he was, but only in a pleasing, supportive manner. Yet, right now, at this restless juncture in time, he wasn't quite sure if he *was* good enough. After all, they were a Triple-A club in the highest level of independent leagues. A league transformed under ex-big leaguers, who were both too old and wearing down or had suffered an injurious setback, or all-star caliber youngsters, who were trying to impress major league scouts and make a name for themselves one day. This league was the last stepping stone before walking into a major league clubhouse with the likes of Tony La Russa or Joe Torre. That's where Jeff Hartes was hoping to fit in.

Jeff stared into the ceiling, listening to Norm make a joke about how he would rather spend an evening with Cliff in the park than go home to Myra. He heard the voices and laughing in the Boston bar on TV, but his eyes were fixed on the ceiling, and his thoughts were on baseball. He rolled over and let his eyes close themselves;

once again hearing laughter after Sam asked Rebecca, 'when was the last time she had gotten laid?'

The next morning, Jeff woke up to his alarm going off at 7:30. His drive to the stadium was only 15-20 minutes (if traffic was flowing), and the team he was trying out for was the Los Angeles Demons; a team he had grown up watching as a kid, and then throughout his years of high school and failed attempt at college. Living in the same city now and so nearby to the Demons was really convenient for tryouts, and he hoped to make it a permanent fit.

The camp started at nine, so Jeff stopped at the local *Mickey D's* and grabbed a couple of sausage biscuits. He made sure to tell the girl at the counter to add cheese to his breakfast. Jeff loved cheese on just about any meal, from breakfast tacos to hamburgers to grated cheese on a chef salad. Melted cheese smothering broccoli didn't hurt either. He slammed down the biscuits despite not being in a hurry.

He checked in with the Demons' front office around 8:40. Since he had some time to kill, he went to the Demon Stadium Hall of Sports, where they displayed the Western League's entire history. Jeff saw that this was going to be the league's fifteenth year of existence. The league was designed for superstars (young and old) to have a chance to participate in a shortened season — less wear and tear on their bodies — while still playing the second highest level of baseball; second only to the MLB. The league was less than two decades old, but was already receiving tons of notoriety and prestige. When the product was good, it sold. Besides, many of the players could be optioned to play in other independent leagues throughout the season.

As Jeff scanned the wall of plaques and team rosters, he paused to read the league's most recent champions: 1995 Western League Champs: *Canada Internationals,* 1996

Western League Champs: *Canada Internationals*, 1997
Western League Champs: *Canada Internationals*, 1998
Western League Champs: *Carson City Gamblers*.

The *Canada Internationals* were disbanded in '97, and the owner took over the Montana Tigers. The Canadian team was mostly composed of major league veterans and Canadian all-stars (not many...). They didn't have the same salary cap and roster regulations, so it hurt the league considerably.

No wonder they dominated the league for three straight years. It would have been nice to play on that roster and be able to get paid over the salary limitations, Jeff thought.

Jeff checked the 1999 team list to see who was in the league for this year. Changes were constantly being made to the league structure, depending on individual team's fan support and income. As a whole, the product was very stable and solid. But every now and then, no matter how good something is, there are always a couple of things (teams) that aren't quite producing as well as the rest.

The North Division contained the *Washington Thunder*, *Carson City Gamblers*, *Montana Tigers*, and the *Cal Gold Miners*. The South Division had the *San Diego Knights*, *Tucson Sun Devils*, *Arizona Scorpions*, and (hopefully) his own *Los Angeles Demons*.

A tall, lanky man with slick combed hair called Jeff into the clubhouse with all of the infielders and told the group to go out on the field and hit. He looked like one of the greasers off of *The Outsiders*. Jeff later found out that the man was one of the Anaheim Angels' top scouts, sitting in the stands and checking out the new season's crop.

Jeff was going to be competing for the two available spots, based on his possible positions, starting second baseman and utility infielder. The Demons were also looking for another catcher and some pitchers, but there were no guarantees on any of the positions. Fresh talent and potential "phenoms" outshone any teams' needs (plus keeping the salary cap down also helped).

Jeff met some of the stadium workers and corporate sponsors standing around behind homeplate sipping on soft drinks and enjoying the tryouts. Through good marketing techniques, the Demons' front office zealously (perhaps overzealously... if that's even a word) kept their business associates and moneymakers happy. And one step for the key to happiness included making them feel involved and part of the team—maybe even part of the decision making in a controlled form.

The tryouts were started with the players running timed 'sixties.' Most coaches and scouts, depending on a player's position, of course, typically demanded the time to be under seven seconds in the sixty-yard dash. Hartes waited his turn, watching the other infielders go, none of them exceptionally fast.

"Jeff Hartes," a man in his thirties called out, appearing to be the Demons' trainer or another form of assistant. Jeff said, 'Right here,' and entered the marked off timing area.

He bent down into a runner's starting position, nodding his head to say he was ready. He waited for the whistle, and then exploded into full sprint. He dashed straight through the finish, slowly braking to a halt. Huffing and puffing, Jeff did a quick maintenance check: *Ankles... good. Knees...still there. Hammy's... never better.*

"Six... five... nine," a man with a stopwatch called back to the Demons' trainer/assistant, who was marking down the times on a yellow notebook.

"Fastest time so far," the recorder said after checking

all the times he'd penciled.

Still got a little speed left...

Hartes' time was only beaten once, by an outfielder who wasn't very impressive in the other drills, especially the cage.

Next stop—fielding and throwing. Hartes did exceptionally well in this drill also. He didn't make any errors during a session of hard hit ground balls or during double play work. His throwing was also fine. So far, he had three of the five stars, even though throwing for a second baseman didn't require the strongest, cannon-like arm.

Taking a break from the physical aspects of the game, the players trying out were now required to show them they could master the mental aspects. Like the NFL combine, they were given a series of timed tests, along with a brief session of learning a few baseball signs and then relaying them back.

Jeff was pleased with his all-around performance in the mental department as well. But he didn't truly know how he fared against the others or how much emphasis the Demons' coaches were placing on that department.

The last drill involved the Demons' assistant head coach, also the pitching coach, who began firing pitches into the batting cage. One by one, players followed orders and stepped into the box to take their cuts, being rated and looked over closely. After about seven other guys hit live, none of them turning heads, Jeff found himself next in line. The curly-haired blond with a dimple in his chin so deep that Jeff could see it from homeplate motioned him into the batting cage. The pitching coach on the mound hollered for Jeff to get in there and take a few hacks.

Jeff Hartes hit the first two out into the leftfield seats, drawing a response from diehard Demon fans scattered in the seats before opening day. He smacked the next few pitches up the middle and finished with some opposite field line drives. *Did I ever quit playing baseball?* he thought. Just like screwing, once you know how, you never forget. Or was that supposed to be riding a bike? Either way—

"Good piece of hitting there, kid," said the assistant coach as Jeff stepped out of the box. That same coach, Larry George, would later compare Hartes' approach at the plate to that of Derek Jeter's. He was willing to fight off pitches and drive the ball to the other field if necessary. He had a rare hitting trait, which was getting his hands through the zone in an inside-out manner, doing whatever possible to take the ball the other way. He used his baseball knowledge to his advantage, never trying to be bigger than the team. His individual stats came second to winning— came second to making a productive out.

"Thanks," Hartes replied, walking toward the dugout to get a drink of H-two-O. The coach began firing pitches to the next hitter, repeating the same pattern of pitches.

After everybody was through getting their licks, Jeff got to meet some of the other players and B.S. for awhile. The first time he met Will, he knew that he really liked him. Will had something about him that was unique, grasping in a way that Jeff knew he could get accustomed to being around if he could only make the club.

Will stood about five-foot-eleven and weighed approximately 190 pounds. His stocky build and muscular toning showed off even better on his dark skin. Will had short black hair (Michael Irvin's style, Super Bowl days, without the lines) and a freshly trimmed goatee. The type of goatee with straight edges all the way down from his mouth to his chin, looking as fresh as though it was professionally groomed. Will was the starting shortstop for the Demons, playing in his fourth season with the team.

Will chatted with Jeff about the team's previous successes and failures and the lack of defense the Demons had at second base. Will said that L.A. went through three second basemen last year, all of them ending up out of the league, and none of them able to field a ball to save their own tail. One of them even had a case of the Chuck Knoblauch, throwing routine grounders over the first baseman's head and into the stands.

Will started to walk away and then turned back. Jeff was going to say goodbye when Will interrupted, "I'm looking forward to working next to ya' rook."

"What do you mean?" Jeff asked, wondering if what Will was saying could be true, wondering if Will was the kind of guy to mess with somebody or not. Jeff didn't think so. The butterflies that weren't there while he was in the batting cage had now begun to flutter in his stomach.

"You made the team, Hartes," Will said back to Jeff with a grin on his face. Will Coleman waived a quick goodbye and jogged towards the clubhouse. Jeff almost started running around in circles, wanting to tell everyone, 'Fuck you, I made the team.' He also wanted to run over to Will and give him a hug.

"But don't go around preachin' it, just letting you know so you won't have to sweat it out," Will shouted before exiting the field, as if he could read Jeff's mind. As if Will knew how excited Jeff was and that Jeff might announce the good news to everyone.

"Thanks, Will," Jeff said even though Will had already disappeared behind closed doors and into the clubhouse. He trotted off the field, and then stopped, dropping to the ground. Jeff smelled the fresh-cut grass and breathed in America's national pastime full throttle. "Looking forward to working with you, too."

II

The next day, after hearing the news of making the Los Angeles Demons squad from Head Coach Skip Bailey himself, Jeff arrived at his first team meeting and practice. In baseball, there weren't very many days off and things got busy immediately. It was Shae's day off (Thursday), though, so they had a nice dinner planned after baseball wrapped up. He saw Will again and met two of the bullpen pitchers, Fred Sanders and Salmon Seavers.

They were both considered veterans, already having been to the show and back. Fred was in his early 40's, and had a chiseled veteran look. He had been to war against some of the best hitters in the American League; McGwire, Mattingly, Boggs, etc... Fred's dark brown hair was receding and had a few streaks of gray above his ears. What was left of his body was flab and softness brought on by age. The only thing he had left were his wits and a magical limb attached to his right shoulder. "I've got to outthink these young punks, including you," Sanders had told Jeff in their earlier conversation.

Salmon was in his late 20's. He was a handsome black man with glowing yellow eyes. You could almost believe that his eyes lit up at night like a cat's. Salmon's work ethic was ritual, and his body showed it. He had a rocket for an arm and his launching pad was his durable and stocky legs. He had a razor bald head that only added to the intimidation others felt around him. And complementing his vigorous look was a jet black patch of hair on his chin. His only pitching problem was that he tended to get a little erratic and wild at times; therefore, he was sent back down by the Giants a few years earlier to work on his control.

After standing around and visiting for awhile, it was time for the team meeting to begin. When Jeff entered the meeting room, he was speechless. *Wow!* he thought. It was bright, he felt like he was in Heaven, and it had an abundance of plaques and trophies. Most of the hardware belonged to the Demons and anything surrounding the organization, but some of the awards were also Greg Viselli's. He was the Demons' Owner/General Manager, and had played a few years in the major leagues as well. Viselli not only knew the business side of running an organization, but also the sporting side. Jeff sat amongst the many players in the room. The sofa was so damn comfortable, he almost dozed off. The meeting got under way.

"Welcome to pro ball, rooks. I'm Skip Bailey, your head coach, and this here is Larry George, your pitching and assistant coach. Now we've already met the new acquisitions from free agency and the sort at our first meeting, before we picked up you, hopefully the last pieces of the puzzle." Skip was aiming his conversation to the four rookies signed from spring training.

"The first thing I tell all my new players are my own personal, three rules: First, show up to practice on time, nothing pisses me off more than players late for practice. Second, play the games a hundred and ten percent. No cadillacing or fucking around out there. And finally, no banging women, especially game regulars, during your hot streaks unless it's your wife. Follow those, and we can look forward to a championship season. We are one of the favorites, ya' know?"

"Hell Yeah, Skip. We'll be ready to kick some ass," replied one of the ballplayers in the back of the meeting room. The words flowed from his mouth with an experienced swagger. He was huge, not all muscle, but not all fat either, just a triple-x large, t-shirt wearing first baseman. At least first base was Jeff's guess, but your guess was as good as his. The "first baseman's" thick beard was a creamy chocolate color, which made him look slightly older than he probably really was. He had short, straggly hair, about the same length as his beard. His left cheek bulged, holding a fresh scoop of Hawken's.

Skip continued, "Now it's time to meet this year's team for all you newcomers. It sometimes helps to get things off on a smoother note. We'll begin with the starting pitchers, Jay O'Dell, age twenty-eight, right-handed. Umm... Thomas Perry, age thirty, another righty. Micheal Tims, one of our rookies we picked up, age nineteen, right-handed. Lake 'Lefty' Williams, age twenty-eight, southpaw. Now for the bullpen, Fred 'Funk' Sanders, age fifty-five."

"Ha, ha, yeah, woo-hoo!" All the players started laughing and shouting when Skip said Fred Sanders was '55.' The aged pitcher only grinned and stared at the coach. Jeff could tell that the two of them had known each other closely, or at least close enough to not take anything personal.

Skip continued once the noise quieted down. "Fred Sanders, age forty-one, right-handed. Salmon Seavers, age twenty-nine, southpaw. Darren Luthers, age twenty-five, righty. Javier Jimenez, another one of our pick-ups, from the Dominican Republic, age twenty-two, righty. This guy can throw some heat. The infielders are first baseman Steve 'Big Daddy' Gunn, —" Jeff's guess was right— "age thirty, second baseman's Simon Luthers, that's Darren's lil' brother, age twenty-three, and our new recruit, Jeff Hartes, age twenty-one. Lives here full time in L.A."

When Jeff heard his name, it sent waves across his

body. It was a good feeling, the first time he really felt like somebody. Jeff Hartes, professional athlete, what a thrill. It sure beat the hell out of anything he had previously accomplished, and this was something he truly did want for himself. His family would be proud as well.

Skip continued, "Shortstop Will Coleman, age twenty-six, third baseman Jason Hicks, age twenty-six, last year's South Division MVP. Across the outfield we have leftfielder Erric Rutherford, age twenty-three, centerfielder Damon Lewis, age twenty-two, rightfielder Billy Goodwin, age twenty-seven, and in reserve is the 'Vet' himself, Brett Chambers, age thirty-five. Behind the plate we have Ron Fetters, age thirty-three, and Bobby 'Leave Tha' Parks, age twenty. He's the final rookie on the team. That's it fellas... no practice today, y'all get a good night's sleep and be back here at eleven-thirty sharp."

Jeff started to leave with the rest of the players, and then Skip said, "Hartes, Tims, Jimenez, Parks. Y'all four need to stay so we can finish working out your contracts."

"Alright," the foursome said simultaneously.

"Hartes, you come in first!"

"Yes, sir."

Jeff entered Bailey's office behind him and sat in a gray metal chair. It was one of those chairs you find at a convention or at a graduation, row after row. The office was nice, small but cozy. The walls were painted a natural wood brown, and the floor was covered with a dark shade of blue carpet. Skip had a few pictures of himself in his baseball days (including a picture of him and Rod Carew), but besides the pictures and a desk, don't forget the chair, the office was pretty much empty.

When Coach Bailey plopped down in his black leather chair behind the desk, Jeff noticed the signs of a so-called 'beer belly' beginning to take form on Skip's body. The coach, with a wad of chewing tobacco tucked up against the inside of his cheek, appeared to have aged rapidly since his playing days. His face was wrinkled, and he carried a two-inch long scar on his neck.

His spectacles hung gently over his nose as he read the contract he was about to hand to Jeff. He skipped through the pages quickly and said, "In this league, most good rookie prospects get around fifteen-to-twenty-five thousand a year, to be honest, Jeff." He continued flipping through pages, apparently reading some few finer points and then proceeded to the next page of the document. Skip stopped scanning the contract and raised his head. He looked at Jeff and said:

"You looked better than most rooks. I've got a feeling about you, and that's not just some corn-fed bullshit. I'm expecting results, so I've decided to put a little preseason pressure on you and up the ante. The club has decided to offer you a little bit more than usual.

"Tell me, Hartes, how does this sound? A two-year contract... thirty-four thousand the first year, and if you have a good year, we'll option you to forty thousand the second year. Uhh, also, you'll get a three-thousand signing bonus. So what do you—"

"I'll take it!" Jeff replied without even thinking. He really didn't care, knowing it was more than he was making (or ever had made), and he could make this money doing something that he loved. *The most beautifully crafted game in the world... the game of baseball.*

"You're sure you don't want to look over this some more? Think about it a little?" Skip asked, raising the contract in his hand.

"Not really, coach. I just wanna' play."

"I like the attitude. That's good shit, Hartes. You gotta' deal," Skip said, extending out his hand.

After shaking hands, Jeff decided to scan through the printed contract. It only took him a few seconds, and then he signed at the bottom, and said, "See ya' mañana, coach."

"Hey Hartes, call me Skip," the coach said, handing Jeff a copy of the contract.

The new second baseman nodded and left the office. When he arrived home, he called his parents to let them know the good news. They were really happy for him. You know how it is… their loser son finally lived up to some of the expectations and did something with his almost totally screwed up life.

Besides Jeff's good news regarding the Demons, there was also some other family things they discussed. His dad told him that Eric had been really working on his hitting in the batting cages. "You should see 'em, Jeff. He's swinging the bat better than ever. You know he always had a great glove and good arm, but now that the offensive part of his game's coming around, it's going to be trouble for those opposing him."

Jeff agreed with his dad about his brother's hot stick. He knew, as his father did, that Eric's defense was superb, but he was lacking offensively if he wanted to hang with the big boys. Knowing that his brother was putting in the hard work pumped Jeff up even more.

Next, Jeff called his admirer, Shae. She was so excited and wanted to go out and celebrate, but her boss had called and needed her to come in and work late.

"Didn't you get my messages, Jeff?" Shae asked.

"Haven't checked 'em yet, but it's okay, I understand," he said. *Shit…* Jeff thought. He wanted to see her so badly, but he also felt exhausted, and sleep sounded pretty damn good itself. "I think I am just going to cook some supper and get some much needed sleep, okay baby?"

"Okay, I'll talk to you tomorrow," Shae said, also discouraged and missing her boyfriend. Her love infatuation responded with 'okay' and then they said their byes.

Jeff cooked supper, throwing a few eggs and bacon in the skillet and putting some toast in the toaster. And don't forget the cheese. He added a couple of slices of cheese to the eggs and bacon, completing the meal. Jeff realized what a mess his apartment was while grease popped in the frying pan.

He hardly ever cleaned up, just when women came over, now just Shae, or when he needed to use something that was dirty, such as clothes, dishes, glasses, so on.... Jeff sat down and started eating supper. All he could think about (besides Shae) was his paycheck. Tomorrow, he was getting a check for three grand. *Three large...I'm going to go buy whatever the hell I want.*

The most money the ex-banker's assistant had ever had in his hand at one time seemed to be around three or four hundred dollars, but a check for $3,000? It was almost too much. *Not really.* He sat there at the table for about an hour longer, thinking, and then he hit the sack.

III

Jeff Anthony Hartes woke up surprisingly fresh at 9:30, to the sound of a ringing phone. He answered the phone. It was Skip telling him practice had changed to four in the afternoon.

Jeff thought this was a good opportunity to grab lunch with Shae, but she was probably at work and too busy (or tired) to meet him somewhere in town. Shae worked only ten minutes from the stadium, but on the other side.

So Jeff decided to eat a late breakfast instead, and then afterwards, head downtown to get some new cleats. After all, he was getting a check for 'three grand' later that day. He ate at *Maria's Diner* and read the morning news. The sports page featured an article on Mark McGwire and whether he could break his own homerun record of 70. *No one's ever going to break that record. Seventy bombs, not a freakin' chance in hell.*

And then a few years later, Jeff would witness Barry Bonds hit 73 homeruns, shattering McGwire's mark. Steroids or no steroids, Bonds could swing a freakin' bat. A little juice couldn't make a bad hitter a good hitter; it did nothing for the hand-eye and so on... but it could make a player's "just-missed it" homerun swing travel just over the fence. But as of today, it didn't matter. The record was an even seventy.

Jeff would soon learn, being inside the ropes, most of the players' opinions of the steroids in baseball. Many of them the same and along these lines: after the strike, fans weren't filling the seats. So Mr. Bud Selig pulled two of the biggest stars, McGwire and Sammy Sosa, into his office, telling them to stick a needle in their ass and hit homeruns. The fans loved it, and the stadiums began to fill again, everyone forgetting the strike. So now baseball's best hitter, Barry Bonds, thought to himself, 'Look at this shit, these guys think they can hit, let's see what the best can do with a little juice.' To keep the story short, Bonds went on to hit 73, win multiple MVP's, and become (performance-enhancing or not) one of the greatest hitters ever. And then the shit hit the fan, steroids became the number one agenda for the media, and Bud Selig had to do what most leaders do, throw everyone else under the bus to save his own ass.

Hartes finished eating. The check for the pancakes and

sausage (plus orange juice) came out to $8.87, and Jeff paid it on the way out the door. He headed back downtown to the Westside Pavilion Mall and Shopping Outlet. He scanned over several pairs of shoes before deciding on a black pair of *Nike's* in the third store he looked in. They were solid black except for a white *Nike* symbol and white laces. Plus, they fit just right. Jeff never was partial to flashy shoes. He preferred plain, but high grade.

As he purchased the shoes, Jeff peeked at some of the newer model baseball gloves behind the counter. 'Maybe I should buy a new glove?' he thought.

On the other hand, Jeff had had his own glove since his senior year in high school, and he realized he wouldn't trade it for anything. Besides, his old glove had many diving catches and leaping grabs still left in it.

What else do I need?

"I guess nothing else," Jeff answered aloud, looking around to make sure no one heard him as he exited the store.

On his way back to the apartment, Jeff stopped and picked up lunch (preparing for the future rather than any immediate hunger) at *Super Ray's Chicken*—the best in L.A.—and then continued home. He relaxed for awhile, occasionally cleaning a few things in his apartment in a disorderly fashion. This stirred his appetite, and he paused to open his chicken box on the counter.

He ate his food, two chicken breasts and a wing combo, a Coke to drink, and then took a short nap until three o'clock. When Jeff woke up, he put on all of his practice clothes, and headed for Demon Stadium. He arrived at the clubhouse around 3:45 p.m. and checked in with management.

The first person he bumped into was Viselli, right outside the clubhouse. Jeff was a little nervous, unsure about whether or not he should talk to Viselli or keep on walking. But the G.M. greeted him first with a warm smile and introduced himself for the second time. The first time Jeff had met him was a brief encounter before the initial team meeting, but this was the first official introduction. Viselli had that distinct look in his eyes (the ritzy clothes he wore with an impeccable ease didn't hurt either) that he always... always... knew what he was doing. Whether it was talking business or baseball or politics, he was a man that knew his stuff. At least he came off that way with his upscale lingo and suave black hair that never moved out of place.

Viselli told Hartes he was glad to have him aboard, and that he used to want to meet all the players before they were acquired; but with Skip, he started making exceptions. "I would trust Skip's judgment as my own," he said.

Jeff enjoyed the chat and liked Greg Viselli. He was just one of those guys you would want to grow up and be. One of those guys you weren't ashamed to go to war for.

Hartes continued into the dressing room and saw the person he and Viselli were just chatting about.

Skip asked him, "How ya' feelin' this morning, rook?"

"Pretty good, coach!"

"Remember, call me Skip. Might as well get out on the field and take some fungos."

"Yes, sir," Hartes replied.

Jeff jogged out onto the field and talked with Will awhile, just ordinary male bullshit. Will's voice was smooth, not snappy or raspy. The words flowed out of his mouth with a swagger, but it was full of sincerity and truth. All the infielders took some grounders, turned two, and learned the practice routine. Practice lasted until just before sunset, nearly all the players tired as hell, but feeling confident about where they stood defensively.

The season was just a week away, today was the third of April, season opened on the tenth. Before everyone left the field, Skip told the players, "Pretty nice practice out there, ladies. We've got five more practices until Arizona. I think we'll be ready. Here are the schedules, grab one and be here one tomorrow for a shit-load of hitting and base-running situations. I'm not trying to get 'Joe College' on you, but I want to make sure we're ready. Also, we'll go over the signs. Have a nice evening. And don't anybody do anything stupid before the season starts, alright?"

"Alright, Skip," everyone replied with a look of guilt on their face. Jeff, almost sure of the answer himself, asked Will what exactly Skip meant about the 'Joe College' remark. Will told him that was what assistant coaches or bench coaches were sometimes nicknamed when they started breaking out the college drills on the pros.

"That's what I figured," Jeff said.

The middle infielder grabbed a schedule, said "laters" to Will and Simon Luthers, and headed home. Simon was a pretty boy only a couple of years older than Jeff. He had bleached blond hair and an innocent face. Most girls could immediately feel the sweet, nice guy vibe coming off of Luthers, whether it was what he wanted or not. To only make matters worse for Simon, his cheeks were rosy and dimpled intensely when he smiled. The perfect sweetheart for any teenage virgin, but beware of the experienced woman—a maneater.

On the way home, the traffic was horrible. There was a big wreck somewhere up ahead, and traffic had slowed to a sudden halt. It was one of those stoppages that turned a fifteen-minute drive into an hour's worth of bad radio.

Jeff could see smoke rising from an eighteen-wheeler about a hundred yards up ahead. The rig appeared to be turned sideways and smashed against the cement wall dividing incoming traffic from ongoing travelers. He stared at the accident – curious if anyone was injured or deceased – as the traffic momentarily began to move before abruptly coming to another halt. While he waited for more signs of flow from the other cars around him, Jeff glanced at the Demons' schedule for the upcoming season. He searched for days off, long home stands, and the ever-exhausting road trips across state lines.

<u>Los Angeles Demons '99 schedule</u>

April 10,11,12	ARIZONA
April 14,15	@Carson City
April 16,17,18	@San Diego
April 20,22,23	TUCSON
April 24,25	WASHINGTON
April 29,30	@Cal
May 1,2	@Montana
May 3,4	@Washington
May 6,7,8	SAN DIEGO
May 9,10	CARSON CITY
May 12,13,14	@Tucson
May 15,16	CAL
May 20,21	MONTANA
May 23,24,25	@Arizona

IV

The traffic eased and Jeff arrived home around 8:40. He fixed supper and watched television, switching between channels. What some people may call channel surfing. He was feeling mildly aroused watching two lions hump the shit out of each other on the *Discovery Channel*, but jacking off after a hard practice was out of the question. He was tired enough. Continuing to watch the wild animal sex, Jeff picked up the phone and dialed Shae's digits.

Mr. Baseball thought of her silky brown hair. And the urge to run his hands over her perky breasts and firm ass was too tempting. Jeff had been with Shae a little over four months now, which was a long time for him. Hell... two months was *long* before this. They felt like they had been together for years. Their chemistry, their insight of what the other was thinking, their love was pure.

She answered the phone, happy to hear from him, and said she was still sorry about having to work the last Thursday. Ms. Kent was still extremely thrilled about Jeff making the team (she was a big fan, told Jeff when she met him that she went to a handful of games the last year before they met) and was ready to celebrate.

She asked if she could see Jeff tomorrow night, and he said, "Okay, I'll pick you up at seven and we can go grab something to eat, then come back to your place, sound good baby?"

"Yeah, sounds like a blast, see ya' then, bye."

She hung up the phone, and Jeff thought to himself: *What a wild lay she has always been. It feels so... so... good to fantasize over the same girl I was sleeping with.*

Even though Jeff had just started sleeping with Shae these last few weeks, she was still the most incredible girl he'd ever been with. He couldn't wait to get back in bed with her (it sounded as if he hadn't seen her in years, when it had actually been less than a week). He went straight to cleaning the apartment (with a serious approach this time) and then to making his bed.

Jeff awoke the next morning exhausted; his head felt like he had a goddamn hangover or something. His clock, which was a baseball diamond encased in glass, with baseball bats as hands and phony-looking baseballs (that looked more like soccer balls) as the twelve times, read 11:37 a.m.

Jeff figured he would get ready and grab a little something to eat on the way to the field. He put on some long pants—Skip had said the team would be running bases, didn't he?—and his white t-shirt which read *15 Reasons Why Golf is Better Than Sex*. The usual clown shirt, with number fifteen saying something like, 'it doesn't matter what the size of your shaft is in golf,' and number eight proposing something to the matter of, 'foursomes are welcomed in golf.' Same ol' clown shit, same ol' shit.

Jeff jumped into his Ford F-150, '97 model—black as the ocean in the middle of the night. It wasn't the greatest vehicle, but it still looked fairly appealing, and it ran consistently. Sometimes, that's all you can ask for. It was one of those vehicles that chicks didn't sleep with you over, but they didn't leave you over, either.

He engulfed a burger at *The Burger Barn*, a local shebang. The double-patty cheeseburger came with bacon, mayonnaise, lettuce, and tomato. It was just the way Jeff liked it, and it was damn good. Next, he headed to the field.

Demon Stadium was only fifteen minutes away from

where the Rose Bowl was held every year. And Jeff had watched some great games there, USC versus cinderella Northwestern, Michigan and Washington State, when Charles Woodson picked off a pass in the endzone to help seal his Heisman Trophy and also helped progress Michigan to a share of the national title with the 'Huskers from Nebraska. Boy there sure have been some dandies in that stadium, lots of memories.

He also remembered meeting the most unique person he had ever been acquainted with. This fellow, Richie was his name, amazed Jeff with his ability to recite verbatim the rosters of all the teams that had ever played in the Rose Bowl. This guy would just ramble on almost unconsciously during a football game when any play or player reminded him of something from the past. There was no end to Richie's memory capabilities; this guy could have gone on and on and on.

Jeff, not Richie, arrived at the park at twenty 'til and went inside the clubhouse to see what was going down. The Demon clubhouse contained about twenty open lockers, a large table with chairs around it, a brown leather sofa (which was softer than a bagful of feathers), and a very nice RCA television hanging from the top of the wall.

Sportscenter was on ESPN, showing basketball highlights from the night before. J. Kidd made a spectacular lob pass to Shawn Marion from half court, and the Suns won. Not paying attention to the television, a handful of guys caught up in some other business. Billy Goodwin, Javier Jimenez, Michael Tims, and Ron Fetters were playing cards at the table. Fetters, with a disgruntled look on his face, appeared to be the only *true* card player. Goodwin and Tims were cracking jokes and laughing the majority of the time; while Jimenez was still learning the language and the game they were playing. But the starting catcher, turning 34 in a few months, wasn't rattled. His face and actions were the same on every hand, and he hardly ever seemed to make a mistake.

The card players were playing a game called *Pluck*. It was similar to *Spades*, but you tried to get tricks that were plucks, two-on-two. Whoever dealt the hand could either bid or pass his bid to his partner, depending on whether or not he had a strong suit (lots of one kind). The team that deals has to take 8 of the 13 tricks; the team not dealing is only required to capture 5 tricks. The dealing team is also allowed to choose the suit, though, and must take over 8 tricks to pluck his opponent. If a team gets one pluck, on the next hand they are allowed to pass the lowest card of one of their suits for one of their opponent's highest card of that suit. If two plucks, they get two cards, and so on.

The pitchers were playing Goodwin and Fetters. The catcher gave Billy another glare as he allegedly tossed down the wrong card.

"Another wrong play, but you'll get it," Fetters added.

"Wat' deed I mece?" Javy asked, now knowing his opponents made a boner move, but he couldn't figure out what was so wrong about it.

"Don't worry, play your cards," his partner chimed in. Jimenez said something in Spanish, and they all laughed. Some laughing because they partially understood him, and others laughing only because of the way the words rolled off his tongue.

Jeff casually walked over to the sofa and sat down next to Will and Erric, who were having a unique discussion of their own.

"Fuck that shit, man, I ain't taking no Ultimate Orange or any of that bullshit," Will said to Erric Rutherford. Rutherford sat on the sofa shirtless, baring his dark, rough black skin and previous muscular toning. Anyone could tell he used to be accustomed to lifting weights and working out daily, but either through aging or drugs, 'E's body toning was diminishing. Don't misunderstand; he still maintained a body that women would get wet over.

The battle scars that Erric carried were a couple of circular whelps on the upper right side of his back. Jeff guessed the scars to either be bullet holes or severe burns from something round, but he wasn't an expert. A few years later, a rapper would come along going by the call name of '50 Cent.' This cat would remind Jeff of Rutherford every time he saw him on MTV or BET.

"You're such a candy ass, Will. Man, all it does is give you energy and put you on a high."

"I haven't used anything my whole career, never, and I ain't—"

"That's why you've hit two-twenty every year," Gunn said, laughing from his locker while sliding his jock strap up his thick, hairy thighs. The first baseman had slid into the clubhouse incognito, and was now getting involved in his share of the fun.

"Screw you, fat fuck," Will responded and everyone in the clubhouse broke out laughing, even Funk, who had been known to never crack a smile, was giggling like a little schoolgirl.

Jeff was spraying laughter out like a water hose watering a flower bed, and he almost fell off the couch. Gunn only smiled back at Will, knowing he was joking, and returned to putting on his gear. Almost everyone else started heading for the door to the field, so Jeff and Will grabbed their gloves and laced up their *Nike's*.

Practice wasn't as bad as the day before, and Jason Hicks hit a couple of 400+ foot bombs to left-center. Jeff recollected that he had never seen someone hit shots like those in live B.P. Not in his high school days for sure, and definitely not during his short stay at Cal.

No wonder the dude was the MVP of the Western League last season. He was like a freakin' animal out there, unleashing the artillery. His golden brown, tanned biceps flexed as he squeezed the bat harder in his hands and wheeled it around like a bamboo stick. Hicks wasn't the biggest guy on the team, but his distinct build made a baseball bat look like a toothpick in his hands.

Not only was Hicks the most valuable player, he was also the ladies' man. He was one of those guys a horny teenage boy saw on television and immediately wanted to imitate to perfection. He could pull nearly any chick, anywhere, any time. Most of his womanizing abilities came right along with his clearly noticeable confidence and swagger. But his handsome, clean face and his soft, brown hair (never gelled, but always appearing perfectly combed) didn't hurt either.

It was 4:20 (four-twenty, nice timing potheads) when Jeff left the fieldhouse and headed home. He wanted to get to the apartment, relax while watching a little of the color box, and then get ready to pick up Shae. She lived about a six-pack away, or 25 minutes across town, for those non-drinkers. Jeff couldn't wait to see her again, just thinking about her made him want to rub one out.

Actually, that was a misstatement. Shae didn't make Jeff want to masturbate. Every other girl he had dated made him want to do that. Shae made Jeff want to cuddle. And that ran much deeper. Those were the things that made someone realize the feelings they had were real.

Chapter TWO
Shae

I

She had gotten lucky. She might even have gotten lucky twice. The second one, though, she wasn't a hundred percent sure of yet. It was too early to tell.

Shae had graduated from a small high school in San Francisco. She wanted to go to college. Hell, her parents had nearly enforced it. But she didn't want to get carried away. She applied to several smaller schools, and Shae, with about a month of high school left, had finally decided on Brandon College.

It was an English literature school by the bay. That was a plus. And it was the perfect blend of coziness along with the "big city atmosphere" surroundings. So Brandon College it was, where she would study to be... an English major perhaps, a teacher, a professor, who really knew?

She fit in with the majority... the norm. She really didn't have any clue to what she wanted to be when she grew up. The problem was... she was growing up too fast. A so-called "ugly-duckling" in high school, or should I use the term "late bloomer?" Either way, boys weren't always on Shae's mind. She didn't start messing around until the end of her junior year.

Her first real sexual experience came right before graduating. Her luck, at the time at least, that she would find someone worth being with, and all the while, he would be going to school at New York University. 'A family tradition,' he had told her. It was too late for any change. He had invited her along; but it was too late for Shae to get into such a prestigious school, and the last thing she wanted to do was to begin the college search and applying to schools all over again.

So they parted ways, promising to keep in touch, but no one ever kept up that bargain. The drastic transition from high school to college, the new friends and new hobbies, the distance, all contributed to making a long-distance relationship nearly impossible.

Shae stood strong. She was motivated with the backing of her folks; she would go to Brandon College and go to class and make impressive grades, responsibly mixing in pleasure when time permitted.

And then the shit hit the fan. Shae fell in love for the first time, now realizing her high school relationship was just a mere fling. The problem... the man was exactly that —a man. It wasn't a fellow student. It wasn't a peer. It was her delightfully charming, incredibly attractive, British Literature professor. The English-born chap carried a slight British accent, just enough to make him even sexier still.

Shae made love with him. She stayed at his delicate cottage with the white-picket fence. They practiced their tomfoolery on a regular basis. She loved him. And she believed that he loved her.

One of the things she was always proud of, even to this very day, no matter how much he could have helped her in class or favored her, Shae stayed honest with herself. And when things did go wrong... so wrong... it was the only thing that truly comforted her. It was a small matter, yes. But to her, it was the simple thing that allowed her to fall asleep at night during the long hours.

Shae never allowed the professor to show favoritism.

She did her work alone—she did it with a passion to show him she could. She wanted him to not only love her, but respect her and her determination. But as I said, it failed, nonetheless.

The professor, like the high school boy, left her. This time, she tried to come with him, but he didn't want her. He was offered a better job at a better college with a better salary, and being in his late thirties, the time to move up was exactly what he had been waiting for. Shae was just a sensual distraction along the way, a pleasurable bump in life's twisted path.

She cried. She lost her motivation. It was hard for her to explain all this to her parents and friends. It was hard for her to drop out of college... she wasn't used to failure—she wasn't used to quitting.

But sometimes life throws you a curveball. Jeff would know. He wasn't a big fan of curveballs; he preferred fastballs low and away, but sometimes you had to make an adjustment (at the plate or in life).

She moved back home and cried some more. The sad part was that the "late bloomer" had finally blossomed into a gorgeous woman, stunning and turning heads. And instead of accepting her beauty or allowing it to help open doors (she had always had the great personality and intelligence to go along with it), she lay around and tried to ignore her parents' harsh words.

And then, she had gotten lucky. She met a guy who was intrigued by her. During her bi-weekly visits to the tanning salon, waiting for the next bed to open up, she engaged in an interesting conversation with an honest man. They talked literature. They talked politics. They connected.

But it wasn't the usual connection. She wasn't entirely attracted to him sexually, nor had he ever made a pass at her. He was the truest man she had ever met, never appearing to have a devious, ulterior motive. They simply enjoyed each other's company, nothing more, nothing less.

And when he finished his internship in San Francisco a few months into their friendship, he landed a job in L.A. with a private law firm. Remaining true, unlike the past men in her life, he brought Shae with him. He helped her pick out an apartment and get on her feet. She found temporary work as a waitress, and then he got her a job as his assistant. Quickly rising in the business, Dave King needed someone to do his busy work and scheduling. Shae enjoyed it because she had someone to talk to without the fear of losing him, and she was also paid well.

Luck had finally found her. At the ripe age of twenty, things seemed to be turning around. And then, for the second time, she believed she had gotten lucky. With Jeff Anthony Hartes...

II

Eager to explode from the lack of seeing Shae (and lack of sex), Jeff was ready to roll tonight. He put on some *Silver Tab* cut-off shorts (several inches past the knees) and a nice ordinary t-shirt. The shirt was cream-white with orange sleeves and black trim. The baseball-slash-soccer-ball clock read just after six, so Jeff finished touching up, moving one last strand of hair over and dabbing a little more Gio Armani on his neck, and headed out.

He arrived at Shae's neighborhood slightly early. She lived in a nice-sized apartment that was about ten times better than his pigsty. It *was* a pigsty before this day—now it was clean. Just in case the party ended up in Hartes'

Bachelor Pad.

The most impressive aspects of Shae's apartment were the lighting and decorations. She had an interior decorator's delicate taste for the finer things. In the living area, there was a glistening crystal chandelier hanging from the ceiling. The lighting structure looked diamond-crested at first glance, and really added to the enlightenment of the room. Shae's furniture was also bold. She had a red leather couch that would hurt your eyes if you stared at it too long. Behind the couch was the dining table, the surface of which was made of smooth glass. Beneath the translucent tabletop, there was a layer of warped glass, shaped like a rippling flag in the wind. The optical illusion caused newcomers to hesitate before putting their wine glass down on the table. They really believed it was wavy and not flat. The black framed chairs complemented the table, also featuring a bent and molded oblong shape.

Instead of stopping at her house right away and rushing her twenty minutes early, which might cause Shae to stress and take longer than if Jeff just let her be, he cruised on by and stopped at the closest flower shop. *Torito's Flowers and Gifts* was small and run down, but Torito or whatever the hell his name was had damn good prices. And he always had what you wanted. At least he did the one time before when Jeff needed emergency flowers. Jeff got Shae six roses that were as fresh as they come, walked back out to the F-150 and started back towards her apartment.

III

He had first met Shae over four months earlier at a nightclub. She was in a tight silk dress that went just past her firm ass. Some individuals might have thought the skirt was slutty or trashy at first glance, but her image and self-confidence made Jeff think otherwise. The short dress was turquoise-green (almost see-through), and the minute he saw it on her he had wanted to take it off and make hot love to her. She was a killer, a fox, and an irresistible brunette bombshell. Her hips swayed and her delicate, sinuous curves played a song to the beat of her body as she danced. Any way you wanted to put it, Jeff Anthony Hartes had wanted her upon first sight.

A lot of men had already tried to dance with her or hit on her with some corny one-liner, but it wasn't working. Jeff went up and talked to her, trying to be himself. The words exited his mouth with a creamy smoothness, not stuttering or wrongly spoken. He was on fire. She said she was exhausted from working all day, and then dancing all night. So they danced a few more times, and then left to his place. They clicked immediately, as couples sometimes do, saving him from dropping the ever-so-dangerous line after line on her.

At his dwelling, they talked and kissed and just had fun. They truly enjoyed each other's company.

No sex.

It was the first time he had just as much fun chatting and kissing and necking and holding her soft, delicate hands as he did having sex. It was now the second time in the past year that Shae felt she had met another honest man, without any "devious, ulterior motives." But this time, she *was* sexually attracted. To Jeff, she was so interesting and bizarre—in a good way. Jeff felt fourteen again, like the touch of her hand would send him exploding through the ceiling.

The rest was history. They clicked, and they would eventually become an item; at least people outside the relationship would think that, and they had had fun together ever since the initial meeting.

Jeff had briefly met Dave King, with his spiked-red hair and puffy frame, never feeling any jealousy towards his relationship with Shae, and this made her happier than ever. She had her two best friends, one was her dear boss, and the other was her treasured lover.

IV

The newly acquired Demon second baseman skipped (not walked), but *skipped* to her apartment door. A little too excited... a little too gay, he supposed, but he was so pumped up to see her after making the Demons' club. He rang her doorbell, one of those little soft buttons ideal to a primer on a push lawnmower. He didn't hear the ring announce his button-pressing inside, so he gave it another try. Still... nothing. So he knocked.

All he could think about was playing pro ball, *her,* getting a hit in triple-A, *her,* and—

"Hey! How are ya' doing, babe?" Shae's voice was like a dream in his head. Similar to someone talking to you after you've just fallen asleep; you can hear their voice and what they are saying, but you don't quite know where the sound is coming from.

"Oh! Hey, uhh, just fine… especially now that I'm here with you."

"Oh, Jeff…" Shae played along. "You've always been such a sweetie."

Jeff grinned and then took a step back, looking his girl over. "*Wow!* You're looking as good as ever Shae!"

"Thanks," the twenty-year-old beauty responded with a shrug and a blush to show Jeff how much he could still flatter her after the few months they'd spent together. He enjoyed knowing that things weren't getting old, and the simplest acts of kindness still got you somewhere. "You know how much you get to me when you compliment me, Jeff."

"Yeah, I know, but you deserve all the compliments because they're true."

"See! There you go again. Sometimes I can't tell what's really sincere and what's bullshit!" And then she smiled and giggled under her breath. Shae couldn't contain herself a second longer. She lunged at Jeff, wrapping her arms around his neck. She locked lips with him, and they stood on the sidewalk kissing. They pulled away and both had a little laugh. They shared "I missed you's" with one another, and then walked out to Jeff's truck. Jeff opened her door, she crawled in (trying not to wrinkle her black skirt or her white buttoned down blouse), and they set off to *Harris' Steakhouse and Grill.*

Expensive? Hell yes. But it was time to celebrate. After all, Jeff was playing for the Demons, and he was with Shae. Not to mention the fact that he also got the hookup at Harris' every now and then as well; explain more on that in a second. 'It doesn't get much better than this!' he thought.

The sun had just set as they approached *Harris'.* It was a stretched liquid of reddish orange and majestic yellow, dropping below the horizon. It was a quarter 'til eight on his clock in the truck—the tiny digital figures that appear on most factory radios. Shae and Jeff went in and waited to be seated.

Jeff tapped the first worker he saw on the shoulder and said, "Excuse me, waiter, is Harris in back today?"

"No sir, he's sure not. But I can tell him you were here if you like?" the waiter (Chuck, read it off his name-tag) replied.

Jeff said, "Yeah, umm... just let him know Jeff stopped by, and that I have some news for him, 'K?"

"Will do, mister, follow me to your table." Before showing them the way, the waiter jotted down the message on the restaurant's front podium. Harris was a lighthearted man, but when it came to business... he meant business. The waiter wouldn't forget the message—not if he wanted to keep his job anyway.

The couple was shown their table. They sat down and visited; catching up on some things they had missed the last couple of days, and then they ordered their drinks and food.

Overall, Shae and Jeff had a splendid time. Shae was as fun as always—possibly more fun with her being excited about dating a professional baseball player—and Jeff firmly believed he was falling for her just a tad. *Just a tad? What kind of stupid person thinks up a line like that?* He didn't know, but if—

"Jeff, Jeff? Hello? Anybody—" Shae said it as if it had been her hundredth time to call his name.

"Sorry Shae, just thinking." She smiled at him as he recoiled with a shy, sweet look on his face. They finished eating. She had the margarita-grilled chicken breast; he had the 12-ounce rib eye. All in all, it was a damn good meal. What else would you expect from Harris? Jeff picked up the check, a little disappointed Harris wasn't here to give them a discount, but figured he would make up for it the next time he came in.

They ended up landing back at his place around 9:45, and both of them immediately crashed on the couch. She reached over and gave Jeff a slight peck on the lips and said, "Thanks for supper, handsome!"

"You're very much welcome," Jeff said as he leaned across the couch and started kissing her passionately. They ended up in his bedroom sleeping together, again.

'How wonderful! How goddamn wonderful!' Jeff thought.

▼

"Rise and shine, sexy boy," Shae commanded.

"Already?" Jeff asked the question, barely loud enough to where she could hear it. It always took him awhile to warm up his vocal chords. So mostly in the morning, he had a tendency to mutter.

He looked up and saw that Shae had a tray with some O.J. and a bowl on it. She balanced the tray with her hands around the sides, waiting for Jeff to move to a sitting position so she could lay the tray down. Jeff sat up and rubbed his eyes. He used his hands to gain leverage and slide his back against the wall—now in a sitting position.

"Yep, baby. I made you some breakfast in bed. The only damn thing you had in the whole house—" Shae motioned towards the kitchen, "—was oatmeal. So I made you a big bowl, fine wit' you?"

"Yeah... plenty fine by me!" And then he grabbed her —she, almost spilling the oatmeal and orange juice all over him, but recovering safely — and pulled her into bed with him.

Shae sat the tray on the nightstand next to the 'crappy clock,' and they gave each other a good morning kiss. Jeff knew his breath didn't smell Listerine fresh, but Shae's orange juice breath made up for it.

She was outfitted in one of his old t-shirts and her own green, lacy panties. Jeff already wanted to rip them off of her like an animal — this early in the morning — but managed to contain himself and just kiss her. They laughed and had a merry ol', jolly ol' time. He ate, she talked and read a magazine, and then he gave her a ride back to her apartment. It was almost time for him to get ready for practice.

"Call you later?" she asked.

"Yeah, after seven."

"Okay. Bye baby!" she responded as she gave Jeff a quick kiss and flitter-flattered inside her apartment. Jeff watched her all the way to the door, every single step. And with each step, her body accentuated her mesmerizing curves and gorgeous legs.

"Bye!" he yelled as her door closed. Loverboy stood there on the sidewalk in awe for what seemed like hours, and then he hopped into the truck. He went back home, messed around, and went to practice at three.

The baseball came and went —

VI

Shae called about seven that night — both agreed on how much they wanted to see each other as soon as possible — and she asked Jeff about the Demons' chances and how he liked the other players so far?

He told her he was confident in himself and those around him, and everything was going really good. Baseball was fun… it was the great game exactly the way he remembered it. Only this time, he was getting paid and playing as a professional. They hung up, nothing much else to discuss, just a pleasant conversation to kill time.

The sixth, seventh, and eighth passed quickly. The April weather was rainy, and the sun struggled to shine. *April showers bring May flowers.* Most of the practices were light, and Shae and Jeff managed to see each other around her work as much as possible. The Demons' practice was canceled for the eighth – due to rain – and the team only had a short practice on the ninth.

The practices were becoming more and more routine, laid back for lack of another phrase. There weren't anymore tiresome or boring drills – A.K.A. 'Joe College' – and Hartes was settling into a comfort zone at second. He still was unsure whether he was one or two at the position, because Simon's defense was downright stellar. Jeff believed he did have a considerable edge swinging the lumber, though, but either way, he was determined to fulfill his role 100% no matter what it might be. He wanted to be considered a five-tool player.

Shae was off tonight (didn't work Thursdays and Saturdays currently, but rather five days a week), so they wanted to do something. They had celebration in mind, since it was just one day away until Friday, April 10th, and the season opener against the Scorpions.

Arizona had a hot prospect in their young centerfielder, Chadley Michael. He was playing in his second season with the Scorpions. Jeff, by chance, had read about his almost unbelievable college stats two years ago at Trinity College in San Antonio, Texas. Michael led

Division-III in batting average, homeruns, runs scored, and was in the top five in runs batted in and stolen bases. It was pretty amazing.

Jeff forgot about baseball for the moment and picked up the phone, dialing the number automatically. "Hello," Shae said, sounding a bit under the weather.

"Hey! What are you doing?" Jeff asked.

"Not a darn thing, why? What ya' have in mind?"

"You sick?"

"No, why?"

"Just sounded different."

"Oh, nah! Just had a froggy in my throat," Shae said, giggling.

"I see, uhh', anyways... wanna' go see a movie to help me get my mind off of tomorrow for awhile?" he asked, zealously awaiting her answer.

"Okay," she said, delighted as ever. Jeff checked the time (4:15 p.m.) and told her they could catch a six o'clock movie—he had seen earlier while reading the paper that most of the flicks were showing at or just after 6 p.m., so he was on the ball. She said that was great and that she'd see him when he got to her place.

"I've got to drive *all* the way out there to pick you up?" Jeff inquired. "The best theater is on my side of the stadium. And traffic is a bitch right now."

"Yes, babe. You have to drive *all* the way over here. And no more complaining, because I miss ya' and want to see ya'."

"Fine, fine. I'll see you soon. I was just joking, anyways."

Jeff got dressed—denim pants and a gray collared shirt—and then gelled his hair. Why gel? Because mousse bothered him; it never seemed to hold worth a shit. You could never drive with your windows down and arrive with the same hairstyle. You could never exert any amount of physical energy without changing the appearance of your hair. So that's why he stuck with gel. The yellow kind, too. *L.A. Looks* for a Los Angeles kind of guy.

Jeff arrived at the beauty's apartment at five-thirty. They got the usual 'hi, hi, how ya' doing, fine, you, fine as well,' out of the way, and then he said, "We should get going, time's a flyin'."

"Yeah, you're right, let's go!" Shae said and jumped into the F-150 through the door he held open for her. You know, trying to be the gentleman that he was.

As always, he had such a grand time with her, he didn't even pass thoughts on the game. They enjoyed a new flick and shared a large order of popcorn, extra butter. After the movie (*The Matrix*, featuring Keanu Reeves and Lawrence Fishburne, two thumbs down), Jeff asked her if she wanted to come back to his place. She said no. She was putting her foot down tonight and wanted him to get a good night's sleep, and not jinx opening day for him. Jeff agreed (not wholeheartedly, but he at least understood the reasoning), took her home, and returned to his apartment.

The night was still young, as they say—who's *they*? *Who knows? Who cares?* So he watched a little basketball, Jazz versus the Lakers. It was a pretty good game. Utah hung around until the fourth quarter, but Kobe and Shaq were too much for the old men. *Go Lakers!* O'Neal dropped 37 on the Jazz and also pulled down 16 boards to lead L.A. to a 104-96 win. Who would have thought that five years later, Karl Malone, "The Mailman," would leave Utah for Los Angeles and join the Bryant and O'Neal, as well as Gary Payton, tandem. And to make matters worse for Laker fans, who would have believed that they would be defeated in the NBA finals by Larry Brown's Detroit Pistons—arguably, piece-by-piece, position-by-position, one of the best starting lineups in NBA history (Chancy, Rip, Big Ben, 'Sheed, and Prince).

After the game, Jeff viewed *NBA2Night* and fell asleep during the San Antonio, Portland highlights.

He awoke at 10:44 a.m., ate some powder donuts (the white, powdery kind that always falls everywhere on each bite no matter how hard you try to prevent it), and thought about the coming game. Skip had said that the starting lineup would be posted right before the game, and he was dying to discover if he was in it or not. Most of the time the coach will let you know if you are playing so you can be ready, but Skip believed a player should be ready every day, whether he was starting or not. Skip had also said that not telling the players the opening day roster would make them more relaxed. But Jeff believed that part of the strategy backfired. He was just as nervous figuring out whether it was him or Simon.

Jeff opened his front door to his apartment, and welcomed the sun into the domain. It was as bright and radiant as he'd ever seen it, neglecting all the rains that had come recently. It was as if the Heavens thought it was a great day for a ballgame as well. The rains most likely caused mudslides and damage somewhere in Los Angeles. Natural disasters never failed, but the Baseball Gods were having no part of it on this day.

Jeff jogged (like someone that is old and incapable of running); he guessed you would call it a jog? Maybe speed-walked? At any rate, he speed-walked-jogged his way to the main office to get the morning's paper. The infielder deposited his seventy-five cents and slowly, but surely made his way back to his dwelling. The paper, *Los Angeles Times*, had all the scores from around the NBA, a major league baseball preview, and a write up on the Demons in the backburner of the Sports section.

Reagan Rothe

Demons Open Tonight With New Faces and New Hopes

The Los Angeles Demons start the '99 season with a couple of new faces in the front office and four new faces on the field.

Kevin Yields, Demons' new assistant general manager, says, "We (Viselli and the coaching staff) are all really expecting a great year, and we believe our chances are very strong."

The Demons also have a new pitching coach, Larry George, who was picked up to aid Head Coach Skip Bailey.

Bailey stated, "We had the second worst ERA (Earned Run Average) in the league last year. Larry should definitely help out that problem as well as a couple of young pitchers we signed."

Those pitchers are Michael Tims, projected starter, and Javier Jimenez, who spent his time away from baseball living in his home country, the Dominican Republic.

The Demons also acquired free agent pitcher Salmon Seavers from the Carson City Gamblers to play the closer role and shut down opponents in the late innings.

To strengthen the infield, the Demons signed two rookies; twenty-one year old second baseman, Jeff Hartes, and twenty year old catcher, Bobby Parks.

The first pitch will be thrown at 7:15 tonight. All of you Demon fans, get out there and cheer on your team.

—Ronald Davison

Jeff was really fascinated to see his name in the *L.A. Times.* He had already seen it earlier in the transactions' page, but that wasn't anything compared to a write-up. This was totally different, wasn't it? Oh, who gives a rat's ass anyways, it felt *different.*

It made him feel more suitable to his role—

Professional athlete, ha ha! Everyone else can kiss my ass right about now.

Thinking about it sometimes was fun, but that wasn't his true demeanor. Jeff remained as humble as ever, no one knowing that he was a minor celebrity or appearing to feel more important than those around him.

Jeff just sat around and rested the morning, slash lunch, away. He watched old reruns of *Three's Company,* never tiring of Jack Tripper and his always predictable antics. On this episode, Teri was Jack and Janet's blonde roommate. Jeff preferred Suzanne Somers' role with Chrissy the best, but Teri was a pretty attractive woman nonetheless. When the show ended, and it was finally time to jet; Jeff threw on some shorts and a t-shirt and then headed to Demon Stadium.

He pulled into the ballplayers' parking lot around four. The players didn't have designated parking spaces, but they typically respected each other's normal parking area and saved the closer spots for the veterans. Just another piece of baseball etiquette and common courtesy.

The team would be taking batting practice at 4:45 and had to be back on the field for the National Anthem at seven. Jeff entered the clubhouse and went to his locker, just in time to witness a guy from *Channel 7 Sports* interviewing Lake Williams, tonight's starter.

Jason Hicks was standing behind the cameraman flexing his muscles and grinning, most apparently figuring he was next. Before the reporter could even start the interview, Hicks had Lake chuckling and distracted. Lake said, "Somebody get that asshole outta' here."

In a leisurely and comical fashion, Gunn trotted over and scooped Hicks up like a mother carrying her newborn baby. Hicks screamed like a banshee as the couple paraded away from the interview session. The rest of the clubhouse laughed at the scene; Williams prepared to answer questions.

Chapter Three
Opening Day

I

"Lake... what do you try to do to prepare for an opening night game in front of more than *three-thousand* people?" the scrawny, never-an-athlete-in-his-life, sportscaster asked him, acquiring his job through knowing the right people or studying his ass off in college. This guy being one of the exceptions and shutting out the college distractions — mostly the partying and sleepless nights.

"Well, Andy, I mainly just try to keep my focus out there and relax just like any other game I've thrown in tha' past. It all comes down to being patient and letting your stuff do the work for you, having faith in your pitches," Lake answered with seniority and experience of someone who had answered questions similar in the past. The interview continued while Jeff moved over to his locker to get his batting practice shorts and shirt on. The reporter kept firing away with the questions. And Lake kept answering them with a familiarity that can only be acquired through years of baseball. He was definitely no 'Nuke Lalooshe...'

"Most definitely. I mean, not trying to throw too many clichés at you, but you always want to give a hundred and ten percent. And you always want to do what's best for the team to win." Lake capped off the interview with a couple of overused classics and returned to his locker to finish dressing.

The undershirt Jeff wore, skin tight like Under Armour, had the Demons' logo on it; a red-faced, devil-looking creature with small sharp horns and staring eyes. The demon had a devious smile on his face that seemed to say, 'I'd love to just snatch you up and eat you whole.' The grimace its face wore reminded Jeff of the big bad wolf in the fable *Little Red Riding Hood.* The Demons' practice shorts were dark blue with a red demon face stitched to the left side of them as well.

For someone who has never been in a professional clubhouse, it's actually somewhat swanky. For one thing, it is much more organized and clean than most might imagine. In the Demons' locker room, there were eight lockers on each side — the east and west sides. The north side was the opening to the restrooms and showers, and the south wall had five more lockers and the door to the front office. The entrance door was in the northwest corner, and the door to the park was in the southeast corner. Hartes' #9 locker was the third one down from the south wall. Gunn's locker was on his left, and Will's locker was on the right. Skip and Larry's lockers were on the south wall, with Wade Smith (the batboy), Fred "Funk" Sanders, and the "Vet" Brett Chambers.

You could say that wall was for the old-timers and the young pups. Not nineteen or even seventeen, Wade was the 14-year-old thorn puller — the kid who got the bats and balls and pulled the thorns out of the player's balls if they asked him to. At least that's what Prescott's coach would say on *Wildcats.*

Will, Erric, Billy, and Damon were watching *Rap City* on MTV. Fetters, the crafty catcher, Simon and his brother Darren, as well as the closer Salmon Seavers, were playing Pluck at the large wooden table at the north end of the clubhouse. Besides Jason (who was now on the Mic for *7 sports*), everyone else was either already outside or getting ready for batting practice.

Jeff grabbed his glove and walked out onto the field where Jay O'Dell, Thomas Perry, and Javy Jimenez (all pitchers) were kicking a little, soft ball around in the air. The stadium seemed to grow magically larger as Jeff's eyes searched it over. This was his baseball Mecca. This was his dream fulfilled and his life made perfect. Even if it was only perfect for this one, impeccable moment, that was enough for a lifetime. You could just smell the ballpark air. Whether the game was going on full-time or the baseball season had ended, the stadium still smelled of hotdogs and cotton candy and plush, well-manicured grass. The verdant green of a freshly cut outfield with specialized mowing patterns for opening day and all-star games.

A few diehards had already taken their seats, getting ready for some baseball action. The sun setting in the west glistened off of the empty stadium seats, causing a slight glare across the field. The smells now grew stronger, bringing a hunger craving in Jeff's stomach.

Jeff debated over what he'd like to send a batboy to order him some grub before—

"Hey Hartes, you ever hacky-sacked before?" Jay yelled from the outfield while he was walking through the little gate that led to the bullpen and then onto the field, interrupting his urge for food.

"Uh-uh," he replied.

Then Perry said, "Well get your just-barely-able-to-drink-beer ass over here and find out."

"Alright, no problem," Jeff said, unsure, just hoping he wouldn't embarrass himself in front of the other players, and the fans, before the game.

He jumped in the circle—a triangle at the time—and

started playing. They were pretty damn good, but Jeff caught on quicker than he would have thought. He slapped the hacky-sack from behind his back with the back of his foot, and Perry knocked it sideways off his head where Jay couldn't make the save.

Perry said, "*Damn!* My bad, man. You sure you've never hackied before Hartes?"

"Positive," Jeff replied as he took the throw off his chest and kicked it back into the air. As the players continued to hacky-sack and relax before game time, the rest of the team began funneling out, and the first group — Gunn, Hicks, Erric, and Will — jumped into the batting cage.

Simon and Jeff took infield fungos at second base hit by Sanders and also worked the double play drill with Chambers. Jeff could see more and more people beginning to take their seats. The first ounce of nervousness entered his body, sending a tingling feeling through his arms and legs. *Just butterflies...*

Demon Stadium could hold 8,000 fans, but only in the playoff games did it ever fill up. Tonight there was an estimated 4,000 to 6,000 people to be in attendance, which was a very good draw. The marketing crew must have been doing their job lately and advertising their balls off.

The first group finished with their round — Gunn and Hicks sending some into orbit for the early fans, who cheered — and then the second group stepped in. This foursome included Hartes, Lewis, Goodwin, and Fetters. The last group to swing was Parks, Simon Luthers, and the "Vet."

Arizona was on the field loosening up and waiting to get their hacks in. As the Demons finished and strolled back into the clubhouse, the Scorpions took the field for their before game B.P.

Back in the clubhouse: 6:45 p.m.

Skip had everyone's attention as he started speaking. "Alright everybody, now I know what you're thinking. You're thinking I'm going to give you a load of shit and take up your pregame grab-ass sessions—" smiles and some small laughter broke out. When everything quieted down again, Skip raised his right hand halfway up to his face, gesturing for everyone to remain quiet in a calm and sincere way.

Skip proceeded, "Well... I'm not. I just have two things to say. First, play your asses off, like the season was riding on it tonight. Play hard and have fun. Second, let's win the son-of-a-bitch and get tha' fuck outta' here!"

Everyone started saying 'yeah baby' and getting themselves pumped up. And then Skip said, "I'm hanging the starting lineup on the Coke machine—" which was on the south wall next to the door leading to the front office. "—as I go out. Go get 'em!" Skip finished his peptalk, and he left the clubhouse, heading to the Demons' dugout. Hartes took a good, hard glance at the lineup card.

Demons' Baseball	April 10, 1999

(1) Lewis   8
(2) Coleman   6
(3) Hicks   5
(4) Gunn   3
(5) Rutherford   7
(6) Fetters   2
(7) Goodwin   9
(8) Hartes   4
(9) Williams   1

When he recognized his name in the eight-hole, electric volts shot up his spine and sent waves throughout his entire body. He was almost positive beforehand that he would get the start, but an individual is obligated to have some doubt. *I mean, c'mon, give me a break.*

Jeff was so damn excited! He was also beginning to get really nervous. But what did he expect?

Do you expect to be perfectly calm in your pro debut?

'Hell no,' Hartes answered his own question in his head. But he was as ready as he'd ever be. And no one was taking this once-in-a-lifetime chance away from him.

II

7:00 p.m.

The player introductions blared over the loudspeaker, and then the *Channel 7 Sport's* radio broadcast with Darrell "The Duke" Marinville started.

"Good evening everybody and welcome to opening night. This is the start of the Demons' fifth year in the Western League. They come in as one of the favorites and have high expectations, looking for their first team championship. I'm Darrell 'The Duke' Marinville, and I'm here to bring you a piece of baseball history," The Duke said, repeating the famous words of Mr. Mel Allen (I'm here to bring you a piece of baseball history).

Marinville loved to throw in well-known baseball quotes or lines whenever he got the chance. It made him feel above the rest when he was able to recite some of the great sports figures' famous sayings or one-liners.

Marinville was the exception to most people and money. He had been offered higher paying jobs and even had a chance to do play-by-play with the San Diego Padres. But "The Duke" loved his gig here and did it for the love of Demon baseball; nothing to do with the material.

"Tonight for the Arizona Scorpions, leading off and playing center, Chadley Michael. Batting second and playing third base, Miles Hunter. In leftfield and batting third, Jake Kimmers. Catching for the Scorpions and batting cleanup, Derrick Hundly. Batting fifth and playing first, Marco Diaz." Diaz was one of those guys you didn't want to piss off: six-foot-five and 245 pounds. He had also been known to whine frequently and argue a call whenever he got the chance. But the infielders always had the pitcher's back in case something went down.

The Duke continued, "Playing shortstop and batting in the six-hole, Hank Hughes. Batting seventh in rightfield, Jeremy Willis. In the eight-hole and playing second base, Nico Chavez. And on the mound and batting ninth for the Scorpions, Eric Ridel." (Pronounced 'Riddle' instead of the more frequent 'Ry-del').

The crowd got their courtesy applause out of the way. You know, the clapping that has no enthusiasm in it, just clapping out of consideration for the team they weren't rooting for. They were ready for the National Anthem to begin, and the season opener to get going. Singing America's song on this night was a cute, blonde-haired teenage girl. She was between the age of fourteen and sixteen, but still drew Hicks' attention. She hit the notes better than average in her newly-bought outfit (a sky blue dress), which was perfect for the occasion.

The crowd cheered and applauded with jubilation as the girl bowed and exited the field. The hidden man in the pressbox (Kyle Queen) announced the Demons' lineup over the loudspeakers as they jogged to their positions, and the estimated 6,000 in attendance gave their home team a warm welcome.

Lake took the mound, threw his warm-ups, and the game had officially begun. The Duke started, "We're under way here in Los Angeles as Chadley Michael makes his way to the plate. A wonderful thing a season opener is, because you now know there's lots of baseball ahead. Lake gets to the rubber, wasting no time here... takes his sign—"

Simultaneously, Queen said, "Now batting, Chadley Michael."

The Duke continued, "—and delivers... fastball outside, ball one. The lefty Michael probably had the take sign on that one, even though it was a ball. Lake readies and stands tall—" around six-one would be a good guess, "—gets the sign, and fires." *Whack!* "Line drive to right, drops in in front of Goodwin. Michael takes his turn as Goodwin's throw comes back in. Leadoff single for Michael. One on, nobody out here in the top half of the first."

The Duke paused slightly, and then added, "Nice piece of hitting there by Michael, turning on an inside fastball with ease."

"You're covering if this fast S.O.B. tries to take second," Will yelled from shortstop to Hartes at second. Michael stood on the first base bag. The second year player's dark brown hair came out of the sides of his batting helmet like a surfer's. His face was handsome, yet rugged, and his nose overshadowed his other attractive features. His calves swelled in his tight pants, and so did his arms. Michael had been in the weight room plenty; he added power and beef to his outfielder speed. *A lead-off man with a little pop...*

"Yeah, alright. I got 'em."

The Duke rolled on again, "Michael takes his lead.

Gunn is holding him on first. Third baseman Miles Hunter up to bat. Williams looks to first, then to home, back to first, this lefty's got a decent move, and delivers.... fastball over the inside portion of the plate, strike one. The right-handed hitter hit two-seventy-three with five homeruns last season with the Scorpions. The pitch... Strike Two! Right down the pipe with another fastball. Lake's using his fastball to get comfortable to start tonight's game.

"Williams comes to the stretch, winds, and fires... Runner's Going! Curve ball low and away, throw to second base! Not in time... Michael safely slides in with a stolen base. One-for-one to begin the season."

The Duke took a drink from his Diet Pepsi. With his thirst quenched, he continued his play-by-play, "One-two count on Hunter, runner on second. Hartes took the off-line throw and made a nice effort to put a tag on Mr. Michael, but it was way too late. Not only can this young superstar swing the bat, but Michael is showing off his baserunning capabilities as well."

"There's the pitch." *Crack.* "Fly ball to shallow left, Rutherford in, makes the catch. No tag chance for Michael, one away now. That was a bad A.B. for Hunter. He's got to get the runner over. Now entering the batter's box for Arizona, the switch-hitting leftfielder, Jake Kimmers."

Will and Jeff were playing around with Michael at second, keeping him on his toes. Hartes slapped his glove in Michael's direction, and then scooped up some infield sand, throwing it in the air, the cool breeze blowing it left to right across the infield. Michael would extend his lead slightly, wait to see if one of the middle infielders slid toward the base, and then draw a step or two backwards. If Hartes and Coleman forgot about him, third base might be his.

Jeff was nervous as hell out there, awaiting a ground

ball or anything to help him loosen up. *Just one easy hop... that will take the edge off and set the comfort zone.* The Duke rolled on, not caring about Hartes' need for relaxation. "Kimmers is batting from the right side off the lefty Williams. Michael playing with Hartes and Coleman, or maybe it's the other way around. The pitch... strike one. A swing and miss from Kimmers. Lake got 'em with the curve ball on that one, changing up his pitch sequence a bit here.

"From tha' stretch, Lake delivers... strike two. Inside fastball that Kimmers must have missed by six inches. Oh-two count on Kimmers. Williams might waste a pitch here. The throw on the way... ball one. That was a slider just a little too far outside. One-two count, Michael on second, one away. The pitch... Strike Three! Two away. Williams struck him out on the *high heat* folks!"

"Two down, baby, two down!" Fetters screamed from behind the plate. Gunn turned to the outfield and extended his index finger and pinky finger (making a *Hook 'Em Horns*), signifying there were two outs.

Over the loudspeaker, the stadium could hear Queen announce, "Now batting for Arizona, the catcher, Derrick Hundly." Hundly took Lake to full-count and then flied out to right, saving the Demons from an early jam.

"Three outs here in the top-half of the first. No runs, one hit, no errors, and one runner left on base. We head to the bottom of the first, zero-to-zero," The Duke said over the radio before a *Budweiser* commercial came on.

When the station was back on the air, The Duke updated tonight's other play. "Earlier today in a day game, Carson City defeated the Thunder of Washington seven-to-two. Norwood Gibbs was the winner, going eight innings and giving up only two earnies. Wayworth was the loser. Aaron Craig went three-for-five with a two-run shot in the fifth for the Gamblers. He also drove in three runs and scored two. Remember that name, sportsfans, because Craig can really play some ball. Couple of night games also under way, San Diego leading Tucson one-to-nothing after two innings, and Cal leading Montana three-to-one after four."

III

Lewis headed to the plate to open Los Angeles' hitting for the '99 season. His height, 5'8", along with his batting stance, hunched and low, appeared to make Lewis the perfect base on balls leadoff man. 'Anyway you can,' one might say. But he wasn't your typical first hitter. Lewis was a free swinger with a little pop despite his thin frame and young face. *The blacker the berry, the sweeter the juice,* Rutherford always told his fellow outfielder, busting his balls with a Chris Tucker, *Friday,* reference.

Back in the dugout, Skip told Lake he was doing a good job, and the main thing was to keep throwing strikes. If he started falling behind in the count, the Arizona hitters would be able to sit on a pitch and drive the ball hard.

"Up to bat for the Demons, centerfielder, Damon Lewis. On the mound for the opposing team, the crafty righthander, Eric Ridel. Lewis in the box, Ridel on the mound. The pitcher gets his sign and fires... ball one."

"Hey Hartes, how ya' feeling out there?" Hicks asked Jeff from inside the dugout. "You look a little shaky over there."

"Feeling tight as hell, just wish I could get a ground ball or somethin' to relax. You know, get in tha' groove," he replied.

"Don't worry about it. I'll get you a ground ball," Williams stated, sitting in the corner of the dugout with his jacket on. Hicks also told Jeff to just relax; he had seen Hartes' defensive capabilities and knew what he could do. Jeff nodded without giving much thought to what Lake and Jason had said. He only wanted to get in the flow of the game, and most of all—stop worrying.

The Duke smoothed along, "Ridel delivers... strike one. Lewis took a fastball right over the meat of the plate. He might have still had the take sign on for the second pitch to help the team get a look at what the pitcher's throwing.

Ridel starts from the wind-up, throws... strike two, Lewis swings and misses. Ridel threw him another fastball inside, and Lewis just missed. A little bit late, perhaps. Damon steps out of the box, stretches a little, and hops back in. The righty winds and hurls." *Smack.* "Ground ball to the left side, Hughes scoops it up and fires to first. One away. I'll tell you one thing I know for a fact sportsfans: even though that ground ball was routine, Hughes is one of the best defensive shortstops I've ever seen step onto a field in the Western League. Last year, he secured many a Demon rallies with his spectacular fielding."

Damon came back to the dugout shaking his head and said, "Motherfucker throws gas! Didn't think he had it in 'em."

"What'd you ground out on?" Rutherford asked.

"A weak ass breaking ball," Damon answered, still very much disgusted with himself. "I should've laid off, man, it was a lil' inside. But seriously, what was this dude hittin' on the gun?"

"Nigga' hittin' near ninety-five. With *that* fastball, he threw you an oh-two curve ball over the plate?" Rutherford responded, but was ready to answer his own question (he actually already knew the answer because Damon had just told him). Erric shook his head. "Nigga's crazy like that sometimes, I guess." The dugout chuckled over what he said as Damon replied 'no shit' with a smile.

As Will entered the box, the Duke started up again, "One away in the bottom of the first, with Will Coleman stepping up to bat. The right-handed batter hit two-ninety-three and scored nineteen runs (in thirty-four games) last year for L.A. Eric Ridel's ready to face his second batter. Coleman digs in, pitcher throws." *Crack.* "Deep drive to straight away center, Michael back, one hands it for the out. Two away. Speaking of Hughes' fielding, that Chadley Michael in center has had a lot of press lately and doesn't appear too shabby a defender either."

"Now batting for the home team, last year's M... V... P... JAAAA-SON HICKS!" Queen announced the third baseman over the speakers as the crowd went wild with jubilation. The fans loved the third baseman with his million-dollar smile and unforgettable charm. Hicks drove the ladies downright crazy while their boyfriends attempted to mimic his classy style and swagger. Also, the avid Demon fan (as well as the knowledgeable groupie) knew that they had better get it while it's hot. Because players as good as Jason Hicks (as good looking) were few and far between. And most sportswriters and reporters speculated that if Hicks had any type of season equivalent to last year, this would be his last season with the Demons; he would be flying first class in the 'Bigs' next year.

The Duke continued, speaking over the air to his Demon faithful with greater enthusiasm than before, "Hicks steps in, crowd on their feet, they love this guy here in Los Angeles. He carries with him an unmatched, unchallenged confidence every time he steps to the plate. Ridel winds and fires." *Whack!* "Deep shot to left, I don't know if it has... Kimmers back to tha' track, reaches up and makes the catch. Three down. Wow! Hicks almost opened the season with a solo shot there, but didn't seem to catch all the wood on it."

"Fuck! Fuck! Fuck! Fuck me dammit!" Hicks screamed at himself on the way to third base. "Goddamn motherfucker, just missed that shit!" Hicks continued 'fucking' himself—baseball term, sort of like chewing yourself out—in Hicks' case, it was more like 'motherfucking' himself as the rest of the defense took the field, and Lake took the mound.

Coleman picked up his teammate, bringing Hicks his glove and cap from the dugout as the third baseman tossed his helmet in the general direction of one of the batboys, most likely Wade. The inning was over.

IV

Lake struck out Diaz, got Hughes to line out to short, and Willis grounded out to Hicks at third. The Demon ace made short work of the five, six, and seven hitters.

The Duke said, "That does it for the top of the second, three up, three down. As we head to the bottom half of the inning, due up for the Demons... Gunn, Rutherford, and Fetters."

The advertisements came on over the air, and Marinville took his headset off for a quick breather. The broadcaster, with thick, flowing black hair, took a sip from his coffee cup and read over some stat sheets. He had gained considerable weight over the past few years, but didn't care. He didn't care because he loved Demon baseball and hanging out with the players. He never once regretted turning down the higher paying jobs, announcing sports. Marinville didn't care about the money; he cared about reliability and dedication. This was rare, but that was his personal dedication.

"Back to Demon baseball with the Duke. The score is nothing-to-nothing in the bottom of the second."

Skip congratulated Lake on another good inning, saying, "You're working the ball good and hitting your spots." Lake nodded, wiping the sweat from his brows and face with a white towel. "You're also keeping their timing off, keep it up, Lake."

"Yeah Skip, no problem. Arm feels as good as ever out there."

"That's good... we're going to try to keep your pitch count under a hundred, though."

"Whatever's best, but I feel great," Lake added, hoping that if things were going well, that coach would give him the benefit of the doubt and leave him in during the late innings.

"Lez' go now Big Daddy, take that fucker deep," Fetters yelled to Steve as the first baseman headed to the batter's box. The catcher spat a black wad of tobacco onto the foul area of the field. And then grabbed his bat to take a few practice cuts.

"Steve 'Big Daddy' Gunn now making his way to tha' plate for the Demons." The crowd rattled and shook the bleachers. "He is a three-time league all-star and has massive power to all parts of the field."

Ridel threw a ball and a strike to Gunn. And then, with a one-and-one count... *Smack!*

"Deep drive to straight away center, Michael ain't gonna' get to this shot! It's off the wall in center! Gunn rounds first, heading to second. He'll come in standing up with a two-bagger. Michael had some trouble fielding the ball off the wall, but he didn't need to worry about the burly first baseman trying to turn that hit into a triple. The ball was quickly thrown back in, but Gunn had already asked for time from the second base umpire. Gunn removes his shin guard as he starts the second with a leadoff double," The Duke proclaimed.

"Thatta' baby, Gunn! Nice shot, big boy," Coleman yelled from the dugout as the rest of the team hollered and could feel the first offensive rally of the year. Rutherford stepped in and did his job. He hit a weak grounder out to second to get Gunn over to third. An out... but a productive one. Ron Fetters came up with one out and Gunn on third.

"Good hitting there by Erric Rutherford, moving Gunn to third. The catcher, Ron Fetters, now batting for L.A.," The Duke trumped from the pressbox, a little fired up now.

Fetters ended up hitting a hard ground ball to third, incapable of scoring Gunn. That brought up Goodwin, who also grounded out, but to second. Hartes was left on deck when Goodwin grounded out, leaving a runner stranded. Goodwin could hear Skip bitching to himself from his chair on the nearest side of the dugout. The end of the dugout that was closest to homeplate.

"Goddamn sonofabitch. Too early in the season for this crap!" Skip was usually calmer than most managers, but not getting the run in from third with less than two outs in a tie ballgame really skinned his hide on this occasion. He stood up and kicked some dirt outside of the dugout, and then sat back down. He turned to Larry George as the pitching coach was walking over from coaching third to sit beside him. "Can you believe that shit? This might just sum up the entire season!"

"We'll be fine," George said, catching a slight smile on Skip's face, but also choosing not to answer the question.

"Gunn said his hammy tightened up on him a little on the double, but was fine."

"If he's fine then why did he mention it?" Skip inquired with good reason.

"Good point."

"Have the trainer check him when he gets back in," Skip said.

"Will do."

The Demons took the field, believing they should have scored and taken the early lead, but that's baseball. The Duke was speaking with a little resentment in his voice now. "Well, well, the Scorpions got out of that jam. Through two, zero-to-zero." After the commercials and network identification, he started again, "Top of the third here in Demon Stadium. We got us a tie ball game, nobody on the scoreboard yet. Other scores from around the league, San Diego now up three-one over Tucson through four innings. And Cal leading Montana six-to-two after six."

"Earlier today, Gibbs was the winner in the Gamblers' seven-to-two victory over the Thunder." The Duke paused for a while, waited for Nico Chavez to get to the plate, and started, "Chavez up for Arizona in the third. In the on deck circle is the pitcher, Ridel."

Williams took Chavez to full count and then walked him. Skip was disgusted, and he wasn't hiding it one bit. His face scrunched up, and the frown that formed showed that his calm demeanor had altered itself slightly. He thought about how good Lake was throwing and then to walk this scrub, unbelievable.

"Un-fuckin-believable. Can you believe that shit, Larry?"

"Pretty bad," the pitching coach said. "He'll be fine."

"Yep, long as he doesn't walk their pitcher, too." Skip

pronounced 'yep' with a long, southern drawl accent. Annunciating the 'y' and then prolonging the vowel sound.

Lake struck out Ridel on three pitches, and Chavez wasn't going anywhere. There was now one out with a runner on first.

The Duke announced, "Michael steps in, one-for-one so far tonight. He singled to right to lead off the game."

Lake Williams wanted the cocky bastard; he wanted him *bad!*

"Hey Jeff, Lake doesn't like these hot shot primadonnas stepping in the batter's box like they've done it for years. These two may have words. I think Williams already hates this fuck," Coleman said from shortstop.

"I didn't know that shit, man," Jeff responded without thinking much into it, but it did seem that Lake appeared more determined against Michael, and what he didn't know then, he knew now. Jeff got set at second, awaiting Lake's pitch.

The Duke announced, "Woah! Fastball high and tight, backing Michael out of the batter's box. He gives Lake a glare and steps back in."

"Told ya' Lake didn't like *this* meat," Will said.

"Damn right," Jeff replied.

Lake got Michael out on a two-two curveball that the centerfielder popped up to Coleman. Two away, Chavez still on first, Hunter batting.

"Third baseman Miles Hunter up for Arizona. Flied out to shallow left his first A.B.," The Duke stated.

Hunter grounded out to Hicks on a 0-1 count to end the top-half of the third. Lake paraded into the dugout without feeling any stress or urgency. That's what good pitchers do. Williams walked the first batter, a minor scare. But instead of panicking, he worried about the next hitters and got out of the inning without any damage being done.

Well, ladies and gentleman, Jeff Hartes was coming up to bat. Holy shit!

He took his practice swings in the on-deck circle; waiting for Ridel to get his warm-up throws in. And then he heard Queen over the loudspeaker, "Now at bat for your hometown Demons, Jeeeffff Hartes!" The crowd gave their courtesy applaud, and Jeff stepped in the batter's box.

All right now, looking fastball. Remember baby, this guy can bring it. Swing the bat, Hartes, let's go. Fastball first... fastball first...

Hartes continued the muttering inside his head as he took his practice swings. His palms were sweaty up against the bat he had recently pine-tarred so the grip would be sticky. His knees felt like jelly; he thought that he might fall over if the pitcher didn't hurry up and throw home.

The righty winded, and delivered... ball one. The conversation in his head started up again.

Okay dammit, fastball outside, now watch this fool come inside with the heat. Bring it, bring it, bring it...

Hartes continued chanting the words 'bring it' as Ridel fired home...

▼

Smack!

Jeff sprinted to first, glancing in time to see the ball roll between the third baseman and the shortstop. He took his turn, thinking about his first professional hit.

Hell yeah! He singled through the right side to lead off his pro career.

"Fuck you Ridel, don't come in on me," Hartes

mouthed under his breath (quiet enough to where he was the only person who could hear it) as Lake made his way up to bat.

"Nice piece, kid," Coach George said, shouting from the third base coach box, beginning to cycle through the signs. "Thatta' way to swing it."

Thanks...

Jeff got the signs from George— *sacrifice*—took his lead from first and steadied himself, not leaning towards second base or first base, but balanced perfectly, similar to identical weight on both ends of a scale.

Ridel glanced once to first, and then again, and finally threw to home. Lake laid down an easy roller along the right side. Diaz fielded it coming forward, and threw Lake out at first with Chavez covering. Perfect bunt. Hartes stood up at second, made sure the throw was on target, and then relaxed.

The loudspeaker man spoke, "Now batting with one away, Damon Leeeewis!" He pronounced the 'eew' in Lewis similar to an Arkansas native yelling Soooo-Weeee Pig. The crowd wasn't riled up, yet, but they weren't mute either. After taking the count to three-one, Lewis drove a ball up the middle. A low-liner that just got over Ridel; Hartes got on his horse and saw Coach George waiving him home.

"Get after it Hartes, c'mon, c'mon!" Larry shouted as the rookie blew by third. Michael fielded the ball clean and came up throwing. The throw was a little wide right (the catcher's right), so Hundly had opened up the plate. The Arizona catcher fielded the throw cleanly and slid back to his left, mitt extended. Hartes slid feet first into home before Hundly slapped him with the tag. It was a no brainer.

"*Safe!*" the umpire bellowed.

Demons one, Scorpions zip.

Lewis moved to second on the throw home; he would remain there, as Ridel struck out Coleman, and Hicks grounded out back to the pitcher.

The Duke capped off the inning by saying, "The Demons managed to get on the board, and rookie Jeff Hartes scores the leading run and the first run of the season for Los Angeles. The score is one-to-nothing as we head to the top of the fourth. Back in a sec with Demon baseball." The prearranged ads/commercials followed.

Kimmers flied out to lead of the fourth, and then Hundly lined out to Coleman. Two away, Diaz up.

"The big lefty steps in for Arizona. He struck out his first time up. Williams fires! Ball one... ball two... ball three... ball four... Williams walks Diaz on four straight with two out in the second. Must have lost focus there," The Duke said, shaking his head even though no one could see him.

"Second walk of the night for Lake. That brings up Hank Hughes, the playmaking shortstop. Lake glances to first, Diaz not going anywhere, and then throws." *Crack!* "This ball is pulled to deep leftfield! Back... Back... It's Gone!"

Nothingness from the crowd, they were completely and utterly silent. The Duke filled in the radio listeners, "The shortstop turned on Williams' fastball and just made it a two-to-one Arizona lead."

Hammerin' Hank trotted around the base path as Lake was storming around the mound. Lake was bitching at himself, using his glove as a buffer. "Fuckin' walk will get you every time, you stupid *fuck.* And then follow it up with cheese, c'mon Lake." He kept up the marching as Hughes stepped on homeplate. The team greeted him with his props for the bomb he just delivered.

"Thatta' baby, Hank! Nice fuckin' piece!" the Arizona players shouted as Hughes fought through their congrats on his way to the dugout.

After Lake settled down, he got Willis to ground out to Hartes at second. *About damn time*, Jeff thought, as he fielded the routine ground ball and threw it to Gunn. The score was now two-to-one, Scorpions up after three and a half.

Ridel made an average start look like shit in the fourth. He walked Gunn on five pitches and then got singled off of by Rutherford to left. Nobody out and catch up. Fetters was oh-for-one so far tonight. He hit a chopper to second that moved Gunn and Rutherford over, and the only play for Chavez was to get Fetters. Ridel then walked Goodwin on five pitches, loading the bases.

"The little hero, Jeff Hartes, up to bat with one out and the bases filled up in the fourth," The Duke rattled to his listeners. He was sure Hartes would step up big here, kind of feeling queasy in the box. "I gotta' good feeling about this one, sportsfans. Our Jeff Hartes scored the only run so far for L.A. and looks to drive in a few right now.

Ridel delivers... strike one. Outside fastball right on the corner, good pitch by Eric Ridel. One away, bases loaded. Hartes, playing his first professional game, has to be feeling the pressure. Ridel throws... ball one. Ridel comes to the plate... ball two. Boy, he sure doesn't want to walk Hartes here, there's nowhere to put 'em. The pitch." *Smack*. "Fly ball to straight away center, Gunn is tagging. Michael makes the catch and fires home. No play as Gunn slows into homeplate to tie this one up at two apiece. It was just too deep for Michael to make a play on Gunn. Count that one as a sac-fly for Hartes. Two down."

"That's the way, baby. Nice job Hartes. That's how to get a run in babee'!" Skip preached to Hartes as he jogged into the dugout from running out his deep fly ball. Hartes got his dibs from Coleman and Gunn and the crew and sat down in the dugout. He watched as Ridel struck out Lake on four pitches to get out of the inning. Once again, the Demons left runners in scoring position, but tied the game nonetheless.

Lake appeared to have found his groove, again. He struck out Chavez, Ridel grounded out to short, and Michael hit a rocket right to Goodwin in right. Three up, three down, as simple as that.

Usually if a pitcher has a rough inning—gets hammered—and gets out of it only allowing one run or no runs, they can get a feel for the game again. That's what Ridel did. He struck out Lewis, struck out Coleman on three pitches, and got Hicks to fly out. No runners for either team in the fifth.

To start off the sixth, Hunter doubled to left-center. The switch-hitting Jake Kimmers then doubled off the leftfield wall, driving in Hunter, retaking the lead. Lake struck out Hundly, and then Diaz grounded out to first. The Scorpions had two away, one run in, and Kimmers on third. Hughes hit a hard ground ball to Hicks, and the MVP booted it into leftfield. Just a lack of concentration on Hicks' part as the Scorpions took a four-to-two lead. Jeremy Willis popped out to second, ending the inning.

Gunn singled to lead off the home team, but they couldn't bring him around to score. Rutherford, Fetters, and Goodwin went in order. Nothing special or fancy about it.

"Eric Ridel has five K's tonight, and has really appeared to come into his own. He's finding the method of pitching that works best against this Demon lineup. Heading to the seventh, it's four-to-two Arizona," The Duke said.

The rest, folks, was crap! I mean total freakin' crap! It was about as hideous a sight someone could have asked for at home and on opening day. The Arizona Scorpions handed Los Angeles a thrashing from here on out.

The visitors scored two more off of Lake and knocked him out of the game. They then scored another run off of Fred "Funk" Sanders, who replaced Lake, making the score seven-to-two and drawing a look of disgust from the majority of the fans. Don't get me wrong, the Demons didn't just give up, it just wasn't their night.

"The Arizona rally accounted for three runs on three hits, and no errors by the Demons. You can really see the look of mere shock on L.A.'s faces out there. We'll be back for the seventh-inning stretch, and let me tell you it really is a stretch from here on out," The Duke said with the slightest ounce of hope left for his team.

The lack of consistency/life/a comeback for the Demons continued... Hartes struck out to lead them off, and then Brett Chambers (pinch hitting for Sanders) popped up to Ridel. Lewis popped up to Hunter to end the inning, nothing happening for the Demons. Javy Jimenez took the mound for L.A., and he did a hell of a job.

Maybe it was Jimenez's pride that kicked in, or maybe it was just his own personal fire that burned inside of him. Whatever the case, his audacity on the mound shut down the Arizona offense. Throwing mostly nothing but straight juice, Jimenez's control was perfect. Cutters riding in on the batter's hands similar to Mariano Rivera. And then two-seam fastballs dancing off the corner of the plate, but no one was able to lay off.

Skip congratulated Jimenez as he came into the dugout after a one-two-three eighth, "Great work Javy. 'Bout fucking time somebody looked like they wanted to win a goddamn ballgame."

Javy struck out Chavez after getting Willis to ground out to second. Then Ridel hit a little rinky-dink dribbler back to Jimenez, and he made the play back to first.

Bottom of the eight; Coleman ended his dismal showing by flying out to Michael in shallow center. That put him at 0-4 on the night; not the way the shortstop had wanted to get things started. Even still, there wasn't a look of dismay on Will's face; the veteran knew there were still 33 more games, and patience was a huge factor during a baseball season.

The Duke presented Hicks' call in the eighth. "Jason Hicks is up, he's really do for something. He's oh-for-three tonight and hasn't looked his best defensively, either. Ball one... strike one... strike two... ball two..."

Crack! "Hicks sends one into high orbit! This ball is leaving in a hurry! Jason Hicks has at least got the remaining crowd on their feet. What a blast from the MVP! Seven-to-three in favor of the visitors, a solo shot for Mister Hicks."

Both Gunn and Rutherford grounded out to bring the game into the ninth. Jimenez threw the ninth just as good as the eighth. He only allowed a single from Michael. That was a broken bat piece.

Bottom nine, Demons still down by four runs. The ninth inning wasn't much better for the team trailing. Hartes flew out to Kimmers after Fetters K'd for the second time, and Goodwin couldn't leg out a ball to short.

The final: Arizona 7, Los Angeles 3.

VI

Jeff made his way to the clubhouse, signing a few autographs along the way, and then waving at Shae as she came down to the bottom of the stands. She saw his hand in the air, leaned over the rail, and said, "Hey! Jeff! Come over here for a sec."

"Hey Shae," Jeff said, trying to show enthusiasm. He crawled into the stands, a little upset at the game's outcome. Shae saw the disappointment on his face.

"I'm sorry, baby. You played a good game, though," she said and gave him a huge hug, wrapping her arms around his neck and swinging her feet in the air.

"Thanks," he mumbled, pulling Shae higher up off the ground and kissing her while a small, blond headed boy tugged at his jersey.

"Can I-I h-have you autodraft'?" the kid, ranging between the ages of three to five, asked with a shy stutter. The young child held the opening-day-game program up for Jeff to sign, with a pen in his other hand. His mom and dad stood a few yards away, smiling as their son took matters into his own hands.

"Of course, my man," Jeff said, taking the program and the pen and signing his picture on page eleven. He handed both items back to the boy as the kids parents walked over to collect him. "Here you go little fella."

The boy smiled and ran to his parents, hugging his daddy's legs. "What do you say now, Peter?" his mom asked him as he buried his head out of sight.

The child whirled around to face Jeff and said, "Tank' you!"

The parents, Jeff, and Shae all got a laugh out of this. The parents also said 'thank you' and were on their way.

"How 'bout you go out with me, and I'm buying. No buts," Shae said, turning Jeff's attention back to her. He pretended to juggle the question around in his head, even though he knew no one could refuse that offer. *Shae made him an offer he couldn't refuse,* he thought. *More lines from Don Corleone and the Godfather family later on, I promise.*

"Sounds good, but let's go to the *Hardball Café* across the street. I mean, that's where all the players usually go to have drinks and get food. So I've heard... that okay?"

"Sure baby. But I'm buying tonight," she said with a big, can't-wait-until-then smile.

"Aight, be out as quickly as I can," Jeff said, and he started back to the clubhouse, his original destination. He signed a few more balls and cards and then went into the fieldhouse. As he entered, he never knew how professional baseball players reacted to a loss until he had seen it first-handed. Sometimes, as a rookie, you truly didn't know what to expect—professional baseball was an entirely different world compared to college or high school.

The players weren't laughing and cracking jokes hysterically, but Jeff could sense the good humor in the air. Hell, anyone could have, it was just that easy to detect the difference between bitterness and glee. He expected shame and disgust, but they acted as if they had won the title today. Don't get me wrong, these guys took their work seriously and understood the circumstances, but they also knew how to shrug their shoulders and say, 'Tomorrow's another day.'

"Fuckin' Fetters lost his job after tonight!" Gunn shouted, and some of the players burst out with laughter. Gunn kept running his shit, as always. "Oh shit, man, I'm too fuckin' funny. Oh by the way, somebody let Will borrow a hit. Sonofabitch went oh-for."

"Haha, oh yeah, oh man!" Everybody broke out with laughter and tears, absolutely no chance to hold it back. "Haha!"

Most people never would have even thought the team would behave like they were after a loss, especially such a revolting one. But most people were wrong, terribly wrong.

They take it one win or one loss at a time. It's such a long season (even a thirty-four game season seems like an eternity) you're going to lose some games. If every player went around with last night's defeat cramping their brains, the sullen look on their faces would show, and most likely rub the whole team badly.

The solution is: stay focused and try not to get down. If it takes partying and having a good time after a loss, then so fucking what! If it takes going home and relaxing to ease the terrible feeling in your gut, let it be! However you choose to handle the situation, it doesn't really matter, just let the season get rolling and show up to play. Let me say that again, though, Show… Up… To… Play…

Jeff showered and cleaned up, prancing to his locker with a blue towel wrapped around his waist. Next to him, Williams told the veteran, Funk, about his performance. Lake said, "I felt good out there until the sixth and definitely the seventh. During the seventh, I felt like I lost total control of my stuff." A lot of players went to Mr. Sanders for advice. Hell, a lot of players just went to each other, sometimes someone else can see what you can't.

"You looked pretty good out there so don't fret over nothing. Just a tough loss, but we'll get 'em next time," Fred Sanders replied to Lake, answering like a true veteran. Jeff put on the same pair of cut-off shorts he wore the other night with Shae, and a Korn t-shirt. Coach walked into the room.

The room silenced itself, awaiting Skip's game review or commands. "I usually don't give speeches after games unless it's really important," Skip said. "Y'all don't get down over that shit, especially the younger players. Come back tomorrow, and we will be ready to get 'em back. Now everybody get tha' fuck outta here and go have a good time." He left the room, and the team finished dressing; tonight's events still ahead. Jeff finished with a dash of *Candies For Men* cologne and headed for the exit.

"Hey Hartes? Watcha' doin' later?" Will asked Jeff right before he got out the door. "Trying to skip out on me and the other old-timers?"

"Naw, of course not. I'm going to the *Hardball* with Shae. That's where everyone goes, isn't it?"

"Yeah, usually. Sucks you had to find out so fast." Coleman smiled. "See you there, then."

Jeff nodded and veered through the clubhouse door. He moseyed on outside and gave the beautiful Shae a big hug again. She looked so damn hot in her tight and not very long blue jean shorts. He wanted to eat her up right there. The young enchanters chatted for a second longer, and then jumped in her car—a silver Mercury Sable. It was pretty damn nice if you asked Mr. Hartes his opinion on cars that women drive.

He liked it, and so did she, so who cares what anyone else thinks, right? They cruised across Gray Street and parked in the *Hardball's* lot. When they got inside, Hicks, Gunn, and Fetters were already at a table, causing a commotion.

"Come and sit with us Hartes. Or does your girl want to sit alone wit' ya'?" Gunn asked him, sticking his tongue out to one side.

He looked at Shae. She looked back at him with a *yes* on her face, and they made their way to the table. It seated about eight, maybe nine, plenty of room for more if necessary. Hartes introduced Shae, and the gang of ballplayers ordered their drinks.

"I'll take Coors Light," Jeff said. "And she will have a...?" He looked at Shae, waiting for her to fill in the answer to the short questionnaire.

She said, "Ummm... I'll have a Coke, please."

"You sure, baby? You can probably drink here. I don't think anyone cares?" Jeff asked, referring to Shae being under age.

"No, sweetie, Coke's fi—" Shae started to respond, but the waitress interrupted.

"Sir? Do you want that in a glass or a bottle?" the perky and very pretty waitress asked, tossing her hair to the side. Jeff didn't know if she was attempting to flirt with him or the whole table, or just working hard for a tip.

"Bottle's fine."

"Okay, be right back," the waitress replied, smiling so bluntly that she was showing teeth.

Hicks tapped her on the side, and asked her what her name was. *Or maybe she was flirting with Jason.*

"It's Britney. And... *you* must play for the Demons?"

"As a matter of fact, I do. Jason Hicks." He slid his hand off the table and towards her.

"Nice to meet you, Mr. Hicks," Britney said, extending her hand to meet his. Jason took her hand and gave it a gentle shake.

"The thumb thing, watch for the thumb thing," Gunn leaned over and whispered to Jeff and Shae, where only the three of them could hear.

"Huh?"

"Look. Hurry."

Jason moved his thumb up and down, softly, caressing her hand with it. Shae rolled her eyes and shook her head. And then Jason smiled, connecting her eyes with his, and said, "Call me Jason, I'm not *that* old." With that, everyone started laughing (some, more so over Jason's comments, some, more at the 'thumb thing'), including the pretty waitress.

She said, "Okay Jason, I'll be right back with your drinks."

From first glance she just looked like a pretty girl, but after getting a good look, she was a beauty! Blonde hair, blue eyes, tall girl, around five foot nine. She also had some of the most incredible legs Hicks had ever seen. They came with a bonus tan that would send any guys' pecker soaring for new heights.

A killer? Hell yes a killer, a straight out walking, talking murderer with a body as stunning as hers was.

Britney brought the professionals (plus Shae) their drinks—Coors Light for Jeff. He sipped on his beer as she set the other drinks on the table with their purchasers, respectively. Hartes glanced at the clock in the bar reading 10:40 p.m.. *Still early,* he thought. Everyone chatted and laughed at Steve's jokes as they consumed their drinks.

"Okay, okay… there were these guys out playing golf," Gunn started. "One guy was like, 'man I got to take a shit.' The other guy said for him to go in the trees. 'Yeah, but what do I wipe with?' asked the first guy. 'Wipe with a dollar,' the second guy told him. The guy went into the trees and came back about five minutes later with crap all over him. The second guy asked, 'What happened?' The first guy said… 'You try wiping with three quarters, two dimes, and a nickel.'"

The entire table started cracking up, especially Fetters; he almost fell out of his chair. It wasn't that the joke was the greatest anyone had heard, but the way Steve presented it with his body language and the hard laugh he released after the punch line (similar to Jackie "The Joke Man" Martling) did the job. Whether it was funny or not, Gunn was going to laugh if he said it.

After the noise diminished, Gunn started up again, "Alright, one more. One day this guy went to the pet store to look around. The salesman—"

"How old was this guy?" Will Coleman interrupted, stirring the listeners' concentration from Gunn to himself as he entered the bar alone.

"Shutup Will, quit fucking up the joke!" Steve yelled back at his infield partner. Will hushed immediately; instead, he took the seat next to Hicks and sat down. The table refocused its attention to the "Big Daddy."

"The salesman came up to him and told him he had the best frog in the whole world. 'This frog gave the best blow jobs out of anybody.' The guy told him he'd take him. He bought the frog and went home that evening. The sales clerk was right. He did give the best blows. Later that night —" Gunn paused and took a sip of his beer, "—that night, the man's wife heard him rattling pots and pans in the kitchen. His wife asked him what in the world was he doing. He said, 'If I can teach this frog to cook and clean, your ass is outta' here!'"

Once again, everyone giggled and laughed like little kids. Hanging out with the team was such a thrill for Hartes. He was so gratified that he was in pro ball and had the chance to be with guys like Gunn, Will, Jason, and so on…

He now understood how Eric, his younger brother, felt when he was allowed to hang out with Jeff and his friends in the high school days. To Jeff, it didn't always seem like that big of a deal. But to Eric, it meant the world. Jeff now felt like the younger brother hanging out with his older friends and being allowed to identify himself in a higher social class.

The group continued to bullshit while Jason got up and went to talk to Britney. Nobody at the table could see or hear what they were talking about, but she seemed fairly interested in Jason's insight on the world. *Fairly interested in his bullshit to get in her pants.* Gunn suggested that Jason was feeding her lines from a script that he had imprinted inside his head.

"So what do you do for fun, besides waitressing?" Jason asked her, unsure if 'waitressing' was a real word.

"Being a waitress, fun? Ha, that's funny," she said laughing, more flirting involved than her really thinking what Jason said was that hilarious. She flicked her wrist and touched Jason's shoulder with her free hand. "Well... sometimes me and my girlfriends go out clubbing or dancing. We also like to go bowling out of nowhere every now and then, too. What else? Hmm... how 'bout you? *What do you do* for fun?"

"Clubbing's not too bad. But I mainly stick to working out and playing baseball," he answered. "I also love going to nursing homes and taking care of the elderly first hand."

Jason tried to hold back the smile he was hiding, but couldn't. The 'nursing home' line was too much for him to handle. He laughed, she laughed, the flirting continued throughout the night.

"How long have you known Jeff?" the burly first baseman asked Shae, starting the table conversation again.

"For around four to five months now. He's such a sweetie. It seems like so much longer, though," Shae replied hugging on her man. Jeff loved it when she was close to him, especially in public. It felt so reassuring— comforting. He wasn't the jealous type, so he didn't mind

Shae dancing without him or socializing with other people, but it was still extra special to have her near him.

He believed his life to be perfect—pro baseball in one corner, and Shae in the other. Earlier when Jeff spoke of perfection on the baseball diamond, he hadn't included Shae. He'd almost forgotten that sometimes life does get a little bit better.

"Thanks gorgeous, you're not so bad yourself," he told Shae, smiling that, 'are-we-gonna-have-sex-later?' smile.

The visiting and laughter went on until around one-thirty in the morning. That is when everyone headed to their destinations. Jeff asked Shae if she was staying with him, but she said she had to go home and get up early for work. She usually didn't work on Saturday's, but she was going to get in some morning work before Jeff's game. Dave King was working on two big cases at the same time, so he needed Shae to do a little overtime. Jeff told her that was understandable, and they departed after a few kisses. He arrived home at around two-thirty in the morning and immediately hit the sack.

Jeff woke up to the phone ringing and grabbed it on the fifth ring. "Hewwo."

"Hey! Sorry to wake you sleepy head, but I wanted to tell you what a good time I had last night before I go back to work." Jeff instantly recognized Shae's voice on the other end of the line.

"Oh... what time is it? Damn baby. It's not even—"

"It's eleven-thirty hun."

"Oh... damn, I see. I thought you had to work early?"

"I did. I said I was calling you before I go *back* to work, silly."

"Oh... I see. Smart girl," Jeff said, being sarcastic but with good humor. "Are you coming to the game tonight? Same time, same place."

94

"Yeah! Sure babe. I get off at one, I'm on my lunch break right now," she said. They said their byes and hung up. Jeff lay in bed thinking about Jason and that chick.

I wonder if she left with him? Hmmm... good question, but no answer—at least not for the time being.

VII

The day zoomed by, and he slept away most of it, drifting in and out of sleep while watching Saturday morning kid's shows. He wasn't a 'cartoon' or 'teenage show' fanatic; it just so happened that was the channel it was on the day before, and Jeff was too lazy to change it. To be perfectly honest, he couldn't find the damn remote.

When he finally got his tired self up for good, he took a little walk to eat some afternoon brunch and grab a paper. Not that the morning's sports news would bring any cheer.

Jeff went to the *Denny's* down the street and bought a Saturday morning paper. He waited to be seated and then followed the waiter to a booth in the corner of the restaurant. Jeff slid into the booth to the opposite side of where it started (it was a round booth), and he opened the paper to the Sports section.

He ordered water to drink, and the 'Moons over my hammy' meal before he started reading the write-up from last night's game.

April 11, 1999

Demons Stung by
Scorpions in Home Opener

The Los Angeles Demons left the field after a disappointing 7-3 loss to the Arizona Scorpions on Friday night.

Eric Ridel (1-0) picked up the win for Arizona, pitching 8 innings and allowing only 3 runs.

Long time Demon Lake Williams (0-1) was rattled in the middle innings and received the loss.

Scorpion shortstop Hank Hughes helped the attack with a home-run and two RBI's, while...

Jeff read a little further down to check his name out and then gave it up. He didn't feel like reading about that shit. Who won? They won. Screw that article. Ronald Davison had been known to sugar coat a loss or twist his words where there was always something positive for the Demons, win or lose. Jeff realized this within the article and didn't care for it. Sometimes, it made the loss feel worse. *Just tell it like it was... we got our ass handed to us.*

At around four, he started getting ready to head to the field. The Demons didn't have batting practice before today's game, so he wasn't in any rush. Just strictly show up and swing the lumber.

Jeff walked outside, a beautiful day for ball, sun shining, calm breeze, no rain in the sky at all. On the drive to the stadium, he picked up a six-piece chicken strip basket at none other than *Super Ray's Chicken* and arrived

96

at the park half past five. As soon as he walked in the door to the clubhouse, he heard Jason and Big Daddy talking about just what he wanted to hear — the outcome of last night's newly acquainted.

"Hell yeah, I took her back to my place!" Hicks told Steve Gunn.

"Did ya' fuck her? You didn't do *that* to the poor girl, did ya'?" Big Daddy replied.

"No-ah," Hicks said, placing much enthusiasm on the simple no. "She said she doesn't have sex on the first night. I said okay, and just figured I would hammer her tonight. Nice girl, though... great legs."

"That is why you need to hurry up and get married," Steve said, secretly disappointed Hicks didn't nail the girl after all. Some laughter arose, expecting some Gunn humor. "I am telling you, unless you have kids, it's automatic."

Will's voice erupted from out of the shower, "Hicks' ass ain't gettin' married unless he gets the girl pregnant and has to. He might even break out the coat hanger to get out of the muthafucka!"

Everyone cracked up; even Jason was hysterical. Gunn's stomach hurt, and he was forced to hunch over mid-laugh.

"Dude!" Jason said chuckling. "I can't believe you just dropped that shit on me. I'm goin' to settle down someday and find me a nice lil' lady."

"Yeah? Well... you're a fuckin' fag, Hicks," Gunn said with one hand holding his stomach, preventing it from aching again. As always, the laughter generated up again.

All the jokes and heckling eventually came to a stop. Hartes, trying to show his sensitive side, asked Jason if he liked Britney or if she was just another lay.

Hicks said, "Sure, she's sexy, pretty interesting, and

would definitely be a nice lay." Once again, the laughter filled the room.

"Shit Jace, that's all you think about," Skip said as he entered the room from the front office. He was already in his coaching uniform and eager to get game two underway. "Okay, listen up real fast, then you ladies can get back to your nine-oh-two-one-oh slumber party. I'm posting the lineup in a sec, and just wanted to tell y'all guys that tonight is a big un'. Let's get back to five hundred and a chance to take the series. Good ball tonight boys."

Skip clapped his hands together, interrupted by Fred Sanders, adding to his pregame pep talk, "Yeah boys, let's play some hard-nose ball and win this *turkey leg*." That, of course, gave everyone another round of laughs.

"Win this turkey leg, holy shit Funk, I knew you were old, but whatha' hell does that shit mean?" Gunn yelled during all the laughter. "I mean, did you steal that one from John Madden and the N.F.L. thanksgiving games?"

Funk told Gunn to shut the hell up as the players scattered out the clubhouse, reading tonight's lineup card on the way out. Jeff glanced, made sure his name was there (thank God it was) and studied the rest of the order.

Demons' Baseball _____ April 11, 1999

(1) Lewis   8
(2) Coleman   6
(3) Hicks   5
(4) Gunn   3
(5) Rutherford 7
(6) Goodwin   9
(7) Hartes   4
(8) Parks   2
(9) Tims   1

Parks, the right-handed hitting catcher, was getting the start against Terry Marks, Arizona's lefty. Goodwin and Hartes both moved up one slot in the order, and 19-year old Michael Tims was on the mound for his professional debut.

Hartes headed out on the field with Coleman and Rutherford. They jogged across the outfield along the warning track, adjacent to the wall, and chatted a bit.

"That Shae girl is a keeper, Jeff," Will said. He was the only one who insisted on using Jeff's first name when talking to him. Almost everyone else on the team referred to him as 'Hartes' or 'Rook.'

"Damn straight," Jeff replied, smiling over the fact that he had gathered Will's praise on the other sex.

"Who da' fuck you talkin' bout nigga'?" Erric said in his usual, quick and hard to understand version of English. What some people might have called Ebonics.

"Jeff's girl," Will said, turning to Jeff. "She coming tonight, right?"

"Yeah, as soon as she can make it up."

The three starters made their pregame lap around the outfield, tossed a little long ball, and then trotted over to the dugout to check out the stat sheets. Will flipped through the stats one page at a time, checking last night's scores and which players had a big opening night.

San Diego beat Tucson easily, 6-1. Cal defeated Montana 8-3. And Carson City won the early game 7-2 over Washington. Besides a couple of well-pitched games, the only real excitement was J.L. Conrad's two dingers and four RBI's for Cal.

The attendance for last night was 6,227 — nice audience for opening night. Tonight, a lot less, but still a fair showing was expected. The faithful had to at least keep coming until the Demons got in the win column.

Kyle Queen stopped the R & B (that was currently playing Ludacris) over the speakers and switched the music to a baseball anthem — John Fogerty's "Centerfield."

"Oh, put me in coach, I'm ready to play... today. Put me in coach, I'm ready to play... today. Look at me... I can be... centerfield! Oh, put me in coach, I'm ready to play... today. Put me in coach, I'm ready to play... today. Look at me... I can be... *centerfield!*"

While the song blared, Queen started to warm up his vocal cords. About three-quarters of the way through the tune, he began, "Good evening ladies and gentlemen, welcome to the second game of the series, featuring the Arizona Scorpions and your own Los Angeles Demons. Don't worry about last night, the Demons are gonna' bounce back strong tonight."

VIII

Queen announced the starting lineups, and Los Angeles took the field. Instead of being tight and ready to shit his britches, Hartes was pumped up. He fielded the ball rolled to him by Gunn and side-armed it to first. The ball made a popping sound as it struck Steve's glove.

"Gametime baby. My house nilga', nine innin's in *my* house, bring allz' you can muthafucka's!" Rutherford chanted as he jogged between short and third, hopping up and down to make sure his legs were loose enough to go.

The Scorpions' roster was identical to last night's lineup, except Marks was throwing instead of Ridel. If it ain't broke, don't fix it. Chadley Michael was still leading off, Miles Hunter and Jake Kimmers following him. Up in the pressbox, the radio waves were filled with the voice of

The Duke, as he prepared to enlighten all baseball listeners.

"The final pregame pitch has been tossed, and centerfielder Chadley Michael makes his way to homeplate. Michael went a peachy three-for-five last night and also stole a base." Tims stood tall on the rubber, winded, and fired.

"Ball one," announced Marinville, "Michael Tims will take the rook deep in the count if he doesn't prove he can be consistent with the fastball. Tims delivers—" Michael was crowding the plate, just looking to distract the pitcher on this one. He wasn't planning on swinging the bat. "—ball two."

Marinville continued to shake his head with disgust as Tims walked Michael on four straight pitches and put the speedy outfielder on first. It was the second night in a row that the centerfielder reached first base to start off the game. Michael stood on the first base bag, removing his batting gloves and holding them in the palm of his hands —fist grip. His chiseled body filled his uniform snugly and frequently drove the ballpark groupies wild. Instead of heckling Michael, the ladies down the first base line usually whistled and asked him for his number.

Michael Tims threw his first strike to Hunter, got the count to two-and-two, and then set to fire.

"Tims sneaks a peek to first, Michael with a good lead, but not a dangerous one. Tims comes to the plate. Michael's going!" *Crack.* "Chopper to third, Hicks fields it clean, fires to first. One away. No chance at getting Michael at second, Hunter moves the runner over on a well executed hit and run. At least it appeared to be a set play to me… who knows? Maybe Michael was going on his own."

Kimmers would fly out to right on the first pitch, also moving Michael. The ball deep enough so that Goodwin, with a very good arm in right, didn't have a play.

The Duke steam-rolled on, "Michael on third, the big catcher Derrick Hundly at the plate. He went one-for-five last night and struck out once. Tims throws... strike one. Tims delivers... strike two. The pitch is on the way... it's outside. Ball two... ball three... full count now as Tims has lost his advantage. The pitch is under way... ball four. Four straight balls after starting the catcher off with two strikes. Hundly takes his free base, the second walk of the inning for young Michael Tims. Diaz steps in grinning, hitless last night."

Diaz mouthed at Tims as he was getting geared up for combat. Diaz cursed at Tims loudly, "Hey rook, yeah you! Throw that pussy-ass breaking shit in here, and I'll take ya' yard! C'mon, bring that shit in here rook." The Arizona catcher was known for his ability to talk the talk, but he didn't walk the walk as often as you might have thought.

"Fuck you," Tims said casually, like he was a machine that said 'fuck you' every time you talked to him. He returned to the rubber, digging a little deeper in the mound's dirt with the heel of his cleat. He ignored Diaz, who was still chirping in the batter's box. This time chatting it out with another rookie, Bobby Parks.

Diaz hit a rocket up the middle, scoring Michael and making it 1-0 Arizona. "I told you rook, don't try to fuck with me boy." Diaz continued talking smack from first base, this time delivering after he had run his mouth. He switched the language from English to Spanish, but never shut up.

Diaz said something in the line of, "No te quiere chingar con migo chingo tu madre."

"Ignore his fat ass Tims and lez' get the fuck outta' this inning," Hicks said from across the diamond, drawing a glance from Diaz. The man on first didn't open his mouth to Hicks, though. No need to fuel Jason's fire, because he knew the Demon third baseman could do some immediate damage.

The shortstop Hughes lined out to Hartes at second to end the top half of the first. The liner looked tough, but there was nothing to it. Hartes jumped a few feet in the air and snagged before it could get in the rightfield alley. The defense hustled back in the dugout, grateful they only gave up one run.

"Good play Hartes," Skip said, not at all frustrated during the initial stages of the game.

"No prob coach, uhhh... Skip."

"That's better. Now let's get the bats going and show these guys our offensive pop."

Nobody on the team knew what Skip said, but everyone felt more suitable in their offensive roles. It all seemed to come in place in only one tiny second of time. The entire dugout was alive. At that very instant, that very moment in time, the team seemed to know they would break out and score numerous runs on these guys.

Hartes markedly felt the same way. He was right!

Lewis singled to right, stole second, and scored on a double in the gap by Coleman. Hicks walked. Gunn took the count to 1-2 when Marks hung a curve ball over the middle of the plate.

"One-two count on Big Daddy," The Duke repeated enthusiastically, sensing a rally. "Coleman on second, Hicks on first, nobody out. Marks checks his runners, then delivers." *Whack!* "Deep drive toward left-center, this ball is back, way back, it's gone! A three-run blast for Gunn, making it four-to-one Los Angeles!"

The inning continued as Marks was ripped through the left side for a single by Rutherford. Then Marks K'd Goodwin, bringing up Hartes.

The Duke presented, "Jeff Hartes steps in trying to

maintain the Demon rally. He went one-for-three last night with a sacrifice fly. Quick move by Marks to first! Not in time. Rutherford slides safely under the tag. Marks scopes first again, then rocket-fires home." *Crack!* "Well-hit ball down the leftfield line... off the wall. Hartes rounds first, Skip is sending Rutherford all the way as the ball took a nasty hop away from Kimmers. Jake comes up throwing, the play at the plate. No chance! R.B.I. double for Jeff Hartes, increasing the lead to four."

Jeff would remain at second, though, as the southpaw retired Parks on a ground ball to short, and got Tims out on a pop-up to the catcher. 5-1 after one, this was the Demon baseball the home crowd could grow accustomed to.

No runs were scored in the second or the third. Tims struck out Willis and Marks in the second and got Chavez to fly out in the middle.

While Marks only gave up a walk to Hicks with two outs after Lewis and Coleman both grounded out to the left side. And then Gunn, who electrified the fans in the first, flied out to straight away center, ending the inning.

There was nothing different in the third. Michael lined out to Goodwin in right, Hunter popped up to first, and Hundly grounded out to short after Kimmers reached base on Hicks' second error of the season.

Rutherford struck out to start the bottom of the third, Goodwin flew out to shallow center, and Hartes hit a dying quail that Michael caught with his body fully extended.

"Oh my, sportsfans, what a diving catch made by Chadley Michael. Unbelievable! I thought there was no way anyone could get to that one. We now have a Western League 'web gem' E.S.P.N.!" The Duke said with much more discouragement than gratitude, since his player was the one that got robbed. "Marks has really settled down after that horrific first inning, allowing only one base runner since."

Diaz woke the crowd up, not with cheers of joy, but with boos all over the stadium after he struck out looking and gave home umpire, Bernie Cavanaugh, an earful, "That was the worst fucking call I've ever seen, and you know it!"

"Keep it up Marco," Cavanaugh replied.

"I will! I can't believe you can be that *bad* after all these fuckin' years of 'piring!" By now, nothing was coming out clear (saying 'piring' instead of umpiring), there was more spittle coming out than proper English.

"One more comment and you're gonna' get run, Marco."

"I got your fuckin' one more comment right here, Bernie!" Diaz said, grabbing his crouch like Michael Jackson always did to drive the ladies crazy. Or because he loved touching that body part, little boys included. But that's just an allegation.

I don't think Diaz was trying to turn on any women at this point, but his message was clear enough that the fans thought he should have been tossed. The boos continued to reign throughout the stadium as Skip rose from his chair and took a step towards the homeplate umpire.

"Are you going to let him get away with that shit, Bernie?" Skip asked the ump, upset that 'blue' was going to let Diaz walk all over him like that.

"I'll worry about that Bailey, don't worry. You worry about your ball club," Cavanaugh replied, pulling his mask back over his face.

"Yeah, you do that," Skip added, retiring back to his chair. "Let's go now, Michael."

Diaz stomped back into the dugout continuing to bitch, but his case was over, next batter up. Hughes singled, but was thrown out at second on Willis' ground ball to Hartes.

"Ground ball to second, Hartes up with it, flips it over to Coleman, Coleman fires to first. Double play!" The Duke shouted all over Los Angeles. "Inning over. Four-six-three double play sending us to the bottom of the fourth."

Parks hit a rocket back up the middle that was snagged by Marks for the first out. Marks sat the opposing pitcher down on three fastballs, putting Tims 0-2 for the night. He walked Lewis, but got out of the fourth without any trouble on a fly ball to left hit by Coleman.

In between innings, the radio commercials were playing 'This Bud's for you, and you, and you, and you!' and 'Bang! The male chick-magnet.' After the advertising, The Duke soothed the listeners with his always fascinating lingual, "Top of the fifth here in Los Angeles. Boy I'll tell ya', it's a beautiful night for baseball, seventy-three degrees with a light breeze blowing in from rightfield. Not a cloud in the sky.

Nico Chavez will start things off for the Scorpions. He is still battling the monkey that is so gently sitting upon his back. Oh-for-four for the two nights combined. Tims sets, delivers… ball one to Chavez. Nico tears up some dirt and digs in, pitch underway." *Whack.* "Slicer down the rightfield line, that ball is in the hole, Goodwin has trouble handling it. Chavez is being rounded to third, the throw on the way. Safe. He slides in with a triple to start off the fifth. Not a bad first hit of the year. I must have jinxed him."

Marks didn't do his job, leaving Chavez stranded after a weak fly to short. But Michael would do his (at least, regarding moving the base runner), hitting a high chopper to second base, where Hartes would have only one option —first base. He fielded it clean and gunned Michael for the second out. Hunter ended the inning with a line out to Hicks. It was 5-2 in favor of the home team.

Marks must have thought he was really rolling, striking out Hicks and Gunn to open the bottom half. But that—I got your number now, so step up and fall down—grin would be wiped off in a heartbeat. He walked Rutherford. Then with a 1-1 count on Goodwin, he made a big mistake.

"The pitch from Marks," The Duke said. *Crack!* "Uh-oh! Not a good sign for the Arizona fans. In *Bull Durham* fashion, that ball must have had a stewardess on board, because it took off in a hurry. Bye-bye Mr. Rawlings! Two-run shot for Billy Goodwin, upping the score to seven-to-two Demons!"

That would end Terry Marks' night. He gave up seven earned runs, walked four, and struck out four in four and two-thirds innings. Now coming in for the Scorpions was another lefty, Japanese native Bruce Yen. He warmed up and then got Hartes to ground out to second, ending the fifth.

Tims stayed on top of his game getting out of the sixth without any harm done.

Yen did the same.

The seventh was boring as well; Tims wrapped his debut K'ing two and finishing seven innings, allowing only two earnies. Darren Luthers would replace Tims for Los Angeles, getting his first action of the year.

In the bottom half of the seventh, Yen showed he was still in command, sitting the Demons down in order.

Michael led off the eight with a hard hit grounder through the right side for a single. He stole second, moved to third on a wild pitch, and scored on Hunter's ground ball to short. Luthers then walked Kimmers on five pitches. Hundly doubled Kimmers in on a 1-1 changeup, making it 7-4. It looked like it was time for a pitcher-catcher-coach meeting, and Skip was on his way.

"Settle down out there, just get a feel for things," Skip said.

"Yeah, I'm alright, I got this guy," Luthers responded.

"Hit your spots," Skip said on his way back to the dugout. He motioned for Salmon Seavers to get up in the pen and plopped back down in his usual place. He discussed the situation with pitching coach, Larry George, asking him what he thought of Darren's pitching. George said that Luthers wasn't following through all the way, leaving pitches up in the zone. It hurt his control and also made it easier for the hitters to pick up and drive somewhere for a hit.

Luthers threw two strikes to Diaz, and then left a 0-2 curve ball over the pentagon, Diaz tattooed it. He wound up with a double, driving in Hundly. The score was now 7-5. Skip, thinking enough was enough, stood up, and called for the lefty (tapping his left bicep with his right hand).

Salmon Seavers came in and struck out Hughes on four pitches. Willis popped out to Hartes at second to get the Demons out of the jam.

"Great job, Salmon," Skip said as Seavers jogged in the dugout. "You've got the ninth, too."

"That's fine wit' me, Skip."

Marty Bell was the new guy on the mound for Arizona, bringing some junk to the game. The guy had no fastball, but was as nasty as they came. He threw a Mussina-like knuckle-curve, though not nearly as deadly. He mixed in a slow sinker and changeup. But his signature pitch was the hook. He threw it with a top to bottom curve rather than breaking left to right (known as a twelve-to-six curve ball based on the readings of a clock). As long as you were extremely patient and sat back on a pitch, he was plenty hittable. But if you approached the at bat too pumped up and trying to kill the ball, you were going to be

Bell's bitch.

Midway through the inning, The Duke updated radio listeners on scores and highlights from around the league. "Carson City improved to two-and-oh, defeating Washington four-three in a thriller. Both starters left the game before it was decided, Carson relief pitcher Lenny Cox got the win, while Washington relief pitcher Mike Peters was handed the loss. In California, Montana evened up the series count one-one, winning 11-6. Montana added four homeruns in their victory. In the late game of the afternoon, San Diego leads Tucson two-to-nothing off a two-run blast by Jacques Martin. That one is in the sixth inning."

Back to gametime, where Bell's breaking shit and change pieces worked the Demons over. Rutherford hit a looper back to the pitcher, Goodwin singled on a dying flair over the short stop, Hartes grounded out to third, but there was no play at second, and Parks popped up to the catcher on a brutal knuckler.

Last inning... last chance for the visitors. But they would have to do it off of a very solid closer.

Chavez singled to lead off the ninth for Arizona. Seavers wasn't rattled, though, knowing he had a two-run cushion and the ability to get a strikeout when needed. Instead, he got something better. Pinch-hitter Derry Wells hit into a double play bringing everyone to their feet, and the stadium to a roar.

The Duke picked up again, "Two outs in the ninth, Michael the last hope for Arizona fans. Seavers brings the gas... strrrrike one! Every member of the attendance is on his or her feet. Seavers stumbles around the rubber, then gets set, winds, and throws... strrrrrrrike two! Oh my, that ball was smokin'. Michael steps out, takes a deep breath, and then stands back in. The pitch... ball one. Just outside the right portion of the plate."

The fans stomped on the metal row of stadium seats in front of them, hollering as loud as their vocal cords would allow. They chanted everything from 'Seavers! Seavers! Seavers!' to 'Strike 'em out!' to 'Let's go Demons!'

"Seavers glares into the catcher's mitt, comes up, and then delivers..." Marinville said. "STRRRRIKE THREE!!! Ball game over, he struck him out."

Simultaneously to The Duke's call, the crowd was going nuts, and the whole stadium was a rockin'. The only thing going through Jeff Hartes' head was 'awesome, freaking awesome.' The speakers were playing the verse, 'Nana-na-na, Nana-na-na, hey hey hey, goodbye!'

"Now we can party tonight," Rutherford said as he was jogging in from center, barely understandable. He slapped Coleman on the back, and all the bench players came out to give everyone dibs on a good game. After banging fists with all the players, Jeff searched the stands for Shae.

"Jeff! Jeff! Over here... you silly brute. Can't you spot me any quicker than that?" Shae hollered, hanging over the fence separating the field from the stands. She dangled over the railing, showing some cleavage. Her cheeks were glowing as she smiled from ear to ear. She was happier than Jeff was over the victory.

"Watch your mouth, sexy!" he retorted.

"Just kidding babe," she said as Jeff yanked her over the fence and gave her a big hug. *Smooch!* They kissed passionately for a lengthy while (the ones that last ten seconds but seem like days), and then chatted while he signed some autographs.

Damn, you sure could get used to this life in a hurry.

The entire team was joking and signing every item jammed into their face by overjoyed kids. Jeff was positive he would end up going to the *Hardball* joint after he cleaned up, but he didn't tell Shae just yet.

"Alright baby, be out in no time," he said, leaving Shae's grasp for the after-game shower session.

"No rush, there are plenty of other cuties out here."

"Real funny," he said sarcastically, but smiling because he knew he was her boy, at least at this point in time. And boys would be boys.

IX

In the clubhouse, Gunn was up to his usual 'shits and giggles.' He was dogging Parks for going oh-for on this night, and making sure the whole team witnessed his long ball. Hartes got naked, showered, freshened up, and told the gang that he would see them at the café.

"Save us a table, dawg," Will yelled from the shower, the water blurring his words.

"You taking your truck, Hartes?" Fetters asked before Jeff could answer Coleman.

"Nah, I'm riding with Shae in tha' Sable."

"Okay. That's cool man, well… save us a table like the idiot in the shower requested."

"Aight, I will," Hartes answered as he went out the door, saw Shae by her car, and immediately went for her. He swept her in his arms, and they kissed again.

"*Hardball*, right dear?" she asked, and he could tell in her voice that she wanted to go hang out with the guys, and that she wanted him to be with her. That was why he loved her, and why he would continue loving her. To coin a phrase that has withstood the test of time; he would love her until the day she died — until the day *he died.*

It mostly came down to the small things you miss when you aren't seriously involved. The things married people become accustomed to: the woman farting in front of the man, her rubbing her unshaved legs against his body and getting 'that's gross' for a reply, the man scratching his balls directly in front of her, him announcing to everyone that she's—

"*Hardball*, right Hartes!?" Hicks shouted on his way out the door.

"Yeah, man," Jeff responded, and then turned back to Shae. "And yes, to you too, baby."

Shae and Jeff were the first ones to arrive, so they (trying to guess the right number) asked the waitress for a large booth, preferably sitting around eight people. She showed them to their table, and they scooted in together, sitting as closely as they would when the table began to fill.

Big Daddy, Hicks, and Fetters showed up next, sliding into the over-sized (fixing to be undersized) booth. Then a couple of minutes after they sat down, Will and Lake came in with a girl dressed in a tight skirt and a revealing top. Will had his arm around the girl's waist as they walked towards the circular booth. She had lighter skin than Will's, slightly resembling Halle Berry with straightened hair. And the ass... was definitely banging. She started to laugh right before reaching the table, gently hitting Will on the arm and shaking her head. She had that look... the look of a girl who loved to cut up and enjoyed life.

"This is Regina, everyone." The normal 'hi's' and 'hey's' that follow an introduction came out. Will proceeded, "Regina, this is Jeff, uhhh... this is Shae, right?" She nodded as if to say yes, and then Will continued to introduce Regina to the rest of the team at the table. Only time would show how their friendship would develop throughout the course of the season. How Will and Jeff would become even closer friends... along with Shae and Regina hanging out when the girls needed a break from their guys.

They took their seats and the laughter began. Where the laughter initiated? That's a simple enough question.

It started with another Steve Gunn comedy def-jam. "Okay, okay, all y'all hush up. I got one for ya'. There was this rich guy and this poor guy who were discussing what they were going to get their wives for Christmas. The poor guy asked the rich guy, 'what are you going to get your wife?' The rich guy said, 'I'm gonna' get her a Mercedes-Benz and a diamond ring.' The poor guy said, 'why would you get her both?' Rich guy said, 'cause if she doesn't like the diamond ring, she can take it back in her Mercedes-Benz.' The poor guy thought that was a pretty good idea. When the rich guy asked the poor guy, 'what are you going to get your wife?' The poor guy said, 'a pair of slippers and a dildo.' The rich guy said, 'why both? That doesn't seem a likely combination.' The poor guy said, 'cause if she doesn't like the slippers... she can go fuck herself!'"

Shae and Jeff turned to each other laughing and then fell on top of one another. Jason slammed his fist down on the table and almost gagged. Everyone else cackled non-stop, saying 'that was a good one Steve.'

Will relaxed, caught his breath, and then said, "Damn Gunn, did you go buy a fuckin' book or somethin' on joke-telling? 'Cause you're the master."

That brought some slight chuckles, but nothing compared to Gunn's hysterics. Once again, the joking and festivity carried on deep into the night. Around 2:00 a.m., couple number one decided they wanted to go back to Jeff's place before they were too sleepy to—(if you know what I'm saying). They weren't the only ones to leave in search of new pleasures, though.

Will and Regina followed right behind their 'fun-and-games' lead, most likely to go participate in their own carnival. Where the Ferris wheel never came to a stop and the rides never ended.

Hicks, who was talking to Britney again, was still alive and going. Britney ended her shift at 2:30, so they (her and Hicks) were waiting until that glorious time. Fetters and Gunn were chit-chatting and downing a few more cold ones before they left—back to their married lives. Shae and Jeff went through the *Hardball's* front door and were cut off by Lake. Williams asked Jeff for a lift home and told him the whereabouts of his home.

"Sure, it's on the way," Shae said.

"Yeah Lake, no prob'," Jeff added, assuring Lake that it was cool with him as well. Although that didn't matter much; Shae had the final say-so in most things.

They cruised with the windows down and the radio blaring, listening to the mix station, 97.7. They dropped off Lake at his destination. It was a community home with several players staying in it: Lake, Salmon, Erric, and Billy. Will had told Jeff that Erric and Billy (the two crazy outfielders) always smoked up the place with some good shit, apparently. Will wasn't as big on weed (only tokin' it up a few times in his younger days) as 'E' and Goodwin, but he didn't seem to mind occasionally hanging with them.

As soon as Lake disappeared behind his door, Shae and Jeff were on each other, necking and kissing vigorously.

"Jeff, let's hurry and get home," she said, pulling away slowly.

"Sounds good to me." All the middle infielder could think about was *let's hurry and get home... let's hurry and get home...let's hurry and get home...*

What if his apartment was her home, too? What if he wanted her to move in? The two of them having a home sounded so damn *amazing*, it was a new *amazing* that he'd never felt until now, but an *amazing* he could get used to.

They sped on their way, made it back to his place (their place) as fast as humanly possible. They barely barraged through the door with their clothes on. Everything was coming off, and it was coming off very hastily.

Jeff tore her shirt off, kissing her breasts. The passion and intensity was running on high. 'Code Red, Code Red, must shut down for fear of overheating'. But the machine didn't turn off; instead, it (they) moved towards the bedroom, supporting each other, and she collapsed back first into his bed. He slid the condom on in record time and was instantly on top, dragging her pants (and panties) down to her ankles.

Shae had on some sexy silk panties, red as roses, tiny as hell. She squeezed Jeff's back with her hands as he rocked forward into her.

"Oh Jeff! Don't stop. Ohhhh God!" Shae moaned.

They fucked wildly, no romantics involved in this rendezvous. Jeff breathed harder as he came closer to the end, biting down on the pillowcase. She screamed and coaxed him on.

"Harder Jeff! Do me Jeff!"

"I'm al... most... there... baby!" The pro-baseball-playing stud came in his protective pouch just as the word 'baby' exited his mouth. He continued pushing, repeating the famous sex cliché 'Oh God' over and over.

"Ooooh sweetie, you're sooo goood!" Shae said, trying to recapture her breath. "Now I know why I want to be with you so bad."

Jeff rolled over, and they lay there on their backs for a couple of seconds, completely naked. He broke the silence,

"Is that the only reason you want to be with me, for the sex?"

"No, of course not. I'm with you because you're so hot... and sweet... and loving... but most of all, the exhilarating sex!"

"Ha-ha, you're so funny," Jeff said, laughing a fake laugh. "But it's an improvement."

"Everything is always better when I am with you."

"Thanks hun'. That's the sweetest thing anyone has ever told me," he said as they cuddled up as one and fell fast asleep.

X

The clock read 11:26 a.m.. Jeff leaned over, no partner.

'Wonder where Shae is?' he thought to himself, still awakening, still worn out. Instead of scanning his head for the answer, Jeff tried speaking out loud in search of it. "Hmm... it's Sunday, she doesn't have work 'til late, where in the wo—"

"You awake?" Shae whispered with her head peeking through his bedroom door.

"Yep, sure am."

She entered the room and crawled under the covers with him. He put his arms around her and embraced her like a teddy bear.

"Love you," he said, without even realizing the words 'love' and 'you' had just come out of his mouth—together even. He kissed her forehead, kind of hoping she didn't even hear him, when she said.

"Love ya' too." *Perfect.*

They dozed, off and on, until he finally arose for game

time. He threw on a pair of shorts and an Eldridge Baseball T-shirt. Jeff had had that shirt since his senior year in high school. It had all the high school players' names from the state championship team he was on: Tommy Moses, Paul Aduka, Gabe Anderson, yours truly, etc. Shae was coming to life too, now, rolling over as she yawned.

"Excuse me."

"You're excused," Jeff commented. "I'm about to head to the field. Are you coming tonight?" Shae sat up, stretching with her arms extended outward.

"I have to get a bunch of papers organized at work tonight and some more stuff for in the morning. Dave's still got both of those cases rolling full steam ahead. He needs all the help he can get, and you know I owe him a lot."

"You *owe* him more than me? The love of your life?" Jeff asked, interrupting in a teasing manner.

"Hush..." Shae laughed. "I won't be able to make it tonight, but... where do you play next?"

"We're off tomorrow, go to Carson City Tuesday."

"Wanna' do something after I get off work then?"

"What time will that be?" he asked.

"Around four, I will just come by about six. We can figure it out then," Shae said, heading from the living room to the front door.

"That's fine, I'll be here then." He walked behind her, leaned towards her and kissed her on the lips. And then he got the tongue he was in store for. "Bye baby."

"Bye," Shae said as she opened the door to go to her car. "Oh wait, do you need a ride to the field, remember your truck's there."

"Taken care of. Simon comes by here on his way. I will get him to pick me up. See ya' tomorrow, bye baby."

"Okay... bye." She jumped in her Sable and drove off. Jeff waited until she was out of sight, and then went back inside to find some grub.

He ate and watched some NBA on NBC. At 5:00 p.m., Luthers honked outside the apartment. Jeff grabbed his bag (after-game clothes, shaving kit, etc...) and locked up. Luthers, with Hartes along for the free ride, cruised to the stadium and pulled into the parking lot at 5:17 p.m.

XI

"Good game, Jeff!" Shae yelled from the stands as he made his way towards the clubhouse and a shower.

"Wow... Hey! I didn't think you were coming tonight?"

"I just got here in the... around the seventh inning. Are you gonna' come give me a kiss, or am I going to have to go home?"

"Hell yeah!" Jeff said and sprinted over to her, kissed her, and casually laughed with her.

The Demons defeated Arizona 7-5 in the third game of the series. Hartes hit his first homerun of his career, and ended up 2-4 with two RBI's. Gunn and Coleman also homered in the victory, while Jimenez picked up the win out of the bullpen. "Hold on a sec, okay Shae? Be right back."

"Okay, hurry up, I miss you already," she replied.

He smiled and jogged up to the pressbox to get the play-by-play tape from Darrell. He wanted to keep the call on his first yard ball, and let Shae hear the action live. Maybe even record it, and send it back home for pops. Jeff thanked The Duke, a true radio guy with long hair and a growing beer gut, for the tape, told him he would make a copy, and then bring it in tomorrow.

"No need to do that, Jeff, I've got one in the copy deck," The Duke said, always in a jubilant mood when the Demons won, and the total opposite after tough losses.

"Alright man, thanks again. I'll see ya' on the road." Jeff closed the door to the pressbox and hopped down the bleachers back to Shae.

"What's that?" Shae asked as he approached her.

"Tape of my homerun you missed. Figured you might want to listen to it. If not, I wanted to keep it anyway."

"Of course I want to hear it, I didn't know you hit one. Damn, that sucks I missed it."

"Maybe next time you'll see my massive power," he said, flexing, and they both cracked up.

They embraced, holding each other while walking to the clubhouse door. He told her the usual; that he would be out as quickly as possible, and then left her. Jeff entered the clubhouse—Skip and Gunn were discussing the game—and went to his locker.

After Skip finished bullshitting, he walked to the center of the room and said, "Day off tomorrow, leaving that night, though. Be here and be ready to go by seven o'clock sharp. Let's go get us some of the defending champs."

Jeff went through his usual post-game routine, and then exited the clubhouse to meet Shae in the parking lot. The homerun-hitting second baseman was re-routed by the *Channel 7 Sports* team—a newsman with a Mic and his cameraman.

"Jeff! Hey Hartes! Gotta' second?" the reporter asked. It was the same guy who had interviewed Lake before the season opener. His name was Andy something, Andy —'Andy Wilkins.' He took Jeff's hand in his own before the infielder could even lift his arm. "Pleased to meet you Hartes."

"Likewise," Jeff responded, and awaited the barrage of questions to begin.

"Starting with the obvious, how does it feel to hit your first professional homerun?" Wilkins asked, jamming the Mic up to Jeff's mouth.

"Uh... basically... just how you would expect it to feel. You know, when you're a kid growing up, you pretend and-and... umm... dream about playing professional baseball and hitting your first homerun. And when it finally happens, if it ever does, it's awesome. It's a great feeling inside. Hoping to have that feeling happen as a much as possible."

"Okay Jeff," Wilkins added, jotting a few notes down, but mostly relying on the camera recording the interview. But taking notes was a backup plan to insure the journalist that nothing could go wrong. A fail-proof, preventive measure. On to the next question, "The Demons are taking a two-game win streak on the road, against the defending champs, Carson City. What's the team's attitude and status heading on their first road trip?"

"Well, I know, speaking personally, that I'm excited about hitting the road and what lies ahead. It's always difficult to speak for the whole team as an individual, but I guess you could say we are ready to get things rollin'. There are a lot of small things we have to get better at and improve on, but winning our first series of the year was a goal we wanted to accomplish, and we did."

"I can understand how it can be so important in this so-called 'Elite' league, playing only thirty-four games," Wilkins continued. "How important is it to take every game seriously?"

"Very important... it's like an N.F.L. season, and like you said, with such a short season, every game is crucial, and any one is as big as another. Most of the guys play in other leagues around the world in the off-season and come here ready for the best baseball you can see besides the majors. We just have to stay focused on our goal, to win a championship."

The interview concluded after a couple of more questions, while Shae lingered in the background, waiting for her sweetie. She was proud of him and enjoyed the mild limelight she was receiving, being his girl and all. After Jeff and Andy said their farewells, he and Shae tried to figure out what they wanted to do. They discussed their options a couple of times, and then Parks and Seavers came up to them with an answer to their problem.

Bobby Parks was the total opposite of the other youngsters on the team. He was rugged, occasionally unshaven (more often than shaved), and was truly dedicated to the nasty habit of dipping. He chewed tobacco nonstop, usually leaving wads of chew running down his chin like black spittle. He was about 5'10", not heavyset, and could run rather well for having 'catcher's knees.' His baserunning was comparable to Jason Kendall. And his dark brown hair was straggly with curls on the end. One might say Parks looked like a hobo with his unfixed hair and puffed out cheeks.

"Hey Jeff, some of the guys are heading to uhh... a club. Which club we goin' to, Salmon?" the catcher said, and then he turned to his friend for help.

"It's *Montello's*. Pretty nice place if you two want to come along. Or meet us there, whatever works best for you," Seavers said. The closer picked up his second save of the season, striking out two in the ninth.

Jeff turned to Shae, gave her a *what do you want to do* look, and said, "It's up to you, baby?"

"I have to work tomorrow, going to some nurse's office to get some paperwork and stuff. But not until like...

fourish. So if I can crash with you—"

"Of course," he said quickly. "We're leaving around seven tomorrow night, so ah... take your car to my place, and we will leave to *Montello's* from there."

Salmon gave them vague directions, but Shae thought she knew where it was. They said they would see Shae and Jeff there and took off.

The lovers went to Jeff's place first, leaving Shae's car behind. They gave each other a romantic look, wondering whether or not they should have a little intimate time before they left. They decided it wouldn't be nearly as fun until they had a few drinks in them and had the despair of waiting so long for what they *longed* for.

They exited the apartment and walked together, holding hands. It was old-fashioned, but the delicate touch of her soft hands made Jeff feel warm inside. He never thought of himself as a 'holding hands' kind of guy, but with Shae (along with everything else), it felt right.

Shae jumped in his truck (black as the ocean on a clear night), and they cruised to the club. It was already late enough for traffic to be fairly light, so the trip to *Montello's* was a breeze.

Once inside the club, they scanned the place over for someone they knew. It had a neon-lighted dance floor with the D.J. playing Sir-Mix-A-Lot's famous rap song 'Baby Got Back.' Everyone was already 'freak-nastying' to the jams as Shae and Jeff made their way over to the table section of the club.

The tables were black with shiny tops. They had six cushioned chairs around each of them. In the middle of the tables sat glass ashtrays and customized matches reading '*Montello's*.' The bar had padded stools and every drink you could imagine on the shelf behind. From 'mind erasers' to 'scotch on the rocks' to 'suicide twists' to 'long island ice teas' to whatever. If you wanted it, it was there. If you knew what was in it, the bartender would make it.

"Yo yo, mister long ball! Get your ass over here," Hicks yelled at the interviewee from across the room. Jason was sitting with the pretty little waitress from the *Hardball.* On her right sat Gunn (who else), and then Seavers and Parks. Fetters and Will were the only other diehards missing.

They started towards the table when Steve stood up and shouted, "Wait a minute! Maybe you should stay over there, Jeff. We just want Shae to join us."

"Suck it Steve!" Jeff said as they drew closer to them. Gunn patted him on the back, and he pulled up an extra chair for Shae. Seven of them now sat around the table, laughing and getting to know each other a little bit more than they maybe should have.

The night carried on until the early hours of the next day. Once again, Gunn had more jokes. Where he heard or remembered all of them? Damn if Hartes knew, but they sprayed out like a nine-hitter's slaps. The group started thinning around 1:45 a.m., when Jason and Britney left holding each other.

"Hey Brit! Be careful! From what I can see in the shower-house, Jason's pretty gift-tudd—" As soon as he was saying gifted, Shae jabbed him in the stomach.

"Shhh... that's not nice," Shae told Steve.

Jason laughed, and so did Britney as they exited *Montello's.* Steve said, "I know, but it still funny."

Everyone agreed on that much, nodding his or her heads. Jeff stood up, taking Shae's hand as he did, and said, "I guess we are heading out, too."

"Well... Shae, I have to tell you the same thing I told Britney, Jeff—" Gunn started before Shae interrupted him.

"I know, Steve."

"Oh shit yeah!" Salmon and Ron said simultaneously.

Both seemed to have awakened from the *too-much-alcohol-in-blood* disease. Laughing now, they leaned back in their chairs and went into their tiresome coma again. Fetters looked like a zombie. His eyes were glazed over with a gallon of Heineken.

The couple, now up and leaving, said their goodbyes; they walked out of *Montello's*, arm in arm. They kissed a time-erasing kiss and jumped in Jeff's truck. Tonight was going to be fun, not just fun, but exhausting. *Thank God tomorrow was a day off.*

Jeff led the sprint into his apartment door, pulling Shae gently behind him. They entered the domain with their lips locked together—she, beginning to yank his shirt over his head, him, still kissing restlessly. She threw the shirt on the floor and undid his jeans. Jeff's pants fell to his ankles. He kicked them off, tossing his shoes across the room behind them. He grabbed Shae and carried her into the bedroom, kissing her all the way.

He tossed her on the bed, unbuttoned her blouse, and threw it over his shoulder. *Like a continental soldier...* he then pushed the thought out of his head. He smiled and returned to Shae, prepared to fully attend to her needs.

She was lying on the bed on her back, wearing only a pair of red panties and a red bra. Jeff crawled his way on top of her in his boxers, knowing she could feel his excitement growing down below. He kissed the exposed parts of her breasts, while sliding her panties off with his roaming hands. She reached into the cozy cove of his boxers, putting both hands around his cock.

"Know what, Shae?" he asked, gritting his teeth.

"What baby?" she responded, taking her hands out of his boxers, and then putting them around the waste-band and ripping them off. A maniacal rage gleamed in her eyes.

"I love you!"

"Love ya' too hun, now fuck me!" Shae replied.

Jeff didn't argue; he did exactly what she had said. He snapped her bra off and began to suck on her hardened nipples. She still had her hands under him, fondling his private toy. She helped him to enter her, and he started pumping. *Damn!* Jeff thought. *I don't even have a condom on; she always makes me wear one.* No time to worry about that now, the most important thing was to make her happy.

Back to sex—Jeff fucked her harder than he had ever before. She pushed upward, moaning and groaning each time.

"Ohhh God Jeff, you are soooo goooood!" she said, carrying all the syllables for a chance to catch her breath.

The love making went on late into the night. The fanatics must have had sex four times before they both crashed like a jet plane running on fumes.

Chapter Four
Another Dream, Road Trip

I

"High fly ball hit by Allen to centerfield. Lewis takes a few steps back, and makes the catch. That ends the fifth, Demons one, Knights nothing. Due up for Los Angeles in the sixth, Parks, Hicks, and Gunn," Darrell Marinville announces to the Demon faithful.

Jogging in from second, I wonder how in the hell I can hear Marinville doing the radio broadcast. After all, Marinville is in the booth, I am standing on the field. The announcer is glassed in and speaking over the radio, I am entering the dugout via the infield. Kyle Queen's voice is the one spilling through the loudspeakers throughout Diego Field, not Marinville's. Queen's the one I should be hearing, along with the fans.

So let me say it again, because it's worth repeating. I can hear Darrell "The Duke" Marinville's broadcast, along with Kyle Queen's announcing over the loudspeakers, and finally, the buzzing of the crowd altogether.

I sit in the left side corner of the always-rectangular bench. I can smell sweat in the air, tasting the cool, refreshing breeze turned sour. The smell reminds me of going to Dodgers games in the early 90s. Me and pops, having the time of our lives while rooting for one of the greatest coaches of my youth, Mr. Lasorda. *But who other than Tommy Lasorda?* And his extremely vocal, and

sometimes outrageous, rants—

I remember I always ordered the same things around the same innings. Right before the fourth or fifth, Dad would make a run to the concession stand and grab a couple of hotdogs and a Dr. Pepper, along with a beer for himself. We would heckle the opposing team's rightfielder from our second row outfield seats, and hope to God that Pedro Guerrero would hit one out in our section. Man, I wanted a homerun ball bad... I never got one. But this jerkoff next to us caught several homers throughout the season. But that's beside the point.

Then I recognize the situation—

My dream is coming to life. Not coming to life in the sense that it wasn't alive before. Because it was... *alive before.*

And not only is it alive now, but it is out to get me. Reaching and clawing with everything it has to pull me in where I can never escape. Once trapped inside, I will become nothing and live a life of nothingness. My head feels like it is going to explode as I try to ignore this burden cast upon me. This noise, these deviations; this current dramatic play I am enrolled in.

My dream *is* coming to life.

Everything is the same: the same noise ringing in my ears, the same crowd buzzing, the same fly ball to center, the same moon smiling at me in that devilish-hateful smile, and the same girl strutting down the steps towards her seat.

I stare at her; she stares back into my eyes. *I know this girl!* But I can't quite place her name with her face. My dream is real. My dream is her dream, whether she appears as a picture show in her mind or not.

Her facial features and details are shady, looking as if someone drew them in with pencil lead and then smudged them with their thumb. Just like a little kid, no matter how hard they try to draw or paint something, it either turns out wrong in the first place or right with a smudge or blots splattered here and there. I just can't place the name. I can't place the name *with* the girl.

WHY... why can't I say her name? Why can't I—

She throws her hair back (so sexy, despite being featureless) and takes another slow step down the stairs. The sex appeal she offers practically emits from her body like rays from a sun. The vibes are essential to knowing her, but unhelpful nonetheless. How can someone without features or details be so sexy? So revealing? I don't know or understand. But she just is.

Is it a possibility that this is where curiosity takes over? Where the mind is so overtaken by not knowing the true identity that it forms its own version, an aberration from the norm. The old version is thrown out—tossed out like an old computer—while the new version takes being. And the new product is guaranteed to sell.

The noise, the overwhelming noise from every direction!

The girl hesitates (the mind maintains the beautiful image), adjusts her bra strap, and then takes another long step down towards the field. My heart is pounding; my mind is racing.

Finally... the noise is silent (it either deafens or my mind's attention is so *engulfed* in this girl that I block the noise out completely), but I am still unable to think straight. A part of me wants to hop off of the bench, run across the field, and exit the stadium.

Please let me live—let me escape out of here.

I just want to run out of this field like a bride running out on her husband-to-be, right at the alter, during the middle of the main ceremony. The bride fleeing down the path between rows and rows of benches, and exiting the church without even looking back once to see the stunned faces of the gallery.

The girl glides down another flight of stairs and then stops to say 'hi' to someone in the stands, someone that looks familiar to her. She knows them, I can tell by the gestures and familiarity in her motions. I watch her without the capability of looking away. My eyes are glued to her movements, without any chance of closing.

The noise, coming from everywhere, is gone. She looks straight into my direction, and oh dear God —

"Not again... wake up Jeff. Wake Up!" Jeff awoke, rising from his pillow and sweating, Shae holding him. "Jeff, what's wrong with you?"

"What's wrong? What? I don't know, why? What... what are you talking about?"

"You were having another dream, saying 'who is this girl'," Shae said, curious about any girl Jeff could be dreaming about other than her.

"What are you talking about?" he said. "I don't remember anything... or any girl for that matter."

"Maybe you should talk to someone about this, because you were shaking really badly and you scared me," Shae said, concerned. He couldn't tell if she truly wanted him to talk to someone or if she was just saying that because she couldn't think of anything else to do or say.

"Never mind, just drop it," he responded, ending the dream talk. "I'm fine."

And they did. For the time being, at least. They had breakfast together inside, rather than going out; Shae cooked up some cheesy eggs (scrambled eggs with Velveeta spread in them). During breakfast, they talked about what Jeff could remember—absolutely nothing that would get them anywhere—and Shae believed this dream to be the second dream Jeff had had, or at least the second dream she had witnessed. No telling how many dreams Jeff had dreamt in all, especially since he couldn't remember a thing.

The rest of the day was spent lazily, watching TV and hanging out. The "dream" chatter had halted, but remained in the back of Jeff's mind for the rest of the day. Shae left to get ready for work around two-thirty and gave Jeff a long, wet, good luck kiss.

"I'll miss you baby, do good in Carson for me," Shae said. On her way out of the apartment, she turned back to Jeff. "Call me?"

"If I get the chance, okay sexy? Love ya', bye!" he said as she gave him a look like 'you better get the chance'. With one last wave, she jumped into her Sable. He watched her drive off down Hickory Street and then went back inside to pack shit up for his first road trip. He was excited more than words could express. He had already been overwhelmed with the hometown atmosphere and playing in the same propinquity of his own domain. Now it was time to be heckled, see new places, and enjoy the best days of his life.

After packing his clothes, shaving kit, and other necessities, he relaxed on the couch watching some early season baseball. On the *Superstation*, the Braves had a 3-1 lead in the fifth against the Phillies. Andruw Jones hit a two-run shot, which was the only excitement in the game so far.

At six, Jeff jumped in his ride and headed to the clubhouse. Traffic wasn't as bad as usual, despite the time and the fact that it was a Monday evening. Guessing that there hadn't been a wreck, for a change, probably helped the flow. Today should be a Los Angeles holiday: 'Idiots finally learned to drive' day. Jeff drove into the Demons ballplayers' parking section and found his spot.

II

"Yo Jeff, bring your ass back to da' back!" Will yelled at Hartes as he stepped into the Demons' road bus. The back was the place to be... that is, if you preferred to not sleep and wanted to drink, party, and gamble. The front, on the other hand, was much more of a relaxing, movie-time environment.

A person could only grasp a true understanding of how awesome this bus was by being aboard one themselves. And if you thought this bus was exhilarating, maybe you should take a ride on a major league baseball team's bus.

There were two 26-inch TV's, one in the front, one in the back. The whole entertainment system was included: the package contained a six-disc CD changer with stereo, a VCR, and a state-of-the-art sound system with 12-inch speakers. The walls of the bus were lined with love seats that folded out into bunk beds. The aisles were carpeted, providing an adequate sleeping place if someone was either too intoxicated, courtesy of a 12-pack of Corona's with limes, or too tired to crawl into a bunk. The water closet was also nice (Jeff thought it to be probably better than his own) and the air conditioning was perfect; colder than ice fishing in your skivvies.

"On my way, bra," Hartes said, walking through the bus aisle towards the end of the giant automobile. The trip to Carson was around a ten-hour drive (approximately 549.8 miles), which gave the team plenty of time to play cards, watch Jerry Springer videos, get fucked up, and then catch some much needed Zs. The pluck game started (five dollars a point), where the losing team might drop ten to forty bucks, and Will and Jeff wound up partners. They lost to Steve and Ron, 11-8, dropping $15 each in the defeat, but got it back and *more* with an 11-7 victory over Simon and Bobby. The last game of the night, Will and Jeff extended their winnings with an 11-4 blowout; the killing handed to Jason and Lake.

The beer went down one after another, and before Hartes and the rookies realized it, they were fucked. As the time neared 12:30 a.m., most of the players in the back (Gunn, Hicks, Rutherford, Fetters, Coleman, S. Luthers, Parks, O'Dell, Perry, Seavers, and Hartes) were buzzing good and getting rowdy over Springer.

"Jerry! Jerry! Jerry!" the crowd in the studio chanted after he made another fat joke about this three hundred plus hillbilly who was marrying a sexy ass model. The model then turned out to be one of his far off cousin's sisters. Just leave it all up to Jerry. The Springer videos started again and again as the team had about a dozen on the bus they could watch. Jeff ended up falling asleep at around one-thirty, but plenty of the others were still going hard.

When he woke up, the Demons' bus was pulling into a Holiday Inn in Carson City, Nevada. The second baseman glanced at his watch and saw that it was 5:08 a.m. The driver had made pretty good time; he must have goosed it the whole way. The 2-1 Demons marched off of the bus like mummies, everybody moving in a trance to get their bags, and then go to their rooms to fall back into a deep sleep.

Skip, knowing the players and seeing how they acted around each other, roomed them according to his knowledge. He did an excellent job, putting Will and Jeff together. Some of the other room pairs were perfect too, like Jason and Steve, Damon and Erric, Billy and Michael, and so on...

Once again, Jeff woke up. This time the trusty timekeeper read 11:37 a.m. He looked over and saw that Will was still out cold. He stumbled into the bathroom, took a leak, dripped it all over his boxers, and then went back to the hotel room bed to lie down.

Jeff awoke a little after twelve-thirty, showered, and got out just as Will was coming alive. "Ahhh... fuck. First road trip is a bitch, man. Sure glad we didn't have to go to Billings."

"Yep, long way," Jeff said, knowing that it was farther than Carson City, but not knowing exactly how far.

Will turned on the television and flipped through the channels. "Wanna' watch this?" Will asked, stopping on the *Master's*.

"Fine with me," Hartes responded.

"You white people always watchin' *golf*," Will added, but left it on the prestigious golf tournament nonetheless.

They watched golf until four (mostly curious to see where Tiger stood on the leader board) and then went to get some grub before B.P. The team left to go to the park at 5:00 p.m.; the game started at 7:30 tonight instead of the 7:15 first pitch time back home. The players loaded up on the bus and headed for battle.

III

"Now back to Darrell Marinville, this is Demon baseball," the recorded message announced after the commercials finished.

The Duke updated the listeners, "Top of the fifth here in Carson City. What a beautiful night. Cool, about seventy-five degrees, with hardly any cloud cover. The ballgame is tied two-to-two, both starters still on the mound.

Last night in the Western League, the Montana Tigers up-ended Tucson fifteen-to-eleven. Clyde Mann got his first Western League win while Sean Tamari took the loss. Moran Gnass hit his league-leading third homerun and also drove in three. Other scores around the league, San Diego improved to four and oh beating Cal in the ninth with a two-out single by Arod Winslow to knock in Timothy Greener. The final was three-to-two." After the scores, The Duke continued to broadcast the game back to Los Angeles where the Demon faithful listened attentively.

IV

Thomas Perry, the 6'3" righty, had gotten the start for Los Angeles, while the Carson City Gamblers threw a right-handed pitcher as well, Ricky Martinez. Martinez got through the first without any harm except a single by Jason Hicks. Lewis grounded out, Coleman struck out; and after Hicks singled up the middle, Gunn popped out to deep leftfield.

Perry also delivered in the first, sitting the Gamblers down in order. Lead off hitter Jessie Kato lined out to right, second baseman David Wayne popped up to Hartes at second, and Aaron Craig (who was hitting .545) hit a hard grounder that Coleman ate up and made the clean throw to first. No runs in the opening inning.

Rutherford and Goodwin both popped out to left on a

total of four pitches from Martinez. And then the Carson City ace got Hartes out on a 2-2 breaking ball that he chopped to short and was gunned down on. The Gamblers scored their first run of the game after Perry walked the clean-up hitter, James Colbrunn, and the fifth hitter, Ivan Gutierrez, back-to-back. Perry struck out Martin Spews, knocking Spews' average further below the Mendoza Line, down to .083.

The next batter, Barry Hunt, drilled a fastball up the middle to score Colbrunn. With runners on the corners, Lionel Silcy hit into a six-four-three double play and helped Perry get out of the inning, only allowing one run to cross the pentagon.

Martinez worked another perfect inning, forcing Fetters to ground out, Perry to strike out, and Lewis to line out to straight away center.

Martinez then led off the bottom half of the third with a broken-bat single to center. Kato singled, putting runners on the corners again. Perry got one-third of the jam out of the way, getting another big 'K' on Wayne. But just as he has done all year, Aaron Craig stepped up again. He drilled a slider to leftfield to score Martinez, changing the score to two-to-nothing. Colbrunn popped up to Coleman, and Gutierrez lined back to Perry on the mound. The pitcher showed off a few of his defensive skills, as his nice snag got him out of another fix. Once again, he only gave up one in what could have been a devastating inning.

Ricky Martinez made his first mistake of the night, walking Coleman on five pitches. Hicks then doubled to left-center, scoring Coleman. Gunn flied out to deep center, moving Hicks to third. Rutherford singled to right, driving in Hicks. But that would be it—Goodwin struck out, and Hartes grounded out to third.

An error by Rutherford in leftfield put Spews on board

in the bottom of the fourth. The catcher, Hunt, hit into a double play, starting with the shortstop. The second Coleman-Hartes-Gunn turn of the night. Silcy walked, but Martinez popped up to the catcher to end the inning.

V

The Duke took over there, live in the fifth. "Due up for the Demons, Ron Fetters, Thomas Perry, and Damon Lewis. Well, fans… we've got a special guest here in the studio. His name is Buddy Clarett, he resides here in Carson, and he is one heck of a baseball historian. Maybe even more so than me… if you can believe that. Buddy's here to possibly share a couple of stories with us. Whatcha' say, Mr. Clarett?"

"Just enjoying the great game of baseball. And be sure to call me Buddy. I may be an old-timer, but I won't stand for any of that mister business." Clarett shifted in his seat and smiled at The Duke, assuring the radio host that he was merely joking.

"Won't happen again… Buddy. So do you have any fascinating tales for our listeners?"

"Well, Darren, I'm sure I could sit up here 'til the end of the game and swap baseball stories, but I know you've got a game to call, so I'll give you a couple of my favorites and then be off."

"Fantastic," The Duke exclaimed. He then picked up the game, as automatic as an ice maker, "Martinez gets on the rubber, stares down the batter, and reads the sign. He delivers… strike one. Mister Martinez has three strikeouts to this point and looks like he is on pace for more. Fetters steps out of the box. He steps back in now with one strike on him, oh-for-one so far tonight. The burly catcher is hitting only a buck eleven so far this year, but looks to get things on track. Martinez delivers..." *Crack!* "Hard hit ball to deep leftfield! Craig going back for it, reaches, it's off the wall! Craig sprints to recover the ball and fires it back into the infield, but not until Ron Fetters has a stand-up double."

"He sure drove that ball, huh Buddy?"

"That he did."

"What have you got for us first?"

"I've got a dandy, Darren. It's about Ted Williams. And what baseball fan doesn't care to hear a story about the 'Splendid Splinter'?"

"Just those damned Yankees, I suppose," The Duke interrupted, drawing a small laugh between them.

Buddy Clarett continued, "It was the late forties. And 'Teddy Ballgame' was batting in the second game of a doubleheader. Uhh... he fouled a couple of good fastballs down the leftfield line into the bleachers... at Fenway. I believe he had a two-two count on him, maybe one-two... either way... that was when he drove another ball down the leftfield line, foul, and into the stands again. You know, Williams was a lefty, and even though he could take the ball to different parts of the field, one of the many reasons he was such a great hitter... maybe the greatest... I don't ever remember seeing him hit that many balls way left of the opposite field."

Perry stepped in and laid down a beautiful bunt to move Fetters over. A bonus sure enough—a pitcher that could bunt. One away with the go ahead run now on third. Damon Lewis would foul off three pitches before walking on an outside fastball. First and third, Will Coleman up to bat.

Marinville allowed Buddy to finish before starting the

call again, "Well... he ended up grounding out to second. Coming back into the dugout, Dom Dimaggio, the Red Sox's centerfielder, asked him, 'Hey Teddy, what the hell are you doing out there? Those fastballs were right there.' Ted Williams replied, saying 'I was trying to nail that damn heckler sitting down the leftfield line, that son-of-a-bee has been on me all game.'" Clarett chuckled that friendly, elderly way. Marinville joined in the jubilee. The baseball historian then added, "Ted must have put a couple of those balls within ten feet of that heckler. Pretty impressive... pretty amazing."

"It sure is... Coleman digs in, batting two-eighty six." After four pitches, the count stood at two-two. Martinez came from the stretch to home. "The pitch... runner goes!" *Smack.* "Chopper up the middle, diving stop by Silcy, fires to first on his knees, no play at second... Safe! R.B.I. single for the Demon shortstop, tying the game."

Hicks lined out to the Spews on third base, leaving Lewis on second and Coleman on first. Gunn then ended Martinez's night with "Pump" number three on the year. The Duke was all over it, "Two down, one-one count on Gunn. Lewis gets his lead on second as well as Coleman. Martinez comes to the plate." *Whack!* "That ball is driven high to straight away centerfield. Goodbye Mr. Rawlings! The Big Daddy strikes yet again, hitting his third homerun of the year.

"A three-run blast off of Ricky Martinez. Wow! Martinez hung a breaking ball over the middle of the plate, and you know the rest!"

Gunn stepped on home and trotted toward the dugout. He was immediately surrounded by the team, receiving fist knocks and pats on his helmet. "Fuck yeah, Gunn, hell yeah!" Hicks yelled at him. "Wooo!"

The Carson fans were dead silent; probably the first

time all year that they had been down and in trouble of losing. Lenny Cox, a crafty lefthander, replaced Martinez on the rubber. The numbers on Martinez were 4 and 2/3 innings, 6 earned runs, 3 K's, and 2 walks.

Six-to-two Demons. Cox got Rutherford to ground out to short to end the top-half of an explosive fifth.

"Big inning for the Demons here in Carson. Lot of action. Mr. Buddy Clarett is still with us, but I believe he's going to make his way back to stands. I'm sorry we couldn't get in some more stories tonight, but that Williams spin was a classic. Possibly tomorrow night, whatcha' say Buddy?" The Duke asked his co-announcer in the booth.

"Sounds good, Darren. The only problem is climbing those steps all the way to the pressbox," Clarett chuckled, rising from his chair. The two shook hands, and then Marinville got back to the game.

There was no answer from the Gamblers in the bottom half of the inning. Besides a one-out single by David Wayne, Kato, Craig, and Colbrunn made easy outs. Perry started to get in his groove, which was damn good for the Demons, but trouble for their opponents.

L.A. sat on a four run lead, supplying nothing in the sixth off of Cox. Goodwin struck out, Hartes flied out, and Fetters hit a dribbler back to the pitcher. Luckily for Los Angeles, Perry worked another scoreless inning. He allowed a double by Gutierrez to start off the inning and then walked Spews.

No trouble for the relaxed starter; Hunt hit a shallow fly to left that Rutherford made a shoestring catch. The fly ball was too shallow to advance anyone. The defensive specialist, Lionel Silcy, popped up to Coleman, once again leaving runners on the first two bases. Two down and two on, the Gambler faithful still had hope and were on their feet.

"Pinch hitting for the relief pitcher, Mih-Key Larrrrrrsen!!!" the name blared over the loudspeaker. The left-handed pinch hitter stepped in to face Perry. Larsen was two-for-two on the year with a double and a single. The crowd loved this hometown boy, too, and supported him every time he got a chance to hack. He had been a fan-favorite coming off the bench for several years now.

"Larsen steps in perfect so far to date, lefty versus righty," The Duke announced. "Perry glances to second, then to first, and delivers.... ball one. Perry winds and fires... ball two. Larsen taps the bat on his cleats, ahead in the count two and oh. Perry delivers... a swing and a miss. Strike one. Got him on a gutsy down in the count slider. The pitch..." *Whack.* "Well hit ball to deep right center! Lewis on the run, sticks his glove out, makes tha' catch! How 'bout that Mr. Silcy, what a play by Damon Lewis to get Perry out of the sixth, and out of the jam."

Lewis came jogging in with his usual nonchalance. "Thanks Damon, nice fuckin' grab," Perry told him and slapped his ass with his pitcher's glove as he stepped down into the dugout.

"Nuthin' to it, holmes," Lewis responded in his usual dialogue, and headed to the water jug.

Over the loudspeaker, the Carson announcer updated the other scores around the Western League. "In the fifth, Washington and Arizona are tied four-to-four. In the eighth, Tucson leads Montana seven-to-three. And completed earlier today, San Diego remains perfect, beating Cal five-to-one."

David Parker was the new pitcher for Carson City. He was right-handed, and threw very hard. Parker struck out Perry to start off the seventh. Lewis walked on five pitches and stole second. Coleman grounded out to second, moving Lewis to third. Hicks came up 2-3 so far on the night and a chance to knock in another run.

Hicks drilled a hard grounder to third that Spews threw away. Lewis scored on the error to make the score 7-2. Gunn popped up to Kato in center making the third out, but not after another run had been tallied.

As the Demons took the field during the seventh inning stretch, a very attractive girl was led towards homeplate. She was the honorary singer for "Take me out to the ballgame." She stood around 5'9" with beautiful, long black hair. She had skinny legs poking out of her tight shorts, but they weren't wobbly or un-sexy; they were just wide enough to wrap around your waist and squeeze you to death.

"Damn!" The first words spoken during the song came from Erric in rightfield. "Sheze' a fine muthafucka."

"No shit 'E', what da' hell you think we was looking at? We sure as hell ain't listenin' to her singin'," Damon responded back to his roommate from center.

Most of the team continued to gaze at the broad in between the warm up. She was finishing up the song with, "It's root, root, root for the Gamblers! If they lose it's a shame, cause one, two, three strikes yer' out at the old... ball... game!"

"Remind me to talk to *that* later." Everyone knew who said it immediately. No one other than Jason yelled the remark from the infield as she walked down the ramp leading towards the concession area. Coleman and Hartes glanced at each other and exchanged smiles; both thinking Jason could probably hit that later tonight.

"I'm gonna' tap that ass all night long," Hicks said as he flipped the last warm-up roller into the dugout, assuring the second baseman and shortstop they had just read his mind. At least Hartes and Coleman had read the sexual part of his mind, which accounted for 95% of it—

give or take a few parts of the membrane.

Perry was peppered all over the field in the bottom half of the inning, allowing four hits, three runs, and walking another. Kato singled, stole second, and scored on an RBI double by David Wayne. Aaron Craig walked. And then Colbrunn hit a hard grounder through Gunn's legs, scoring Wayne. Ruling was E-3, and the score was 7-4. The runners held at first and third with Ivan Gutierrez batting.

Perry got behind in the count 3-1 and grooved a fastball that Gutierrez ripped to left. It dropped in for a single, knocking Craig home. With Luthers and Sanders in the pen, Spews would probably be the last batter Perry would face (whether he got him out or not). The third baseman hit a rocket right to Coleman at short. Will caught the line drive, but Colbrunn made it back to second using good base running skills for a first baseman.

Pitching coach, Larry George walked to the mound, "Nice job out there kid, the bullpen will close 'em down for ya'."

"I've still got some stuff left, Larry," Perry replied, not really attempting to persuade anyone to keep him in the game.

"We're going to turn this one over to D.L. He'll get the job done. Go grab a seat, baby."

"Hit The Road Jack" started up across the ballpark as Perry slowly dragged himself to the visitor's dugout. "Don't you come back no more, no more, no more, no more... Hit The Road Jack and don't you come back no more..."

George headed back to the dugout, allowing more time for the pen to get warm. And then, as soon as he disappeared, Skip Bailey began his rehearsed march to the mound. The Carson fans booed as he crossed the third base line. Skip, before reaching Perry on the hill, tapped his left bicep, making the call for Luthers, who was the only pitcher up in the pen at the moment. Sanders had just sat, cooling his arm. Luthers had an 81.00 earned run average, throwing only a third of an inning so far and giving up three earned runs.

He struck out Hunt (two away), and then Silcy flied out to end the seventh.

"Thatta' boy Darren," Larry told him as he jogged into the dugout. "Way more relaxed out there this time, huh? And using your stuff. Keep it up, kid."

Rutherford popped up to first in foul territory to open the eighth. Parker walked Goodwin, and then Hartes walked to the plate.

"Jeff Hartes strides towards the batters' box here in the eighth inning. The score is seven-to-five in favor of our Demons," The Duke announced back home.

"He is oh-for-three tonight and looks to add more to the Demons' lead. Parker checks to first, big lead for... throw to first. Got 'em! Goodwin was caught leaning, and the overpowering righty nailed him. Two down now, no count on Hartes."

He stepped out of the box, took a deep breath to get his air supply back, and then stepped back into the war-zone. *Nice freakin' job, Billy.*

The Duke relayed the events as they happened, "Parker to the wind up now, gets his sign, and comes to the plate." *Whack.* "A line drive through the third base side. Craig jogs up to field the ball on the ground as Hartes takes his turn at first. Two-out single for the seven hitter."

Fetters hit a two-hopper right at Colbrunn, who took it to the bag himself for the third out.

Luthers dealt again in the bottom of the eighth (*dealt in lead,* Roland might have said in the *Dark Tower* series), striking out Gorley, the pinch hitter for Parker, getting Kato to line out back to the mound, and forcing Wayne to ground out to Hartes on a one-two sinker. He threw 1 and 2/3 innings of relief, allowing zero runs or walks, and had a pair of punch-outs.

Los Angeles didn't make any effort to increase their two-run lead when Alvin Snider, a right-handed relief pitcher, struck out the side in the ninth. Pinch-hitter Bobby Parks on four pitches, Lewis on five pitches, and Coleman on four pitches.

"Boooo, boooo!" the crowd echoed throughout the stadium as Seavers jogged to the mound. "Boooo!"

The reason: Salmon played the last two years with Carson City and left for a bigger paycheck. Which was very understandable, based on (1) the small contract he had had with the Gamblers and (2) his ability to close out games. The once fan favorite here in Carson, now on the other side, was something the hometown crowds could never tolerate. As a fan, you just felt betrayed. You spent your hard-earned money to come out to the park and bring your family and kids, to watch stars like Seavers. And when they moved on with their life, you felt abandoned. So then you proceeded to... "Boooo... Boooo!"

"Fuck yeah," Will shouted from short, just loud enough for the infielders to take in. "Salmon loves this shit."

Hartes smiled back at him and got ready for Seavers to close this bitch out. Salmon didn't start off the way you wanted a pitcher to, walking Craig on four straight. Colbrunn then singled to right, moving Craig to third.

Seavers struck out Gutierrez with a nasty slider for the first out. Spews hit a weak chopper to first that Gunn could only get the third baseman on. Aaron Craig crossed homeplate to cut the lead to one. Two outs, tying run on second, and Barry Hunt at the plate.

"How many times do you see this, sportsfans?" The Duke asked his listeners. "Carson pitcher Antonio Smith is jogging out to run for Colbrunn. Oh... man, I love this game of baseball. A pitcher running for a position player."

"Seavers stares into Fetters' glove, paying no attention to Smith on second. He gets the sign and fires... strike one. Hunt watched that outside fastball zoom by. Salmon comes set, delivers... strike two. Swing anna' miss. Another outside fastball that the catcher just couldn't catch up with. Two strikes, the Gambler fans making all the noise they can. Seavers fires... ball. A little upstairs on that one, trying to get the batter to chase the high offering. Salmon rares back and hurls...

Strike Three! Strrrrrrike Threeeee! The Demons have defeated the defending champs seven-to-six! What a game, what a game!"

The visitors gathered at the mound to celebrate the victory. The triumph was their third straight, and moved L.A. to 3-1. The Demons formed a pair of lines—half of the team on one side, half on the other—and walked down them giving each other high fives and 'dibs' in a conveyor belt motion.

"Wonder what tha' fuck there is to do in Carson?" Parks said, strutting down the line with his right hand fist connecting to Hicks's.

"Don't worry... there is always shit to do and ladies to bang," Hicks replied to the catcher, arising laughter throughout the line.

"'Specially the seven innin' stretch hoe," Rutherford added, drawing a shaking of the head and a smirk from Skip. The congratulations ended, and the players and coaches headed back to the dressing room.

Before all of the team exited the field, Skip added, "If you paid half as much attention to the game as you did those rah-rah sluts, we'd never lose again."

Rutherford, Hicks, and Lewis turned around, assuring themselves that Skip was joking. The manager gave them a 'just keep walking' smile, but followed it with a small chuckle.

"Son of a bitch," Damon muttered in a friendly manner. He ducked his head as he walked through the door to the clubhouse and down the short tunnel.

VI

In the clubhouse, some of the guys were talking about going to Reno in the morning and gambling before the game while others were talking about what was cooking tonight on the town, and the remainders were just showering and dressing.

"I can't believe that fucker Martinez hung that shit up with two runners on," Gunn said.

"That ball had some fuckin' juice in it man," Goodwin said from his locker, referring to Gunn's three-run shot, and then pretending to inject his bicep with a needle. And a bicep it was, when Goodwin flexed, the fainted blue veins bulged and his muscles cracked against his paler skin. If he hadn't taken steroids at some time in his life, *that* would have been a surprise. Going against his good build was his fair skin. Complementing his good build was his long, sticky brown hair. Goodwin sweated a lot in his Demons' cap, but that wasn't always the reason his hair looked unwashed. He didn't always have time for showers, or a shave for that matter. He claimed to be too busy. Or in his words, 'I just need a quick toke on the bugler.'

"We all saw it, Steve, we don't need a replay," Coleman added. But Gunn ignored his comment rather than firing a customary missile back.

Hartes finished dressing, dabbed a little Polo Sport on, and then walked to the bus. 'Well what do you know?' Jeff asked himself. From where he was sitting in the bus, he could see Jason talking to the "Seventh-inning stretch" girl outside the field. The rest of the team was slowly crawling onto the bus, but only Jason remained talking to the chick.

"That muthafucka'," Erric yelled from the front of the bus. "I wanted to hit that shit man, now dis' white honky neck's stealin' my hoe." Gunn started the uproar of laughter, soon everyone followed.

Skip peered into the back of the bus and said, "Somebody go out there and get Hicks. I'm tired of waiting in this dump." Will leaned out the bus and told Jason to get her number, see what she was doing tonight, and hurry his ass up.

"Bye beautiful, call me in room 216 in about an hour," Jason said to the tall, black-haired girl as he made his way to the bus, showing off his award-winning grin to her just before he disappeared into the player carrier. He said the "call me" part with such confidence that there was no doubt in the cocky fucker's mind that she wouldn't call. Of course she would, he was Jason freakin' Hicks.

"Okay, see ya' later," she replied and sprinted back to where her friends stood visiting, appearing very excited over being talked to by a Triple-A third baseman. Returning league MVP on top of that.

Jason came aboard the bus grinning ear-to-ear, high-fiving a couple of players on his way to the back. "What did I tell you fools, no hooya' can resist Jason Hicks."

"I don't care if you fuck her or not, Jace, but at least help a nigga' out and tell her to bring sum' friends,"

Michael Tims preached, a bold rookie move, as almost all of the other riders agreed.

"Especially hook up Will," Gunn said instantly, everyone waiting eagerly to see where Steve was going with this. This was his opportunity to break the cease-fire he had signed earlier. "He hasn't gotten a piece of ass on the road since that sista' with gold teeth and stretch marks on her tits rode him last year."

Do you even need to be told what the team did next? The answer's no, but the information was leaked, anyway. Hartes collapsed out of the love seat onto the floor, holding his sides. Hicks, who had been standing in the aisle, leaned his head against one of the bunks; sounding as if he was crying, the laughter was so fierce.

Salmon dove into one of the bunks and started kicking the top of it (the bottom of the bunk above him) while twisting and turning with hysterics. Only Will, and maybe a couple of others in the front who already had their headphones on, weren't amused. Will just sat down, knowing he got ripped, and then started laughing with the rest of the team.

"I'm gonna' fuck you up, Big Daddy. You just wait and see. Don't close your eyes tonight or any night soon," Will warned him, holding in his own glee. "And don't let that shit get back to Regina."

The team bus pulled into the Holiday Inn parking lot and came to a stop in the back of the hotel. The players headed to their rooms, and began planning the paths they were destined for this night.

"So what's up tonight, kid?" Will asked his fellow infielder as he crashed down into his bed, the one closer to the bathroom.

"I don't know yet, man," Jeff said to Will, thinking about his question some more. "I need to call Shae for one thing, then I guess I will just see what happens."

Will turned on the television and flipped through some channels before stopping on his (and Jeff's, as well as the rest of the team's) favorite, *Sportscenter.* He saw Jeff had picked up the phone, so Will kept the volume low. Hartes looked at the numbers on the phone, then to Will. "Shit man, I need to get a calling card."

"Stop and rob right across the street. They should have 'em," Will said, glued to the Master's highlights.

"Good idea," Jeff said, sprinting out the door, down the stairs (screw the elevator — too slow), through the lobby, and across the street to the gas station.

He saw Erric and Billy in the store already supplying themselves for the munchies later. 'E' had two bags of Funyuns, a Slim Jim, a large coke, and a Snicker's Bar, while Billy had a box of Lil' Debbie's Devil Cakes, some cheese crackers, and a couple of bottled waters.

They asked what Jeff was doing, and he told them that he didn't have a clue as of yet. "But if y'all find something hot, give me a holla'?"

After their supplies were purchased, Jeff stepped up to the counter and asked the lady for a $10 calling card. It had sixty minutes of use anywhere in United States on it, so he figured what the heck. This *was* before the cell phone mayhem began. The second baseman snatched the card up and sprinted back across the street, through the lobby again (smiling at the girl in her mid-thirties behind the counter; *somebody might hit that*) and climbed the stairs to room 224.

He launched himself into the bed, rolled over, and picked up the phone. Jeff dialed the numbers on the calling card, followed the prompts, and then pressed Shae's home number.

Ring — ring... Ring — ring.

"Hello," Shae's voice never sounded better. It didn't take much for her to get him going.

"Hey sweetie, we won."

"That's good baby, how did you do?" Shae asked.

He told her that he had gone one-for-four with a single. She said, "That's good," whether it had been or not. They talked about their relationship a little, how much they missed each other, and how they couldn't wait to see one another. Jeff told her how he wouldn't be home til' early in the morning on the nineteenth. Shae said good luck, and they said their goodbyes, and then hung up.

"So are you going to do anything tonight or not?" Hartes immediately questioned Will after his conversation with Shae. Will sat up, looked around the room, and then said:

"Fuck no. You enjoy your first road trip, go out and have a good time. My ass is watching sports, sports, sports, and then getting some sleep. I'm going to eat some breakfast and lift in the morning, anyway. You should go to Hicks's room, see if he's talked to that chick yet."

Jeff said okay and started out the door when Will added, "Room 216."

"Yeah... I know. Late."

"Late, bro."

He walked down the indoor hallway past three other doors, and then stopped at 216 and knocked, even though the door was creaked open. "Come in," someone said from inside in a gentle, tender voice.

Jeff pushed the door open, and what he saw next would have been a Kodak moment in anyone's photo-album. Jason—appearing picturesque—was posing on his bed. He was lying on his left side with his left arm bent to where it held his head upright. His right arm was relaxed on his side, despite being flexed.

Once he realized it wasn't the person he was truly waiting for, the pose ended instantaneously. Jason sat up and stuttered, "I... I... thought you were that chick." The tone in his voice had now risen. "What the fuck, Hartes? Shit man, stop spoiling my grand setting."

"Sorry Hicks," Jeff said, laughing. "The one from the field or what?"

"Yeah... her name's Alyssa," Jason responded.

Jeff could hear the water running in the shower, so he speculated that's where Steve was.

He inquired, "So what's the deal bro?"

"Here's the scoop. That chick, Alyssa, is on her way over here, and I guess we are going to a bar or club or someplace she knows," Jason said as he motioned with his pointer finger in the location they might be bound for tonight.

"Any friends?" Jeff persisted, but not really caring whether she did or not. Jason casually pranced over to the sink, grabbed some cologne off of the counter, and squirted it two times in his own direction. He then waved his arms around in small circular motions and proceeded to walk through the area he had contaminated with his love potion.

"Not coming here with her, but she said we'd prob'ly meet up with them."

Jeff nodded, told Jason he was tired, anyway, and then moved along down the hall. "Shoot that *Motherfucker!*" The yelling was coming from room 221, across the hall. "Kill him, *kill him.* Don't just stand there."

The middle-infielder, peeking his head in the room, saw Tims, Erric, Billy, Damon, and Parks. Four of the five were sitting on the floor with their backs against the beds; they had gaming controllers and were fiercely grasped by the game they were involved in. Billy (the only one of the five not playing) was sprawled out on the bed talking shit to Parks.

"Bobby-O, if you don't kill somebody real soon, I'm gonna' take that controller from you and beat your fuckin' ass with it!"

Jeff snickered to himself, just loud enough where no one else in the room knew he was there yet. He made his way farther into the room, and sat next to Goodwin on the edge of bed number one.

Billy was the first one aware of Jeff's presence in the room and hollered, "About fuckin' time... give Hartes your controller and find a new hobby, Bobby-O."

The other three playing expressed their amusement in a daze, laughing because it was the thing to do, but never losing focus on the killing of each other. Jeff watched as Damon shot Bobby in the back of the head with his Sniper Rifle.

"I quit!" Parks said, throwing the controller to the floor. He motioned for the newcomer to step in (get some, Hartes), and Jeff picked up where he left off.

The group played *007* on Nintendo 64 long into the night. Jeff honestly believed he saw the sun shining through the curtains before he had made his way back to 224. Hartes fumbled the key card in his hands, recovered, inserted it into the slot, and went to sleep.

VII

Jeff awakened to a rattling noise, followed by an electric buzzing sound. He opened one eye, saw Will turn in his direction, and Coleman's mouth began to move. "Wanna' go get some grub with me this morning?"

"Uh-uh." The only words that would come out of Jeff's

mouth as he rolled back over, pulling the blankets over his head. He didn't stir again until Will returned from breakfast and working out a couple of hours later.

The day went by slowly, the roommates both curled up in their own beds, watching the Master's. Tiger struggled on the final day, shooting 75, and finishing one over par for the tournament. They watched until Jose Maria Olazabal, the Spaniard, put on his second green jacket, edging out Davis Love III and Greg Norman, and then Will and Jeff hustled to the bus.

The Demons arrived at the field and entered the clubhouse to change. Everyone's attention and thoughts were on Hicks (that's *if* they hadn't already found out). Jason had taken a dump the whole bus ride from the hotel to the ballpark, so no one had had a chance to question him on his after-game performance.

Perry broke the silence, "How was last night?" he asked Jason.

"Not too bad, not too bad... you could say it was doggie-licious." Jason smiled, thrusting his pelvic area forwards and backwards, his hands clamped into fists, almost as if he was skiing. But we all knew Mr. Hicks didn't go skiing last night, he went riding. "I fucked the shit out of her and her bucktooth friend while Simon and —" Hicks started cracking up. " —and 'duh Javy watched through the window. I left that fucker creeped open and laid the wood to those hoes!"

"Holy shit, that's crazy! Two hoes?" Will asked, shouting, while Simon and Javier nodded their heads, confirming Jason's story.

"It's crept, you dumb focker," Gunn added.

"Who gives a shit?" Jason responded, and went back to the story. "Hell yea', two hoes. That's not even my favorite part. It's the fact that her last name was Suarez, adding a lil' Mexican flava' to the evening. My lil' seniorita!" Jason started the laughter like tossing gasoline on an open flame; the room exploded once an individual came in contact with the hysterics. Jason was pumped up over his accomplishments, dancing around the room.

The discussing and details on Hicks's wild ride continued until everyone funneled out onto the field. The chatter carried on throughout the pregame stretches and warm-ups, and the game was under way. Another great night for baseball; it was time to get it on again.

Los Angeles, like the night before, jumped out on Carson City early, only to give up a two-run blast in the bottom of the sixth, and wind up losing the game. The homer was Barry Spews' (Carson's third basemen) second on the night, leading Carson City to a 5-4 win. Hartes didn't drive in anyone or score any runs, but ended 4-4 with four singles—a career high in hits. Not a bad night despite not producing any runs. Jason hit his second homerun of the year on his first at-bat of the game. Nonetheless, the Demons were defeated.

The only positive for The Duke and Demon listeners on that night was another epic baseball story from Buddy Clarett. This one revolved around the great Satchel Paige and his ability to take the field with only a first baseman and a catcher.

The Los Angeles Demons packed up the gear, let the assistants stack it neatly below the bus, and then they proceeded back west to San Diego on somewhat of a sour note.

VIII

The team's road trip festivities resumed as usual, everyone knowing San Diego was still undefeated and that they couldn't roll in there on a down phase and take this series. The Knights' pitching had been stellar so far to date. The Southern California journalists were comparing their Triple-A staff to the Atlanta Braves three-man combination of Maddux, Glavine, and Smoltz. San Diego featured lefties Jerod Wilkes and Robert Anderson, and righty Erwin Hammel.

Everyone who had been around the baseball circle knew Wilkes and Hammel as they went back in forth between the "Big's" and the Western League. Wilkes's injury proneness and ailing shoulder kept him from being a big league starter, while Hammel lacked the control. But here in the Western League, they were top notch, cream of the crop, superb aces.

For Anderson, this was his first year in the Western League, but he had pitched with the Louisville Bats the two years before. He was left-handed for one thing, and another very solid arm in the Knights' rotation.

Back on the bus: the trio of Jason Hicks, Steve Gunn, and Jeff Hartes managed to slam down two cases during the long night. Peer pressures a bitch, Hartes soon found out. He always had his drinking kicks while he was in college at Cal and failed out, but never engulfing so many at one-thirty in the morning. Hicks, Gunn, O'Dell, and Perry kept the action going (telling stories, sharing good times) the longest, well after Hartes passed out half on, half off of his bunk. The two pitchers had to jump into Jeff's rotation to keep the party alive and to keep Hicks and Gunn from relying only on each other.

The freezing cold air blowing down on him from the AC vents was enough to wake him up about an hour before L.A. reached their destination. Jeff lay there, staring into the emptiness – actual the bottom of the bunk above him – and thinking about Shae. He thought of her smooth, tanned body. Her breasts glistening in the lamplight (or candlelight if it was a special evening) as he ran his hands steadily over them.

Shae's smile, always welcoming, always bringing out the best in her lover. Always bringing out the best in his true self and his true wants and desires. It was simple; Jeff wanted Shae more than any girl he'd ever come in contact with in his whole life. She didn't force him to act different around her, and he didn't deviate from his normal self. She just made him *feel* different around her.

But why now? *When I can get the hoes, cheat on the road, whatever I wanted...* But he didn't want it. He only wanted Shae.

The bus stopped, the engine shut off. He glanced out the window. Daylight... *shit.* The sign read Radisson Hotel, Harbor View. Players began to stir around him and stretch their wearisome bodies. The team funneled off the bus and waited for Skip to tell them their room numbers. Will and Jeff stood in the lounge together, holding their luggage, eyes glazed over from the lackadaisical sleep they had just gotten.

Skip commenced to passing out the key-cards, starting with Hicks and Gunn, then to Goodwin and Tims, then to Parks and S. Luthers, and next to Coleman and Hartes. Will took the cards from coach as Skip continued with his task of handing them out, and Will led the journey up to the room in search of more sleep.

IX

"We head to the bottom of the ninth with the score Los Angeles two, and unbeaten San Diego two." Marinville gave the call to all the home listeners. He was still riding on a high, hoping the Demons could hold San Diego here and win in extra innings.

"Due up, when we return, for San Diego, the seven, eight, and nine hitters, Kramer, Greener, and closer Treplow. We'll return with Demon baseball in just a minute."

The Knights' star closer, Rich Treplow, had to bat (or be pinch hit for) in the ninth. This was another aspect in the Western League that made it more comparable to the major leagues than the minor leagues. No designated hitter. This required the coaches to actually have to strategize and be careful not to use too many players early in the game; since their rosters weren't as deep as the majors.

In the stadium, the crowd was going ape-shit, especially this idiot down the rightfield line. Heckling at its finest, "Hey Good-Bar! Hey Good-Lookin'! Hey boy, I'm talkin' to yew!" Billy really got the heckler riled up in the fourth when he earlier gave him the finger. A league fine coming. "Hey Billy Boy, why don't you show me that birdy again, he's gotten more hits than you have this year!"

Goodwin focused on the ninth, ignoring the imbecile. But the imbecile kept it coming. "Hey John Good-Man, when are you gonna' cut that hair, boy?"

Goodwin couldn't contain himself. He lifted his cap off his head and tossed his hair, allowing it to just bounce on his shoulders. The idiot down the rightfield line fired some more one-liners and continued heckling. Goodwin just smiled and focused on the game.

Hartes fielded the last rolled ball by Gunn, side-armed it back to first, and got in position for Phil Kramer. Skip was yelling from outside the bench, "Let's go Darren, throw strikes." Seavers was now up in the pen, just loosening up his arm in case of a save situation or lack of pitchers in extra innings.

Luthers looked in, waited for the third baseman to step in the box, and fired. Ball one. The pitch under way... ball two. The second baseman tapped his glove and hollered through the crowd, "C'mon forty-five, hum now, let's go baby." Forty-five referring to Darren's uniform number.

Strike one... ball three... ball four...

Kramer trotted down to first base; the winning run was on board for the Knights. This brought the already loud fans to their feet and cheering more.

"Next fly ball hit to rightfield is going to be your doom Good-Son! Your hair is gonna' git' in yer' eyes and you are gonna' drop the ball, idiot!" Goodwin kept silent, focusing on the big inning.

Marinville kept the faith, "Luthers checks the runner, winds and delivers... strike one on the outside portion of the plate. Oh-one count to the second baseman, Timothy Greener. The switch-stick Greener batting from the right side off of the lefthander, Darren Luthers.

The pitch... ball one. One-and-one. Both the batter and pitcher get their signs. The pitch..." *Whack.* "Hard grounder to third, Hicks fields it cleanly, *and loses* the ball pulling it out of his glove. Both runners safe. The winning run in scoring position and the crowd is going wild."

Hicks shouted something not fit for children's ears into the pocket of his mitt. And then he stood in his position at third base with a look of utter disgust on his face. That error on the MVP got the heckler off of Goodwin's back as the asshole started in on Hicks. He was shouting from the rightfield bleachers, loud enough, that Hicks could hear him on third base.

The Knights left closer, Rich Treplow, in the game, and the son-of-a-bitch did his job. Treplow laid down a perfect bunt heading towards first base. Gunn ran up on the ball but had no option except back to first. Hartes caught his throw for the first out, but San Diego now had runners on second and third with their leadoff hitter coming to the plate.

"Pretty clever decision there by San Diego's Head Coach, Donald LaRue, letting the pitcher stay in the game to move the runners," The Duke said, agreeing with the result of the play. "Now up to bat for the home team, centerfielder J.J. Frazier. He's one-for-four tonight with a single, but we should see a walk here." Luthers pitched to the batter, instead, with the infield playing in. He evened the count on the hitter with a slider that Frazier swung and missed on.

"He's pitching around you J.J., you've got to be smarter than that," The San Diego skipper advised from the Knights' dugout, referring to Frazier swinging at a ball.

"Two-two the count, Kramer on third, Greener on second. The pitch by Luthers." *Smack!* "Drive up the middle! Hartes dives, but it's out of reach. Kramer comes in to score, and he's met at the plate by the whole Knights' dugout. San Diego wins three-to-two, tough luck for our Demons." The Duke paused, attempting to allow the loss to soak in.

"A nice piece of hitting by J.J. Frazier. That pitch might have even been a ball outside. Three-to-two Knights, a bottom-of-the-ninth victory."

That was how game one ended in Southern California.

San Diego's Waylon Ponds, who went 3-4 with a solo homerun and 2 runs batted in, producing the only big highlights. Damn, the Demons wanted that one bad, *real bad.*

Nothing much happened that night. Hartes followed up the road routine and called Shae; let her know that he went hitless, and that they had lost. She said she had already known because it was her night off, and she had listened to Darrell Marinville's broadcast.

But tomorrow was another day, Jeff had told her. And with another day comes another game (and hopefully not another dream)....

Did I remember the dreams? Really?

Jeff didn't know. Of course, he believed in them. Or at least, he believed that he hadn't been sleeping consistently. Shae wouldn't lie to him. Not over something like this. And if he was dreaming... and if he was unable to remember them.... then why did he have this empty feeling in the pit of his stomach, in the back of his mind, that the dreams meant more.

I shouldn't feel anything if I don't know. I shouldn't even care.

But I do....

Chapter Five
A Midnight Message

I

"Dammit to hell! OUCH!!!" the elderly, broken down man screams as his coffee mug tumbles from his hands and onto his legs, spilling a full cup of coffee and singeing whatever white hair still remains under his faded pajamas. The dull, pale mug (which has McNally Sales printed on the side in bright blue) bounces off of his thigh and shatters onto the hardwood floor. The old man leans back in his recliner, gritting his teeth, and trying to ignore the burning sensation that is his lower body.

After the intense pain lessens, he checks the time in the study. The clock reads 10:13 p.m. *I guess it's about time to take a break for a little while,* the aged figure thinks. He slowly launches his body upward out of his most comfortable seat. The man stumbles his way through the doorway leading from the study to the living area and then on towards the kitchen. The kitchen is one of those that women (or chefs) love, the full counter and cabinet space with an island bar in the center, surrounded by three stools. But the man travels to neither of the cabinets, nor the bar, he settles for the pantry closet where he gathers up a broom and dustpan.

He makes his way back to the mess he has made; thinking, *oh how much Shae always loved that kitchen. She would have just died in it if she had the chance.* Now this brings some sadness to the current house cleaner. "She could have died in the kitchen if we could have ever gotten her out of that awful hospital room," he mutters to himself as he begins to sweep the glass into the pan.

"There... all done," the man speaks to himself while emptying the dustpan into the trash-bin. Talking out loud, with no one else around, has become a daily ritual. Besides, if he didn't speak to himself, how would he remember what he sounded like? So he chatters on, "Now I reckon a hot bath might do some good."

II

The water splashes as he gently settles down in it, hoping it's not too hot for him. It automatically shuts off once the water level reaches a specific height—another one of these futuristic devices that the old man never quite fully grows accustomed to. For the most part, technology has passed him by, and he lives his daily life with things of the old. But Shae was more evolved, in with the new. So a few things slip by his watchful eye, and now he is alone and doing his best to deal with these unfathomed *machines*.

Jeff Hartes tilts his head back against the wall, raises a white towel with his left hand, and drenches the water from the towel down his forehead. Motionless now, Hartes just wants a moment of peace and quiet before remembering again. It's more arduous on the mind than one might expect. The time passes quite slowly, and then Jeff opens his mind (his thoughts) back to 1999.

Where was I? He thinks for a couple of minutes, and then remembers. *Oh yes, we had just lost the opener to San Diego. What a shame. The date was... hmmm... the date was April 16th, 1999, that's right. And I believe it was a Thursday.*

He pauses, and then turns the hot water knob with his foot, on a low drip, but the water automatically shuts off. He shakes his head, dripping water and sweat, and removes the stopper briefly to allow some of the water to drain. He returns the stopper to its designated spot and release hot water until the tub is warm again. He leans back and then uses his foot to turn the knob clockwise again, halting the water's flow before it can do so itself by closing the valve and returning his bathroom to complete silence.

This is where things begin to get fuzzy. He assures himself, and then continues with his thoughts. *Fuzzy? More like shady. Or maybe hazy. Yes, hazy's a good word. But why? Why do things stop here? Doesn't matter, though, I've got the scrapbook and notes to help my mind.* He convinces himself that he'll never know the answer why, and thinks on regardless.

I remember the beginning of my season so well, and the end even better. But why are some of the middle parts fuzzy/shady/hazy? Forget it Hartes; just think of the more important things, details aren't as necessary in the middle to get the whole picture. They just ease the story along. As long as you remember the beginning, some of the middle, and the end, just like the essay papers you turned in during college. Half-ass to say the least. Maybe that's why I failed out and... forget it. Just focus on the important stuff. You have to catch the reader early, be interesting enough for him to take the long ride, and then dazzle him at the end. That's me... that's my story!

He slides his body forward until his head is underwater. He then resurfaces, and shakes the water off his hair and out of his eyes. No signs of a receding hairline anywhere. "Goodwin. Yeah, the rightfielder, he's who I was thinking about when I spilled my coffee."

III

"I remember... we lost. I had called Shae, and we had just chatted for a little while. About what, I couldn't tell you. Then Will and I were sitting in our room after eating at Wendy's. That's where Goodwin comes into my thoughts. So that point is where I will continue... remembering," Hartes says aloud, but all alone in the bathroom. And then, as if told to shut up by his elementary teacher Mrs. Zane ('Z' for short), Hartes stops speaking, and begins to reflect on the past, saved within his thoughts.

Simon came in the room, told us to hurry up, Goodwin was being arrested. The silly fool was always dicking around. Will and I sprinted down the Harbor View hallway banging on Gunn and Hicks' room along the way, yelling at them to hurry up and follow us. We asked Simon how he knew, and he said he saw Billy and 'E' arguing with a cop, and then the police officer handcuffed the rightfielder. Jeff and Simon flew down the stairs, using the rails as a balance beam, and came to a 'thud' landing on the sidewalk below.

We could see the cop's car lights from where it was parked on Front Street. The policeman had Goodwin chest first against the hood, and was talking to Erric. Another cop stood off to the side, just watching the situation unfold. I remember arriving worried, and then the laughter began. We asked what happened, and Erric answered in gibberish. He said something like "Dis' stupid mofo started takin' a pizz right 'ere in da' fuckin' street

|

man. And den' when Officer wha's his name arrived, Billy showed him his dick. I ain't freakin' makin' it up eider!" The rest of the night was spent laughing over the incident, and bailing our outfielder out of the Oakland County Jail.

The next day was another game. Skip had caught wind of Goodwin's incident and just shook his head without uttering a single word. *Skip might have said more; but that night, I'm fairly positive we handed San Diego their first loss; but as I have told you, this is where my memory fades. Strange, isn't it? I guess a person can't expect to remember every day of his life within a distinct year.*

Hartes sits up in the tub, loosening his rusty joints and muscles, and then eases himself back in the water. "I need to go see if I still have all of my box scores from that season. I know Shae cut them all out and put them in a scrapbook for me, but I'll have to find them."

Hartes wonders where in the attic they might be. After picturing them in the back corner of the attic in a cardboard box, he rethinks leaving the bathtub at this moment. "Maybe later. I'll just go on as best I can and get the games' box scores when I can't think anymore."

That does sound right, though; we beat San Diego for the first time, and then lost to them the next night before heading back home to L.A. Once back in Los Angeles, we had one or two days off. Shae and I made love one whole day. A smile arises on Mr. Hartes' face, almost touching his ears. *We made love like rabbits. I couldn't tell you how many times... exactly. But it was more than four. Lying in bed with her, watching movies, chatting... it was so great.*

How long had it been since he had made love? That was a good joke there. But remembering making love with Shae could really do the trick sometimes.

It's coming back to me now. I believe I may have

came... 'nutted' for the young folks, about seven times that day. I also remember spending a whole day with Will and Regina. So we must've had two days off. Shae and Regina... oh yes... they immediately clicked, and this wouldn't be the last time we all went or did something together. We became a traditional foursome that could be seen anywhere from Harris' Steakhouse to Montello's to The Bayview.

Shae and Regina would begin to sit in the stands together and cheer on their hubbies. I believe they even made a road trip together. Oh yes, they did. Where? I can't really remember. But they did this... uhh... don't really know what to call it. They played this little game or stunt or prank, where neither of them would stay the night with Will or me. They got their own room, and had an "all-girls slumber party." They went out with us, but refused to sleep in our beds, telling us "you are road roommates; we plan on keeping it that way." They thought it was so damn funny.

After our days off... and after spending some quality time with each other (Will, Regina, Shae, and I), we had a three-game home stand against the Tucson Sun Devils. Lake got his first win of the short season pitching eight shutout innings in game one. I can't remember who won games two and three, but I can remember Lake's handsome black face and short hair, always groomed neatly before one of his starts, and his rubber arm, which never tired and could throw a 175 pitches if needed. Our record was five-and-four after Lake's victory. We were over a quarter of the way through the season.

Following the series with Tucson, we traveled to... umm... maybe we stayed home. Like I've said, things aren't as crystal clear in the middle of my mind. Washington? That's it! We played the Thunder. Where?

*How many games? Who won? I just can't remember. But I
do remember where we stayed at on our next road trip, the
Howard Johnson at "Bay Bridge." I remember Regina,
Will, Shae, me; Regina, Will, Shae, me. We spent more and
more time together. Every chance we got. Shae and Regina
even sat together at the games, cheering for their hubbies. I
mentioned that already, didn't I? Well... shit, it's worth
mentioning twice, I suppose. Real pals.*

*Hmm... what else? Oh, of course, the dreams. Yes sir, I
had a couple of more dreams. No... let's say four to six
more dreams throughout the next few weeks. I can't
remember these, though, only knowing that they were the
same at the start and got farther along with the women
strutting down the steps and the NOISE that almost drove
me to the loony bin. Shae was always curious how I
couldn't remember any of them when she asked me to
remember them the mornings after, but how I could
remember most of them perfectly afterward. And also 'til
this day. I told her...*

"I guess it's because it's over now," Jeff says audibly,
wanting to hear his voice one more time. "And I've just got
to go get those box scores and whatever the hell else is up
there because I can't remember shit anymore."

IV

Hartes steps out of the bathtub, dripping wet, and reaches
for his favorite towel — a midnight blue shade. It wasn't the
color so much as the towel's linen, never scratchy, always
fluffy and comfortably soft. A sensor beeps, and the water
begins draining automatically. *Whooptie-doo.*

The kids these days were using some newer, fancier

towels that dried almost immediately after use. It soaked the water right up; the towel contained some special chemical that treated the sponged water, allowing an individual to use the same towel for a month before it needed a good wash.

Jeff would have no part in these new-aged technological advances unless he didn't have much of a choice. He stuck to his own. Simplicity, right alongside comfortableness, is usually all an older person needs.

He dries off quickly, not wanting to forget to go get his scrapbook, but in his old age, you never know. He didn't have any symptoms of memory loss or Alzheimer's when he was thinking of 1999, except for the middle of the season, of course. But recently, he would sometimes forget things that were just on his mind. Short-term memory loss, one might call it, but Jeff supposes everybody has a little bit of that in them. Aging just made it occur more often. An example: something as simple as getting up to fix a cup of coffee—once in the kitchen, he didn't know what he had come for.

So he makes his way out the bathroom door as speedily as he can with aged legs, moving towards the pull-down ladder leading to the attic. The ladder unravels bit by bit and comes to rest with a soft thump. Jeff—not getting any younger—climbs up the ladder step after step until reaching the top. He's more careful than in his younger days—falling wouldn't be a few bumps and bruises anymore. It would probably result in a broken hip or something worse. He finds the joist (2 x 6), beneath thin plywood, that he wants to walk on in the direction of the boxes, and continues on his errand.

Upon reaching the dust-covered, cardboard packages, Hartes bends over, stretching his back, and then straightens. "Ah-ha, I found you!" he says in jubilation, reaching for the box closest to him. The retired second baseman rummages around for a minute, then locates what he's been searching for.

Jeff flips through the first book, sets it aside, and then opens the second. "Badabing!" he exclaims, still using an old Andrew "Dice" Clay line that would leave the youth of today clueless about what he was referring to. Upon finding the scrapbook Shae gave him forty-three years ago, Hartes feels relieved. He begins to blow the dust off, realizes it's not getting the job done, and then brushes it with his hands instead. Gently removing the clumped debris with a meticulous swipe, wary that the pages may have signs of deterioration, Jeff thinks of the scrapbook as the "incredible signifier of time passed." *Everything here, just the way I expected it to be.* Hartes commences on finding the facts his mind has scrambled.

Jeff stops somewhere right before the middle of the scrapbook, recognizing the date—April 17, 1999. *This is where things aren't as good in my mind. This is where things began to get fuzzy/shady/hazy.* Hartes scans each box score, hoping to retain that perfect memory.

THE SCRAPBOOK

```
April 17, 1999
DEMONS            H  AB R RBI AVG
cf Lewis          1  2  2  0  .240
ss Coleman        1  2  1  2  .296
3b Hicks    (HR)  2  4  1  2  .346
1b Gunn           2  4  0  1  .292
lf Rutherford     0  4  0  0  .250
2b Hartes         0  4  0  0  .333
rf Goodwin        1  4  0  0  .200
c Parks           2  4  1  0  .231
p O'Dell          0  2  0  0  .000
 ph Chambers      0  1  0  0  .143
KNIGHTS           H  AB R RBI AVG
cf Frazier        0  3  0  0  .323
ss Winslow        1  3  1  0  .280
lf Ponds    (HR)  2  4  1  1  .333
rf Martin         1  4  0  1  .305
1b Garrido        0  4  0  0  .247
c Degginger (HR)  2  4  1  1  .299
3b Kramer         1  4  0  0  .271
2b Greener        0  4  0  0  .202
p Hammel          0  3  0  0  .167
 ph Garces        0  1  0  0  .333
W- O'Dell (1-0)  S- Seavers (4)
L- Hammel (1-1)

Los Angeles 5, San Diego 3
```

April 18, 1999

DEMONS	H	AB	R	RBI	AVG
cf Lewis	0	5	0	0	.200
ss Coleman	2	4	2	0	.323
3b Hicks	2	3	0	0	.379
1b Gunn	0	3	0	0	.259
lf Rutherford	0	3	0	0	.222
2b Hartes	0	1	0	0	.321
ph S. Luthers	0	3	0	0	.000
rf Goodwin	1	3	2	0	.217
c Parks	2	4	0	3	.294
p Perry	0	2	0	1	.000

KNIGHTS	H	AB	R	RBI	AVG
cf Frazier	0	5	0	0	.273
ss Winslow (HR)	1	3	1	1	.295
lf Ponds	1	2	2	1	.352
rf Martin (HR)	1	3	2	2	.317
c Degginger	0	3	0	0	.270
3b Kramer (HR)	2	4	1	3	.295
1b L. Allen	1	2	0	0	.667
ph Garrido	0	2	0	0	.259
2b Greener	0	4	0	0	.154
p Heilmann	0	2	1	0	.000

W- Heilmann (1-0) S- McCall (1)
L- Perry (1-1)

San Diego 8, Los Angeles 4

April 21, 1999

SUN DEVILS	H	AB	R	RBI	AVG
ss Bonham	0	3	0	0	.375
c Talley	0	2	0	0	.197
lf Maldonado	0	4	0	0	.244
cf Greggs	0	3	0	0	.287
rf Vargas, Jr.	0	3	0	0	.255
1b Pudd	1	3	0	0	.229
2b Carter	0	3	0	0	.157
3b Rozier	0	3	0	0	.291
p Tamari	0	2	0	0	.000
ph Bueller	1	1	0	0	.333

DEMONS	H	AB	R	RBI	AVG
cf Lewis (HR)	1	4	1	1	.206
ss Coleman	0	4	0	0	.286
3b Hicks	0	2	0	0	.355
1b Gunn	0	3	0	0	.233
lf Rutherford	0	3	0	0	.200
2b Hartes	0	3	0	0	.290
rf Goodwin (HR)	1	3	1	1	.231
c Parks	1	2	0	0	.316
p Williams	0	3	0	0	.143

W- Williams (1-2) S-Seavers (5)
L- Tamari (0-2)
Los Angeles 2, Tucson 0

April 22, 1999

SUN DEVILS	H	AB	R	RBI	AVG
ss Bonham	1	3	0	0	.368
c Talley	0	3	0	0	.171
lf Maldonado (HR)	3	4	1	5	.289
cf Greggs	2	5	0	0	.302
rf Vargas, Jr.	2	4	2	0	.276
1b Pudd	3	5	1	0	.276
3b Rozier	3	3	2	1	.334
2b Bueller	1	5	0	0	.250
p S. Benes	0	3	0	0	.000

DEMONS	H	AB	R	RBI	AVG
cf Lewis	1	5	0	0	.205
ss Coleman	1	4	1	0	.282
3b Hicks	2	4	0	0	.371
1b Gunn (HR)	2	4	1	2	.265
lf Rutherford	1	3	0	0	.212
rf Goodwin	0	3	0	0	.207
2b Hartes	0	2	0	0	.273
c Parks	0	4	0	0	.261
p Tims (HR)	1	2	1	1	.143
ph Chambers	0	1	0	0	.125

W- S. Benes (2-1) S-Valentin (2)

L- Tims (1-1)

Tucson 6, Los Angeles 3

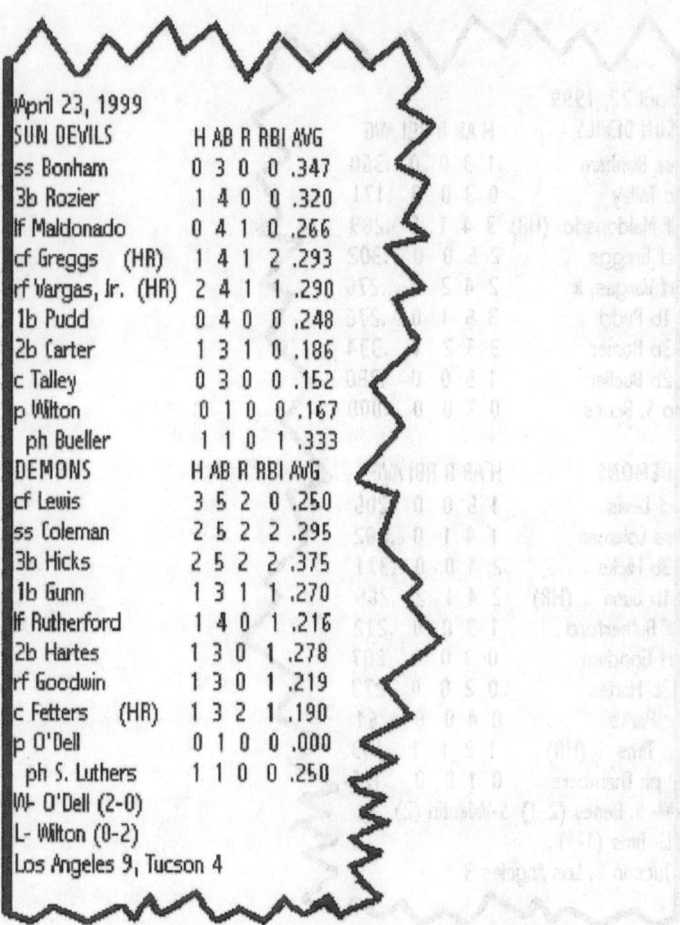

```
April 23, 1999
SUN DEVILS         H AB R RBI AVG
ss Bonham          0  3 0  0 .347
3b Rozier          1  4 0  0 .320
lf Maldonado       0  4 1  0 .266
cf Greggs    (HR)  1  4 1  2 .293
rf Vargas, Jr. (HR) 2 4 1  1 .290
1b Pudd            0  4 0  0 .248
2b Carter          1  3 1  0 .186
c Talley           0  3 0  0 .152
p Wilton           0  1 0  0 .167
 ph Bueller        1  1 0  1 .333
DEMONS             H AB R RBI AVG
cf Lewis           3  5 2  0 .250
ss Coleman         2  5 2  2 .295
3b Hicks           2  5 2  2 .375
1b Gunn            1  3 1  1 .270
lf Rutherford      1  4 0  1 .216
2b Hartes          1  3 0  1 .278
rf Goodwin         1  3 0  1 .219
c Fetters    (HR)  1  3 2  1 .190
p O'Dell           0  1 0  0 .000
 ph S. Luthers     1  1 0  0 .250
W- O'Dell (2-0)
L- Wilton (0-2)
Los Angeles 9, Tucson 4
```

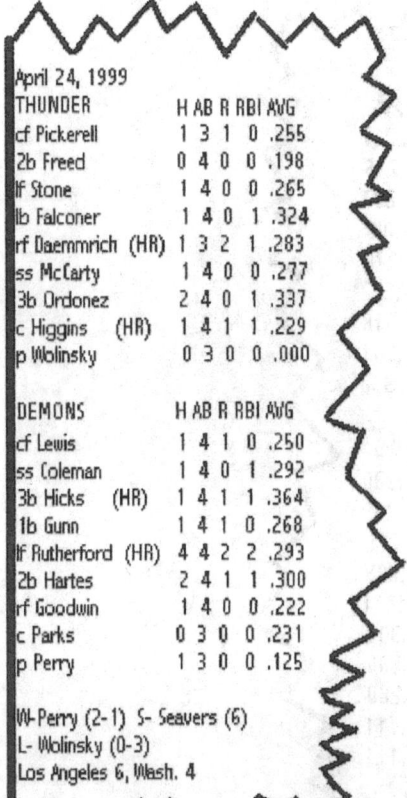

April 24, 1999

THUNDER		H	AB	R	RBI	AVG
cf Pickerell		1	3	1	0	.255
2b Freed		0	4	0	0	.198
lf Stone		1	4	0	0	.265
1b Falconer		1	4	0	1	.324
rf Daemmrich	(HR)	1	3	2	1	.283
ss McCarty		1	4	0	0	.277
3b Ordonez		2	4	0	1	.337
c Higgins	(HR)	1	4	1	1	.229
p Wolinsky		0	3	0	0	.000

DEMONS		H	AB	R	RBI	AVG
cf Lewis		1	4	1	0	.250
ss Coleman		1	4	0	1	.292
3b Hicks	(HR)	1	4	1	1	.364
1b Gunn		1	4	1	0	.268
lf Rutherford	(HR)	4	4	2	2	.293
2b Hartes		2	4	1	1	.300
rf Goodwin		1	4	0	0	.222
c Parks		0	3	0	0	.231
p Perry		1	3	0	0	.125

W- Perry (2-1) S- Seavers (6)
L- Wolinsky (0-3)
Los Angeles 6, Wash. 4

April 25, 1999

THUNDER	H	AB	R	RBI	AVG
cf Pickerell	0	4	0	0	.217
2b Freed	1	3	1	0	.215
lf Stone	2	4	1	0	.287
1b Falconer	0	4	0	0	.300
rf Daemmrich (HR)	1	4	1	4	.278
ss McCarty	1	4	0	0	.272
3b Ordonez	0	3	0	0	.318
c Higgins	2	4	0	0	.251
p Mahoney	1	3	1	0	.333

DEMONS	H	AB	R	RBI	AVG
cf Lewis	0	5	0	1	.226
ss Coleman	1	4	1	0	.288
3b Hicks	2	4	1	0	.375
1b Gunn	2	4	1	1	.289
lf Rutherford	2	4	1	0	.311
2b Hartes	1	3	0	2	.302
rf Goodwin	0	4	0	0	.200
c Fetters	3	4	1	1	.280
p Williams	0	2	0	0	.111
ph Chambers	0	1	0	0	.111

W- Williams (2-2) S- Seavers (7)
L- Pollack (0-3)
Los Angeles 5, Wash. 4

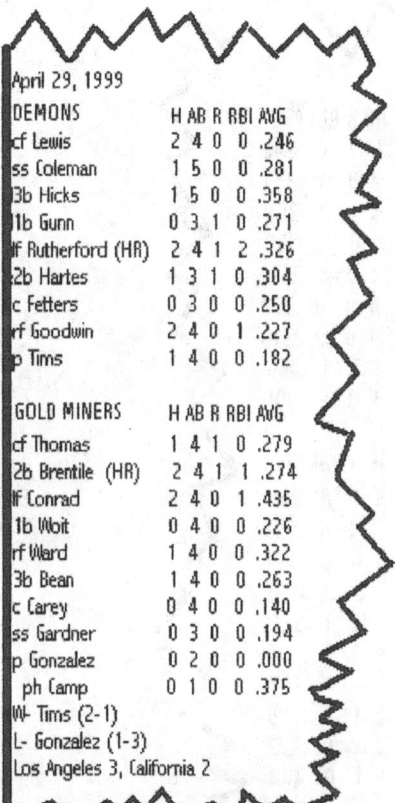

April 29, 1999

DEMONS	H	AB	R	RBI	AVG
cf Lewis	2	4	0	0	.246
ss Coleman	1	5	0	0	.281
3b Hicks	1	5	0	0	.358
1b Gunn	0	3	1	0	.271
lf Rutherford (HR)	2	4	1	2	.326
2b Hartes	1	3	1	0	.304
c Fetters	0	3	0	0	.250
rf Goodwin	2	4	0	1	.227
p Tims	1	4	0	0	.182

GOLD MINERS	H	AB	R	RBI	AVG
cf Thomas	1	4	1	0	.279
2b Brentile (HR)	2	4	1	1	.274
lf Conrad	2	4	0	1	.435
1b Woit	0	4	0	0	.226
rf Ward	1	4	0	0	.322
3b Bean	1	4	0	0	.263
c Carey	0	4	0	0	.140
ss Gardner	0	3	0	0	.194
p Gonzalez	0	2	0	0	.000
ph Camp	0	1	0	0	.375

W- Tims (2-1)
L- Gonzalez (1-3)
Los Angeles 3, California 2

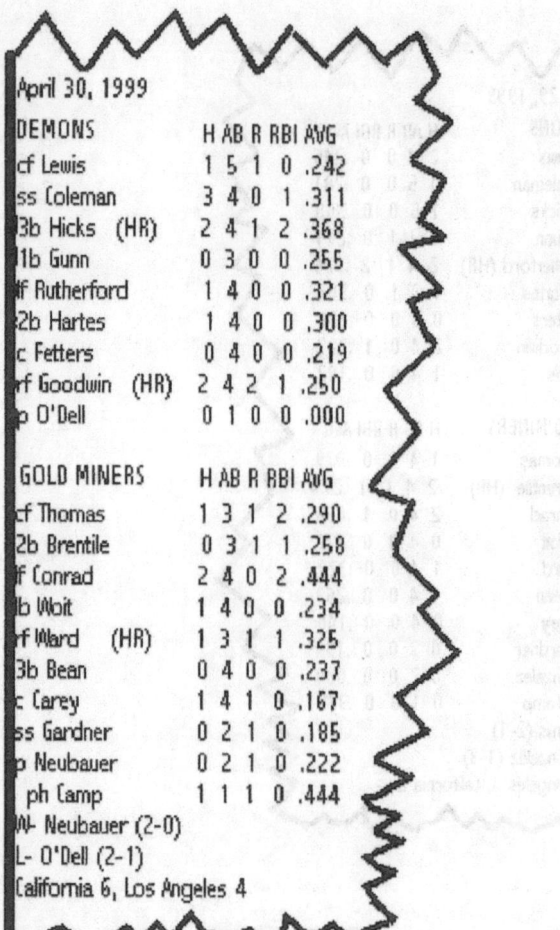

```
April 30, 1999

DEMONS              H AB R RBI AVG
cf Lewis            1  5 1  0 .242
ss Coleman          3  4 0  1 .311
3b Hicks    (HR)    2  4 1  2 .368
1b Gunn             0  3 0  0 .255
lf Rutherford       1  4 0  0 .321
2b Hartes           1  4 0  0 .300
c Fetters           0  4 0  0 .219
rf Goodwin  (HR)    2  4 2  1 .250
p O'Dell            0  1 0  0 .000

GOLD MINERS         H AB R RBI AVG
cf Thomas           1  3 1  2 .290
2b Brentile         0  3 1  1 .258
lf Conrad           2  4 0  2 .444
1b Woit             1  4 0  0 .234
rf Ward     (HR)    1  3 1  1 .325
3b Bean             0  4 0  0 .237
c Carey             1  4 1  0 .167
ss Gardner          0  2 1  0 .185
p Neubauer          0  2 1  0 .222
 ph Camp            1  1 1  0 .444
W- Neubauer (2-0)
L- O'Dell (2-1)
California 6, Los Angeles 4
```

May 1, 1999

DEMONS	H	AB	R	RBI	AVG
cf Lewis	1	4	0	0	.242
ss Coleman	0	4	0	0	.292
3b Hicks	2	4	0	0	.377
1b Gunn	1	3	0	0	.259
lf Rutherford (HR)	1	4	1	1	.316
2b Hartes	0	4	0	0	.278
rf Goodwin	1	4	1	0	.250
c Parks	1	4	0	1	.233
p Perry	0	3	0	0	.091

TIGERS	H	AB	R	RBI	AVG
ss Brown	1	3	1	0	.320
2b Grace	1	3	1	1	.383
rf Petty	0	4	0	0	.218
lf Gnass	1	4	0	0	.262
c Marbury	1	4	1	1	.267
1b Frerck	1	4	0	0	.260
cf Lucas	1	4	0	1	.269
3b Rogers (HR)	2	4	1	1	.308
p Mann	0	3	0	0	.083

W- Mann (3-1)   S- York (5)
L- Perry (2-2)
Montana 4, Los Angeles 2

May 2, 1999

DEMONS	H	AB	R	RBI	AVG
cf Lewis	3	5	2	1	.268
ss Coleman	2	3	2	2	.309
3b Hicks	1	5	1	0	.369
1b Gunn (2HR)	3	5	3	6	.288
rf Rutherford	1	5	0	1	.306
2b Hartes	2	4	1	0	.293
rf Goodwin	0	5	0	0	.228
c Parks	1	4	1	0	.235
p Williams	0	1	0	0	.083

TIGERS	H	AB	R	RBI	AVG
ss Brown (HR)	2	4	1	3	.336
2b Grace	1	4	0	0	.372
rf Petty	1	4	1	0	.225
lf Gnass	0	4	0	0	.243
c Marbury	1	4	0	1	.265
1b Frerck	1	4	0	0	.259
cf Lucas	1	3	0	0	.267
3b Rogers	1	3	2	0	.311
p MacNelly	0	2	0	0	.167
ph Wasserman	0	1	0	0	.167

W- Williams (3-2)
L- MacNelly (1-3)
Los Angeles 10, Montana 4

Mid-Season Standings
May 3, 1999

NORTH	W-L	GB	Streak
(1) Carson City	10-7	-	L-2
(t2) Montana	9-8	1	L-1
(t2) California	9-8	1	W-3
(4) Washington	5-12	5	L-2

SOUTH	W-L	GB	Streak
(1) San Diego	12-5	-	W-2
(2) Los Angeles	10-7	2	W-1
(3) Arizona	9-8	3	W-3
(4) Tucson	4-13	9	L-4

League Leaders
May 3, 1999

Batting Average
1. J.L. Conrad, Cal .416
2. Aaron Craig, CC .385
3. **Jason Hicks, LA** **.377**
4. Stephen Grace, Mont. .372
5. Waylon Ponds, SD .357
6. Joey Bonham, Tuc .341
7. Arthur Brown, Mont. .336
8. Chadley Michael, Ariz. .332
9. Jessie Kato, CC .331
10. David Falconer, Was. .328

Homeruns
1. J.L. Conrad, Cal 8
t2. Stephen Grace, Mont. 6
t2. Steve Gunn, LA **6**
t2. Waylon Ponds, SD 6
t5. Jason Hicks, LA **5**
t5. Moran Gnass, Mont. 5
t5. Jacques Martin, SD 5
t5. Rob Rogers, Mont. 5
t5. Bruno Woit, Cal 5
t5. A. Vargas Jr., Tuc 5
t5. Jake Kimmons, Ariz. 5
t5. David Falconer, Was. 5

League Leaders Cont...
May 3, 1999

Runs Batted In
1. J.L. Conrad, Cal   23
2. Waylon Ponds, SD   20
3. Stephen Grace, Mont.   19
t4. Jake Kimmons, Ariz.   18
t4. Steve Gunn, LA   **18**
6. Jacques Martin, SD   17
t7. Aaron Craig, CC   13
t7. Will Coleman, LA   **13**
t9. David Falconer, Was. 12
t9. A. Vargas Jr., Tuc.   12
t9. Derrick Hundly, Ariz. 12

Runs Scored
1. Stephen Grace, Mont.   18
2. Waylon Ponds, SD   16
t3. Chadley Michael, Ariz. 14
t3. Aaron Craig, CC   14
t3. J.L. Conrad, Cal   14
t6. Miles Hunter, Ariz.   13
t6. Damon Lewis, LA   **13**
8. Jason Hicks, LA   **12**
t9. Ivan Gutierrez, CC   11
t9. J.J. Frazier, SD   11

League Leaders Cont...
May 3, 1999

Stolen Bases
1. Dom McCarty, Was.   10
t2. Chadley Michael, Ariz.   7
t2. Damon Lewis, LA   **7**
t4. Ivan Gutierrez, CC   5
t4. Jessie Kato, CC   5
t4. Arthur Brown, Mont.   5
t4. Alon Thomas, Cal   5

Wins
t1. Jerod Wilkes, SD   4-0
t1. Maxwell MacKenzie, Cal   4-1
t3. Eric Ridel, Ariz.   3-0
t3. Robert Anderson, SD   3-0
t3. Clyde Mann, Mont.   3-1
t3. Ramon Ontaro, CC   3-1
t3. Lake Williams, LA   **3-2**
t3. Sandy Benes, Tuc.   3-2
t9. 13 Players with two wins

League Leaders Cont...

May 3, 1999

E.R.A.

1. Jerod Wilkes, SD — 1.66
2. Maxwell MacKenzie, Cal — 1.97
3. Robert Anderson, SD — 2.48
4. Norwood Gibbs, CC — 2.89
5. Kevin Ryan, Mont. — 2.91
6. Eric Ridel, Ariz. — 2.95
7. Enrique Sierra, Ariz. — 3.14
8. Sandy Benes, Tuc. — 3.24
9. Ramon Ontaro, CC — 3.27
10. Grant LeDuc, Was. — 3.53
11. **Lake Williams, LA** — **3.63**
12. Clyde Mann, Mont. — 3.66

Saves

1. **Salmon Seavers, LA** — 7
2. Binner Wilson, CC — 6
3. Chuck York, Mont. — 5
t4. Rich Treplow, SD — 4
t4. Charlton Markel, Cal — 4
t6. Mayflower Smith, Ariz. — 3
t6. Frank Johnstone, Was. — 3
8. Eduardo Valentin, Tuc. — 2

v

Jeff's eyes begin to burn slightly from concentrating on the box scores and stats too vigorously. The stinging his eyes feel now are similar to how they felt when he used to eat the Grande Nachos from *Taco Bell* and rubbed jalapeño juice in them.

He closes his eyes, re-opens them, and then brushes off the tears starting to swell on his face. He adjusts his body to a more comfortable position (leaning against the acute-angled wall rather than sitting Indian style) and lets his mind wonder.

Why does something about May third ring a bell? He contemplates the question, rolls it around in his head, and focuses on finding an answer.

Maybe it has something to do with Shae?

Or the dreams?

Or the next game?

Damn, damn, damn... "That's it!" he shouts in the shadowy attic, stirring a mouse from under a chest. It scatters across the attic floor with unmatched speed and balance, hiding once again behind a pile of junk. Jeff pays no attention to the rodent, but says, "It's the next game that brings back my memory. The game I got four hits in and hit a two-run homer to win it."

Hartes scurries from stud to stud—a rejuvenated youth—and then descends the ladder leading back to the hallway. He is just dying to go sit in his recliner and reminisce over the '99 season some more, where his thoughts are conjured without much strain. With his full train of thoughts and memory restored, Jeff feels totally capable of vividly retelling his glorious, yet one-of-a-kind, season.

"Plump," the sound made as the old man plunges into his chair. He pulls the lever on the right side of the recliner, causing it to slope backwards, and folds his arms behind his head. He sits for a minute or two, stretched out. He then returns his hands to his lap, fumbling through the scrapbook pages once again. He flips through the middle of the book, trying to find his place.

"Let's see here. May third I believe. We were ten-and-seven, right behind San Diego, right at the halfway point of the season. Our game was in Washington against the Thunder, and nineteen-year-old Michael Tims was starting for us. I had called Shae right after lunch, before she went in for work on a Sunday, and let her know I would be back on the fifth and that we had the whole day off together. Then Will and I went across the street to a bar called *Tacoma's Best* and shot a couple of racks of pool. I got my ass kicked four out of five games in 8-Ball, but took two out of three during our 9-Ball session. Before we headed back to the hotel for a quick nap, we drank a Coors Light together and chatted.

After our nap, we scarfed down some burgers from Fuddrucker's, and then got on the bus heading out to Stone Stadium (named after a famous local guitar player, Henry Stone, who died of AIDS at the age of 29). We got to the fieldhouse, got dressed, and—"

VI

"Knock, knock... knock, knock." A noise that can only be derived from a hand folded in a fist striking something wooden. "Knock, knock."

Who in the hell would be knocking on my door at midnight? Jeff asks himself, not a clue to who it would be, and then decides to find out by asking the knocker. "Who is it? What do you want? Don't you see what time it is?"

No response from behind the door.

Jeff pulls himself out of the recliner once more, aggravated to say the least. He goes to the door. He sneaks a peak through the curtains covering the window next to the front of his house, and recognizes the knocker to be some sort of mail carrier. *Hmm... better see what this guy needs.* Jeff unlocks the deadbolt first, then the doorknob, and cracks the door open a couple of feet wide.

"Mr. Jeff Hartes?" the knocker-slash-mailman asks. At first glance he appears to be no older than fourteen. With a face full of freckles and curly red hair, he couldn't be over twenty. But a second look at his build and height would make you change your guess to eighteen, nineteen at the most.

"Uh-huh," Mr. Jeff Hartes replies.

"I have a letter for you. I blew a tire out earlier, but I wanted to make sure you still received your letter A.S.A.P."

"You couldn't have delivered in the morning?" Hartes questions, still irritated from having to leave his memory behind—also his comfortable recliner.

"Well... I should have had it here by six o'clock. I'm terribly sorry. Madd Mail Service guarantees its delivery, one way or another, rain or shine, snow or —"

"I get the point," Jeff interrupts.

"And plus," the carrier continues, "The guy who sent it through us said it was important. Very important. That's why I reconsidered bringing it here tomorrow and tried to get it here as fast as I could."

The youngster remains shivering with clattering teeth

from nervousness over his mistake—plus the chill in the midnight air. Jeff, never being a typical "red ass" baseball player, eases the kid's stress as well as his own.

"Alright, fair enough," Jeff says, taking the letter from the delivery boy and waving his hand at him in a gracious manner. The delivery boy says bye, as does the man at the door, who then proceeds to get out of the cold and back to his thoughts. He takes one more peek at the letter; thinking, *I can't believe someone actually delivered a letter at midnight?* He considers opening it, and then decides to wait. *Can't forget what I was thinking about now, can I?*

On his way to his "Numero Uno" seat, he lays the letter on the coffee table. *Important my ass, nothing is important when you're seventy-four and shit on yourself every time you try and fart. Now where was I?*

Chapter Six
Hartes Delivers

Hartes backhanded the grounder, flipped it to Coleman on second, and the shortstop hurled it to Seavers on first.

Crack! "Big Daddy" Gunn continued to send the B.P. pitches from Larry George into orbit.

Smack! Hartes fielded another ball and turned two again. *Crack!* Another big swing from Gunn, lining one off the centerfield wall.

"Girl you looks good won't you back that ass up... you'ze a fine muthafucka' won't you back ass up... call me Big Daddy when you back that ass up... girl who's you playin' wit', Back That Ass Up!" Lewis sang for Steve as he jogged in from shagging fly balls in center. Damon tossed his glove aside, and reached for the wood.

Standing outside the batting cage, directly behind homeplate, Lewis told Gunn, "My turn to show you who has the real pop on this club." Gunn, Hicks, and the rest of the guys around the cage broke into laughter, while Damon gripped his bat as tightly as he could and took a couple of practice swings.

Will and Jeff worked on double plays until it was their turn to hack. They took their cuts with the other two in their group (Parks and Chambers) and headed down the third base path to the clubhouse to get dressed for the game.

Jeff was sliding his socks up his shins when O'Dell started to crack up, followed by several others. Hartes turned his attention to the hysterics, and saw one of the funniest things he'd ever seen.

Salmon was striding naked from locker to locker flexing his body. Looped over the head of his abnormally large package was one of those tiny football helmets that you get out of a quarter machine. The helmet (New Orleans Saints) was bouncing on top of his cock, being held on by the football helmet's small, white chinstrap.

The closer turned in Jeff's direction, flexed his chest muscles with his arms behind his head, and said, "Must be nice to not have to wear a cup tonight. I've got 'The Helmet.' Woah!" Salmon pronounced the word very similar to the *woah* of Joey Lawrence on that stupid television show, *Blossom*. "Must be nice!"

Jeff, with the rest of the team still in the clubhouse, doubled up with laughter. Perry broke the hooting and hollering, "Couldn't you have least saddled up a better team than the Saints on your tally-whacker?" Everyone chuckled, awaiting Salmon's response.

"Must be nice to just have quarters lying around, you know. Wow! I could only afford one helmet for one cock," Seavers replied squeezing his "junk," but making sure the Saints didn't fall off. "I mean, c'mon, must be nice to drive a Mercedes like Thomas. Wow! Must be nice!" The words "wow" and "must be nice" came out of Seavers' mouth without him even knowing. They were just fill-in words. They were used like a scared or nervous public speaker said "umm" or "uhh" during every break in their speech.

The fun and games carried on for about fifteen more minutes, and then it was time to get serious. Well... not really serious-serious, sort of serious. Do your job on the field and at the plate, and then nobody will bitch.

II

"Singing the national anthem tonight, Ms. Marie Summers," the man hidden in the Stone Stadium pressbox announced. The entire infield gaped at Ms. Summers—a long good look at that—as she began to sing; her eyes were a cool blue, her hair a sunny brown, and she had a sweet look of innocence on her pretty face, speckled with a few light freckles that took nothing away from her beauty and only added a little more to her charm. The Demons' heads turned to their third baseman.

"Uh-huh," Hicks said, already knowing what everyone was snapping their heads his way for. And then Hicks said what everyone was 99.9% sure he would say, "Yeah, I'll fuck her after the game if she's not careful."

He then directed his eyes between the flag and Marie's ass. No laughter, just smiles as no one would dare burst out during the national anthem. Ms. Summers finished, received her applause with a quick bow, and the umpire calling the balls and strikes shouted:

"Play Ball!"

"Good evening, sportsfans. Welcome to another day of Demon baseball," The Duke relayed back to the home audience. "It's a near perfect day, only a few clouds in the sky. The temperature... well... not too hot, not too cold. Before we get to tonight's lineups, I'll update you on the two earlier games being played. In Carson City, Antonio Smith holds a four-to-one lead over Cal going into the seventh. J.L. Conrad hit his league leading ninth homer in the fourth. A solo shot for the streaking outfielder. Down in Arizona, where the red-hot Scorpions play host to Tucson, the score is three-to-two in favor of the Sun Devils. Tony Maldonado broke the two-two in the sixth." Marinville reached for a switch in front of him, clicked it on, and waited.

The recorded message played, "One-and-two the count on Maldonado. Score still tied two-to-two. We're in the top half of the sixth. The pitch under way..." *Whack!* "Deep drive to left-center field. Michael and Kimmons chasing, but not going to run this one down. A solo shot for Tony Maldonado silencing the Arizona fans and breaking the tie."

"That was Arizona's own Kip Kravitz with the call," The Duke interrupted the pre-recorded broadcast. "Now to the starting lineups. Leading off and in center for the Demons, Damon Lewis. Batting second and playing shortstop, Will Coleman. Hitting third at third base, Jason Hicks. Batting clean-up and covering first base, Steve Gunn. In the five-hole, playing leftfield, Erric Rutherford. Hitting sixth, the second baseman, Jeff Hartes. Replacing a resting Billy Goodwin and batting seventh, the rightfielder, Brett Chambers. Catching and taking his cuts from the eighth spot, Bobby Parks. And on the mound, hitting ninth, Michael Tims." Darrell Marinville proceeded with the Washington Thunder's batting order and defense in the same manner, told the Demons' fans not to go anywhere, and went to commercials.

"We're back with Demon baseball. This is Darrell "The Duke" Marinville bringing you all the action. The last meeting between Los Angeles and Washington favored the Demons, who won five-to-four. Ron Fetters led the charge, going three-for-four, scoring a run, and also driving one in." Simultaneous to the Duke's announcing, Lewis marched towards homeplate.

"Centerfielder Damon Lewis leads off for the Demons.

Lewis, who is hitting two sixty-eight with one homerun and thirteen runs scored, digs into the box. He's not hitting for average as well as he would like to be, but he is still producing the runs. His on-base percentage is over a hundred points higher than his average. He'll be facing the lefty, Grant LeDuc. LeDuc, the Aussie, is two-and-oh on the year with a three point five-three earned run average."

Lewis got set in the batter's box, eyed the pitcher, and took a few cuts. LeDuc rolled the ball around in his hand, received his sign, and fired. Ball one. The bench chatter got underway, "Humm now... humm now... let's go Damon, lead us off baby."

Salmon, maintaining his high from earlier in the clubhouse, started in on the pitcher for the Thunder.

"Hey La-Duck! You like duck? Duck down and get you some! Wow! Must be nice to get some every now and then. God knows it's been—" Salmon cut himself off as the Washington pitcher snuck a quick glance into the dugout, and then re-channeled his focus on the batter. One of the things that made Salmon's use of tongue so hilarious was how slow and smooth it rolled out of his mouth. He paused, he accented the wrong words, he was the darker version of Larry Merchant. Sometimes you just want to say, 'Hurry up and finish the damn sentence already!'

LeDuc delivered another ball, making the count 2-0. He shook his head, appearing to disagree with the homeplate call. He paced around the mound, before regrouping himself and returning to the rubber. Salmon didn't let him off that easy.

"Wow! You know... I should grunt that hard when I pitch La-Duck. Maybe I could throw low eighties, too. At least bring it if you're going to grunt, you know. I mean damn, throw a little harder!"

Every "wow" and "you know" Salmon said became

slower and less understandable. Almost better than the Larry Merchant comparison, Rutherford always said Salmon's words came out similar to the late rapper, D.J. Screw, who was always cutting up famous or new rap songs and slowing them down to a grinding, but relaxing beat.

His face did fit the voice, though. Although a handsome black man, he had large jaw bones and puffy cheeks. His body wasn't fat, but it was much softer than most of the other athletes. He had lightning, diamond-colored eyes, and the crazy bastard even bleached his black hair to—in his words—"intimidate the other team's batters."

LeDuc eventually walked Lewis on five pitches, bringing up Coleman. Coleman dropped the sacrifice down on the first pitch, moving Lewis to second and making the first out of the game. Hicks flied out to deep left, unable to move the runner, and Gunn hit a hard grounder right back to the pitcher, ending the top of the first.

Marinville with the call, "The Demons leave one stranded heading to the bottom of the first. Due up for Washington... Pickerell, Freed, and Stone. It's nothing to nothing. We'll be back in a flash with Los Angeles Demon baseball."

Washington also left one stranded in their first try of the night. Tims struck out Pickerell to start off the bottom half of the first, but Leonard Freed singled through the right side off of a 0-1 slider. Freed then moved to second on a wild pitch, but Stone and Falconer could not bring him home. The leftfielder flied out to shallow center, and the first baseman grounded out to Hartes at second.

Zero runs produced in the first, as well as the second and the third, as neither team's offense could get things kick-started.

Hicks singled to start off the fourth for Los Angeles. Gunn, leading the team with 18 RBI's, struck out. Rutherford hit a chopper, moving Hicks and making the second out of the inning. And then Hartes stepped up to the plate.

"LeDuc checks Hicks at second, turns, and then delivers home. Ball one. Jeff Hartes singled his first time up off of LeDuc, raising his batting average to three-oh-five. LeDuc's pitch... strike one on the outside corner, one-and-one."

The second baseman stepped out of the box, checked the signs one more time. *Nothing, swing away,* and advanced back into the chalk-outlined hitting area.

"Hartes is ready, so is LeDuc, the pitch underway." *Smack.* "A shot to leftfield, Stone charging, won't get there. He fields it cleanly and fires home. Hicks slides, the ball is off line, one-to-nothing Demons. An R.B.I. single for the second baseman."

Hartes didn't advance any further than first as Chambers lined out to second, ending the Demons' attempt at a rally.

In the bottom of the fourth, the Thunder answered. Tims showed his first signs of struggle when he walked Falconer and Daemmrich to open the inning.

"Dom McCarty steps in for Washington, runners on first and second, and nobody out," The Duke proclaimed. "The speedy shortstop is hitting three-oh-one and leads the league with ten stolen bases. A base hit here would definitely bring the handful of people in the stands to life. Tims pays no attention to the stocky first baseman getting his lead from second. Instead, he checks the sign, and delivers... strike one. Right down the shoot. The pitch underway... strike two. A swing and a miss by McCarty."

Marinville cleared his throat while Tims strolled around the rubber trying to pump himself up. "Tims is back on, checks first, then Falconer at second, and delivers... ball one. McCarty taps his bat on his cleats, re-enters the box, and awaits the pitch. Strike Three! He struck 'em out! One away now in the fourth."

Ordonez couldn't move the runners either. Hicks knocked his hard ground ball down, stepped on third base, and side armed the ball to first. Gunn's stretch wasn't enough as Ordonez beat the throw by a step. With two outs, the catcher Marc Higgins came to the plate. Tims worked the count in his favor, but hung a slider that Higgins laced over Coleman's head.

"Rutherford runs the ball down in the gap. He turns and fires it in. No chance to get Daemmrich. Coleman cuts off his throw, making sure Ordonez doesn't try to score from third," The Duke announced as Coleman flipped the ball to the pitcher. "The Thunder have tied the game at one." But one was all Tims allowed in the fourth, 'K'ing LeDuc to end the inning and leaving two on the bases.

The Demons and the Thunder both went scoreless in the fifth. A hit from Parks for Los Angeles, and a hit from Stone for Washington was the only excitement.

Hicks led off the sixth with a single, but Gunn followed with a grounder to short, setting up an easy 6-4-3 double play. Rutherford ended the Demons' chances with a fly out to rightfield.

The Duke summarized the bottom of the sixth for Washington. "Los Angeles is going to have to make up some ground now. Tims has been knocked out of the game, and the damage has been done. It all started with a walk to Falconer. Daemmrich doubled him home, and scored consecutively on a double by McCarty. After Ordonez popped out, Higgins sent Tims packing with a two-run shot off the scoreboard above the leftfield wall. Darren Luthers entered the game for the Demons, halting the Thunder's charge. Luthers sat down LeDuc and Pickerell in order, closing the book on Washington's four run sixth."

The next two innings were fairly quiet. The Demons chalked up one run when Hartes crossed homeplate due to a double by Chambers. The score now stood 5-2 Washington, heading into the last inning.

III

"Let's go D. Lewis, get us started now," Hartes yelled, wanting to find some hope in the ninth, but none yet. Damon singled up the middle to open the inning, bringing up Will, and then bringing the hope that was needed.

Marinville wasn't sure if there was life on the Demons' bench or not. But he wasn't concerned with how much or how little life the team had. He believed, and sometimes, that's all that matters. "Making his way to the plate, Will 'The Thrill' Coleman. Coleman is hitting three-twelve with thirteen ribbies on the season. Washington's closer checks the speed-burner over at first, Lewis has seven steals on the year, and then Johnstone fires home." *Crack!* "This ball is hit hard, way back, way back, gone! A two-run homer for Coleman! His second of the year, closing the gap. This game is now a one-run ballgame."

Coleman rounded third, hopped on home, and was greeted immediately. "Nice shot baby, nice fuckin' hammer!" Gunn told him as he gave him some dibs (connecting fists) and made his way to the on deck circle. No joking involved that time, Steve was pumped.

Hicks connected on a crowd-pleaser high into center.

But the wind brought it back enough for Pickerell to make the grab in the warning track. One away with Steve Gunn approaching the pentagon. Gunn took Johnstone to full count, and then struck out swinging. Two away in the ninth.

Erric Rutherford was the Demons' last hope. The hope that Will mustered was dwindling. Rutherford fouled off two straight 1-2 sliders, and then got the fastball he wanted. L.A.'s leftfielder drilled the outside fastball to the opposite field for a two-out single.

"Nice fuckin' piece of hitting 'E.' Let's go Hartes, bring 'em home," Coleman shouted as the whole dugout was now up and rowdy.

"Hartes has been on his game tonight folks," The Duke blared, feeling something special. "He's three-for-four with a run batted in. Hartes gets settled in, looks over at Skip, and then wheels back towards Johnstone on the mound." The rambunctious Thunder fans in the stadium, and nearer the outlining of the field, could definitely see the sweat mounting on the closer's face as he continued to wipe his brows. He paced back and forth behind the mound, calming his nerves.

Thunder skipper Brandt Shaw gave no signs of going to the bullpen, much less warming someone up. He had faith in his closer.

Hartes called for time, sticking one leg beyond the chalked boundary. *C'mon you fuckin' pussy, this is what it's all about!* He briefly shook his head in a jerky fashion, *let's go,* and then he advanced back into the batter's box.

"Hartes steps back in, glaring at Johnstone," Marinville stated. "The pitcher looks to first, back to home, to first again... Throws to first! Not in time. Rutherford easily slid in before the tag from Falconer. Johnstone's trying to pick up his fourth save on the year and trying to pick off the runner so he doesn't have to face another hitter. The pitcher shakes off his sign, then nods, and checks Rutherford again. Turns to plate and fires... ball one. Missed on the inside corner.

"Johnstone steps off the rubber, grinding the ball down between his hands. He's back on, and delivers... ball two. The fastball got away from him a little and sailed high. He comes to the stretch, and throws... strike one. Fastball over the middle of the plate. Two-and-one count on the second baseman."

Hartes' mind presently only spoke two words: *Bring it, bring it, bring it, bring...*

"Johnstone fires home."

Fastball! The word echoed in his head. *Whack!* "Hartes SMASHES one down the line," The Duke screamed. "If it's fair it's got the distance. FAIR BALL! HOMERUN FOR JEFF HARTES! Holy mackerel, the Demons take the lead six-to-five! JEFF HARTES IS MY PERSONAL SAVIOR TONIGHT!"

Hartes rounded first, pumping his fist in the air.

"Hell yeah, motherfucker!" he hollered as he touched second base. He could see Will was already out of the dugout, jumping up and down and shouting things at Hartes that he couldn't interpret. The second baseman jumped on home and was surrounded by the rest of the team, everyone slapping his helmet or pushing him in the back.

"Goddammit' Hartes, that's what I'm talking 'bout!" Gunn bellowed above the rest of the excitement. It was Hartes' turn to shine, his turn in the spotlight, and his turn to keep this team headed towards a championship. He was half-carried and half-shoved off the field—back into the dugout.

Even Skip was hootin' and hollerin'—a rare

phenomenon during game time for the hard-nosed, veteran-style manager whose idol was the legendary Billy Martin. Coach loved to shoot the shit off the field and before games, but seldom did he become this riled up in the course of a game. By the shimmering expression on his face, the whole team could tell he was excited. His already large nose appeared to be bigger and glowing before the excitement. He wasn't entirely overweight for his age; his skinny ankles, bird legs, and average waist were overshadowed by his hanging beer belly.

Hartes sat on the end of the bench, trying to catch his breath and allow the moment to take hold. He watched as Chambers grounded out to second for the third out. And then jumped up and jogged out to his position for the last half of the ninth. His heart was still pounding hard, but it was time to play defense. For the Thunder, there was no bouncing back. In other words, Coleman's homer hurt, but Hartes' bomb broke their hearts.

Jimenez sat them down as they came up, one-two-three. He closed for Seavers, who was suffering from slight fatigue in his throwing arm. Los Angeles moved to eleven-and-seven with the win, gaining a game on San Diego. They would have one more game with Washington, travel home for a day off on the fifth of May, and then get ready for one hell of a series with the Knights.

IV

The fluorescent glowing blue and green sign read, *'Club Silverstone.'* The letter 'C' was blue, the letter 'l' was green, the letter 'u' was blue, and so on... The sign sat perched high above the building, lighting up the whole street block.

The drivers had led the ballplayers through a maze of intersections, back roads, and smoothed areas (not even official roadways) so that Hartes wasn't even sure he was in the same town anymore. They were all the way across town. When the cars had finally come to a standstill, they found themselves in an enormous parking lot off of Saint Helen's Avenue.

Seavers, Coleman, and Hartes killed a 12-pack of Bud Light just on the ride over, leaving them to believe that if they had time to hammer down twelve beers, how many did Gunn, Hicks, and Jimenez swallow down? Nonetheless, they stepped out of the car. Will and Jeff crawled out of the backseat, while Salmon (supposedly resting his sore arm) remained in the front seat, getting his groove on with Tiffanie.

A voice from the car parked behind them shouted, "*Silverstone*? Looks like a winner to me. Time to get my freak on." Gunn walked in front, followed by Javy, and then Jason and Marie (O' say can you see...) brought up the rear.

Tiffanie hopped out of the driver's side seat and said, "I'm ready to get *my* freak on too, Steve." Big Daddy smiled, presumably thinking how much he would love to get in her panties. But being the faithful husband that he was, the girl wouldn't even get to first base (how ironic?) if she chose him as her "lay" for the night.

The eight of them arrived at the door, paid the ten-dollar cover charge—Gunn picked up Hartes' cover, saying "you are my hero," referring to the bomb Jeff hit, and giggling, and Salmon and Hicks picked up the ladies' cover. They entered the nightclub. The place was already jam-packed and in full swing. The techno blared over the speakers; ravers' danced with plastic, glowing neon wristbands and necklaces; and the bar section was full of heavy drinkers.

"This is too gay," Gunn said. Seavers laughed, seeming to be the only person who heard him. But then Hicks shrugged in agreement.

Hicks added, "Gay may be right, but the pussy in here is endless."

On the left side of the club were about six pool tables, a few dartboards, and several pinball machines. The tables and games were divided by a circular constructed bar with twelve black stools evenly arranged around the bar, nearly all of them occupied.

To the right of the gaming area—if someone were facing the back wall from the entrance—was the dance floor. It was separated into three different levels: the highest raised area was on the exterior, and the lowest, ground level, raised area was in the extreme interior of the configuration. Beyond the dance floor, lined against the back wall, were two DJ stations and ten, fifteen, and twenty-foot high light stands. The lights changed from red, blue, green, yellow, and white while flashing all around the dance floor. The lights flickered on, off, and then danced around the people like a jackrabbit escaping gunfire.

On the far right hand side of the nightclub was the full bar area with a multitude of drinking tables. The bar covered the whole wall along that side and featured over eight bartenders splashing down drinks. The tables were all round and wooden with ashtrays and matches in the center of them. Some of the tables were spacious enough for four chairs, while others could hold eight.

Parallel to the entrance was a twisting staircase leading to the second floor. This floor was hollow in the middle— cut out for visual to the first floor—with a white rail preventing people from falling onto the dance floor below. It contained two small bars, a few tables, and more places to dance or rave.

"Where to first?" Hicks asked, carrying his voice over the constant roar throughout the dance club. Will, Javy, and Jeff shrugged their shoulders, not really worrying about where they went as long as the beer continued to flow.

"Let's go chill at the tables over there," Steve suggested, pointing in the direction of the main bar area. No one answered vocally, but they all started in that route.

The player's club sat at one of the larger tables, conversing and drinking. Hicks had that look on his face that said, 'I'm already in with the National Anthem girl' as he continued chatting with her. Tiffanie, Marie's friend, had narrowed down her decision to the two guys flirting with her the most. Ms. Tiffanie's options were between the twenty-two year old rookie, Javier Jimenez, or the veteran closer, Salmon Seavers. If Seavers had any seniority pull with the women like he did in the clubhouse, it was all over for the young Dominican.

"Isn't Shae going to miss you not calling tonight?" Steve asked, facing towards Will and Jeff.

"Not at all," Shae's sweetie replied, almost yelling.

"Why's that?"

"Because I already called her, dickhead," Jeff said. He stuck his tongue out at Steve and scrunched up his face, acting retarded. "Der-da-der!"

Steve waved his left arm back at Jeff, meaning *whatever asshole*, or something close to that line, and chugged the rest of his beer.

The boys kept buying Marie and Tiffanie drinks, plus the ones they were downing themselves. Both girls were very sexy before the club, now they were becoming "Perfect 10's." They were both about the same height, somewhere around 5'5", and both had pretty, young faces. Innocent, but easily recognized as fake. Marie had a hair color (dirty blondish/brownish) similar to Jason's. Perhaps they used the same shampoo and conditioner and groomed their hair likewise. Tiffanie had the bleach blonde, tacky but classy look going on. Slightly too much dark eye shadow and rose rouge on her cheeks.

Before too long, Hartes was staggering to the bathroom to take one of those orgasm pisses. You know, the piss that is so ready and willing to spray out that it feels better than an orgasm. Jeff stumbled, hit his head on the wall above the urinal, and pulled out his buddy.

Hartes aimed and then fired, "Ohhh... that's better," he moaned as he zipped his pants back up and exited the bathroom. Jeff's vision was beginning to blur, but finding the table wasn't a problem.

"Who needs another one?" he asked everyone except Jason and Marie. They were on the dance floor getting freaky with one another. "Huh? Speak up?"

"One here for sure," Will answered. And then he checked the rest of the table. "Looks like we could all use one." Tiffanie and the fellows all nodded.

"Alrighty then... I'll be right back." Hartes traveled to the bar, hoping to not look too ridiculous, and ordered another round. The pretty little waitress said she would add it to the tab and bring them right over.

The boozing and visiting prolonged deep into the next morning until the club closed at three. Someone speculating that the group stayed out until early the next morning was sort of a redundant statement. Only because it would be a deviation if they didn't make it past midnight. Because normally, they did.

Upon leaving, Hicks drove Marie's ride, and Will steered Tiffanie's. Hartes sat in the front seat with his roommate while Salmon and Tiffanie already started to mess around in the back. It looked like the veteran was victorious in the battle of love. He pulled the right strings and defeated the rook.

The second baseman faded in and out of reality, listening to Salmon chat about a previous sex incident. "You know... so this chick's mom walked right in while her daughter was giving me a blow job, right. Like I said before, her whole family was like real strict, Church of Christ... in other words, crazy." Tiffanie laughed at the reference to the family being crazy, ignored the part about Salmon getting head, and then Salmon continued...

"Must be nice, you know... her mom, like immediately dashed out tha' door. Cristina was like oh my God, what just happened. 'Your mom walked in on you suckin' my shaft,' I said. Woah... and then laughed my ass off. Then her mom popped her head back in and called her to come outside. And then blah-blah-blah, you know, she came back in and was all upset and like cryin.' I asked her if she told her parents that she had followed their advice. She was like what are you talking 'bout. I said, 'Must be nice, but dad? You always told me to use my head when it came to sex.'"

Hartes remembers the car erupting with laughter, so he decided to join in.

And then next thing he saw was Mr. Toilet again. But this time, it was his other head spewing out something—vomit. He hurled over and over again, hugging the sides of the hotel john. Will asked if he was okay, Hartes mumbled yeah, and Coleman said he would be back in a second.

The rest of the night Jeff didn't remember. Will told him the next day, after reading the morning paper, that Jeff crawled out of the bathroom on all fours. He then wallowed around on the floor for awhile before finally pulling himself into bed and passing out on top of the sheets.

Coleman also said, "Salmon boinked Tiffanie while Javy and I watched through the curtains. I can't believe I did that shit, but it was sooo funny. He was laying the wood to her man, you should have seen it. Steve kept coming in and out of his room saying he couldn't watch *Sportscenter* because Jason and Marie were going at it under the sheets and giggling and shit. What a fuckin' crazy night, man! I haven't even heard what the smokers' did." Referring mainly to Goodwin, Rutherford, and Lewis.

Hopefully, none of them got arrested this time...

Chapter Seven
Failure is an Option

I

"High fly ball hit by Allen to centerfield. Lewis takes a few steps back, and makes the catch. That ends the fifth, Demons one, Knights nothing. Due up for Los Angeles in the sixth, Parks, Hicks, and Gunn," Darrell Marinville announces to the Demon faithful.

Jogging in from second, I wonder how in the hell I can hear Marinville doing the radio broadcast. After all, Marinville is in the booth, I am standing on the field. The announcer is glassed in and speaking over the radio, I am entering the dugout via the infield. Kyle Queen's voice is the one spilling through the loudspeakers throughout Diego Field, not Marinville's. Queen's the one I should be hearing, along with the fans.

So let me say it again, because it's worth repeating. I can hear Darrell "The Duke" Marinville's broadcast, along with Kyle Queen's announcing over the loudspeakers, and finally, the buzzing of the crowd altogether.

I sit in the left side corner of the always-rectangular bench. I can smell sweat in the air, tasting the cool, refreshing breeze turned sour. The smell reminds me of going to Dodgers games in the early 90s. Me and pops, having the time of our lives while rooting for one of the greatest coaches of my youth, Mr. Lasorda. *But who other than Tommy Lasorda?* And his extremely vocal, and

sometimes outrageous, rants —

I remember I always ordered the same things around the same innings. Right before the fourth or fifth, Dad would make a run to the concession stand and grab a couple of hotdogs and a Dr. Pepper, along with a beer for himself. We would heckle the opposing team's rightfielder from our second row outfield seats, and hope to God that Pedro Guerrero would hit one out in our section. Man, I wanted a homerun ball bad... I never got one. But this jerkoff next to us caught several homers throughout the season. But that's beside the point.

Then I recognize the situation —

My dream is coming to life. Not coming to life in the sense that it wasn't alive before. Because it was... *alive before.*

And not only is it alive now, but it is out to get me. Reaching and clawing with everything it has to pull me in where I can never escape. Once trapped inside, I will become nothing and live a life of nothingness. My head feels like it is going to explode as I try to ignore this burden cast upon me. This noise, these deviations; this current dramatic play I am enrolled in.

My dream *is* coming to life.

Surely I do *recognize* the situation —

Everything is the same: the same noise ringing in my ears, the same crowd buzzing, the same fly ball to center, the same moon smiling at me in that devilish-hateful smile, and the same girl strutting down the steps towards her seat.

She looks straight into my direction, and oh dear God, it can't be —

"Time Out!" The umpire shouts as a big bouncing ball, full of air, flies out of the stands and onto the field. This turns my attention off of the girl, and back on the game.

Bobby Parks is batting for us in the top of the sixth. He flies out to left. I then watch as Hicks doubles to center, trying to get a rally going, but Gunn strikes out and Rutherford grounds out, ending the top half of the inning.

I zombie-like jog back out to second base, trying to figure out what is happening to me. I steer clear of looking into the stands while I am playing second; placing my attention on what I am supposed to be doing (playing baseball). I turn to glance at the scoreboard in center. The board reads 1-0 in our favor. The pitcher, Wilkes, leads off the bottom of the sixth with a grounder down the first base line that Gunn dives for, catches, and hurries to the base for out number one. The next batter, Frazier, walks for San Diego and then steals second. I catch the throw from Parks, slap the tag, but it's not in time.

Lake makes his first mistake. I watch as he delivers a chest high fastball that Timothy Greener belts to right, scoring the tying run. I clap my glove, keeping the runner on second on his toes, but it isn't necessary. Williams strikes out the next two hitters, Ponds and Garrido, to end the sixth.

I come up to bat in the seventh, leading off—the *noise,* which is quiet for one inning of action, comes to being once again inside my head. It has returned with a vengeance— full throttle. It is a repeated buzzing sound, infecting my mind. *What is going on?* I ask myself. *Get your mind on the game, you're batting in the biggest game of your life.* Before I can gather my thoughts, and myself, I have two strikes on me. I can hear Marinville calling my at-bat over the radio. *It's just not possible.*

"Two strikes now on Jeff Hartes. He's oh-for-two tonight, having struck out twice already. Hartes has been a leader down the stretch here for the Demons, but struggling to get the ball on the bat so far tonight." The San

Diego pitcher Jerod Wilkes winds and fires. I swing... and miss. "Strike three. Hartes has the hat-trick and it's only the seventh inning."

I feel like quitting. It's as simple as that. My mind is racing and my heart feels shattered. Not like being dumped by your horny little high school fling, but shattered as in pierced with a bronze-tipped spear. I look down and see blood on my uniform. It is all over my chest. *The spear must have penetrated my skin and hit a major organ... The Heart.* I close my eyes. I wish the blood away. I open them. It is gone, but my heart still aches — along with my head.

And *the noise* isn't getting any easier to deal with. I not only want to quit, but to run, just run away. Scared? You can say I am, very easily to say that in fact. I mean, there is this *fucking noise* echoing in my brain, this girl I do recognize, but cannot place her fucking name, and I am failing my team. I am letting them down after all the hard work and dedication we've committed ourselves to. After a gut-wrenching and emotional roller coaster of a season, what more do I need? I mean, for real, put Chambers in to pinch hit for me.

My pops once said, 'There are some people who believe they are going to fail, Jeff. And then there are those who believe that failure isn't an option. Sorry to tell you Jeff, but failure is. And it is easier to fail than succeed.' No shit pops. Failure seems to be the only option I am being dealt.

— Failure is an option —

Hicks says something along the lines of 'its okay Hartes, you'll get 'em next time' as I plop down on the bench. A player I don't recognize walks over and grabs the sides of my face. His hands don't touch me in a fierce, jerking movement trying to get my attention, but a soft, gentle placing of his hands on my face. As in the case of trying to show pity yet remorse.

He moves his hands to my shoulders. I place my head in my own hands, somewhat ignoring the kind gesture. The unknown man removes his hands from me and whispers, "Will's watching you, bro."

And then he jogs to the end of the dugout, grabbing his bat and helmet and joining the on deck circle. I try to silence my mind, but nothing appears to be working. This is hell, and I am —

II

Jeff didn't remember passing out, or most of the throwing up. But he did remember waking up. He was sweating all over, his head stung with pain, and Hartes knew that he had dreamt the dream. For the first time, he felt it inside him. Shae *was* right. But it's not like he ever doubted her. Of course, he couldn't recall any of the details until many years later, but he knew either way. It was just a feeling.

His legs wobbled as he tried to stand. The old saying 'my legs feel like Jell-O' was entirely accurate this morning. Pressing one hand against the bed nearest the bathroom and his other hand on the floor, Jeff ascended upward. He rose to full height, felt his left knee buckle, and crashed gently on the bed. Will began to stir out of his own sleep, made a clearing-his-throat *uhh-kuhh* sound, and moved no more.

Hartes rolled over and crawled to his pillows, aching head and all. He entered the sheets for the first time, as his drunkenness allowed him to pass out on top of them earlier. Jeff rested his head on top of the two pillows, and then leaned forward again to check the time. The frequently used hotel clock displayed 9:14 a.m. Jeff eased back into the indention he had previously created in his pillow, now snuggling beneath the blankets, and slowly drifted off to sleep.

III

"Order me an ice tea," Coleman said. "I'm gonna' go get a newspaper." He left the table located in the bar section of *Chili's* and darted through the restaurant's front entrance.

The hostess gathered four menus, brought them to the table, and asked, "I thought there were four of you?"

"There is, he-uhh... went to go get a paper," Parks replied to the hostess, who then proceeded with taking the player's drink orders.

"Oh... okay. What would you like to drink, sir?"

"Tea please."

"I'll take a Coke."

"I'll have a water and a tea, and my friend out there wants a tea also," Jeff said, looking out the window to see if Will had bought a paper yet.

"Okay, I'll be right back with your drinks. Your waiter will be with you in a second to take your food orders," the hostess—one of those *special* restaurant workers who didn't write down your order until she got out of sight, showing off her job skills—walked down the aisle, turned the corner to the fountain drinks, and disappeared. Will entered the front door with a smirk on his face. When he got close enough to talk in a normal voice, not shouting, he publicized:

"Looky-here, Hartes made the front page," Will

flipped the *Tacoma Daily Tribune* onto the table and slid into the booth. The hero picked up the newspaper before Bobby or Simon could, and saw a picture of himself stepping on homeplate with the team surrounding him— similar to ants enveloping a beetle that has angered them. After viewing enough of the photograph, he redeployed his attention to the article.

May 3, 1999

Thunder, Lightning, But No Hartes

The Washington Thunder had all the "heart" and ingredients to win except an answer for Demon rookie, Jeff Hartes.

Hartes collected four hits on five at-bats, drove in three runs, and hit a two-run homerun in the top of the ninth to win the game.

The Thunder led the Demons 5-2 in the last inning, but a two-run blast from shortstop Will Coleman with nobody out, and then the homer by Hartes with two outs, sealed the four run comeback for Los Angeles.

Javier Jimenez (2-0) pitched a scoreless ninth and picked up the win for L.A. Frank Johnstone (0-2) blew his second save of the year, getting the loss for the Thunder.

Continued on... page 4.

—Eric Hargrove

The rest of the write-up was the game storyline and a paragraph setting up tonight's game, O'Dell (2-1) versus Wolinsky (1-3). The waiter appeared, took their orders (baby back ribs for the second baseman), and Will fired up the conversation.

"Aight fellas. I heard this joke from Gunn the other day while we were shagging balls. I guess I'll try to carry the load when he's not around." Will paused to drink his ice tea. "A guy is out fishing too long. He's racing home over a bridge doing eighty when a cop catches him on radar and pulls him over. The guy says, 'Give me a break, I'm on my way to work, and I'm late.' The cop says, 'What do you do for a living?' The guy says, 'I'm a rectum stretcher.' The cop says, 'A rectum stretcher? What does a rectum stretcher do?' The guy says, 'People call me when they need to be stretched. I go to their house, start with a couple of fingers, then a couple more, then a whole hand, then two hands. Then I slowly pull them apart, further and further, until it's a full six feet across.' The cop says, 'What the hell do you do with a six foot asshole?' The guy says, 'They give him a radar gun and stick him at the end of this freakin' bridge.'"

The table, barely alive, was still able to hoot and holler loud enough after Will's joke that people's heads turned. Bobby put his index finger directly over his lips and went, "Shhh." Nobody listened. They just kept on howling over the six-foot asshole.

The waiter returned with the food and asked if they needed anything else. The Demon quartet told him no, and he left to wait on another table. Hartes engulfed his ribs, but only put a small dent in the fries and corn. His stomach still ached (probably alcohol poisoning) from last night's activities.

They finished their meal, tossed enough money on the

table to pay for the food and drinks, plus ten dollars extra for the tip, and then left the restaurant. Jeff shivered at the frigorific blast of wind blowing out of the west. The clouds had darkened, and the group could smell rain as well as feel the moisture in the air.

Jeff looked at Will's face, and the smile that erupted on it meant only one thing. In the famous words of Kevin Costner's "Crash" Davis in *Bull Durham*... "Rain out," the four of them said simultaneously.

If it had been five or six years earlier, one of us surely would have responded with 'Jinx, you owe me a Coke,' or the rated-R version 'Jinx, you owe me a blow.' But either way, the forecast was rain; and maybe plenty of it from the looks of things.

Will and Jeff spent the rest of the time, the rain now pouring against the windows of the hotel, in room 186 watching Simon, Bobby, Erric, and Billy switch off kicking each other's ass on the Playstation. They were playing Tekken, one of those mono-e-mono fighting games.

The rain didn't let up; but the game couldn't be called until the umpires said, so the Demons rode out to the field, awaiting the decision. There really wasn't any debate, the game would be canceled, and it was just a matter of waiting it out. To kill the time, some of the team played pluck, while others stood in the dugout watching the downfall. You know what they say, "No place rains as much as Seattle." The Demons weren't exactly in Seattle (more like Tacoma), but this was still Washington.

The game was finally called about an hour past the seven o'clock start time. Because no one was fatigued from baseball and it wasn't even past nine o'clock, this bus ride home was going to get rowdy. The beer cans' caps were popping off and the cards were on the table, ready to be shuffled. No time for pluck tonight, it was high stake's poker all the way home, unless you went bankrupt and decided to crash for the night.

The six players in the game were Hicks, O'Dell, Rutherford, Fetters, Seavers, and Hartes. Jason threw the cards around one card at a time until Fetters got the jack. "Your deal, catch," Jason said to him, sliding him the cards.

Gunn and Coleman lay on the top bunks on the outsides of the poker table, heckling the card players (no hints or cheats, though), beer in each hand.

"Give me a cut 'E,'" Ron said, sliding the cards to Erric. The leftfielder cut near the center of the deck; Fetters topped it off, and called the first game of the night. "Seven-card stud, deuces wild, two-dollar gruber."

"Kelly Gruber?" O'Dell asked, laughing.

Fetters shook his head, ignoring the remark. He dealt everybody the two cards down and then the third card showing.

"A gruber is an extra card at the end for cash, right?" Seavers asked the dealer in slow motion, each word its own.

"Yessum... two dollars to be exact," Fetters replied and then faced O'Dell, who was still smiling over his Blue Jay's one-liner. "Your king is high card, start the betting."

O'Dell opened with fifty-cents on his king, and everyone matched. Hicks and Hartes folded after the fifth card when Jay had two kings and a deuce up. The game continued, and the other players kept sealing Jay's max bets.

"Last card fellas, down and dirty. Just the way Willy likes 'em," Fetters said, passing out the final and seventh card face down. Erric, saying, 'must be nice to get an extra card,' threw in two bucks for his gruber, looking to be working on a straight flush. He had a 3, 4, and 6 of diamonds, plus a wild deuce. He was missing either a 5 or

7 of diamonds or another deuce. He didn't draw it, and O'Dell took the first hand with four cowboys.

"Thanks for the charity guys, my wife loves it," O'Dell said chuckling.

"Woah! Your wife loves this too!" Seavers responded, standing up and grabbing his crotch. The poker players all laughed and waited for Salmon to shuffle the cards.

"The next game is three... five... seven! Ante up fellas, right on," Seavers announced. Poker lasted through three cases of beer, and around five hours passed before the game finally shut down.

The rookie fled from the table early, losing around thirty-five dollars. But a restless, fresh meat named Bobby Parks quickly filled Hartes' vacancy. Salmon appeared to be slightly ahead, but Mr. O'Dell was raking in the dough after what seemed like a string of full boats. Hicks, Rutherford, and Parks each donated around $250 to the winnings, and Jay almost certainly had seventy-percent of that in his stack of bills.

IV

The team arrived at the Demon clubhouse just before sunrise. Hartes ambled to his truck like a zombie, hopped in, and headed to his apartment. Jeff arrived without even knowing, staggered to the bedroom, and crashed out dead to the world. He woke up after lunch, one-ish to be more exact, and checked the answering machine.

The first message was from his mom, saying that his dad, little brother, and her were coming to the next home game. She said she loved him, and told him to call her back as soon as he got home.

The next message was from Shae. Jeff's girl said she would be off of work at four o'clock sharp and for him to drop by her place around five. Hartes contemplated over watching television or going back to sleep. Sleep won the battle, and it only took him ten minutes to fall back sound asleep.

This time, the ringing of the phone woke him. He rotated his body to face the other way, grabbed the phone off the hook, and said, "Hello."

"Hey honey, what's up?" The voice on the other side was Shae's. Hartes looked at his baseball clock. *Four-thirty? Damn,* he thought, before Shae interrupted him, lost in his own world. "Jeff? You there?"

"Yeah baby I'm here," he answered. "I was just checking to see what time it was. Can't believe it's so late. I overslept a little. But I'll—"

"I'm on my way over there," Shae butted in. "I figured you were tired, so I decided I would just come stay with you. Okay luvva'?"

"Fine with me darlin," he said, throwing his legs over the edge of the bed. Jeff had to piss really badly; a farewell from Shae would be clutch right about now.

"See you in a lil' while, love ya', bye," Shae said, hanging up the phone.

Jeff mumbled goodbye, *that was clutch,* and then rushed to the bathroom. He peed for what seemed like a half hour, and then threw on some shorts and his favorite T-shirt (Eldridge High School, state champs baby!). *Guess I better clean some of this shit up.* He picked up some dirty clothes and carried them to the hamper. Next, he gathered up all of the used glasses and dishes and put them in the sink. *That'll do for now.*

Hartes flopped down on the sofa and pressed power on the controller. The only thing on the agenda was "Trick

Shot" pool on ESPN. It's comparable to playing "H.O.R.S.E." in basketball. One pool shark calls a shot and has to make it in two tries. Then the other player gets two tries to match. They each receive a point if they make the shot, and then the pool hustler who shot second chooses the next trick shot. And so on and so on until somebody reaches twelve points, or fifteen points… doesn't really matter.

But before Jeff could even get involved in the show, Shae knocked once out of politeness and then used her key to unlock the door and come inside. "Hey sweetie," she said, giving him a swift peck on the lips and a big hug. "I talked to Regina earlier, and she wants to know if you and Will want to go out with us?"

"*Us?* Sounds like you're going with or without me, anyways."

"Shutup, silly, you know I was counting on you going."

"Sounds good. I'm sure Regina will inform Will of the plans," Jeff responded, sweeping her off of her feet and laying her back first on the couch. "But until then… I missed you."

"Missed you too, baby."

"And I'll have to tell you about my passing out night."

"Oh really? Must've been wild."

"Not as wild as this," he took Shae by the hand, leading her from the living room to the bedroom. And Hartes closed the door behind them. For no apparent reason, since they were alone at last.

V

"Hurry up Jeff, we're going to be late," Shae commanded while he fixed his hair in the bathroom.

"I'm coming, I'm coming," he insisted. "Oh shit, girl... I've got to call my parents. Hold on one *more* minute."

Shae sighed and fell down onto the couch. "Just hurry baby, I hate being late."

Jeff dialed home, getting his mother. "Hey mom, I got your message." He waited for her quick response and then followed with, "And if you and dad and Eric want to come up tomorrow, that'd be great."

"I think we'll just do that, Jeff Anthony. Your father and I will get a room, and Eric can stay with you if that's okay," his mom replied wholeheartedly.

"Yeah that's fine, Mom. The game starts at seven-fifteen. I'd love to chat tonight, but I'm kinda' in a rush," Jeff said, glancing at his watch.

"Okay dear, I'll let you go. We'll see you tomorrow. Bye."

"Bye Mom." Jeff tossed the phone precisely on the hook, and then ran to tell Shae he was ready.

"Let's go baby, whatcha' waiting on?" he asked her with a grin on his face. He hurried out the door, and then turned around and looked at Shae as if it was her fault they might be late.

"Hush," Shae said, trying to hide her smile from showing.

The four of them ate dinner at *Harris' Steakhouse*, and on this occasion, Harris was there. He had the same full head of hair flowing over his ears and pony-tailed in the back. The rugged facial hair look had turned from brown to brownish-gray, but if anyone could pull it off, Harris could. He still walked the same, slightly hunched over and balancing on his toes.

Six years ago, when Jeff was only fifteen, Harris and his father had been business partners. They split the earnings from their restaurant fifty-fifty. Harris had asked Jeff's father to move to Los Angeles with him to expand their restaurants and increase their bank accounts, but Mr. Hartes didn't want to move. He enjoyed the small town life too much.

So on exceedingly friendly terms, Harris left the restaurant to Jeff's father and took his share of the saved profits. And the place he opened was the prominently famed eating establishment they were at right now.

Harris and Jeff discussed the old days. He asked how Jeff's father had been. Hartes informed Harris he would have a chance to ask his dad himself tomorrow night at the game. Harris was thrilled at the idea of seeing one of the games and his ex-partner again.

"I'll even leave you and the missus free passes on the guest list," Jeff told him on the way out of the steakhouse. A small price to pay for the free meal Harris just gave them. 'Dinner's on me,' he had said while they were dining. And they were all extremely grateful for Harris' generous gesture.

Next they moved to drinking and conversing at *Rocky LaRue's* (a local sports bar) for a few hours. The middle infielders shot a couple of games of pool. Will stomped Jeff once again, while the ladies gossiped over how good their men were in bed or whatever new rumors they could conjure up. The foursome departed right before midnight, Shae with Jeff, Regina with Will.

VI

"You know what, baby?" Shae asked her man in bed. Jeff, trying not to drift off to sleep, opened his eyes.

"Sup," he muttered into the pillow, barely getting that much out.

"I really, really love Regina. And Will, too... I think Regina and I are going to have some great ladies' nights out in the future."

Hartes lifted his head up and stuck his tongue out at her. "Izzz 'dat all you boddered me fo'?"

"Be quiet and go to sleep then. You're such an ass!" Shae responded, slamming her back down on the bed and closing her eyes.

"I thought I was a sweetie?" he inquired.

"Shut up Jeff!" Shae screamed in laughter. She lay there in bed, thinking about her new friends—thinking about Jeff. She was incredibly happy. She loved her man. She loved her job. She had one terrific male friend (and employer), and now she had a best girlfriend.

Jeff's snoring kept her up. Thinking.

But the bed bugs must have finally bitten, because she now joined him in a grand slumber.

Chapter Eight
Family Vacation

I

Shae and Jeff relaxed in bed most of the next morning. What you might call sleeping in. He didn't have to be at the field until 5:30 p.m., since they weren't having batting practice or taking infield before the game. When the couple finally began to stir, the phone rang.

Jeff didn't feel like answering, so he let the machine do its job. He checked the message—mom. She said they were leaving Desert Shores for Los Angeles about one o'clock. They were going to leave earlier than expected so that they would have plenty of time to eat and shop around downtown. Shae and Jeff then dressed and left the apartment in search of some fast food.

"I feel like getting something quick. McDonald's, Jack in da' crack, Steak 'n' Shake, Subway—" he asked Shae before she interrupted him.

"The last one, Subway," she answered, excited about a delicious, yet healthy and nutritious meal. "The rest of them are nasty."

Jeff ordered the foot-long ham and cheese sub combo, and Shae had the 6-inch B.L.T. combo. *Not enough meat on my sandwich... never enough meat at Subway.* After their nice, peaceful brunch, Shae dropped him off at the field. She said she needed to hurry and finish some paperwork so she could make it to the game tonight and meet his parents. Hartes told her to bring his truck if she wanted, so she wouldn't have to go back to the apartment and switch vehicles. She said that was fine, and that she would see him tonight.

II

The glove-steady second baseman entered the clubhouse to another episode of "shower talk."

Steve told Coleman and Lewis, "You've got to see that chick that Jace was with on his day off, man. But listen to this first... Suzanne and I went out to this bar last night, some place out in the middle of nowhere, just to have a relaxing night out. Anyways, my wife and I are having a few drinks, talking. And Jason walks in with this gorgeous blonde girl, in this tight black mini-skirt. I was going to try to make myself unseen, but my wife had already started to wave at Jason. So I bitched her out... nah, not really." Steve paused, pulling his undershirt and tights out of his carry bag.

And then he continued his story, "This chick, her name wassa', umm... fuck. Fuck her name, she was hot. So being the wonderful friend I am, with my wife also egging me, we invited them to sit with us. Jason agreed, and they sat in our booth."

Jason stumbled in through the door, wearing only a pair of Oakley's and Nike shorts. No carry bag, no gear. His tan glistened as the sun behind him appeared to be pushing him through the entrance. "There's the man of the hour right now," Gunn said, turning towards Hicks.

"Are you already telling them about my chick, you fucker?" Hicks asked seriously, holding the straight face as long as he could, and then began to laugh and hold his stomach. Before Gunn could respond, Jason turned to Wade Smith, the head batboy, who was bringing in the freshly washed uni's, and said, "Hey bro, can you go get my gear out of my jeep?"

"Sure... no prob," Wade answered.

"Good kid —" Hicks started, but Gunn jumped in.

"I sure am talking about her, dickhead. Back to the story," Steve replied, and then asked Jason:

"What was her name?"

"Kassandra. With a 'K'... who knows?" Hicks answered. "At least that's what the bitch kept saying. I should have taken her to get me a Pepsi."

"Alright, yeah that's right," Gunn continued. "Hold that Pepsi thought for the younguns. Well my wife and Kassie started chatting like women do. My wife got to the question of 'so what do you do for a living Kassandra?' She hesitated, thought it over, and I guess she decided not to lie to her new man because the bitch straight up said, 'well... I used to be an adult dancer, but I wasn't making enough money. So now I make adult videos!'" The hysterics initiated amongst the few that had already arrived at the field. Including Goodwin and O'Dell, who had just walked through the clubhouse door. Gunn contained his laughter, his face turning red beneath his beard over the idea of what he was going to say next.

"Jason spit out his beer on the table. Said, 'what the fuck, you make pornos?' My wife maintained her composure, but I couldn't help but crack up. Then Jason started laughing his ass off, and she just straight got up, told Jason and me 'fuck both of you if you can't appreciate what I do.' And then Suzanne giggled.

Jason didn't even really care that she was in porn, it just slipped out like that, sounding bad and all. Kassie, the porn star, stormed out of the bar, and called a cab... I guess. Because Jason said fuck her, and the three of us had a good time."

More laughter followed. Thomas Perry and Darren Luthers entered near the last portion of the story, but it was enough for them to join in on the hilarity. Parks asked the question that some of the younger players were curious about. "What do you mean, take her to get a Pepsi?"

Hicks filled them in. "That's where you take some groupie who's worn out their welcome with the Demons, and drive her to the nearest convenience store on your route to the field or wherever. You say, with a sweet tone, 'do you mind going in and getting me a Pepsi, I'm really thirsty.' And when the bitch goes in the store, you drive off."

"And that, my friend," Gunn interrupted, "is taking the bitch to get a Pepsi."

The amusement continued all the way onto the field, and all the way to game time. Where in the back of his mind, Hartes wasn't thinking about the pornstress, or the Pepsi background, but he *was* thinking about the dreams.

Not that he could ever remember anything from them, but maybe this time he could. Jeff was thinking that he knew something; some small piece of information or data that was in some way connected with all of dreams. *Wasn't it San Diego that was in my dreams? And baseball?* He didn't know for certain. Thinking about it virtually felt reminiscent of a dream. But the idea of the *Dreams* and *Baseball* linking together appeared factual in his mind. *If there was only some mnemonic tool to facilitate my memory,* he thought; realizing he had heard the word mnemonic on a talk show earlier that morning. And then he resolved the whole matter by changing his constellated and gathered thoughts of dreams; switch gears completely,

ready to see his parents, ready to see his brother, and Shae
getting to meet them.

III

Immediately upon leaving the clubhouse to the field, Jeff
recognized his dad and Eric leaning against the rail that
separated the field from the stands. His brother, hanging
over the fence, pointed in his direction and said something
to their dad.

Jeff's dad threw one hand casually into the air and
motioned for him to head over there. Jeff broke into a
controlled jog — loosening his hamstrings and calves before
the first pitch.

"Hey man, what's up?" Eric shouted as his brother
drew closer to them.

"Not much. Just getting ready to deal with the
pressure of playing in front of my family," he said and then
laughed. He hugged his dad over the barrier and said,
"'Bout time you made it out for a game."

"I know... I know. And don't worry about playing in
front of us, you'll be fine," Pops encouraged. They chatted
about the usual family things. Jeff's father said his aunt
was running out of money because she purchased too
many scratch-off tickets and lottery tickets. She had always
been addicted to gambling, not the betting on sports games
type of gambling, but spending her money at casinos, more
often than not the slot machines.

Jeff's little brother was excited when he told him Skip
wouldn't mind if he sat in the dugout during the game. He
could bullshit with Wade, since they were near the same
age. Eric looked very similar to Jeff, except he had lighter

hair and a few more pimples. He hopped over the fence, and Hartes introduced him to Will, Steve, and Parks as they passed by towards the dugout.

Jeff's mother journeyed from the top of the stands toward the field with ice-cold sodas in one hand and nachos in the other. She got to the rail, handed the food and drinks to her husband, and gave her son a big hug.

"Shae should be here anytime now," he said.

"Okay, Jeff. You know how much your father and I want to meet her," she said. "Especially since she is one of the few girls you're going to actually let us see."

Both father and son chuckled at this comment. They were most likely thinking of the time that Jeff told his dad in an altered, comical voice: 'I don't like bringin' da' hoes home 'cause they aren't goin' to be around that long.' And then pops had responded by saying, 'You're full of shit, son, you're probably a homo.'

Jeff told his parents that he had to go throw and stretch before the game, and that he would see them right after. Eric helped shag balls that were overthrown and also assisted the everyday batboys. Wade felt like a foreman, as he had another helping hand with carrying equipment to the dugout. Hartes' little brother thoroughly enjoyed hanging with the pros and feeling like part of the club.

The second baseman warmed up his arm, firing the hardball back and forth with Will as they had done all season. His mom, meanwhile, snapped picture after picture with her new camera her husband had bought for her birthday. Her oldest son had gotten her a card, a candle, and a plant with red flowers.

IV

"Nice hit 'Big Daddy'," Eric congratulated Steve after his two-run blast in the fourth.

"Thanks, my man. It was nothing," Steve gave Jeff's brother a high-five on his way to taking a seat at the end of the bench. Eric sat back down in his spot; his face lit up with joy.

The Demons were ecstatic as well; they had built up an 8-2 lead over the Knights. Damon was having a career night out in centerfield, already 3-3 with three runs scored, three RBI, and a homerun. Rutherford ended the five-run inning with a fly out to left, but the damage had been done.

San Diego rallied with three more runs in the final five innings, but never threatened the Demon lead. Goodwin and Lewis both collected three hits apiece, while Jay O'Dell picked up the win (3-1). The Los Angeles Demons had now pulled to within a half game of the South Division lead.

Of course, Jeff's parents had something special already planned for the nightly festivities. It included going out for dinner, with Shae forced to tag along, and long hours of visiting.

V

"So as I was saying, Jeff was only five, but it was just so-so funny." Shae laughed the hardest out of everyone, mainly because everybody else at the table had already heard the story a zillion times before.

"That's so cute, Mrs. Hartes," she said. "I'll be sure to tease him about it all the time."

The food arrived just in the nick of time, as Jeff's mother's stories were becoming tiresome to him—along with the rest of the family. The dinner fivesome had practically ordered every item on the menu, covering two appetizers and five different entrées. The food ranged from Bennigan's famous *Monte Cristo* club sandwich to ribs to chicken fried steak as well as the potato skin apps.

"Steve's really funny, I hope I am as good a first baseman as he is when I get older," Eric said as everyone was enjoying their food. "Plus, all the girls will be all over me."

"Eric?" Mrs. Hartes said with a smile arising on her face. The rest of the table chuckled at the thought of young master Eric picking up the ladies. His dad even nudged him on the shoulder and said:

"That's my boy, start as early as possible."

A different sort of laughter carried on the rest of the dinner session. Not the usual drinking, chatting about the other sex, nasty jokes, that occurred with the baseball team, but a more casual, pleasant night out. Grant it, the stories weren't as hilarious or violent or sexual, but they fit the soothing occasion. Jeff was happy his family could finally take a brief vacation and visit him. He was happy they could meet Shae.

Shae and her sweetie followed his parents back to the hotel and said their goodnights for the time being. Jeff asked Eric if he wanted to come stay with them; he actually said stay with him to his parents, but really meant hanging out with Shae and him.

He jumped up and said, "You betcha'."

Mr. and Mrs. Hartes both agreed that it would be fine, just as long as everyone was careful. The couple and little brother headed to Shae's apartment to watch some movies and socialize. Eric was full of news that he needed to share with Jeff. He wanted to talk about all kinds of things he had been doing while his bigger brother was away. You know… the important stuff in life.

Like how his University of Southern California franchise was doing on *NCAA football* for the Playstation. How he had hit his first homerun last week in little league. Jeff already knew this, Mom had been sure to mention it first thing on one of their phone conversations. Eric also told Jeff that he had made him as a character on his *Triple Play '99* baseball game. He said that Jeff played second base for the Oakland A's and was hitting .276 with two homeruns just a few games into his season.

Jeff listened to his brother intently. Back at home, a few years ago, he would have gotten tired of Eric's nonstop chatter about video games and made up characters. But today, missing his family and brother, he just listened with open ears at whatever Eric had to say. He could have talked all night and Jeff would have stayed up with him — just talking away the night.

Eric finally dozed off to sleep around two in the morning, watching *Silence of the Lambs*. Well, not really watching, more like curled up on the couch snoring his ass off. Shae and Jeff both laughed when Eric finally silenced. One second he was telling them another baseball story, and then the next minute… out cold.

Shae was also ready to call it a night; she was scared of Hannibal Lector and couldn't take anymore serial killers. The ferocious cannibal would keep anyone awake with his horror-filled smile and hateful, raspy voice.

Shae and Jeff made love quietly, not wanting to awake Eric. Afterwards, they fell fast asleep in each other's arms.

VI

The next two days with the family were spent shopping and chatting, and even Mrs. Hartes and Shae got an opportunity to have a day all to their selves. The Demons split games two and three of the series with San Diego, losing game two, 6-1, but winning the final game, 6-5.

Jerod Wilkes (5-0) remained undefeated, throwing nine innings of one-run baseball in the six-to-one Demon loss. There weren't any long balls hit in the game, but San Diego leftfielder, Waylon Ponds, finished with three hits and two runs batted in.

A gutsy performance from Lake Williams (4-2) in the final game put Los Angeles only a half game behind once again. It also gave the Demons the rubber game, taking the three-game series. Lake threw nearly 130 pitches in the game, another aspect that showed how crucial every game was. There were a handful of dingers; for Los Angeles, Hicks hit his sixth, Rutherford hit his fourth, and Goodwin also hit his fourth. For San Diego, Kramer hit his fourth, and Garrido hit his first. Salmon Seavers, recovered from his sore arm, got his eighth save of the year.

VII

After the third game with San Diego, Jeff got the season-to-date stat sheets for Eric, who had wanted to see all of the player's information on the year. The papers included batting average, homeruns, runs scored, and every other major statistical category. It even had the last game's box score and the league standings already updated into its figures.

Eric said thanks as he took the sheet from his brother and gave him a hug farewell. Jeff's parents and Eric were going to stay the night in town, but they were destined back to Desert Shores first thing in the morning. Dad had to get back to business and get some major household chores finished. Mom just wanted to get home and make sure the house was clean, Jeff was sure of that.

The next morning, bright and early, Jeff's family headed out of dodge. Eric pulled out his stat sheets and read them the whole way home, memorizing their names and numbers; if he came back to watch some more games, he would know everybody ideally.

The Western League sheets were as follows:

Western League Standings
(MAY 9, 1999)

North Division	W-L	GB	WP%
Carson City	14-9	--	.609
Montana	11-11	2.5	.500
Cal	10-12	3.5	.455
Washington	6-14	6.5	.300

South Division	W-L	GB	WP%
San Diego	14-8	--	.636
Los Angeles	13-8	.5	.619
Arizona	12-10	2	.545
Tucson	7-15	7	.318

TEAM STATS HITTING — Los Angeles Demons

	AVG.	HR	More...
Chambers, Brett	.143	0	1 RBI
Coleman, Will	.301	2	17 Runs, 16 RBI
Fetters, Ron	.206	1	7 Runs, 3 RBI
Goodwin, Billy	.275	4	11 Runs, 9 RBI
Gunn, Steve	.280	7	20 RBI, 14 Runs
Hartes, Jeff	.329	2	12 RBI, 8 Runs
Hicks, Jason	.329	5	15 Runs, 13 RBI
Lewis, Damon	.295	2	18 Runs, 8 SB's
Luthers, Simon	.250	0	--
Parks, Bobby	.261	0	6 RBI, 3 Runs
Rutherford, Erric	.308	4	13 RBI, 11 Runs

TEAM STATS PITCHING — Los Angeles Demons

	W-L	ERA	More...
Jimenez, Javier	2-0	2.87	
Luthers, Darren	0-1	5.97	
O'Dell, Jay	3-1	4.41	
Perry, Thomas	2-3	4.36	
Sanders, Fred	0-0	5.23	
Seavers, Salmon	0-0	2.13	8 Saves
Tims, Michael	2-1	4.58	
Williams, Lake	4-2	3.91	

May 9, 1999

Gamblers Searching for Pair of Aces

The Carson City Gamblers (14-9) come into town with a two and a half game lead in the North Division and precognitions of sweeping the two-game series tonight and tomorrow night against the Los Angeles Demons (13-8).

"We always look forward to competing against a team that plays our style of ball," said Gamblers' coach Dennis Herring. "They (Los Angeles) split the earlier series with us back in April, but I expect both teams to be much improved since that time."

Getting the game one nod for the Demons is Michael Tims (2-1, 3.98); he will be facing Carson's righthander, Ricky Martinez (0-3, 7.14).

A key player to watch for the series is Demon rightfielder, Billy Goodwin. Goodwin has gone 6-12, with one homerun and three runs scored since the club's day off on May 3rd.

Getting off to a good start tonight will be an important factor in the series if the Demons are going to catch San Diego.

"We definitely have to start off hot tonight and get Michael (Tims) some help," said Los Angeles Coach Skip Bailey. "He's been throwing his heart out without much run support so far. With him on the mound, tonight's a huge game in our run at the South."

—Ronald Davidson

236

VIII

The Demon fans rose to their feet not once, not twice, but *three* times for shortstop Will Coleman during their first game against the Carson City Gamblers. Bringing you the calls and not letting you miss any of the action, Darrell "The Duke" Marinville— *who other?*

"Deep shot to leftfield—" *Channel 7 Sports* aired the pre-recorded call (three calls to be exact) by Marinville later that night on their show: *Los Angeles Sports Flash.* " —Way back... Oh Baby! Will Coleman has hit his third homerun of the season and has tied the game one-to-one. Martinez tried to come inside on Coleman and paid the price."

The next at-bat: "Coleman has homered already once tonight. The pitch from Cox... Hit Well To Straight Away Center... Larsen to the wall... Jumps up... No chance! A two-run homer for the shortstop, his second of the game, upping Los Angeles' lead, six-to-three!"

And if that wasn't enough, *Channel 7 Sports* fed your need for more with one last call from The Duke...

"Bottom of the eighth, two runners aboard. The count on Coleman is two-and-one. Remember folks, he is three-for-four with a pair of homeruns. Snider checks the runners and delivers..." *Crack!* "THIS BALL IS SMOKED TO LEFTFIELD!!! IT COULD BE... IT'S GONE!!! I DON'T BELIEVE IT! WILL "THE THRILL" COLEMAN BLASTS NUMBER THREE, NUMERO TRES, ON THE NIGHT!!! Three dingers for Coleman! The Demons now lead twelve-to-five in the bottom of the eighth... OHHH MY!"

The score would remain the same as the Demons took game one 12-5. Coleman ended up with 6 RBI's to go along with his bombs. Rutherford also homered and drove in 3 runs. Tims bettered his record to 3-1, striking out nine over seven innings of work.

Lost in the action was Carson City's centerfielder, Mickey Larsen, hitting two homeruns on back-to-back at bats. Ricky Martinez was handed the loss, his fourth of the year. Martinez had yet to get a win.

One of the best aspects of Will's huge game was that Regina (along with Shae) attended the game and neither of them missed a thing. They jumped up and down and screamed when Coleman hit his third bomb in the eighth, Regina even saying something like, 'Will's gonna' get some good lovin' tonight.' Shae nodded approvingly, and figured she might as well celebrate her friend's good game, *with* Jeff.

IX

Maggie Perry was on to something when she showed Shae Kent how to look up the Demons play-by-play on the Internet. Jeff, never being the most helpful and thinking kind of man when it came to small things as this, never bothered to find anything out; including checking the Demons' scores online.

Jeff just shrugged his shoulders while Shae scolded him, in a sweet and constructive manner. 'Things would have been *much easier* on late nights, Jeff,' she had said, 'if I didn't have to keep turning my radio up and down so Dave wouldn't get so upset, thinking I wasn't focusing on his next court case hard enough. Also, the radio wouldn't be bothering anyone else working in the same building.'

It wasn't like Jeff was withholding information; he too,

had just found out. Maggie had passed the news on to Shae and Regina while they were sitting (player's wives section) in the stands during the first game against the Gamblers. She told them the name of the website, www.girlslovedemons.com, and how to open the "currently updated" page during the game. She said it was so easy, and that the girls who were doing it were longtime Demon fans just wanting to give something back to the community.

And yes... Maggie said "girls." Supposedly, they sat either in one of the luxury boxes or at the top of the bleachers with a laptop computer. Their names were Gina and Gabby. Rumor had it that they even sunbathed down the leftfield bleachers (opposite of the Demons' clubhouse) during the day. The reason they could get away with all of this and have such pull... their father was General Manager, Greg Viselli.

How Jason Hicks hadn't caught wind of these girls, and how they managed to steer clear of him, was a miracle. Reason one: the girls weren't even in their twenties yet, Gabby was still in high school. And reason two: they weren't the average groupie—they tended to not hang around the clubhouse and their dad too much at the stadium. They pretty much kept to themselves.

They loved the ballpark, they loved their baseball, and they found something worthwhile to do during the games. *Daddy's little girls,* keeping the play-by-play on their laptop so all the Demon faithful could keep up with game. No tickets, no radio—No problem. Let Gina and Gabby Viselli do "the work" for you while you focused on your own work. Or if you were just relaxing at the house, keeping up with Jeff Hartes, or Will Coleman, or Lake Williams, or whoever your favorite Demon player was, would be easy, via the Internet.

X

Now knowing, using the Internet was how Shae followed the next game and her lover's performance. She was now happier to work at the office late, moving around from room to room with a bounce in her step. Of course, nothing could beat actually being at the park, but this kept her out of trouble. She simply put the Gina and Gabby's play-by-play on one of the unused computers in the main office, and hopped in to check the score when she got a quick break. She didn't have to listen to The Duke drag on about the "beautiful weather" or "baseball's pastime" — don't misunderstand, Shae loved Marinville, she just didn't have the time to listen to him wander.

She wanted the score, and fast. And now with bonus features, she could check Jeff's stats along with whoever else she wanted. It was fantastic, and Shae couldn't resist checking the game update every time she passed by the office.

The final game results looked as follows:

1999 Los Angeles Demon Baseball
Carson City (14-10) versus Los Angeles (14-8)
May 10, 1999 at Los Angeles, California (Demon Stadium)

Carson City starters: cf Kato; 2b Wayne; lf Craig; 1b Colbrunn; 3b Spews; rf Gutierrez; c Hunt; ss Gorley; p Gibbs;

Los Angeles starters: cf Lewis; ss Coleman; 3b Hicks; 1b Gunn; lf Rutherford; 2b Hartes; rf Goodwin; c Parks; p O'Dell;

Carson City 1st – Kato grounded to short (1-1). Wayne singled up the middle (2-0). Craig struck out looking (2-2). Colbrunn flied out to left (1-0). *1 LOB.*

Los Angeles 1st – Lewis lined out third (2-0). Coleman flied out to right (0-0). Hicks homered to center (3-1). *Demons 1, Gamblers 0.* Gunn struck out swinging (1-2). *0 LOB.*

Carson City 2nd – Spews walked (3-1). Gutierrez sacrifice bunted, moving Spews to second (0-0). Hunt doubled to left, scoring Spews (2-1). *Demons 1, Gamblers 1.* Gorley struck out swinging (0-2). Gibbs lined out to short (1-0). *1 LOB.*

Los Angeles 2nd – **Rutherford** flied out to center (0-0). Hartes grounded out to third (3-2). Goodwin popped out to pitcher (2-1). *0 LOB.*

Carson City 3rd – Kato walked (3-1). Kato stole second base on second pitch. Wayne sacrifice bunted, moving Kato to third (2-0). Craig homered down leftfield line, scoring

Kato (1-0). *Gamblers 3, Demons 1.* Colbrunn struck out looking (1-2). Spews reached on error by Hicks (1-1). Gutierrez flied out to right (1-1). *1 LOB.*

Los Angeles 3rd – Parks homered down rightfield line (2-1). *Gamblers 3, Demons 2.* O'Dell infield singled to left side (1-1). Lewis grounded into double play (0-0). Coleman struck out swinging (1-2). *0 LOB.*

Carson City 4th – Hunt walked (3-1). Gorley singled to right, moving Hunt to third (1-0). Gibbs popped out to short, no runner's move (1-0). Kato tripled to rightfield, scoring Hunt and Gorley (2-1). *Gamblers 5, Demons 2.* Wayne struck out swinging (1-2). Craig singled through left side, scoring Kato (3-2). *Gamblers 6, Demons 2. Sanders enters the game to pitch for Los Angeles.* Colbrunn struck out looking (1-2). *1 LOB.*

Los Angeles 4th – Hicks grounded out to short (0-0). Gunn grounded out to second (1-0). Rutherford walked (3-2). Hartes lined to short (1-1). *1 LOB.*

Carson City 5th – Spews flied out to center (1-1). Gutierrez struck out looking (1-2). Hunt popped out to first in foul territory (0-2). *0 LOB.*

Los Angeles 5th – Goodwin singled to left (0-0). Goodwin stole second base on first pitch. Parks struck out swinging (2-2). *Fetters pinch hits for Sanders for Los Angeles.* Fetters homered to left-center field (2-2). *Gamblers 6, Demons 4.* Lewis grounded out to second (1-0). Coleman flied out to center (1-1). *0 LOB.*

Carson City 6th – *Luthers enters the game to pitch for Los*

Angeles. Gorley grounded out to short (3-1). *Silcy pinch hits for Gibbs for Carson City.* Silcy struck out swinging (1-2). Kato walked (3-2). Kato stole second base on second pitch. Wayne singled to right, scoring Kato (1-1). *Gamblers 7, Demons 4.* Craig flied out to deep center (0-0). *1 LOB.*

Los Angeles 6th – *Parker enters the game to pitch for Los Angeles.* Hicks singled to leftfield (1-0). Gunn walked (3-1). Rutherford grounded into double play, Hicks to third (1-1). Hartes flied out to right (1-0). *1 LOB.*

Carson City 7th – Colbrunn struck out (2-2). Spews lined out to short (0-0). Gutierrez doubled to right-center (0-1). Hunt singled up the middle, scoring Gutierrez (1-0). *Gamblers 8, Demons 4. Jimenez enters the game to pitch for Los Angeles.* Gorley grounded out to second (1-0). *1 LOB.*

Los Angeles 7th – Goodwin struck out looking (0-2). Parks grounded out to third (1-2). Jimenez struck out swinging (1-2). *0 LOB.*

Carson City 8th – *Larsen pinch hits for Parker for Carson City.* Larsen doubled to right-center (2-0). Kato grounded back to pitcher, no runner's move (0-0). Wayne homered to leftfield, scoring Larsen (1-0). *Gamblers 10, Demons 4.* Craig flied out in foul territory (2-1). Colbrunn struck out looking (1-2). *0 LOB.*

Los Angeles 8th – *Snider enters the game to pitch for Carson City.* Lewis singled to center (1-0). Coleman singled through left side (2-0). Hicks singled to center, scoring Lewis (1-1). *Gamblers 10, Demons 5.* Gunn struck out swinging (1-2). Rutherford grounded into double play (1-

1). *2 LOB.*

Carson City 9th – Spews homered to center (1-0). *Gamblers 11, Demons 5.* Gutierrez struck out swinging (0-2). Hunt grounded out to second (1-0). Gorley grounded out to first (1-1). *0 LOB.*

Los Angeles 9th – Hartes reached on throwing error by Gorley (1-1). Goodwin grounded into double play (0-0). Parks flied out to deep left (2-0). *0 LOB.*

Game over – Gamblers 11, Demons 5…

<u>Score by Innings</u>
Carson City...........0 1 2 3 0 1 1 2 1 – 11 11 1
Los Angeles.........1 0 1 0 2 0 0 1 0 – 6 9 0

Chapter Nine
A Good Walk Spoiled

I

"Hartes, Jace, whoever's listening," Perry said, trying to gather the attention of some of his fellow teammates. "My dad wants me to fly home to Houston for the day off and play a round of golf with him, and he's invited whoever wants to come with me. He told me to bring some of you hackers. Maggie has a baby shower to go to, anyway. So who's in?" Maggie was the pitcher's wife.

"I'm *fuckin'* there," Jason said.

"Count me in," Bobby added.

"No fuckin' brainer man, I'm goin' wit' it," Erric yelled above the splashing of the running water in the shower. "I'M IN, I SAID!"

"We heard you the first time!" Steve hollered back.

"Jeff? Steve? Up to it?" T.P. asked; welcoming all the guests he could get.

"I'll have to check with Shae, but—"

"Aww... how cute?" Several players remarked in a synchronized fashion.

"But anyways... as I was saying," Jeff retorted. "I'll prob'ly be on that plane whether she wants me to go or not." Jeff was speaking out of his ass now, and he knew it. Either way, he still wanted to go swing the sticks; it had been awhile since he had been on the golf links.

"I can't," Steve said, unwillingly. "I mean, I want to,

but tomorrow is me and Suzanne's anniversary. Sucks for me."

"Damn, Big Daddy. I can't believe you'd even consider tryin' to skip out on your anniversary. That's just cold dawg," Will added to the mix. "Plus, Mrs. Gunn will kick your muthafuckin' ass to the curb!"

"She isn't kickin' shit to the curb. Is she, Wade my man?" The batboy came into the room to gather the uniforms and other dirty laundry.

"She sure isn't, Big Daddy," Wade Smith hollered, cruising along. "Not that biatch!"

Heads turned. Gunn's eyes widened. "Watch it, you little peckerhead sumbitch. Get outta' here." Steve swung his wooden bat at Wade without any intention of delivering pain as the batboy scurried away with the clothes' cart, pushing it through the open door.

"Sooo… once again, who's all in?" T.P. inquired one last time. He watched for hands or nods or any other signal from the players notifying him that they were in. "We got me, Jace, Bobby-O, 'E', and Hartes… maybe. Good enough. With my dad too, that will give us two threesomes."

II

"Please gentlemen, this way to your seats," the sexy stewardess said, leading them to the first class section of the jet plane. "Have a nice flight."

In the famous words—in dedication—of Salmon Seavers, "Must be nice to ride first class!"

"Nigga' say *damn*, T.P. Your ol' man sure knows how to treat his guess," Erric said in his own gibberish. "Ridin' first shimmy like this is da' shit. Hell, I might shoot sixty-seven today."

"On the front nine, maybe. You fuckin' pussy," Bobby said and laughed, using the oldest golf joke ever thought up. But that one-liner was like a fart, it got a laugh every damn time.

Parks now understood his days as the soft-spoken rookie were over. Jason winked at Jeff and Thomas, signaling them to watch his next move. He gently grabbed the brunette flight attendant before she exited the front cabin of the plane.

"Excuse my friends and their rude behavior, miss... miss umm?" Jason asked her, awaiting an answer. Jeff wondered how Hicks could so easily conjure up the energy and sexual drive before six-thirty in the morning. She swung around to face him, and said:

"Missus Abbott. Pleased to meet you." The ring now showed itself, glowing on her finger with diamonds. "And the rudeness is a norm amongst first-class passengers. So don't sweat it." She looked into Jason's eyes one more time, no sign of love at first sight here.

"My name's —" she turned back around and left the front section through the dividing door " — Jay-jay... son." Hicks tailed off at the end of his name, rolling his eyes at the rest of the Demons.

"Smooth. Very smooth," Jeff said, grinning from ear to ear. "I'll bet you she's waiting to blow you in the shitter as we speak."

"Shut tha' fuck up, Hartes." Jason collapsed into his aisle seat and picked up a magazine. "She's probably a dike with a wedding ring as a cover up."

III

The golf-bound athletes arrived at Houston Hobby Airport at 9:40 a.m. This was the smaller of the two airports in H-Town, but more convenient and less crowded to get in and out of. They waited by the luggage drops to pick up their cased golf bags, and then proceeded to the loading/unloading section outside the airport's front entrance.

Mr. Perry waited for them with two vehicles. The first one, a chrome BMW, 325SI, and the second one, a dark blue Lincoln Navigator. He drove the beamer while one of his personal drivers steered the larger luxury vehicle. Once again, this got a complimentary remark from Rutherford.

"Thanks Erric," Mr. Perry replied. "Sorry you fella's had to land at this shithole of an airport. These were the fastest tickets I could find. I hope the first class made up for it?"

"Hell yea, sir. It was great," Rutherford answered.

"Yessir… appreciate everything," Hartes and Parks followed. The only person who hadn't said anything in awhile was Jason. He appeared to still be mourning over the fact that he couldn't rejoin the "Mile High Club" with the married stewardess.

The group packed their bags into the vehicles. Thomas and Jeff rode with Mr. Perry; and Jason, Erric, and Bobby followed them. They didn't stop to grab anything to eat, as they all engulfed the courtesy breakfast—omelets—on their flight. They left the airport heading immediately to *Houston National Golf Club* and their 10:57 tee time.

The golf course was in tiptop shape, and running fast

as hell. The greens were blazing fast, reading easily over a "10" on the Stimp meter. The fairways were hard and slick, but flawless for links style golf. Everything on the course was awe-inspiring; the views left one feeling invigorated.

The course featured links golf at its best, with no trees, but wispy wind-blown rough (burnt brown to accentuate the greener fairways) around five to six inches high and rolling hills with severe, quick slopes, instead. The greens —a deep verdant—were all tucked in either low spots or elevated in secluded high areas, with multiple layers ensuring that the players clubbed themselves ideally. Each hole was also surrounded by two-storied and three-storied homes, occupied by no one other than the rich and famous.

The first threesome to go off the number one tee box was the Lincoln Navigator team: Jace, Bobby, and 'E'. They loaded up their carts with ice chests of cold Coors Lights on the way to the first tee box. The first hole was a straight-ahead par four, playing just less than 400 yards.

Jason was the only one of them to hit the fairway, lacing a low draw that rolled for days. Erric sliced his into the right rough, near the driving range, while Bobby found the beach. It was early in the round, but a bystander watching *this* group would definitely think of the movie, *Caddyshack*. Bobby even dropped a quick one-liner after Erric's teeshot, saying, "Gambling is illegal at Bushwood, and I never slice..."

The match was set for a dollar a hole, double-birdies and triple-eagles, lowest score from each team. Meaning, that every winning birdie doubled the hole value while eagles tripled it. The teams were identical to the pre-made threesomes set up before the round.

Team one left the first hole with a par, as Jason hit the green in two and two-putted from around thirty-five feet away. Team two followed with a par as well; Mr. Perry lipped out a short birdie putt and had to settle for the tie.

"Nice par, Mr. Perry," Jeff said, after sinking his putt for a double-bogey six.

"Call me Erwin, Jeff. Mister is an overused prefix."

"No problem," Jeff said, hopping into his cart and heading to the second tee—riding single.

As the front nine flowed along, Jeff thought the course to be breathtaking. Especially since he was all over the place with his shots; he truly got his money's worth—not his money of course, just a cliché. His favorite hole on the front side was #8. It featured a straightaway tee shot with high mounds on both sides of the fairway. If your shot went slightly errand, you might get a great kick off the hills and wind up in the middle of the short grass. But, if you strayed way right or left, you were toast. The shot would feed even farther away from its original path and end in the deep stuff.

The green on #8 was another superb aspect of the immaculate course. It was cut out from a three to four foot high wall of grass, which led to an elevated, pearl white sand trap. The green was a peninsula inside the raised bunker, as the sand trap enclosed three quarters of it—the whole backside and right and left sides.

So basically, if you hit it long or to either side, you were faced with a bunker shot from above the green instead of the typical uphill sandblast. Oh by the way, Jeff hit his shot left into the bunker. And he didn't manage to save par, he took a double on the par four.

Thomas made the only birdies for the second team, delivering one on the par-five 6th hole and another on the 9th. Erwin, Jeff, and Thomas won seven of the first nine holes with two doubles (birdies), while Jason, Bobby, and Erric got drunk up ahead and only pulled off two holes with one double. A lonely birdie from Hicks on the long par-three 7th.

Don't misunderstand the front nine, it had its laughs and goodhearted conversations; but the back nine got a little bit crazy. The mixture of alcohol and losing badly settled in; team one opened up the floodgates with some help from outside influences.

On the par-four 14th hole, Erric tattooed a three-wood from the right side of the fairway over the back of the green. His ball fell off the raised green and rolled just off the edge about three yards or so. Fortunately, or unfortunately, depending on the player's game, the deep stuff grabbed his ball before it could roll further down the hill. Jason and Bobby were both short, so they didn't see the guy behind the green when Erric came driving up.

Erric saw a middle-aged man with a white shirt tucked into faded blue jeans holding Erric's Titleist Balata. The man, who seemed to have come out of nowhere—just appeared from thin air— was tossing the golf ball in his left hand.

"Hey foo', you got my ball," Erric said, walking toward the guy and up to the green.

"Oh... jou' playin'?" The Panama-Jack-hat-wearing newcomer, with jet black hair, asked Erric, appearing to have no clue he was on a golf course.

"Yea, I'm playin', nigga'. Wha' da' fuck do ya' tank I'm doin'?" Erric was getting aggravated at the man's ignorance. With the combination of getting his ass kicked on the golf course and alcohol in his system, he was ready to dance if this guy wanted.

And then he smelt something familiar; something very close to home. The smell of reefer escaped from the man like perfume. Erric scratched his head and smiled.

The individual in front of Erric dropped the ball to its previous location and raised his other hand to his lips. He took a quick puff from the joint and let the smoke filter through his mouth and nostrils. The guy apparently didn't care about smoking a doobie in the wide open with golfers passing by.

"Now we'ze talkin', man. Give me a hit of that 'J'," Erric said, dying for just one drag of the hippie lettuce.

"I can't, need it for my work, holmes," the unnamed person responded.

"Your work? What kinda' work needs weed, foo'?" Erric asked, as Jace and Bobby followed their noses over to their teammate.

"Gots to go build a flower bed."

"Holy shit, dawg." Erric erupted with laughter. "You're fuckin' kiddin' right?" He thought that was the funniest shit he had heard in days. You couldn't write better comedy than what that idiot had just said. Bobby and Jason joined in the hysterics, realizing where the distinct aroma was coming from and understanding what the guy had just issued from his mouth.

The smoker simply shook his head and sat down in the grass, puffing on his joint. The threesome finished up the hole while the pothead just stood back and enjoyed watching some golf. He even clapped when Bobby sunk his bogey putt from five feet. When the first group drove to the 15th hole green, the unknown person disappeared into the quiet neighborhood, not letting group two in on the fun.

"Hartes and those other fuckers will never believe that shit," Jason said, laughing on the next tee box.

"Never," Bobby replied.

And then one hole later, if the pot-smoking gardener wasn't enough, Parks spotted a sunbather. Right off of the 15th fairway, a girl with short blonde hair and a pink bikini was reading a magazine in her backyard, basking in the sun. Jason actually saw her first, but he was trying to remain focused on his second shot—perhaps, still stunned from the first class burn. That's where Bobby stepped in and took over the show.

The catcher, hammered to say the least, drove over to her fence, which was made of black steel with carved spires at the top. He jumped out of the cart and walked up to the barrier protecting her privacy. "I don't mean to bother you, miss, but I think my balls went in your yard."

The sunbather let her book—one of the Sue Grafton alphabet titles, *G is for Gumshoe*—fall to her waist and looked at the Bobby amusingly. "Excuse me?"

"My balls? See... I hit a ball—" Bobby gripped the top horizontal railing of her fence, balancing momentarily, and then prepared for lift off. "Do you mind if I come in?"

"Shhhure, but there's a—" She wanted to inform him that there was a gate on his left, but Parks had already scaled the obstacle. Quite the nifty move for someone as blasted as he was. She looked him once-over and then wrapped herself in a long, white towel. "Now what is it you needed?"

"My ball. Umm... I'm sorry, my name's uh... Bobby," the catcher said, trying to work his magic, but stuttering slightly. He extended his hand gingerly and took the girls into his own, raising it to his mouth. The sunbather watched curiously, excited by the fact that he was going to kiss her hand like she had always seen in the movies.

"I'm Ashley," she said as Parks placed his lips on her hand. She was tickled by the move, but tried her hardest not to let it show. She didn't want this younger individual to think he already had her in his pocket, did she?

"Very nice to meet you, Ash," Bobby said with an innocent charm only someone under the age of twenty-one could present. Somehow he still maintained an innocent and young look, despite the raggedy hair and stub on his face. The girl, Ashley, looked like an actress he had just seen on the big screen the other day, but he couldn't think of the name.

"As I was saying, I thought I hit my ball into your yard. But apparently not," Parks' words came out of his mouth like someone reading Lord Byron for the first time. The annunciations were on the wrong words, and the sentences didn't flow smoothly. But either way, he stumbled on, "Better get back... back to my round before my friends get mad. Cameron Diaz!" Parks shouted 'Cameron Diaz' with great excitement.

"Huh?" the sunbather asked, startled.

"Oh... sorry. That's the actress you reminded me of. I just thought of it." Parks fidgeted with his hands. "Not a big deal."

"Thanks, I suppose."

He smiled his best smile and gave Ashley a small wave before turning around. He took one step back towards the golf course, and then she said, "Wait! That's it?" Thinking the Demon catcher may not have heard her, she continued, "I, uh, uh, would like to see you again."

Parks eyes lit up. *It fucking worked, man,* he thought to himself before spinning back around to face her once again. "Yea? I'd love to see you, too."

Bobby realized who she reminded him of now. It wasn't Cameron Diaz at all — well... maybe the hair... or hair color. It was a different actress. Ashley's face was identical to Juliette Lewis's, everything matching except for the short blonde hair. The Demons had recently watched the remake of *Cape Fear* with Robert DeNiro and Nick Nolte, as well as Ms. Lewis, on one of the road trips. And this was what reminded Bobby.

Ashley hurried inside her house through a sliding

glass door and returned in under a minute. She carried a paper and a pencil, planning on exchanging numbers. 'I didn't even have to drop the Demon's bomb on her,' Bobby thought.

"Before you give me your number and all, I need to tell you I'm not from here," Bobby said, awaiting her response, but thinking those were the last words he should have said. Hicks would have never said anything that stupid. He searched her eyes for the question, 'where are you from then?'

IV

As Parks' conversation with his new acquaintance continued, Hicks and Rutherford were waiting on the green, allowing the other threesome to play through them.

They told father and son Perry and Hartes what the hold-up was, as all five of them moved to the par-three 16th. They sat a few yards away from the tee box, impatiently awaiting Parks' return, but knowing they were in no hurry.

"I guess we can wait when pussy is involved," Erwin said. He chuckled to himself as the Demon players joined in immediately. He seemed a good enough guy, but the comment surprised a few of the players.

A fivesome of older men were hitting off the tee box, playing boringly slow as they were barely able to walk back to their carts. "Y'all fellas go ahead and hit," the gray-haired man said, realizing the group approaching him wasn't a group of five like his own, but two separate parties.

Thomas, Erwin, and Jeff pulled out their club of choice

and walked to the tee box. Thomas hit first on the 183-yard par three, playing downwind. He stuck a six-iron about fifteen feet right of the pin, pleasing the gallery of elders. Next to hit was Hartes, as Mr. Perry was changing his mind and switching clubs.

Jeff smoked a five-iron that flew the green and landed in the tall grass. "Fuck me," he murmured, and then raised his voice. "I hit a freakin' five iron. How the hell did I fly it?"

"Whadga' you hit young 'un?" the man nearest the tee box asked, sitting legs-crossed in his cart. He wore a faded, blue-striped collared shirt that was cream-colored because of too many days at the links.

"I hit a five iron, sir," Jeff answered politely. The old man grinned and nudged his co-rider in the side.

"I hit a five, too," he bellowed with a raspy, dry voice. "A five fucking wood!" All of his playing partners, except one—the one hard of hearing and missing the joke—and the group playing through exploded with laughter.

"You know the difference in young golfers and old golfers, don't you?" he proceeded, not really wanting an answer because he was about to give it as the punch line. "Old golfers have stiff wrists and a limp peter, while young golfers have limp wrists and a stiff peter." This time, the laughing frenzy and madness was so thunderous that the gathering could probably have been arrested for disturbing the peace.

After everything calmed back down, Erwin hit his ball just off the left side of the green and into the short rough. The threesome thanked the men for allowing them to play through as all eight golfers drove to the green. Hicks and Rutherford waited behind, wondering if Bobby was getting in a quickie back there.

V

"Where are you from then?" Ashley asked. She presented Bobby with just the question he had been searching for.

'Just tell the truth now, idiot,' Parks thought.

"I'm from San Diego. But right now I'm playing pro baseball in Los Angeles with a triple-A team called the Demons." Okay... there it was... Parks said it. She did ask, though. But yes, he dropped the "Demons bomb," hopefully getting him in for good.

Her facial expression dampened — most likely over the location, not the occupation — but one could tell she was still very much interested in her new friend. Parks saw this, "Maybe I could come back with my friend and visit you."

"Or *maybe*... I could come and watch you play?" she asked, not sure exactly what words had just escaped her mouth. "I mean, uh... I know it sounds outrageous, but I'd like to see you again. Plus, my friends and I take long trips all the time."

Bobby left Ashley his number and took her number, folding it up and sliding it into his wallet. Something overcame him that he couldn't resist — the urge to kiss her. He didn't hesitate. Hell, he had nothing to lose from it. He put his hands on her side; she allowed him to as a trance overcame her.

He leaned forward, realizing her mouth was moving his way as well. He planted a kiss on her lips, forcing the tongue on contact. She kissed him back like they had known each other for years.

She pulled away, overwhelmed, and said, "Wow... that was... nice," Parks agreed. "Call me, Bobby."

"I will." She threw the catcher a rapid wave and fluttered away inside her house.

Parks stood still for a moment, still excited over the unexpected events. When his legs returned to walking state, he hopped the fence and got in his cart. He didn't finish the hole; he hoped Jace or 'E' posted a good enough score to match the other team, that was kicking their ass.

He rolled up to the par three where his teammates on the baseball field and golf course waited for him. He told them all about what had just happened; the story thrilling Jason the most. Hicks had been known for doing something analogous to what Bobby had just done.

"We should go back and double team her," Hicks said. Erric laughed.

"Ha-ha... funny. You're just mad I got her number," Parks retorted.

"Yeah?" Hicks questioned, looking at Rutherford beside him. He then turned back to Parks and pointed at him. "And you're a faggot if you don't want to hit that shit with me."

"A faggot? Because I don't want to have sex with another dude next to me? Your reasoning is ridiculous."

Hicks smiled, saying, "Who said anything about you having sex? I was going to pound her while you rubbed my back!"

Rutherford kicked the golf cart's dash with his soft spikes and then banged the roof with fists. Parks couldn't think of anything else to say. Hicks was too quick on the draw... too witty with comebacks.

VI

After finishing up the round of eighteen holes, the two teams compared scorecards to see how much the Perry's-Hartes combination won. Jason, Erric, and Bobby each owed the winners $12.00 apiece; the losses weren't too expensive, especially since the round was on Mr. Perry.

Keeping things friendly.... if the stakes got too high, then things could get personal. And with that, things could turn ugly. Keeping it on the friendly side, especially when too much alcohol was involved, was never a bad thing.

The golfers left *Houston National* at three-thirty, all of them making sure to truly say 'thank you' to Erwin Perry — whose hospitality was more than anyone could have asked. They drove the two vehicles back to the airport with plenty of time to spare. Bobby now wished they were staying the night, for reasons all too clear. The flight back (first class all the way) was scheduled for 5:25 p.m. They would arrive back in Los Angeles sometime after dark and get ready to hit the road to Tucson first thing in the morning.

Chapter Ten
A Stroll in the Park
-Old Days of Baseball-

I

Jeff had Shae pick him up at the airport around 9:15 p.m. He thanked T.P. for the trip, and told him that he truly had a wonderful time. The rest of the guys all had rides as well, so Jeff and Shae didn't have to worry about dropping anyone else off.

She said that she missed him and wanted to do something different tonight. She knew it was late. And that Jeff had to be tired. But she just had the urge for something else tonight, especially since her man was going out of town the next morning.

She gave Jeff one of those heart-warming, sympathy looks before she even told him what she had planned; before even hearing the words leave her mouth, he couldn't refuse.

Jeff and Shae strolled through the park, hands locked together. The park lights lit the way like colossal-sized candles. The weather was delightful; a clear, moonlit sky with scattered clouds and a cool breeze. They walked along the cement path surrounded by perfectly cut hedges — no worries amongst them.

Shae thought about how much she was in love with Jeff. Cute, wasn't it? She now realized for the first time in her life that if Jeff asked her to marry him, she would. She didn't yet know the hard times that would bestow them. She only knew what she wanted now. No hesitation, no pause, just a heart-warming smile followed by a simple *yes*.

Her thoughts moved from marriage to work. She tried to remember what she had to do this upcoming week and realized that it wasn't much. But she didn't want to spoil a good walk with thoughts of work. She only wanted to feel her lover's hand clasped in her own and enjoy the day to the fullest enlightenment possible. The night was beautiful, the temperature was perfect, and she enjoyed the exercise while breathing in some fresh air.

Jeff, on the other hand, was blank. His mind didn't work at the present moment, and he only breathed in the spring smells and fresh night air. The path took a turn to the couple's left and started downhill. In the immediate distance, the park opened up to a clearing. The opening welcomed the couple, with bright lights and the chit-chatter of sportsfans. There were baseball fields on the left and a large field with playground equipment on their right. The little league fields were lit up like festive houses on Christmas Eve.

They walked with ease and comfort, the path was hard yet smooth. Its consistency allowed the walker or jogger to not worry about a twisted or sprained ankle. Speaking of joggers, a guy with a white headband and headphones passed by the couple, sprinting down the hill and eventually out of sight.

The baseball fields were still almost a half-mile away, as the hill began its sharp decline. Kids, looking like diligent ants at work, were scattered across the baseball diamonds and outfields, enjoying the little league season. Jeff remembered the days of using minor league baseball to escape from reality.

His mind was now alive. The smell of the concessions and sweaty uniforms stirred his insides. Like the lights shining on the field, he was also lit up.

Yes, his childhood was a good one, but every teenager has his or her problems. Jeff had his share of problems during his second season of youth ball. That's the year his younger brother, Eric, had an infection in his pancreas. Jeff, believing Eric might not live through the illness, couldn't cope with losing his only sibling. He spent the days at school thinking about his brother and not thinking about his work. His grades dropped, his lack of interest wasn't doing anything positive for himself or his family.

The only thing that took his mind off of the real world and the trouble that comes with it was baseball. It's funny how some things can take you away from reality. Drugs and alcohol being some harmful ones. But there were also good ways to cope with stress. Young Jeff had found one in baseball.

Oh man, how he loved the sound of an aluminum bat going *Ping* as someone struck the Rawlings. Nothing in this world soothed his mind or diverted his grief-stricken thoughts better than America's pastime.

II

It had just turned 1990 three months earlier —

New Year's was a blast, better than ever. I remember sitting with my brother for most of the evening and visiting, but then heading out for my first real night with the opposite sex.

I was going to my friend's party and expecting to enjoy myself. His name was David; and he was the brave

boy that dared to throw a fiesta with *girls*. Girls, girls, girls
— this was going to be something new, yet exciting. I had a
boner all the way to Albuquerque, and it wasn't going limp
anytime soon.

The party was supervised; after all, we were only in
our younger stages of our teens. Hell, puberty was trying
to set in. It would have been kick-ass if it wasn't, though.
Supervised... that is. The girls were plentiful. And I had
my own already handpicked. She was the prettiest girl in
the seventh grade, and all the boys would have loved for
Felicia to even acknowledge them.

Felicia and I had flirted and held hands at school on a
couple of occasions, but never more than that. Neither of
us thought of each other as "going steady" or whatever
junior high or high school term fit the bill. I spent most of
my time worrying about baseball, and Eric. I didn't have
time for girls... yet.

I met Felicia at the party, since I couldn't exactly drive
her, being under the age and all. It took me about twenty
minutes or so to locate her and her long, blonde hair. Her
A-cups weren't matured yet, but they were perky and
enough to get a handful. I didn't think I would get that far.
Her skin was a milky-white, with filled out thighs and
calves, not fat, but nicely proportioned to the rest of her
body. Her face was tender and smooth, framed by her
evenly cut bangs.

She smiled at me from across David's living room,
motioning for me to come and talk to her. We said our
bashful hellos, and I hugged her. I didn't know if it was
appropriate at the moment, but she smiled afterward.
Good enough for her, good enough for me.

The night was young. Beer young? Not quite. But it
was still pre-midnight, and who knew what trouble we
could find. We chatted and danced and fell in the kind of

childish love that some might call "puppy love." It was way too early in our lives for real love or true love to take place. It was especially early for a thing I liked to call, *"Passion!"*

A person can only say that they love someone so much and for so long. The word can become overused and redundant. And sometimes, you just simply want more emphasis.

But how can one say that they love someone more than another? You might ask. They can add the word "passion," and say they love them with a *passionate* love no others could ever follow. I never did love Felicia passionately, but Shae was right on the verge of arriving there.

The night flew by as my half-husky grew from about three and a half inches to five. I thought it was humongous at the time; not knowing any facts of penis sizes or any comparisons on the rest of mankind.

As soon as midnight struck, I planted the worst—best by my standards at the present time—kiss right smack dab on Felicia's lips. She smacked her lips tightly together and returned the favor, smooching me back. We kissed for an eternity—not really. That kiss would never have stood up to the kisses that followed in years to come.

After the kiss, Felicia and I faded away like the sun in the evening. Slow as a sunset, yet impeccable. The sun has not once failed me during my lifetime. It is as pure and definite as day and night.

And then Felicia disappeared out of my life forever, not willingly or by choice.

III

Enough about Felicia and young love, it's time to go back to the spring and what it brought along with it. I had always loved baseball when I was young, but never with ahh... umm... *Passion!* The "passion" came after my brother's sickness and my own personal problems. I needed an escape, baseball was there for me as the outlet, and I fell in love with the game forever.

I loved double plays, homeruns, popcorn, southpaws, cold beer (not in my youth), cotton candy, sacrifice bunts, and every other aspect that made baseball special. I despised the designated hitter, guaranteed contracts, playing for the money rather than the love of the game, and pitchers who didn't come inside.

As I said, springtime was in the air. And the baseball fields were jam-packed. Although it was barely spring, Desert Shores was dealt one of those extreme weather conditions. The sun was fierce; the heat rose from the sandy infield like water evaporating from a boiling pot.

The grandstands were scattered with fans cheering on their little heroes. Some of the parents, siblings, and friends watched field one, while others focused their attention on fields two and three. The sports complex was assembled similar to a giant pie with four evenly cut slices. The first slice was field one, and the second and third slices were fields two and three, respectively. The fourth piece of the pie was the entrance and parking lot.

I scooped up another handful of sand in my glove, allowing it to trickle out of my mitt and back to its origin. I then adjusted the brim of my hat and slapped my glove with my throwing hand.

"Let's go Bobster, come on big two-three," I said, shifting a couple of steps to my right and covering any ball hit up the middle.

"C'mon baby, strike 'em out, Bobby," the rest of the infield and dugout joined in harmoniously. The batter was "Terrible" Tommy Jeffries, one of the most feared kids in all of minor leagues. Hell... he was even feared throughout the neighborhood. "Terrible" was the only kid to ever hit the ball over the leftfield fence and into the city's public swimming pool. Not only did his rocket shot clear the fence, but the bomb took a swim about fifty feet further up. It was one hell of a blast.

Bobby helped himself out on the mound, throwing a 2-0 curve ball that Jeffries took for strike one. There were two outs and bases loaded in the fifth inning. To this day, I still remember feeling something extraordinary about to happen — something unexplainable.

A pulse of electricity vibrated through my body as I repositioned myself at second base. Before I could even think about what had come over me, Bobby delivered the pitch.

Crack! The ball was hit as another shot of adrenaline filled my body.

I streaked to my right, seeing the hard grounder headed up the middle. I felt my calves flex as my rubber cleats clawed into the dirt surface. *There is no way I'm getting to this one.*

I took one final stride towards the second base bag and then laid out. Fully extending my body, I dove for the ball with eyes open and glove outstretched. I reached as far as possible as the side of my body struck the ground. My eyes shut, and I let out a brief grunting sound.

I backhanded the grounder, trapping the ball in my

glove for an unbelievable diving catch. Moving as quickly as I could, I hopped up and pitched the ball to Sammy at second. Sammy snagged the toss for the final out, getting us out of the jam.

I bet you thought that I was just here to brag about my diving catch. Well... you thought wrong. I'm here to brag about more. I excelled in every aspect of baseball, not just in the field.

Another two innings went by before I came up to bat in the bottom of the seventh. The last inning of baseball for our league — save the nine inning games for the big boys. With a runner on third base and the score even, I trotted to homeplate.

Throughout my little league career I had never been shining like I shone on this day. With two hits, both doubles, and a multiple-run saving play, I showed the locals I was becoming a premium player. An early blossoming before a high school calling that would leave most dazzled. My stardom was on its way.

The pitch count was two-and-two, with one out accounted for. "Hanky-Spanky" Young was getting his lead from third as I dug in for the next delivery. No one was really sure why we called him "Hanky-Spanky." I know for a fact it wasn't because he got laid all the time. He would have a hard time with his curly, always messed up, red hair and pimpled face.

The Pirates pitcher threw an inside fastball that I tattooed off the leftfield fence, driving in the winning run and leading the A's to victory. A game-winning RBI to go alongside the doubles and the diving stop.

I didn't dream about the game-winning double, my third of the game, nor did I dream about any of my games before my professional debut. But I did dream about something else that night; something that just struck me for

the first time since it originally happened.
I can't believe I didn't think of this before.
I honestly can't believe —
It fits in perfectly… like a puzzle.
I just honestly can't believe —
I feel so stupid now.
I just honestly can't believe I didn't think about the incident before now.

IV

As Jeff and Shae finished their stroll through the baseball facilities, they headed back west into the second stage of the park area. More trees, more overgrowth. The lighting dimmed, but it was still illuminated enough to keep anyone from feeling frightened. Their bodies cast shadows on the pavement, forming an 'X' around them as the lights hit from every angle. They walked on.

Their shadows became less visible as the path turned into a spongy grass trail that led them deeper into the trees — into the woods. The route was surrounded by thorny brush with overhanging vines covering the entrance. A few yards ahead, the trees opened to their right, revealing a small, cascading waterfall that splashed quietly in the heart of the copse. The shallow pool that the water descended into contained two golden lamps sticking out on each side. The lamps added to the overall scenery, carrying a light of hope with an infinite clarity.

The couple succumbed to the darkness and benefited from nature's way of relaxing one's stressful self. The only sound that disturbed the peaceful Los Angeles style jungle was the smoothness of birds chirping. It was consistent, and the harmonious sounds were catching. The city traffic and hellacious sounds of downtown were left far behind.

"We ate pizza, and I saw Felicia for the last time before..." Jeff said, tailing off at the end. He bowed over, gripping his knees. Pain struck his stomach as he felt like vomiting. The memory hit him so fast that he wasn't prepared for its arrival.

Shae immediately grabbed him, thinking that he was having some sort of seizure or attack. "Jeff, Jeff! Are you okay?"

"Yeah... one second," Jeff strained to speak, trying to gain his balance. "Something happened in... when I was younger... in nineteen-ninety. Something that I haven't thought about since that time."

"What, Jeff? What is it?" Shae asked, concerned.

Jeff stood straight up and stretched his arms to their full length. He rolled his neck once and then closed his eyes. Letting his eyelids reopen, he looked at Shae, deep into her own eyes. He took her hands into his own, and began.

I can't believe I forgot about Felicia.

V

"Felicia was the girl that I had a crush on when I was little. We thought we were in love. You know, stupid kids, not having a clue what love really was. Not really caring or thinking that far ahead, just enjoying the time and place you were trapped in. I spent the days at school thinking about her and the evenings playing baseball while my little brother was shut up in a hospital bed."

Jeff paused, trying to gather all the information

swimming around inside his head. The data was attacking his brain like bees swarming on an uninvited pest; he was an uninvited visitor who disturbed them and their honeycomb's peace.

"Go on, hun'," Shae said.

"Well... I *have dreamed* before," Jeff continued. "I *dreamed* about the girl's... death before it happened. I know, I know. It sounds strange, but it's true. I really did. I blocked it out because it had really happened, and I didn't want to believe it. It felt like it was my fault because I didn't do anything to stop it."

"What girl, Jeff? Felicia?"

"Yes. She was killed in a car accident while I was playing ball. I mean, I saw the car and-and everything. It was a faded red truck, with uhh... blots of cement plastered to its sides. I know... because the details remain vivid in the back of my mind. I think it was the S-Ten model made by Chevy, but I'm not completely positive. It's not important, anyways.

"I saw it go by as I was warming up between innings. I thought to myself, 'That's the same car I dreamed about last night.' Then I turned to Sammy at short and said, 'Hey Sam, that's the exact fuckin' truck I had in my dream, man. You know... the one I told you about today.' Sam said, 'No shit,' and the conversation ended as the ump said play ball.

"About two minutes later, we heard the screeching of tires and... uhh... scree-screaming. The game was stopped as... umm... most of the fans cleared the stands to see what the hell was goin' down. Somebody yelled somethin' about callin' the paramedics and that a lil' girl had been badly injured."

Jeff stopped on the verge of tears. Shae hugged him and rubbed his back with her gentle hands. She whispered in his ear, "You knew it was Felicia, didn't you?"

"Yes," Jeff said sadly. "And then I forgot the whole thing ever happened. Just like that, it left my mind. My parents had been stressed over Eric, and it was easy to forget about others problems when I had so many of my own. And so many around me."

Shae comforted Jeff as they slowly headed back home. Only a few words were spoken between the walk and the ride to her apartment.

They spent the rest of the night at Shae's apartment. Neither of them mentioned the childhood dreaming incident again, but they did keep track of the Demon baseball dreams. Those dreams came more frequently as the season grew longer, and Jeff knew when he had had one. He just had no idea what they meant or the details that were hidden inside of them.

VI

This is hell, and I am in it.

I sit with the palms of my hands collecting my tears. Running my fingers through my hair, my cap falls to the dugout floor. *C'mon Jeff, snap out of it.* The reoccurring noise of everlasting fear and torture continues, diverting my attempts to gather myself. Escape is impossible.

With my eyes shut, I sit in on the bench and let the visions come. And trust me; they arrive without any layovers or delays. I see Will. He's taking batting practice, trying to drive balls out of the park. Shae is sitting beside me now, with her hand on my back. Will, still hacking away, turns and smiles at me. Shae kisses my cheek and smiles as well; heart-warming and full of pleasantries.

I'm now eating with the crew: Jason, Will, Regina,

Steve, Lake, Shae, and myself. We are laughing and drinking and—

A dark alley...

Silence—

A piano playing, but the sound it makes isn't coming from anywhere. It's coming from everywhere.

Shae and I are making love. Her stomach is boiling hot as I touch my tongue to it and lay my face against it. The trials of love are tested once more as I enter her. Shae lets out a small scream of ecstasy, arousing me to no end.

The lovemaking is over. I'm watching television from the bed. 'My bed,' I think. 'Or maybe Shae's?'

Shae enters the room, tray in hand. She brings me breakfast in bed, but it doesn't feel like breakfast time. It seems much later. I eat the bacon, eggs, and toast without asking the time; Shae reads a book next to me. The cover reads *The Key to Midnight,* by Dean Koontz.

She flips through the pages as I finish my meal. 'You done, hun?' she asks. I nod in reply, leaning back against my pillow. I let my body become entirely motionless as my thoughts unwind.

Nothingness now—

No noise, no voices that shouldn't be heard, no girl in the stands, nothing but my loneliness in the hushed room.

'I would trade my eternal loneliness for some peace and quiet,' I think. Right about now, I would swap anything to just be able to get away from here. Away from the pressures of the world and away from my inevitable failures.

And then it happens yet again. The noise returns with more enthusiasm than before, distinctly resurfacing in my head. The constant buzzing is earsplitting; it shatters the insides of my brain.

"Jeff, Jeff," the voice sounds so far away; I fight the

noise and ignore it momentarily. Stirring me out of yet another dream, I turn to look over my left shoulder and see Eric leaning over the rail. But Eric doesn't look like the same little brother I always remembered; he appears enlarged. His face grows in and out like a pulsing artery — th-thump, th-thump, th-thump — his body swells as he emits a golden shield around him.

This new change makes him look like an angel. *A guardian angel sent to protect me.*

"Jeff, goddammit! I'm not your guardian angel, I'm your brother," he shouts, but only I am able to hear him. Everyone else in the dugout is focused on Erwin Perry, at bat with a four-iron in his hands. "You've got to wake up, Jeff. You can do it! We all believe you can! Shae does! Will did! We all do!"

And I see it now. Inside this uncontrollable, eerie world between my eyes, within my skull. This isn't *a dream.*

Wrong —

This isn't *the dream.* It's just your standard Sunday morning paper, coffee with creme, pancakes with syrup, type of dream — border lining the realm of nightmare. I close my eyes within my dream.

I'm back in bed. Alone. But it isn't my bed. Well... at least it isn't my current bed in Los Angeles. It's my twin-sized fortress surrounded by mom's hand-sewn pillows of old little league shirts. I'm lying under my baseball-themed bedspread. There is a book on my nightstand. I pick it up, reading, Mario Puzo's *Fools Die.* The character, dressed in a mobster's style, centered on the cover, has his chin touching his chest, allowing his gangster-brimmed hat to hide his face. He lifts his head and smiles. The grin has turned this harmless bad dream into a nightmare.

Shit...

I'm frightened for the first time—trapped in this nightmare. All walls surround me. I can't find my way out of this madness. My last thought...

Will...

VII

Jeff snapped his head forward, rising up off his pillow. Sweat bubbled on his forehead and ran down his chin. His heart raced in his chest like a caged animal trying to attempt jailbreak. This last dream wasn't the same. It wasn't one of *them*. But like Felicia's, it could have significance—a greater meaning. And it was more intense; he could at least feel that much.

But not much more. Man, what the hell is going on. He got up slowly, trying to find out where he was. Jeff glanced around the poorly lit room, and realized he was at Shae's place, in the comfort of his true love.

Shae was next to him—asleep. He decided there was no need to wake her. And also... no need to tell her. She had worried about his dreams enough. And this one wasn't even along the same line. It wasn't even in the same ballpark. *Nice baseball pun, Jeff.* He could feel it. He knew it.

Shae's magical wall clock grabbed his attention in the darkness. It didn't only have the time glowing in holographic numbers; it also had the day of the week and date. The calendar clock combo read... May 12, 1999, Tuesday, 3:37 a.m. Each part, the date, the day, and the time, were stacked on top of each other vertically.

The holographic wall clock also featured an alarm, of course. It played beautiful, sweet music to the ears, which definitely topped the "alarming" threat from most early morning "wake-me-uppers."

Jeff sat up in bed, careful to not disturb Shae, yet. There wasn't much use for more sleep. Shae was taking him to the stadium parking lot in less than an hour, anyway. The Demons had a nine-hour drive to Tucson ahead of them; there was plenty of time to sleep on the bus.

So Jeff simply relaxed in the dark. As much as one usually ponders when there isn't much light or sound around them, this time it was ironic. Jeff didn't think of much. Sure, a few thoughts of the dreams, and of baseball, and of Shae crossed before his brain, but nothing with longevity. He enjoyed the time, wishing it could last longer —not delving the deeps of his atypical subconscious.

He heard a car honk outside. *Crazy bastards, it's four in the goddamn morning.* He smiled to himself. As no one else was awake to see it. And no one else could hear his thoughts.

Shae awoke to the alarm at four-thirty. She mumbled good morning, went to her closet, threw on a pair of jeans over her lacy thong, and then reached for a bra. She grabbed it, reconsidered putting it on (as she was already wearing a ladies tee), and then tossed it back in the closet.

Who needs a bra at this hour? Jeff thought, smiling again.

They rode to the field without much conversation. Shae was obviously still in a sleepy daze as Jeff drove his truck.

They said their goodbyes, hugged, kissed, and hugged again. Shae, now behind the driver's seat, waved farewell and headed back to her apartment for some more sleep before going to the firm.

"Let's go, bitch," Fetters said, greeting the second baseman at the bus's entrance and carrying a steaming cappuccino.

"It's on," Hartes muttered, ascending the first step to Tucson.

Chapter Eleven
A Day Off

I

Lack of sleep appears to finally haunt the tired, weary old man.

Yes… it truly is a struggle, as he attempts to do the complete opposite of what he normally goes through with during the after hours. Customarily, he tosses and turns, wondering when his eyes will finally close and his thoughts cease to exist.

But this night, he paces beside his bed as he has already vacated his favorite chair. He wants to stay awake. He wants to keep remembering. He wants it so much because he knows how close he is to the end; the end where he unravels his final tales and his insomnia ceases to exist. At least he thinks remembering the past will cure his sleeping disorder. *I guess I should say I hope, I hope remembering will allow me to sleep.*

Sleep is the last thing on his mind. But he knows he must sleep eventually. He thinks?

His back aches, his joints sting, and his head hurts from constantly remembering the pains of the past. The weight of his eyelids increases dramatically as the clock ticks away the morning hours of the next day. His veins are running on battery acid.

He eventually collapses into his bed rear first and rolls over on his back. A mild spasm passes in his lower back, but figuring as much, the pain doesn't bother him. He shakes his head in disgust, as if to say, 'quitting already, you poor excuse for an old man.' *Insomnia comes with the territory.* He rests his head on his down pillows, and tries his hardest to keep the thoughts channeling, wanting to stay awake more than ever. He's afraid of the darkness that lies ahead; *terrified to remember—petrified to forget.*

Irony finally kicks in as he drifts into an elderly slumber; snoring, coughing, irregular breathing. He sleeps through the rising of the sun and daylight's greeting. The clock—fancy and digital, not the sports clock of the past—flashes continually as a ticker, displaying 9:46 a.m. He can't believe that he slept so late; today shattered the record he previously owned within the last five years or so.

Must be the dreams... just thinking about them.

Jeff Hartes sits up in his bed with the new day's thoughts beginning to swell in his brain. He pushes them aside, as he needs a day off. At least a morning and lunch away from the pain that is coming. The pain that is unforgettable—can wait until tonight.

Jeff's heart, as well as his mind, predicts a severe aching. Like a storm brewing in the west, it is coming fast and will be unstoppable. So as people would take cover and prepare for the worst—Jeff does the same, just in a different manner. His method is rest... resting his heart, resting his mind—taking a day off from the pain.

Using the side of his nightstand and his expensive memory mattress that Shae yearned for, he elevates his body out of the bed and moves toward the bathroom for an everlasting leak. His ankles are slightly swollen and his knees ache, but he moves with the ease of someone who has become unaware of this reoccurring nuisance.

Relieving himself in the morning with a half-husky (yes... it still works) and a bodily system full of coffee and water is the closest, and best feeling he gets to an orgasm. The lengthy, body-draining piss tingles his sides and makes his legs quiver similar to ejaculating. Of course, it could never replace sex, but he has to settle for less than in the past, these days.

He flicks the flush lever down, realizing he catches a few drops in his pajamas, but doesn't really care. Jeff leaves the restroom for the kitchen to get his McNally Sales mug and brew some "Good Morning America." He wasn't much of a coffee drinker during the dreams. He despised the thing he called "black liquid death." But with age... things change. And his need for a pick-me-up, home brewed or Starbuck's, existed nowadays.

He sits at one end of the dining table, never seeing nor remembering the letter he has placed at the other end. It was lost in the rubble of magazines, receipts, and previously paid bills. And also lost in the garbled thoughts inside his head.

After his coffee is ready, he drinks it alone, as he has done regularly for the last year and a day. Jeff isn't the type of man anymore who simply pretends to enjoy other's company, for the sake of being polite, and mingle at the local cafés. He just simply wants to quietly enjoy his new favorite drink and watch anything dealing with sports on the television.

The coffee, black as a moonless night, goes down as smooth as always. *I'm not going to think about the Demons, I'm not going to think about the Demons, I'm not going to think, period.* Jeff says this over and over in his head, reassuring his mind that the day—the day off— ahead won't be interrupted by the past.

He snatches his tanned-leather jacket off of the coat rack and proceeds out the front door. His guess is fairly accurate; it isn't as cold as he previously thought, but the slight breeze from the north chills the spring air. He begins his walk down the street, not needing a vehicle to travel a few blocks. Jeff leaves behind his cozy home in search of a relaxing day and his only true friend still alive.

At least, he thinks it's the only true friend still around.

II

Upon arriving on Texas Avenue, Jeff bends down to grab his knees as fatigue overcomes him. Not an overwhelmingly long walk for him; Jeff just hasn't been himself since... well... you know. A slight stage of dizziness passes as he now holds his lower back. The elderly man appears to be trying to straighten up by putting leverage on his back and hoping his body bends the way it is supposed to.

"Jeff... you alright?" another man, in his late fifties, shouts from the house directly parallel to the street. The younger fellow charges off of his porch and towards the road with a worrisome look planted on his face. "Jeff, hey man!"

He gently places his hands on his friend's back, awaiting Jeff's next move. Mr. Hartes straightens up a little bit more, and turns his head to an angle that faces his dear friend. A spell of laughter comes over him, and he chuckles with half-glee and half-pain. "Ha-ha, uh, ha-ha, uh-uh!"

Leslie Paxton shakes his head in disbelief, and then joins in the laughter.

"You should wear your shit like that when we go eat lunch, Leslie," Jeff says, referring to Leslie's shaving job. His left cheek is clean and smooth, his mouth and chin are rough and bristly, and his right cheek is covered with puffy, white Barbasol. The shaving cream begins running down his neck as Leslie responds to Jeff's comical comment.

"If I didn't have to sprint out here and save your old ass, maybe I could've finished shaving. And then maybe I would have been able please you. You old, blue-haired asshole."

"I can't believe you still shave the old-fashioned way," Jeff adds, smiling. "I thought you're the one trying to be innovative."

"Innovative my ass."

Both of them cackle loudly, possibly disturbing the quiet, still-German neighborhood. They help each other down the sidewalk leading to Leslie's house, one with a basement, and disappear from the street. Once inside, Leslie returns to the bathroom to finish what he started earlier. His restroom is in the front part of the house, facing the street. To his shaving mirror's immediate left is a small, framed window. This is the opening that allowed Leslie to see Jeff hunched over in the road.

"How long 'til you finish shaving? Because I'm freaking starving."

"Not long, my friend. Patience has never been your best virtue," Leslie points out to his friend of nearly fifteen years. The two pals feel as if they have been *To Hell and Back*, right alongside Audie Murphy. Jeff helped Leslie through the trials and tribulations of his own wife's death three years ago. And now Leslie has been repaying Jeff in a twisted, ironic kind of way, as Shae died a day over a year ago.

The loss of their spouses only brought the two friends closer, and they spent all their time away from being alone with their own thoughts, with each other's thoughts. Both of them had so much in common that when they argued with each other, they were on the same side the majority of the time.

Leslie played in several different semi-pro football leagues, but never made it to the big time. He told Jeff that he never experienced anything like the dreams during his football years, but did come across some weird shit.

"There. All finished," Leslie says as he rinses out the sink of hair and shaving cream. He grabs the nearest towel from the rack and dries his coarse skin. "Let's go and get some grub. Ready?"

"Sure am."

The two of them end up leaving Leslie's house for an eleven o'clock meal. Once again, a vehicle isn't necessary.

III

"You remember how I told you that it was nearing *that* time in my life in which I wanted to try and rethink everything that happened to me in *that* one special year?" Jeff asks, neither needing nor waiting for a response from Leslie. "What I'm trying to say is... I've spent many restless nights thinking about that strange... that magical... that one-of-a-kind year. It's like I've been forcing my mind to gather all the facts. To gather, uhh... everything I can remember."

Jeff leans back in his chair. "I think all the pieces are together, like shards of glass magically transforming back into a broken vase. The time is now, Leslie, and I've been at it, all last night. All yesterday. All the week before. My mind won't allow me to rest anymore without releasing... releasing nineteen ninety-nine."

"Really?" Leslie responds, drawing a look of interest

on his face as he sets down his spoon and rubs his chin with his right hand. He gets a tiny bit of chili on his face, not realizing it had gotten on his fingers. Jeff disregards telling him for the time being. Leslie asks, "How's *that* coming?"

"Good... so far. But the painful parts are on the way."

"You know, Jeff, you really should have written all this down. Or found someone to write a book about it."

"I-I-I-uh... don't think it was meant to go down that way. On paper, that is." Jeff leans back in his chair, pondering deeply. He stares at the *Check's* chili on Leslie's chin, still ignoring the thought of mentioning it so he can remain on topic. "This is the way it's supposed to happen. I truly believe that, Les. *Remembering...* One. Last. Time." The words leaving Jeff's mouth in their own simple sentence, a hesitation between each of them, emphasis on all of them.

"If you say so, Jeff."

"I do, my friend... I do. And I'm sure glad this place still serves an unhealthy meal when you need one."

IV

Leslie returns to his chili (meat and beans in chili sauce poured over spaghetti noodles). The way the chili is made at *Check's* has been just a minor adjustment in Jeff's life since the move from Los Angeles, California to Louisville, Kentucky. Jeff, meanwhile, stops eating his fried bologna with cheese, and just thinks. He stares at the walls of the less-than-busy cafe.

He catches a glimpse of an athlete's picture that he recognizes... Scott Padgett. Padgett was a shooting guard for the Kentucky Wildcats when they won the national championship. *Funny,* he thinks for no apparent reason.

Jeff picks up the check at "*Check's*" —not trying to be redundant. He and Leslie, on a sudden whim, decide to go gamble.

"I haven't been to Caesar's in awhile, whatcha' say? A horn bet for old time's sake?" Jeff asks his friend, referring to a type of bet in *Craps,* while closing the café's door behind them.

V

Caesar's—near Kentuckiana.

The casino boat, much improved with all sorts of digital and voice-command upgrades, was just across the Ohio River, separating the Kentucky and Indiana borders. Jeff and Leslie had walked back to Leslie's house, jumped in his 2046 model Caddie, and taken the forty-minute drive across the bridge to gamble.

They parked valet; forget walking any further to get to the casino because once inside, they would still have a good hike to the actual boat—gambling area. They had to pass the numerous gift shops, expensive restaurants and excellent buffets, casual twenty-four hour café's and cigar stands, and finally, take the escalator down to the riverboat where the slot machines hummed, the dice rattled off the boards, and the cards were shuffling. And during that entire journey, they also picked up some cash from an ATM.

"I.D., sir?" the young casino patron asks, without yet raising his head to look at the person waiting to travel through the turnstiles. The entrance from the under twenty-one area to the over twenty-one area is roped off with false gold stanchions. Jeff laughs, never reaching for his wallet.

The kid, in his mid-twenties—at least a child to Jeff and Leslie—looks up and doesn't ask for identification again. He motions for the two friends to proceed inside the boat.

"Oooh, man. Brings back some good memories," Jeff says, taking in the scene. The only place that could lighten him up like a battery, chilling his spine, more than a casino is the baseball diamond. To Jeff, walking out of the clubhouse and onto the flawlessly manicured grass to perform in *his* chapel is still the greatest feeling alive. It doesn't matter how long it has been since he'd played. The feeling—the memory of the feeling—will never fade... never go away.

"Better than the ones ahead, for you, at least, huh?" Leslie asks, not trying to spoil the mood, but simply securing the current mindset.

"Most of them," Jeff responds, ending that topic and quickly changing subjects. "What first, Les?"

"I think I'm going to relax at the Blackjack table, you in?" Leslie follows his friend's question with one of his own.

"Maybe in a little while," Jeff answers. He points in the direction behind Leslie, an invisible beam leaving Jeff's finger and just clearing Leslie's right shoulder. "I've got some old business to take care of at the Craps' table."

Leslie turns around and sees the stickman waving his glorious rod. "Dice out," the man shouts as another high-roller blows on his magical fist and flings the cubes. Leslie turns back to Jeff and nods.

The ex-second baseman for the Demons... and then briefly with the Twins... passes by his younger friend and proceeds to his table of choice. Meanwhile, Leslie ventures off to the $10.00 minimum Blackjack table, sitting in one of the vacated, padded-black stools.

Jeff, also choosing a $10.00 minimum, finds a slot to stand in on the left hand side of the Craps' table. The stickman is to his right, with one person between them. Before getting his chips, he turns to see where Leslie went one last time. *Don't see 'em. No biggie...*

He turns back to the table as the shooter on the opposite rolls again—a six. Jeff tosses a couple of hundreds on the table, saying, "Give me two-hundred please."

"Changing two-hundred," the boxman says, taking the money and forcing it into a cash box below the table. He slides the chips to the dealer on Jeff's side of the table. The dealer checks their count, and then pushes them to the wall in front of Jeff.

Jeff picks up the chips and stacks them neatly in the racetrack-like rack. He waits for the shooter to either seven-out or pass his roll; it's bad luck to jump in during the middle. The shooter fires the dice down to his end—a five.

"Five-alive... another pass!" the stickman proclaims, dragging the two previously shot dice back towards the shooter. The dealers, meanwhile, are busy paying off the winning bets and pulling the losses. "Hot shooter, hot shooter!"

Jeff decides to jump on board, hoping the shooter has more passes in his right arm. He puts a thirty-stack on the pass line, riding the good side. "C'mon shooter, early seven or eleven," he says aloud in a whisper.

The man with the dice is a black fellow in his late twenties. He's wearing a dark-blue winner's jacket and sporting several gold chains. His watch, also gold, gleams next to the fist entrapping the dice. He appears to have a posse of four or five other guys cheering him on—all black but one. The dice fly out of his hands, striking the wall near Jeff, and reveal themselves—an eleven.

Thatta' baby!

"Press it," Jeff tells the dealer, meaning to leave the thirty he just won next to the thirty already out there. Therefore, his pass line bet is now sixty.

The shooter's posse jumps up and down, hollering some more. Jeff looks down at his end of the table again, seeing the massive stack of chips in the young black man's slot. And they weren't ten dollar or twenty dollar chips, either. They were fifty pieces and C-notes, and he had about fifteen large altogether.

Jeff rides the shooter for another twenty minutes or so, and two more passes later, before the black man finally craps out. While the high-roller's stack is now around twenty-five grand, Jeff is pleased with his winnings so far. He's up about one-fifty.

"Nice rollin', man!" Jeff shouts across the table as the dice are passed to the next shooter. The black man takes Jeff's compliment with a nodding head, and then others at the table follow suit.

"Very nice!"

"Superb dice, my man!"

"Good shit, bro!"

All but one. The one everyone at the table hates— despises. It is a guy on Jeff's dealer's immediate left. The belligerence and angst of a sore loser gleams in his eyes and shines on his face beneath the dimmed-cylinder lights. The reason... this angry man bet against the shooter the whole time. He wanted to be alone, thinking his system or method of betting was right. Sometimes, my friend, but not today. He wouldn't be sharing in everyone else's glee.

The black man started to leave the table with his posse

engulfing him and protecting his winnings. Chips stuff his jacket pockets, practically flowing over the hemmed edges. He momentarily disappears in the crowd a few yards from the table.

The next shooter grabs the dice as the bets have been placed. Jeff, staying true to form, lays forty on the pass line. A little more than before, but not trying to get greedy with a new roller.

This is where the *real* action begins. Jeff will subsequently remember the new shooter, an elderly woman with too much licorice red lipstick, beginning to raise the dice in her throwing hand. Simultaneously, the stickman yells, "Dice out!" Within seconds time, the black man, winner's jacket full of rich chips, pushes through the crowd around the table and throws a handful of chips on the table, shouting, "Five Grand On Boxcar's!"

As soon as the words exit his mouth, the dealer nearer to him bellows, "No bet! No bet!"

Meanwhile, the dice are flying through the air towards Jeff's end of the table. They hit table first, clank up against the side wall, and then spill to a stop. Jeff sees one six by the come line. His eyes widen as he searches for another—a twelve.

Six-six... holy shit!

"Boxcar's!" the stickman exclaims, staring between the dealer and the young black man.

"Boxcar's! Motherfuckers!" the black man screams in ecstasy. "That's thirty-to-one in this mofo!" His chains bounce against his neck and chest as he jumps up and down, pumping his fists.

"A hundred an' fifty gees! Oh shit!" His posse joins in the frenzy, hugging and also leaving their feet.

The dealer, with an overwhelming look of sadness on his face, bitterly says, "No bet, sir... no bet."

The words don't exit his mouth with much authority or strength. They are said feebly and very quietly. The black man stops his celebrating, staring at the dealer with an unsure glare. "What did you say?"

"No bet, sir."

The mayhem begins. The black man grabs the dealer, one hand gripping his dress shirt while the other hand wraps around the tie. "No bet my ass, you motherfucker!"

The boxman is out of his chair now, trying to separate the two. The other dealer also joins the confrontation, backing the boxman. The black man's friends now swarm the dealer trying to deny them their winnings. Jeff watches as bodies collide, grabbing and pushing. The black man releases his right hand, cocks it, and throws a much anticipated right hook. The punch lands flush on the dealer's left cheek, driving him back into the boxman and causing both of them to spill downward.

The posse jumps in, letting their hands fly freely as well. The fracas is out of control. It's time for the big boys to step in—and sure enough, here comes one the pit bosses. He grabs the first hood he sees, bending the punk's arms behind his back. The pit boss throws the black man's friend —the white one—down to the flashy-patterned carpet. He radios for security while grabbing another fighter.

Jeff watches with bewilderment. Too old and too stunned to try and help. A couple of security guards come from behind the cashier's cage and begin helping the casino employees in their struggle. The pit boss has now gotten the black man, the instigator, bear hugged and finally under control. While the security guards separate bodies, the second dealer helps the boxman, who is slightly bloodied, and the other dealer, very bloodied and bruised, to their feet and away from the crazy scene.

Another security guard joins the action. Instead of

heading right to the middle of it, he smartly decides to try and clear the area. He asks all the Craps' players who were on that table to stay together, for questioning if need be. He then tells everyone else that everything is okay, and that they can go about their business, continuing to gamble.

Jeff stands in the newly formed circle of Craps' players, shaking his head in disbelief. A kid, with an innocently youthful face that shouts 'I'm barely of age', breaks the silence, "Can you believe that dude rolled the boxcars?"

"Pretty crazy," another man, older, responds while taking a drag off his cigarette.

"Pretty crazy is right," Jeff adds, joining the conversation. At that moment, Leslie walks up.

"Hey, what's going on? I've been trying to get through all the people to see if you started this mess?" Leslie says jokingly.

"Les... it's just too much to explain right now," Jeff says, shaking his head at his friend. Now walking towards the group is the pit boss that first started helping the unforeseen situation. He is on the heavy side, with a perfectly trimmed goatee and short brown hair. He's wearing a pair of dark-tinted shades – slightly crooked from the scuffle – on his friendly face.

"Everybody okay over here?" he asks as the security guards begin to haul off all members of the brawl.

A harmony of 'yes's' follow. "Alright," the pit boss says. "Well my name's Miller. If anybody needs anything, just let me know. I'll have someone else over here asking some questions if you good folks don't mind."

Nobody moves. Usually people can't wait to get away from an inconvenience. But it must have been their curiosity that kept them waiting around to eagerly help solve the current situation. Curiosity killed the cat. And what is good for the goose... forget it.

Jeff starts filling Leslie in on what happened. His eyes widen as the story gets further and further along. He must've been sharing the same disbelief that Jeff felt earlier. While the storytelling is taking place, a female dealer begins asking a few of the people questions. This seems somewhat silly to Jeff, mainly because all casinos have the "eye-in-the-sky" watching every move. All the Caesar's head security would have to do is watch the replay.

After about thirty minutes of just standing around and bullshitting—with Leslie now up to date on what happened from several different angles—the Caesar's pit boss, Miller, finally lets the bystanders move along.

"I think I've had enough excitement for one day," Jeff says, ready to get back to his home and relax... and *remember.*

"Sounds good," Leslie agrees. "Guess it's time to get outta' here." They both head for the exit. Leslie asks, "So how'ja finish anyways?"

"Not bad... not bad at all. See... ol' Boxcars there was on one hell of a run before the shit hit the fan. I nearly doubled up."

"That's good," Leslie responds as they ride the escalator back up to the casino entrance, obviously waiting for Jeff to return the question. Which, he does.

"How did the Blackjack table treat ya'?"

"Not bad... not bad at all." They smile simultaneously, now walking through the plethora of restaurants, stores, and other entertainment and too out of breath to laugh. Leslie continues, "I double-downed a couple of times with nine-two, and both times drilled the face card. Caught a couple of Blackjack's as well. I-uhh finished like fifty up."

"Sounds like an all-around nice day at Caesar's," Jeff deducts.

"You can say that again," Leslie concludes. And then mumbles, "You can say that again."

VI

Jeff and Leslie stop at *Morton's Steakhouse* in downtown Louisville to celebrate their winnings with the best steak around—the best meal... period. After their filet's, two tired old men, one slightly older than the other, drive back towards Germantown. Leslie drops Jeff off at his house. And they go their separate ways after a long day together.

Jeff walks to his door, pausing at the top step of his porch. He looks up at the spring sky, scattered stars beckon to him. They tell him it's time... time to remember some more. Time to get back to the task at hand. Time to get back to the story.

People are waiting for you, Jeff... to finish the tale. The voice in his mind is Shae's. A tear develops from his right eye and rolls down his rough cheek.

He swipes it away, then takes the last step and proceeds through the front door. Dark, but still light enough to see his way across the living room, Jeff walks a few feet before pulling the string on a rustic lamp. He then heads to the bathroom, needing to relieve himself.

"Ahhh... all done," he speaks aloud. Jeff heads for one thing, and one thing only—his favorite chair.

His thoughts channel back to 1999. He pulls the lever on the recliner, raising his feet and leaning back. Sleep won't find him. Not any time soon at least. *This is Darrell "The Duke" Marinville bringing you another edition of Demon baseball...*

A smile surfaces on his face. He is afraid. He knows it

will hurt. Either way, he must go on.

The time to remember again is now... there's nothing else worth thinking about in the present.

Except... perhaps...

A letter lying on his coffee table.

(Bottom of the Inning)

Chapter Twelve
Darkness Lies Ahead

I

"High fly ball hit by Allen to centerfield. Lewis takes a few steps back, and makes the catch. That ends the fifth, Demons one, Knights nothing. Due up for Los Angeles in the sixth, Parks, Hicks, and Gunn," Darrell Marinville announces to the Demon faithful.

Jogging in from second, I wonder how in the hell I can hear Marinville doing the radio broadcast. After all, Marinville is in the booth, I am standing on the field. The announcer is glassed in and speaking over the radio, I am entering the dugout via the infield. Kyle Queen's voice is the one spilling through the loudspeakers throughout Diego Field, not Marinville's. Queen's the one I should be hearing, along with the fans.

So let me say it again, because it's worth repeating. I can hear Darrell "The Duke" Marinville's broadcast, along with Kyle Queen's announcing over the loudspeakers, and finally, the buzzing of the crowd altogether.

I sit in the left side corner of the always-rectangular bench. I can smell sweat in the air, tasting the cool, refreshing breeze turned sour. The smell reminds me of going to Dodgers games in the early 90s. Me and pops, having the time of our lives while rooting for one of the greatest coaches of my youth, Mr. Lasorda. *But who other than Tommy Lasorda?* And his extremely vocal, and

sometimes outrageous, rants—

I remember I always ordered the same things around the same innings. Right before the fourth or fifth, Dad would make a run to the concession stand and grab a couple of hotdogs and a Dr. Pepper, along with a beer for himself. We would heckle the opposing team's rightfielder from our second row outfield seats, and hope to God that Pedro Guerrero would hit one out in our section. Man, I wanted a homerun ball bad... I never got one. But this jerkoff next to us caught several homers throughout the season. But that's beside the point.

Then I recognize the situation—

My dream is coming to life. Not coming to life in the sense that it wasn't alive before. Because it was... *alive before.*

And not only is it alive now, but it is out to get me. Reaching and clawing with everything it has to pull me in where I can never escape. Once trapped inside, I will become nothing and live a life of nothingness. My head feels like it is going to explode as I try to ignore this burden cast upon me. This noise, these deviations; this current dramatic play I am enrolled in.

My dream *is* coming to life.

Surely I do *recognize* the situation—

Everything is the same: the same noise ringing in my ears, the same crowd buzzing, the same fly ball to center, the same moon smiling at me in that devilish-hateful smile, and the same girl strutting down the steps towards her seat.

She looks straight into my direction, and oh dear God, it can't be—

"Time Out!" the umpire shouts as a big bouncing ball, full of air, flies out of the stands and onto the field. This turns my attention off of the girl, and back on the game.

Bobby Parks is batting for us in the top of the sixth. He flies out to left. I then watch as Hicks doubles to center, trying to get a rally going, but Gunn strikes out and Rutherford grounds out, ending the top half of the inning.

I zombie-like jog back out to second base, trying to figure out what is happening to me. I steer clear of looking into the stands while I am playing second; placing my attention on what I am supposed to be doing (playing baseball). I turn to glance at the scoreboard in center. The board reads 1-0 in our favor. The pitcher, Wilkes, leads off the bottom of the sixth with a grounder down the first base line that Gunn dives for, catches, and hurries to the base for out number one. The next batter, Frazier, walks for San Diego and then steals second. I catch the throw from Parks, slap the tag, but it's not in time.

Lake makes his first mistake. I watch as he delivers a chest-high fastball that Timothy Greener belts to right, scoring the tying run. I clap my glove, keeping the runner on second on his toes, but it isn't necessary. Williams strikes out the next two hitters, Ponds and Garrido, to end the sixth.

I come up to bat in the seventh, leading off — the *noise,* which is quiet for one inning of action, comes to being once again inside my head. It has returned with a vengeance — full throttle. It is a repeated buzzing sound, infecting my mind. *What is going on?* I ask myself. *Get your mind on the game, you're batting in the biggest game of your life.* Before I can gather my thoughts, and myself, I have two strikes on me. I can hear Marinville calling my at-bat over the radio. *It's just not possible.*

"Two strikes now on Jeff Hartes. He's oh-for-two tonight, having struck out twice already. Hartes has been a leader down the stretch here for the Demons, but struggling to get the ball on the bat so far tonight." The San

Diego pitcher Jerod Wilkes winds and fires. I swing... and miss. "Strike three. Hartes has the hat-trick, and it's only the seventh inning."

I feel like quitting. It's as simple as that. My mind is racing and my heart feels shattered. Not like being dumped by your horny little high school fling, but shattered as in pierced with a bronze-tipped spear. I look down and see blood on my uniform. It is all over my chest. *The spear must have penetrated my skin and hit a major organ... The Heart.* I close my eyes. I wish the blood away. I open them. It is gone, but my heart still aches—along with my head.

And *the noise* isn't getting any easier to deal with. I not only want to quit, but to run, just run away. Scared? You can say I am, very easily to say that in fact. I mean, there is this *fucking noise* echoing in my brain, this girl I do recognize, but cannot place her fucking name, and I am failing my team. I am letting them down after all the hard work and dedication we've committed ourselves to. After a gut-wrenching and emotional roller coaster of a season, what more do I need? I mean, for real, put Chambers in to pinch hit for me.

My pops once said, 'There are some people who believe they are going to fail, Jeff. And then there are those who believe that failure isn't an option. Sorry to tell you Jeff, but failure is. And it is easier to fail than succeed.' No shit pops. Failure seems to be the only option I am being dealt.

— Failure is an option —

Hicks says something along the lines of 'its okay Hartes, you'll get 'em next time' as I plop down on the bench. A player I don't recognize walks over and grabs the sides of my face. His hands don't touch me in a fierce, jerking movement trying to get my attention, but a soft, gentle placing of his hands on my face. As in the case of trying to show pity yet remorse.

He moves his hands to my shoulders. I place my head in my own hands, somewhat ignoring the kind gesture. The unknown man removes his hands and whispers, "Will's watching you, bro."

And then he jogs to the end of the dugout, grabbing his bat and helmet and joining the circle. I try to silence my mind, but nothing appears to be working. This is hell, and I am —

—I am in it.

The shapes moving on the field blur. It's an abstract painting with unclear colors. The creamy-white ball — fuzzy — travels to the area of second base. It then disappears in a hazy brown. It reappears in the air this time, flying towards first base. Garrido snags it out of the air, and the shaded blue man signals the second out, Goodwin. The blurriness continues as I watch the Demons' next batter, an unfamiliar character, swing his tanned lumber, looking like a darkened mirage, and drive the creamy-white fuzz to leftfield. It disappears again in the brown. Ponds begins his jog in, his movements appear like someone looking through distorted, warped glass. The top of the inning is over. I pray for my vision to clear — to return.

I shake my head, close my eyes, and rise from the pine. A slang term, as San Diego's benches were a padded, metal bleacher. My prayer is answered.

I head back out to second base, immediately making a play on Kramer as he hits a rocket grounder right at me. Tossing it to Gunn at first; if it didn't happen with such instinct, such habit, such ease, I probably wouldn't have been able to make the play. But my body is still a seasoned machine. It is a weapon of past repetitions, and it is still working... at least, working better than my twisted mind.

"One out in the seventh," I hear Marinville call back to the Demon faithful; the radio listeners who weren't fortunate enough to make the inner-state drive. I hardly see the next two at-bats; my mind wanders. *Failure is an option, Jeff. All this, everything you've fought for all season, sliding away...* And then, a different voice, one full of warmth, sincerity, and "truth." *You have to snap out of it, Jeff. I believe in you. Will believes in you. Everyone is rooting for you.* I look around to see runners on the corners. Lake must have given up back-to-back singles. The voice continues... *Jeff? Jeff? You have to believe, Jeff. You must—*

And then like a shot of pure adrenaline, the sound of wood colliding with rawhide alerts me. I see the ball heading up the middle. Lake tries to make a play, but can't get his glove down quick enough. I dart to my right, towards the second base bag. Cutting the ball off on the edge of the infield grass, I turn to flip it to the man I don't know. The teammate covering second is new to me; I've never seen him until earlier, when he tried to console me in the dugout. Never pulling the ball out of my glove with my hands, using my padded leather as the initiator, I quickly toss the ball to the shortstop covering second. He takes the perfect pass and fires it to first.

"DOUBLE PLAY!" Marinville shouts, his excited voice splitting my ears as I tumble forward, rolling in the plush, manicured grass. I hear a scream of pleasurable joy, and look up in time to see Lake raising his fist as he animatedly hops off the mound and sprints to the dugout.

Marinville's unbelievable voice in my head, followed by Lake's cheering yell, quickly turned into a disappointed hush as the Knights' field quieted. I run back to the bench, receiving pats on the back and words of praise, but never truly knowing who gave them... or understanding... because...

Because I see *her* again. Standing. Clapping. Cheering. *For me?*

Of course it's for me.

I duck my head away, under the dugout roof. I simply can't take it. Not knowing—not knowing her name. This time, I'm sure, I even recognize the person she is sitting next to. But his name, all the same. *All the same.*

"Nice fuckin' play!" Gunn taps me on top of the head and takes a seat next to me.

The words trail away in my mind... "fuckin' play"... "in' play"... "play"...

I bury my head in my hands. I see my face in my palms—reflecting like a mirror. Reflecting like a gleaming pond. I can't bear to see it. I feel shame and disappointment. *Sure, I just made a play... but it's only postponing the failure. Failure is an option, Jeff.*

Failure is an option. *Failure is—*

Ⅱ

Jeff awoke, sweating. How in hell could someone be pushing bubbles of warm liquid out of their skin when the AC was blowing right on them? Full blast.

Damn, it's cold. And I'm sweating.

Jeff now realized the irony. He knew...

He'd dreamed again. *Man... such an intense dream for a bus ride.* Light tried to enter through the tinted windows, but not much got in. He wiped the window adjacent to his bunk, covered in frost from the air conditioning, and peered outside.

He looked back down at his watch — 2:15 p.m. Shaking his head and rubbing his eyes, he watched as they passed what appeared to be a large, city park. Christopher Columbus Park to be exact.

"Rise and shine," Parks said in a backwards country voice that reminded Jeff of the movie *Deliverance.* The catcher was reading a *Playboy* in the bunk across the aisle.

"We in Tucson, yet?" Jeff asked.

"Just entering the city limits... I think," Parks replied. "Gonna' call that girl from the golf course after tonight's game." The catcher changed the subject completely. First confusing Jeff, but then the second baseman caught on.

"Oh... yea. Good —" Jeff was interrupted by Hicks, storming down the aisle.

"You call that bitch tonight, you're a fuckin' retard!"

"What?" Parks asked, not grasping the relationship between calling her and being mentally handicapped.

"Two-day rule, faggot," Hicks filled the catcher in, holding the deuce up with his right hand.

"He's right," O'Dell opened the shitter door in the back, a few bunks deeper in the bus, and concurred.

"Shutup," Hicks snapped, pointing at the pitcher. "You're married. And close that fuckin' door! It smells awful."

A couple of the other players sitting in the back agreed. O'Dell followed suit, closing the restroom door.

"Muss vee niice... to vunn de phole teem." The words, apparently 'must be nice to run the whole team,' came from Seavers. They left his mouth muffled by his head being face down on his pillow. He was lying stretched out in his bunk, just now waking up and including himself in on the discussion.

Hicks ignored Salmon's comments and sat on the edge of Bobby's bunk. "Put your bunk up, laddie, so we can have man-to-man talk."

Hartes laughed in his own bed. The catcher followed Hicks' order, and the two of them sat there going over the game plan that would get Bobby laid—that would get Ashley, the sunbather, to come up and watch a Demons game.

Hicks advised his young apprentice all the way to the Marriott Tucson "University Park" Hotel, by the Arizona Wildcats campus. Skip, in a surprising, yet good-spirited move, kicked open the door separating the front of the bus from the back. He said, "You ladies need to hurry up and get your shit in your rooms so we can get to the field and get in some early B.P."

No one said anything. Hicks waved Skip farewell, acting as their leader and signaling that everything was under control and that the back of the bus would be ready.

It didn't take the players long, once they got their key cards from Larry George. Will and Jeff tossed their luggage in the room, changed out of their bus clothes and entered their practice gear, Demon tee, Demon shorts.

The bus was off again, headed to East 22nd Street and Sun Ray Park—

III

Back home, in Los Angeles, Shae was working back-to-back late nights in the law office. There were several other employees trying to catch up on deadlines as well, so Shae didn't want to try and find the game on the radio, afraid that the noise might disturb someone.

Instead, following the same procedure as the last time she couldn't make a Demons' game, she put the broadcast on the Internet, letting Gina and Gabby Viselli feed her the story lines from each night.

She would browse through her paperwork, and then, every so often, glance at the computer screen to see any updates made to the Demons' broadcast page. This is how Shae Kent kept up with her favorite baseball team for two straight nights – the first two games against the Tucson Sun Devils.

The games unfolded...

1999 Los Angeles Demon Baseball
Los Angeles (14-9) versus Tucson (7-17)
May 12, 1999 at Tucson, Arizona (Sun Ray Park)

Los Angeles starters: cf Lewis; ss Coleman; 3b Hicks; 1b Gunn; lf Rutherford; 2b Hartes; rf Chambers; c Fetters; p Perry;

Tucson starters: ss Bonham; 1b Pudd; lf Maldonado; rf Vargas, Jr.; cf Greggs; 2b Carter; 3b Rozier; c Talley; p Benes;

Los Angeles 1st – Lewis lined out to center (2-1). Coleman flied out to right (0-1). Hicks flied out to deep center (0-0). *0 LOB.*

Tucson 1st – Bonham doubled to left-center (1-0). Pudd struck out, failed sacrifice (1-2). Maldonado struck out looking (1-2). Vargas, Jr. grounded out to second base (2-2). *1 LOB.*

Los Angeles 2nd – Gunn flied out to center (0-0). Rutherford struck out swinging (1-2). Hartes fouled out to first base side (2-2). *0 LOB.*

Tucson 2nd – Greggs grounded out to third (1-1). Carter fouled out to first base side (1-2). Rozier flied out to center (1-1). *0 LOB.*

Los Angeles 3rd – Chambers flied out center (0-0). Fetters grounded out to second (3-2). Perry singled to right (2-2). Lewis grounded out to shortstop (1-1). *0 LOB.*

Tucson 3rd – Talley flied out to left (1-1). Benes flied out to shallow right (0-1). Bonham infield single (2-0). Bonham thrown out stealing by Fetters (1-0). *0 LOB.*

Los Angeles 4th – Coleman struck out looking (3-2). Hicks singled to left (0-0). Gunn flied out to deep center (2-0). Rutherford grounded out to third (2-2). *0 LOB.*

Tucson 4th – Pudd reaches on Hicks throwing error at third (2-0). Maldonado flied out to shallow left (1-2). Vargas, Jr. flied out to left (2-2). Greggs grounded out to first (1-1). *0 LOB.*

Los Angeles 5th – Hartes flied out to right (2-2). Chambers flied out to center (1-0). Fetters flied out to center (1-1). *0 LOB.*

Tucson 5th – Carter homered to left (2-0). *Sun Devils 1, Demons 0.* Rozier singled to left (2-0). Talley tripled down rightfield line, scoring Rozier (1-1). *Sun Devils 2, Demons 0.* Benes grounded out to third, runner stayed (1-2). Bonham singled to center, scoring Talley (1-1). *Sun Devils 3, Demons 0.* Pudd flied out to left (1-1). Bonham stole second on second pitch. Maldonado struck out swinging (1-2). *1 LOB.*

Los Angeles 6th – *Goodwin enters the game to pinch hit for Perry, and will play rightfield for Chambers.* Goodwin grounded out to second (1-1). Lewis struck out looking (1-2). Coleman grounded out to short (0-0). *0 LOB.*

Tucson 6th – *Sanders enters the game to pitch for Los Angeles.* Vargas, Jr. walked on five pitches (3-1). Greggs flied out center (3-1). Carter doubled to left, Vargas, Jr.

scores (2-1). *Sun Devils 4, Demons 0.* Rozier grounded out to third (1-1). Talley grounded out to short (0-0). *1 LOB.*

Los Angeles 7th – Hicks tripled off centerfield wall (1-0). Gunn flied out right, runner stayed (1-1). Rutherford singled to left, Hicks scored (0-0). *Sun Devils 4, Demons 1.* Hartes walked on five pitches (3-1). Sanders struck out bunting (2-2). Fetters grounded out to first (1-1). *2 LOB.*

Tucson 7th – *Valdez enters the game to pinch hit for Benes.* Valdez flied out to shallow center (1-1). Bonham grounded out to third (2-2). Pudd struck out swinging (2-2). *0 LOB.*

Los Angeles 8th – *Gonzalez enters the game to pitch for Tucson.* Goodwin singled to right (2-2). Goodwin stole second on first pitch. Lewis homered down leftfield line, scoring Goodwin (3-2). *Sun Devils 4, Demons 3. W. Hughes enters the game to pitch for Tucson.* Coleman doubled to right-center (1-0). Hicks grounded out to short (1-1). Gunn reached first on infield error by Bonham, Coleman moved to third (2-2). Rutherford struck out swinging (1-2). Hartes struck out swinging (2-2). *2 LOB.*

Tucson 8th – Maldonado flied out to right (1-1). Vargas, Jr. doubled to right (2-0). Greggs doubled to center, scoring Vargas, Jr. (2-0). *Sun Devils 5, Demons 3. Jimenez enters the game to pitch for Los Angeles.* Carter flied out to left (1-2). Rozier struck out looking (1-2). *1 LOB.*

Los Angeles 9th – *Valentin enters the game to pitch for Tucson. D. Luthers enters the game to pinch hit for Jimenez.* D. Luther walked on seven pitches (3-2). Fetters grounded into double play (1-1). Goodwin flied out to center (2-2). *0 LOB.*

Game over—Sun Devils 5, Demons 3...

<u>Score by Innings</u>
Los Angeles..........0 0 0 0 0 0 1 2 0 – 3 7 1
Tucson................0 0 0 0 3 1 0 1 x – 5 9 1

1999 Los Angeles Demon Baseball
Los Angeles (14-10) versus Tucson (8-17)
May 13, 1999 at Tucson, Arizona (Sun Ray Park)

Los Angeles starters: cf Lewis; ss Coleman; 3b Hicks; 1b Gunn; lf Rutherford; rf Goodwin; c Parks; 2b S. Luthers; p Williams;

Tucson starters: ss Bonham; 2b Carter; lf Maldonado; rf Vargas, Jr.; cf Greggs; 3b Rozier; 1b Bueller; c Talley; p Wilton;

Los Angeles 1st – Lewis grounded out to third (1-1). Coleman flied out to left (1-0). Hicks struck out looking (1-2). *0 LOB.*

Tucson 1st – Bonham infield singled to short (1-1). Bonham thrown out at second by Parks (1-0). Carter doubled to left (2-0). Maldonado doubled to left-center, scoring Carter (2-1). *Sun Devils 1, Demons 0.* Vargas, Jr. flied out to center (2-2). Greggs struck out swinging (1-2). *1 LOB.*

Los Angeles 2nd – Gunn fouled out to first base side (3-2). Rutherford singled through left side (1-1). Goodwin homered to right, scoring Rutherford (3-1). *Demons 2, Sun Devils 1.* Parks walked on four pitches (3-0). S. Luthers hit into double play (1-1). *1 LOB.*

Tucson 2nd – Rozier struck out looking (0-2). Bueller tripled to right (1-1). Talley sacrificed flied to center, scoring Bueller (2-2). *Sun Devils 2, Demons 2.* Wilton struck out swinging (1-2). *0 LOB.*

Los Angeles 3rd – Williams flied out to shallow center (1-1). Lewis grounded out to second (2-2). Coleman walked on five pitches (3-1). Hicks homered to center, scoring Coleman (2-0). *Demons 4, Sun Devils 2.* Gunn struck out looking (1-2). *0 LOB.*

Tucson 3rd – Bonham bunted for a hit (0-0). Carter hit into double play (0-2). Maldonado tripled to right (1-1). Vargas, Jr. homered to right, scoring Maldonado (3-1). *Sun Devils 4, Demons 4.* Greggs struck out looking (0-2). *0 LOB.*

Los Angeles 4th – Rutherford walked on six pitches (3-1). Goodwin grounded out to third, force at second (2-2). Parks flied out to left (1-0). S. Luthers homered to left, scoring Goodwin (3-2). *Demons 6, Sun Devils 4.* Williams singled through right side (1-2). Lewis homered to left, scoring Williams (1-0). *Demons 8, Sun Devils 4.* Coleman flied out to deep left (2-2). *0 LOB.*

Tucson 4th – Rozier grounded out to short (1-1). Bueller struck out swinging (1-2). Talley flied out to center (2-1). *0 LOB.*

Los Angeles 5th – *S. Hughes enters the game to pitch for Tucson.* Hicks homered to center (1-1). *Demons 9, Sun Devils 4.* Gunn flied out to center (1-0). Rutherford struck out swinging (1-2). Goodwin walked on eight pitches (3-2). Parks grounded out to short (2-2). *1 LOB.*

Tucson 5th – S. Hughes reached on S. Luthers error (1-1). Bonham infield singled, runner moved (2-2). Carter homered to left, scoring S. Hughes and Bonham (3-1). *Demons 9, Sun Devils 7.* Maldonado struck out swinging (1-1). Vargas, Jr. flied out to left (3-2). Greggs grounded out to short (0-0). *0 LOB.*

Los Angeles 6th – Luthers flied out to center (1-0). *Hartes enters the game to pinch hit for Williams.* Hartes doubled to right-center (2-0). Lewis singled up the middle, first and third (2-2). Coleman sacrifice flied out to left, scoring Hartes (3-1). *Demons 10, Sun Devils 7.* Hicks lined out to third (2-2). *1 LOB.*

Tucson 6th – *Sanders enters the game to pitch for Los Angeles.* Rozier popped out to short (1-1). Bueller flied out to shallow left (1-1). Talley doubled to left (3-1). S. Hughes struck out swinging (0-2).

Los Angeles 7th – Gunn homered to left (1-0). *Demons 11, Sun Devils 7. W. Hughes enters the game to pitch for Tucson.* Rutherford grounded out to third (1-1). Goodwin singled to center (0-0). Goodwin stole second on first pitch. Parks grounded out to short (1-1). S. Luthers grounded out second (2-2). *1 LOB.*

Tucson 7th – Bonham lined out to first (1-2). Carter popped out to second (2-2). Maldonado grounded out to short (1-0). *1 LOB.*

Los Angeles 8th – Sanders singled to right (2-2). Lewis sacrificed bunted, Sanders to second (1-0). Coleman struck out swinging (1-2). Hicks struck out swinging (2-2). *1 LOB.*

Tucson 8th – Vargas, Jr. flied out to center (2-1). Greggs grounded out to short (2-2). Rozier reached on error by S. Luthers at second (2-2). Bueller doubled to left-center, scoring Rozier (2-1). *Demons 11, Sun Devils 8.* Talley doubled to left, scoring Bueller (1-0). *Demons 11, Sun*

Devils 9. Seavers enters the game to pitch for Los Angeles. W. Hughes struck out swinging (0-2). *1 LOB.*

Los Angeles 9th – Gunn lined out to third (1-0). Rutherford grounded out to short (1-1). Goodwin walked on five pitches (3-1). Parks flied out to left (2-2). *1 LOB.*

Tucson 9th – Bonham grounded out to third (0-2). Carter walked on six pitches (3-2). Maldonado homered to left, scoring Carter (2-2). *Sun Devils 11, Demons 11.* Vargas, Jr. flied out to center (1-1). Greggs struck out swinging (0-2). *0 LOB.*

Los Angeles 10th – S. Luthers flied out to shallow center (1-2). *Chambers enters the game to pinch hit for Seavers.* Chambers struck out looking (1-2). Lewis singled to right (2-2). Lewis stole second on third pitch. Coleman struck out looking (2-2). *1 LOB.*

Tucson 10th – *O'Dell enters the game to pitch for Los Angeles.* Rozier struck out swinging (1-2). Bueller flied out to left (0-2). Talley flied out to right (1-1). *0 LOB.*

Los Angeles 11th – Hicks lined out to first (1-1). Gunn grounded out to second (2-2). Rutherford singled to left (2-1). Goodwin tripled to right, scoring Rutherford (3-2). *Demons 12, Sun Devils 11.* Parks flied out to right (1-0). *1 LOB.*

Tucson 11th – *Jimenez enters the game to pitch for Los Angeles. Pudd enters the game to pinch hit for W. Hughes.* Pudd flied out to center (1-1). Bonham flied out to right (1-1). Carter walked on six pitches (3-2). Maldonado flied out to center (1-0). *1 LOB.*

Game over — Demons 12, Sun Devils 11…

<u>Score by Innings</u>
Los Angeles..........0 2 2 4 1 1 1 0 0 0 1 – 12 15 2
Tucson................1 1 2 0 3 0 0 2 2 0 0 – 11 13 0

IV

"Hello sportsfans, this is Darrell "The Duke" Marinville here to bring you some more Demon baseball," The Duke opened, ready to call the rubber game between Los Angeles and Tucson. "If you weren't able to listen last night, you missed one heck of a game. Lots of action... lots of homers... and lots of runs. The Demons took an eleven-to-seven lead into the eighth, only to let it slip away when the Sun Devils scored two in the bottom of the eighth, and then two more in the bottom of the ninth off of Salmon Seavers. That was his first blown save of the season.

But then, in the top of the eleventh, Billy Goodwin stepped up with a two-out triple, driving in Erric Rutherford. This would be all the Demons needed, as Javier Jimenez came in and sealed the deal. Demons twelve, Sun Devils eleven. Jay O'Dell, one of L.A.'s starters, got the easy win (4-2) coming out of the pen and ailing a tired relief staff. Wally Hughes received the loss (0-4) while Jimenez picked up his second save of the year."

The Duke continued to announce the starting lineups and other pregame stats as the Sun Devils took the field. Hartes hopped to the top of the dugout steps, back down again, and then back up to the top ledge one last time, feeling a little livelier than usual. Perhaps it was because he had finally gotten a good night's rest. After the long, extra inning game the night before, Hartes wanted no part of the Arizona town. He stayed in and slept, mostly watching ESPN reruns of *Sportscenter.* Coleman didn't go out, either. But instead of sleeping in, Will went to the hotel weight room to do some lifting, and then ate breakfast. Hartes, along with the majority of the team, was busy sleeping.

"Lovely night, fellas," Gunn said, putting a hardball in his glove, and then setting his glove on top of the dugout — the crest furthest away from the grasping hands of the stands. Lewis headed to the on-deck circle along with Coleman. They were both swinging with the weighted donut, and Hicks stood halfway up the steps, "in the hole."

"Did you hear what 'E' said this morning?" Coleman asked Hicks, both getting loose just outside dugout.

"Nah, I must have been out," Hicks responded.

"I didn't catch all of it, I was sleepin' a little, too," Coleman started, stopping to spit in the short grass. "But a couple of the honkies—" Hicks already began to laugh, expecting something hilarious "—were arguing with Salmon on what movie to watch this morning, when Erric jumped up out of his bunk and shouted, 'How come all the white players always want to watch *8 Seconds* and all black players always want to watch *Friday*? Damn! Pick something else!'"

The two shared a good chuckle. Hicks shook his head, saying, "Pretty damn funny." Even Damon Lewis, who was headed for homeplate, couldn't keep back a smile.

It was gametime.

"Demons centerfielder, Damon Lewis, strides towards homeplate to get this game underway," Marinville relayed over the waves. "Game three... both teams trying to stay alive in the playoff race. The Demons need to win to stay in second, and ahead of the Arizona Scorpions. And the Sun Devils just need to win... period. Beating the Demons for a second time and taking the series would go a long way in their desperate playoff chase."

"Let's go now," the dugout chatter began. "Let's get somethin' started, D. Lewis."

Davey Helton, a tall, 6'7", lanky lefthander with loose

pants and a live arm was on the hill for the opposing team. His numbers, 1-2 with a 5.08 ERA, didn't truly reflect how good his stuff could be when he was on. He was a little wild, and a bit of a head case, this was his downfall — and the downfall of many great players that weren't in the Big's — but the upside remained.

"The first pitch underway... ball one. A fastball a few feet off the outside of the plate. Lewis is hitting three-fourteen with four homers, and also has nine stolen bases. Helton, slow but steady, winds and fires... ball two. Another fastball, another miss. Lewis crouches a little more in the box. He's going to force the lefty to throw a strike here. Helton comes home... strike one. Fastball right down the pipe. Two-one the count on Lewis. Helton shakes his catcher off, a little early for that business if you were asking me, delivers." *Smack.* "Line drive to centerfield, Kenny Greggs charging and *sliding* to make the catch coming forward. A nice play for the Tucson defense to start the game. One away, tough break for Damon Lewis. Robbed of a lead-off single."

Greggs lobbed the ball to the shortstop, padded down his slightly dirty pants, and then returned to center. The burly centerfielder might remind a baseball fan of Wily Mo Pena playing the outfield. Rare, with plenty of speed to go along with a huge frame.

Will Coleman stepped in. And for the second time tonight, Helton fell behind in the count. Coleman then drilled a three-one fastball to right-center, the ball rolling all the way to the wall. He would stand up at second with a one-out double, bringing up Jason Hicks.

"Hicks has started to pick up where he left off last season," The Duke announced. "He collected two hits two nights ago, and then hit two homers last night. His average is up to three-fifty on the season, and he now has ten homeruns. This will be the third season in a row that Hicks has reached the double-digit plateau; fans might be searching for his name on a major league roster sheet next year."

Hicks copied Coleman's at bat. Except, his double hit the middle of the wall in left-center as he turned on the wild Helton. And the first run, one for the good guys, crossed home. Steve "Big Daddy" Gunn, who had been in a slump of late, couldn't break out of it as he grounded out to third, causing Hicks to stay put on second. Rutherford then flied out to left, ending the top-half of the first and leaving Hicks stranded.

Michael Tims, 3-1 with a 3.93 ERA, was on the mound for the Demons. The young, hard-throwing righty had been the most consistent starter all year. His only problem, besides an occasional walk, had been giving up some untimely homers.

Tims first faced Joey Bonham, the speedy shortstop, who continued his hitting streak with a line-drive triple that just went over a shallow-playing Lewis' head. Bonham has had three hits in each of the first two games against L.A., and he was now batting three-sixty.

"Fuck me," Lewis said disgustingly. He shook his head at Rutherford, not believing he let Bonham, zero homeruns in his career, drive one over his head.

"Shake it off, nigga'," Rutherford said from leftfield. "You played 'em in da' right spot. Lucky fucka' just laced one. Tims'll be aight."

Howie Talley, the catcher, grounded out to Coleman for the first out, but Bonham scored to tie the game at one. Tony Maldonado, a pure hitter who was slumping like Gunn, singled on a bad oh-two pitch from Tims. The early trouble continued as Anthony Vargas, Jr. doubled. Lewis had trouble picking up the ball out of a damp warning track, and couldn't get it in quick enough to stop Maldonado from scoring and giving the Sun Devils the lead.

The excitement in this series had been endless, and the run scoring seemed to be on pace again. Tims, now a little rattled, walked Mike Carter on five pitches. There were runners on first and second for centerfielder, Ken Greggs. Tims finally helped his cause as Greggs hit a hard grounder to Coleman, who flipped it to Hartes, and then back to first for the six-four-three, inning-ending double play.

Standing outside the batter's box, Hartes adjusted his helmet several times. He tapped his cleats with his bat, stepping in the chalked rectangle with his right hand holding "time." He situated his feet, digging in just enough until perfectly comfortable.

"Hartes leads off the second for Los Angeles," The Duke announced. "He's batting two-ninety nine with two homeruns. Helton, who got out of the first allowing only one run, delivers the first pitch... ball one. One-an'-oh on Hartes."

Hartes bounced his bat on his right shoulder. The second pitch was underway... and it was ball two. Hartes momentarily stepped out of the box, refastening his gloves — a la Nomar — and then got ready for the third pitch.

C'mon you fucker... you've got to get that fastball over now... bring it, bring it, bring it...

"The pitch from Helton." *Crack!* "That ball's driven to deep leftfield... way back... way... It's Gone!" The Duke joyfully exclaimed. "A solo shot for the rookie at second base, tying the game!"

Hartes took his turn around first base, firmly slapping his gloved hands together. "Thatta' baby," he said under his breath. He touched them all and was greeted at home with a forearm bump from Goodwin. Fetters patted Hartes on the helmet as the second baseman made his way back into the dugout.

Giving dibs and receiving praise, Hartes said, "Fucker's fastball's not so good when you sit on that shit two-oh! Keep trying to come in, meat!" The last comment, dropping the "meat" bomb, was shouted back out onto the field, drawing a stare from Helton on the mound and Pudd at first base.

"Woah! Just keep your head in the game, Long, Tall Sally!" Seavers yelled from the other end of the dugout, picking up his teammate.

Helton turned away from the Demons' dugout and muttered something no one could understand. Either way, it was now two-to-two, courtesy of Hartes' third four-bagger of the season.

Billy Goodwin followed, flying out to center for the first out. Fetters then stepped in, pulled one down the rightfield line, but got robbed on a nice play by Vargas, Jr. near the foul wall separating the playing field from the crowd. Tims then singled, showing the fans he still had a little "bat" to go along with his live arm. The top of the order was back up with two outs, but the inning went no further. Lewis struck out on seven pitches after fouling two back into the stands, leaving Tims on the pond.

Lawrence Rozier led off the bottom of the second with a fly out to shallow center. Mills Pudd, hitting .278 with 3 homeruns, walked on five pitches. He tried to steal second, apparently missing a sign from the third base coach as it looked like he thought the pitcher, Helton, would be bunting. A bunt and run, perhaps? Something was wrong, and Pudd paid the price, getting hosed out by Fetters. Helton struck out to end the second.

Coleman grounded out to first on an attempted check swing to start the third. Jason Hicks, hotter than two mice screwing in a woolen sock, hit his eleventh blast of the year, a rocket shot to right-center that landed out on a passing street in downtown Tucson. The Demons now had the lead, three-to-two. Gunn walked next as Helton was still disturbed over giving up his second deep ball of the game. The tall lefty battled back, though, striking out Rutherford and then getting Hartes to pop up to short, ending another one-run inning for the visitors.

Bonham lined out to right, trying to take the ball the other way. The catcher, Talley, then struck out on three blazing fastballs from Tims. Third in the inning, and trying to get a two-out rally started, was Maldonado. He singled in the first and came around to score on a Vargas, Jr. double. But nothing this time around; he popped up to Coleman to end the third, one-two-three.

Goodwin, opening the fourth inning, grounded out to second. Fetters flied out to Vargas, Jr. in right for the second time. And to end the inning, Tims popped out to shallow right. Three up, three down for Helton.

Anthony Vargas, Jr. tied the game to lead off the bottom of the inning, hitting a low-laser down the leftfield line that barely cleared the fence. It was his tenth homer of the year. Carter and Greggs both struck out behind the Sun Devils' slugger. Rozier ended the inning, flying out to Lewis.

Lewis flied out to Maldonado in left for the first Demons out. Coleman followed with a line out to Bonham. Hicks, two-for-two with a double and a homer, then grounded out to third. It was the eighth straight batter retired by Helton.

Pudd singled up the middle for Tucson. He was then successfully bunted over by Helton, not confusing the signs this time. With a runner on second and one out, Bonham flied out to center, not deep enough to advance

Pudd. Talley followed, walking. And then Maldonado struck out swinging with two runners on; Tims keeping the game locked at three.

Gunn, showing signs of fatigue and sore knees, proved the doubters wrong with a hard hit double to start off the sixth. Rutherford grounded out to second — a productive out, moving Gunn — for the first out. Jeff Hartes up to bat, one-for-two with a solo shot.

Alright, you fucker... you crossed me up last time with a first pitch slider... but not this time... bring it...

"Ball one," The Duke relayed to the Demon faithful. He was pumped, hoping Hartes could do whatever it took to get Gunn, not the fastest runner, home from third.

Slider again? Hmm... bring that weak ass fastball you bitch... bring it, bring it, bring...

"Helton checks Gunn at third, fires." *Smack!* "Hartes drives one to left-center with plenty height! Greggs and Maldonado chase... It's Outta' HERE!" The Duke called, wanting to say 'chasing', but not quite getting it all out. "The second homerun of the night for Jeff Hartes, a two-run shot taking the lead! That's the second baseman's first multi-homer game of his short career."

"C'mon wit' it!" Hartes shouted, stomping on home, giving Goodwin the forearm shiver for the second time. If he was at Demon Stadium, he might have received a curtain call, but not here in Sun Ray Park. Instead, he listened to the fans boo Helton as he was jerked from the game.

The numbers on Helton, besides throwing two solid innings, weren't good. He threw 5 1/3 innings, struck out two, walked one, and allowed five earned runs. Coming in to relieve was Danny Gonzalez, 0-1 with a 5.73 ERA.

Goodwin flied out to center and Fetters struck out looking, ending the top of the sixth. Los Angeles Demons

5, Tucson Sun Devils 3.

Vargas, Jr. led off for Tucson, flying out to left-center. Carter followed, lining out to center on a ball that Lewis probably only had to move a couple of steps on. Greggs singled on a two-strike curve that Tims hung over the plate. Rozier then hit an infield chopper that bounced over Tims' head, and neither Coleman nor Hartes had a play anywhere. Two on, two outs; Tims dug deep. Pudd, with a single on the night, couldn't rally the Sun Devils. He grounded out to Coleman, who took the matters into his own, stepping on the bag at second for the final out.

Parks pinch hit for Tims, closing the books on the Los Angeles starter. Tims' line was six innings pitched, with five K's and two walks, allowing three earned runs.

The backup catcher lined a shot right over a leaping Rozier's head at third, leading off the seventh with a single. Lewis, without any sign from Bailey, laid down a perfect sac bunt, moving Parks to second. It was always nice when someone played team baseball, not worrying about their stats, without being instructed to do so. Coleman grounded out to second, but moved Parks one bag away from his wishful destination. Hicks, still swinging that hot lumber, ripped his second double of the game, driving in his third run of the game. Gunn flied out to end the seventh.

"Now pitching for Los Angeles, the twenty-five-year-old lefthander, Darren Luthers," The Duke updated the listeners. "He started the year struggling, but has begun to throw a little better of late."

And throw better he did. Luthers struck out two (Tucson pinch hitter Marcus Bueller and then leadoff man Joey Bonham), and subsequently ended the quick inning getting Talley to pop out to Fetters. Six-to-three after seven, in favor of the visiting club.

Wally Hughes entered the game for Tucson, 0-4 on the season. He walked Rutherford. But then got a break as Hartes hit a hard liner right at the second basemen, Carter, who then snapped the ball back to first, doubling up Rutherford. Goodwin's sour night finished with a backwards 'K.'

Luthers pitched another scoreless inning. He walked Maldonado, and gave up a singled to Carter after getting Vargas, Jr. to fly out, but other than that, no threat from Tucson.

Los Angeles couldn't add to their three-run lead in the last inning, getting only a leadoff single from Fetters, but then nothing more.

Salmon Seavers sprinted out to the mound from the outfield bullpen, showcasing a 2.13 ERA and 8 saves. He would have the chance to take the league lead in saves with one on this night. To accomplish this, he'd have to go through Pudd, Enrique Valdez, pinch hitting for the pitcher, and then Bonham.

Seavers struck out Pudd on four pitches, giving a fist pump on the mound. The Demons' closer was obviously a little more fired up than usual, most of it being that he was still tasting that bitter blown save from the night before. He wasn't about to let it happen again. He dug in deep, grinding his spikes into the front of the rubber.

The youngster, Valdez, just signed within a week, grounded out to Hartes for the second out of the inning. Last hope… a streaking Joey Bonham. But Seavers got Bonham, at least, he thought he did. The Sun Devil centerfielder flied out to right, but Goodwin had trouble with it, losing it in the lights as the ball bounced off the outer part of his glove. A little hope for Tucson, maybe?

That ended quickly as Talley broke his bat on the second pitch, hitting a weak ball back to Seavers on the hill. The pitcher scooped it up barehanded and hurled it to Gunn. Game over, Demons 6, Sun Devils 3.

Michael Tims went to 4-1 on the year while Davey Helton dropped to 1-3. Salmon Seavers picked up his 9th save, and Jeff Hartes hit his 3rd and 4th homeruns of the season; his first career multi-homer game.

V

"Ohh-right," Perry said, smashing a can of Bud Light on the wooden arm rest beside him. "What's on the Dee-El for tonight?"

"A little dick action, if ya' want some," Parks responded, standing in the Demons' bus's aisle. The club had just left Tucson around thirty minutes before, happy to come out of there winning the series after losing the first game. The shy, soft-spoken catcher, Bobby Parks, with the special training of Jason Hicks, had now come full form in the back of the bus revelries.

"You're funny, rookie," Perry said. "Now get me a goddamn beer. Seriously... we playin' some cards or just boozin'?"

"Man... T.P., hold on, bra, hold on," Seavers interrupted, motioning with his left hand — open palmed — for Perry to 'take it easy.' "Must be nice to be ready to pah-tee b'fore we even get outta' tha' city!"

Hartes, momentarily resting in his bunk, snickered. Hicks tapped the second baseman on the shoulder, saying, "Put your bed up, bitch... so I can sit down."

Hartes rubbed his eyes and then rolled out into the aisle. The two of them raised the unfolded bunk and tucked it back into the bus's wall. "Give me a beer," Hartes shouted at O'Dell, who was guarding the ice chest. The pitcher stood up, lifted the lid, and asked:

"Bud Light, Coors Light, or Nati' Light?"

"Coors," Hartes answered. O'Dell fired it; Hartes snagged it out of the air with his right hand.

"Nice snatch," Hicks said, laughing. "Hey Jay, buy me beer, too."

"You son of a bitch," O'Dell said as he sat back down on the closed ice chest. "You could have told me before I closed it, asshole!"

"Yeah, yeah. Just give me a damn Bud Light," Hicks requested.

"Where's Gunn?" Perry asked, rejoining the conversation he initiated earlier. Currently, the back of the bus contained Hartes, Hicks, Seavers, O'Dell, Parks, Coleman, who was reading *Sports Illustrated* in his bunk, Fetters, who was killing beers like water, and Perry himself.

"I don't know," Fetters finally joined in. "But there must be one hell of a movie or something going on in front. This fucker's light in the back."

"Scared to hang with the big boys," Parks said, grabbing his package with one hand and scratching his nose with the other.

VI

Another hour of the ride passed. The beers were going down in a fury. The back of the bus remained intact, only adding another regular, Rutherford, to the excitement. No cards as of yet. Just swapping stories and killing time.

"How many have you had already, Bobby-O?" O'Dell

asked, tossing him another from the beer well he so diligently protected.

"Like... eight... I think," Parks said.

"Holy shit," 'E' observed. "That's too many for a rook."

Amazingly, Parks didn't think so, shaking his head. But if you watched him rise from his seat and try to walk down the aisle to the bathroom to leak, with an unsteady bus, you might not agree with the catcher's reasoning. Rutherford was just about to comment on Parks' swaying when the door separating the front of the bus to the back swung open.

"Well... I be damned!" Perry said from the cooler.

"No way!" Rutherford added with surprised disbelief.

The rest of the crew turned their heads; most of them already thought the opening of the door was just Gunn finally coming to his real home. But they were wrong. The man smoothly strolling down the bus aisle, without showing any signs that the high-passenger vehicle was moving, was none other than Lake Williams himself—proclaimed ace of the Demons' staff.

"How's it goin' back here, fellas?" Lake asked, smiling from ear to ear because he knew what was coming next.

Hicks jumped up and almost hit his head on the top of Hartes' bunk. He stood in the aisle in front of Lake, right between Perry and the beer. "Bout time you made your one and only trip to the back of the bus with the big boys."

"Yeah... well... I figured now was as good as any to keep the mo' in our favor. Plus, I don't have my next start 'til the eighteenth against Washington." Lake paused. "Say, it's pretty quiet back here, though. I figured a couple of you would already be butt-naked, starting with the foreplay first."

"We've been waiting on you," Coleman joined in the

conversation, rising up from his magazine and sitting upright. Before Williams could counter, Gunn had his arm around the pitcher's neck from behind. It might be the only time, and the last time, that the burly infielder ever snuck up on anyone. But everyone was still in a bewildered state, not sure if their eyes were playing tricks on them or not. Lake Williams in the back of the bus with the "wild bunch" was quite a shock.

Gunn pulled the starting pitcher down into one of the bunks, partially rolling on top of him. "Get your fat ass off of me," Lake hollered, everyone laughing.

The two of them sat nearest the dividing door; Lake appearing to make sure he was close to an exit for a quick escape if necessary.

"Beer?" Perry asked, standing up and raising the ice chest's lid.

"Thought you homos would never ask," Lake said, holding out his hand.

"What kind?" Perry asked, pulling out the Bud Light and Coors Light only, knowing Lake's "high class" ass wouldn't dare touch a Natural.

"Bud's good."

The card games initiated — with a shot of new blood for a change as Lake took a shot at his luck. He played for a few hours and then headed back to the front where he belonged, searching for some needed sleep. He was commemorated for his journey into the unknown by everyone who was still awake or hadn't yet passed out. He felt like a war hero returning home, passing through the masses of supporting crowds honoring his bravery. He was a little buzzed, but sober enough to hide it in the front and maintain his business-only manner for the others to see. Hell, they wouldn't want to see that their hero had gotten a chink in the armor. Even if it was only once a season.

VII

L.A. vs. Cal, May 15th, 1999.

In the dugout, some between-inning chatter broke the silence. "So much for Lake's keeping the fuckin' momentum. This is brutal... just brutal," Hicks said, leaning slightly forward and peering down the row of teammates.

"Yeah... I'm freaking tired," Rutherford acknowledged, "Lake kept me up past my bedtime."

The veteran utility player, Brett Chambers, let out a rare chuckle. Some of the other players were laughing as well.

"Got a laugh out of that guy," Coleman said, pointing at Chambers. Will then stood up and yelled, "Let's go Billy, get something started now!"

He clapped his hands together, drawing comical looks from most of the dugout, especially Gunn. "What?" Coleman asked, a smirk on his face.

"Nice, very nice," Hicks said, most likely expressing in words exactly what Big Daddy was thinking. Coleman sat back down on the pine, watching Goodwin strike out.

"Shee-it," the shortstop said, seeing the third out, and not wanting to get right back up and jog to his position.

"Somebody play third for me," Hicks said, shaking his head with an amusing facial expression, but in disgust.

The Demon players lackadaisically made their way onto the field for the top of the fifth. Skip might have yelled something motivational, but he had already been tossed from this one. Filling in, and sitting with arms folded and legs crossed, Larry George remained silent.

The score was Gold Miners thirteen, Demons nothing. It's baseball. It was simply one of those days. Better to smile about it and not let it eat at you rather than get down and let it affect your play for the rest of the season. If things stayed the way they were, it would still only be one down in the loss column. Whether it was a defeat by twenty runs or by one run, it counted the same in the standings. Baseball players understand this. They know and live by the code—one day, one game... at a time.

That same code applied to Skip Bailey. And for those reasons—one, not wanting to get so pissed to where it might result in saying or doing something damaging to the team or players; and two, not really wanting to watch any more of this garbage—Skip decided it was best to hit the showers. With the Demons already down by eight runs in the third, Skip watched Sanders walk in a run on a close ball four. He had had enough. The Demons' coach jogged out to homeplate, almost begging Ed Phelps, the head umpire, to toss him and toss him fast. Skip got what he wished for, receiving an immediate ejection after kicking some dirt and throwing around some amusing profanities.

The fans, following right along, cheered Skip's arguing and then booed the ump's ejection of him. Skip stormed through the dugout, still cussing and knocking over a Gatorade cooler. He went to his office and leaned back in his chair. He lit a cigarette and took one puff, not even putting the game on the radio. He outed the smoke, then simply leaned back and went to sleep.

The final score was sixteen-to-one. Not pretty at all, but nobody hurt. The Demons would find a way to bounce back tomorrow and pick up where they left their road trip off—the way they'd battled all season. The only real things of note for the Demons was their lonely run, a solo shot by Bobby Parks late in the game, and the pitching performance by position player Brett Chambers. The "Vet" stepped in and ailed a tired bullpen, throwing two full innings and only allowing one run.

Jay O'Dell, appearing fatigued because of his extra inning relief job two nights before, got the loss, dropping to 4-3. Julio Martin got the victory, improving to 3-1 on the year and lowering his ERA to 3.85. J.L. Conrad, the hottest hitter around, smacked his league-leading 14th homer.

VIII

It's amazing how quickly things can change. The twisted hands of fate reach down and encircle something so dear to you, choking it in its deadly grasp. And then to remember the times before things change. So bittersweet. You want to hold on to them and embrace them and touch them and never, ever forget them.

But it hurts. The pain can be so unbearable. Moving on is the hardest... the most defeating part of this wicked situation. True, you should *never* truly forget the things that haunt your mind or tear at your chest. You have to make peace with them and realize them for what they are, "missing memories."

They are like the dreams. They are there. They are real. They happen... because Jeff feels it in his soul. They are, as Shae sometimes referred to them, "missing memories." Deep inside the darkest crevice of the mind, of the brain, one knows these thoughts, searing as they may be, are still there—remaining. They remain with us for life. They will always be there as the sun will always rise.

The hard part—

Recollecting these "missing memories..." these bad

times, and speaking about them rather than allowing them to burn inside and boil. It is healthy to clear one's thoughts, to let it all out. It seems so much easier to just forget. Or at least to pretend to forget. But doing things the easy way isn't always what's best. Sometimes, you just have to suck it up and live for those bad memories, for those things that cause you sleepless nights.

Be strong, for the darkness lies ahead.

Chapter Thirteen
Will's Last Grounder

I

"The home crowd is on their feet. Two away, nobody on for the Gold Miners. Seavers appears to be having trouble with the signs. Parks calls for time, and jogs out to the mound. While the pitcher-catcher conversation continues, we'll check in with our station identification." The automated message that says this game was brought to you by so and so played, and then Marinville's voice rolled back on.

"We're back here with Demon baseball. Seavers from the stretch... ball one. The crowd is really into it tonight, making themselves heard all the way to downtown. Seavers delivers... strike one on Gardner. One-and-one the count. What a game this has been tonight? Los Angeles one out away from the 'W'. Seavers comes home." *Whack.* "Hard hit grounder to short. Coleman fields it cleanly and fires to first. Got 'em! Ballgame over! The Demons have upended Cal seven-to-four. Thomas Perry picks up his third win of the year, and Salmon Seavers gets his tenth save."

Marinville cycled through the rest of the game stats—Will Coleman finished with three hits and a three-run home. He then previewed the Demons' next game, a make-up with Washington on the 18th, after informing the listeners there wasn't a game the next day. He then finished his broadcast, "This is Darrell 'The Duke' Marinville signing off of another edition of Demon baseball. Goodnight all."

Hartes proceeded to the showers for his usual post game routine. Shae, who usually worked a few hours during the day on Sundays, had already asked for the day off since the Demons were also not playing baseball on that day. The inseparable couple had arranged an entire day together, and they were positive they would make the most of it.

Instead of undertaking the conventional itinerary after the game—which was to the *Hardball* and also becoming very redundant—Shae and Jeff elected to go to dinner with Will and Regina. The special occasion? I guess you could say, 'A celebration of friends.'

The four of them congregated at *Mia Piace*, a prestigious and cozy Italian restaurant in Burbank, featuring scrumptious delights with generous portions. The average cost of a meal per person was around $45.00, but the quartet wanted to commemorate a magnificent and growing friendship. They wanted to go all out.

They toasted and celebrated for nearly two hours, *Mia Piace* never tiring of their company. The height of the conversation came when Will and Regina said they had something special to announce, but they wanted to wait until the news was official. Shae and Jeff said they understood, but were secretly very curious to what it could be, and dying to hear.

After some final chitchat, the group departed the fancy restaurant. Will and Regina ended up at her apartment, turning off ahead of Jeff and company, and Shae and her man ended up at his place. The other two, positively, would perform the same exploits of zeal that Shae and Jeff were more or less about to perform on each other.

II

The lovers didn't screw that night. They made *love*. They both agreed to leave the rough sex until the day off. But that night, Mr. Hartes and Ms. Kent made passionate, fanatical, and avid *love*. And then instead of falling into a deep slumber afterward, they talked. About what? No one could tell you exactly, today. But at the time, it seemed most important. Consisting mostly of pillow talk and hearsay Jeff would have guessed. But how many times has Jeff Hartes stayed up and chatted following sex? Probably... never.

Shae and her man finally fell asleep around five in the morning. He awoke at eleven-thirty to another incredible breakfast-in-bed courtesy of Ms. Shae Kent. She walked in wearing one of his faded white t-shirts and a pair of hearted boxers, carrying a dish of food in one hand, a glass of orange juice in the other, and the *L.A. Times* folded under her arm.

"Why thank you so much dear," Jeff said, sitting up in bed, with nothing on but the sheets.

"What makes you think this is for you?" Shae inquired, not hiding her smile very well.

"Because you're the best," Jeff answered, right on cue. "Thank you, baby."

"That's right! And you're welcome, hun. Anything else I can get for you?" Shae asked.

"No baby, this is fine." She leaned down to his level, he kissed her lips gently, and then he kissed her cheek. And last but not least, Jeff nibbled on her ear whispering, "This is perfect Shae, I love you so much."

"Love you too, Jeff," she responded, fluttering her eyelashes and tossing her hair over her shoulders. "I'll be right back to join you in bed, I've gotta' go get mine."

Shae sprinted out the bedroom door and headed to the kitchen. Jeff grabbed a piece of bacon and chewed it until it passed down his throat. Then he used his fork to gather some scrambled eggs, which traveled down his esophagus as well.

He then flipped the newspaper opened to the Sports page. He opened to the Western League section and checked last night's scores and the current standings:

<u>Scores—May 16, 1999</u>

L.A. 7, Cal 4

W - Perry (3-4), L - MacKenzie (4-3)

S.D. 2, Arizona 1

W - Wilkes (7-0), L - Ridel (5-1)

Mont. 8, Wash. 4

W - Mann (6-1), L - Wolinsky (3-4)

<u>Scheduled Games—May 17, 1999</u>

Washington @ Montana, 7:05 p.m.

Tucson @ Carson City, 6:35 p.m.

WESTERN LEAGUE STANDINGS

NORTH	W	L	GB
Carson City Gamblers	15	12	0
Montana Tigers	15	13	1/2
Cal Gold Miners	14	15	2
Washington Thunder	10	17	5

SOUTH	W	L	GB
San Diego Knights	20	9	0
L.A. Demons	17	11	2 1/2
Arizona Scorpions	13	16	7
Tucson Sun Devils	8	19	11

Shae reappeared as Jeff was putting the paper on the nightstand. She hopped in bed, still being careful not to spill anything, and started in on her own breakfast—just scrambled eggs and toast, no bacon.

III

Will and Regina underwent analogous activities during their night together. But in place of breakfast-in-bed, they went out and ate at *George's*. Will had pancakes and sausage while Regina had a ham and cheese omelet. Reading the *Los Angeles Times*—with the Demons' victory on the backburner of the paper—Will felt Regina's feet between his legs.

He smiled, looking up from the paper. Regina smiled back, using her foot as a massaging apparatus. "We need to take this back home," Will said, slightly aroused.

"Alright, sugar," Regina said, halting the kinkiness and sliding out of the booth. "Gotta' go to the bathroom."

Will nodded and also got up. He paid the check at the register. And then the pair of lovers headed back to Regina's apartment for a quickie.

"That was niiice…" Regina said, putting a little twang on the last word, as she dressed for a day on the town. She motioned for Will to hurry up and get ready as well, and he followed her lead.

Regina said she wanted to take him shopping and buy him some new clothes. Will didn't oppose. Instead, he tried on one stylish set of attire after another. Before the shopping concluded, Regina had purchased three new dress shirts: one black with gray trim, one dark blue, and one white with a red and yellow Polo logo, two pairs of Khaki pants, and some shiny new black boots, Sketchers.

The shopping spree finally ended when Will stopped Regina from going into another clothes store and said, "Baby dis' is plenty 'nuff already. Thank you so much. But let's juss' go back to your place and get it on."

Regina grinned, and then said, "You're welcome, sugar. And that's a great idea." She took her man by the arm, marched him to the car, and they drove back to her apartment for an afternoon of pleasure and entertainment.

The last time... she would ever have sex with Will Coleman.

IV

Shae set her finished breakfast plate on the nightstand, crawled out of bed, and said, "Why don't you come help me wash dishes?" Jeff placed his dish on the floor, rolled over on his stomach, and buried his head into the pillows. "*Jeff!?* C'mon... please babe?" Shae asked with the sweetest, most sympathetic voice she could muster.

Jeff rotated his body until he was facing her, and she gave him one of those droopy eyes, sagging frown faces. The ones that little children use either to get something they want or right before they are going to cry. Jeff opened his mouth to say no, and then hesitated. The stupid look on her face was actually working; Mr. Macho was falling for it.

"Okay whatever," he said.

Shae wrapped her arms around his body, kissing his face all over. "You're such a sweetie, Jeff," Shae said, pulling him out of the bed with all of her strength. At first, she was supplying all the effort and drudgery, but then Jeff willed himself out of bed, and alleviated Shae's exertion. He transported his unclothed body to the dresser, catching a few glances from Shae's attracted eyes. Jeff slid on a pair of shorts and put on some low-cut socks.

"My feet are cold, hun," he said. Shae then situated the

dishes to where they were balancing on top of his folded arms and dragged Jeff into the kitchen.

"You know, I usually don't do dishes on my day off," he suggested. Shae glared at him with a pair of evil eyes that were as fallacious as they come. Then she giggled and said:

"You used to not get any ass on your day off, either!"

"Oh... *Is* that a fact?" Jeff responded, half-asking and half-agreeing.

"I believe it to be," she said, sticking out her tongue, and then ramming it downward into Jeff's throat. Initially, she did the kissing as he was caught off guard. But once the pro athlete grasped the situation, he quickly improvised, and the intense kissing contest began. He dropped the dishes sideways into the sink. They crashed with a bang, but didn't chip or break. The whole time, he kept his concentration on Shae and her supple lips.

Jeff yanked away from Shae's embrace, and while trying to catch his breath, managed to say, "Screw the dishes, finish them later."

He boosted Shae onto a small—yet large enough for this delicate job—cutting table and crawled up her body. His lips immediately reconnected with hers, and his hands started to roam about her body. As soon as she could feel his thin pair of shorts pressing against her, she tenderly laughed, and said:

"Uh-oh, Jeff's being a naughty boy."

"Sure am," he replied, squeezing her bare breasts under *his* shirt, which she was wearing. "You aren't being such a good girl yourself."

"I know," Shae said, ending the conversation. She snatched his shorts off and threw them across the room. Jeff removed her boxers—*his* boxers; another one of his items of clothing she delved in wearing—and sucked on her neck, his hands feeling the heat intensifying between her thighs.

V

"You were wonderful as always, Will," Regina said, lying with her head on her man's chest. Will ran his fingers across her face, to her lips, as she took them in her mouth and began running her tongue all over them.

"I'm always wonderful, girl. You know that," Will responded.

The time ticked by slowly as the couple rested in bed together, recuperating from the energy exerted earlier. Regina suggested that they should watch a movie together; Will acquiesced. Will and Regina watched what Will might have told the guys in the clubhouse to be a "chick flick." The two lovers fell asleep within the first thirty minutes of *Untamed Heart.*

They wouldn't awake until around eight o'clock that night, where Regina would say the last words she'd ever say to her man.

VI

Shae relaxed on the couch, watching *Friends'* reruns while Jeff finished up the dishes. He placed the last plate in the dish rack and grabbed a Coors Light out of the fridge. "Want something to drink Shae?" he asked her, still holding the refrigerator door ajar.

"No thanks, babe. But I could use some Ibuprofen or

Tylenol. My back still hurts from that damn table." Jeff chuckled at that comment, but not loud enough to where she could hear him.

"Okay," he said, still smiling—still thinking about screwing on the kitchen table. He made his way to the bathroom to get her some pain relievers. He opened the medicine cabinet, grabbed the first bottle he saw—Aleve—and went back into the living room. "This do?"

"Yeah, sexy, this is fine. Thanks." Shae held the bottle up close to her face, debated between taking two or three pills, and then she swallowed three down with Jeff's Coors Light. "That should do the trick."

Nothing like taking medicine with alcohol, Jeff thought. Jeff snickered to himself one last time, still amused over the fact that he had made a girl take some pain medicine after doing *it.* He took his seat on the sofa besides her, and they watched *Lost Love Found* on the Lifetime channel. In other words... a "chick flick."

VII

8:26 p.m.

Will woke up, rolled out of bed, and walked to the bathroom to relieve himself. When he returned to the bedroom, Regina was sitting up, rubbing her barely-awake eyes. Will inched his way under the covers, kissed his girl on the forehead, and said, "I'm not even sleepy anymore."

"Me neither," Regina responded. "And if you're not tired anymore, why don't you run to the store and pick up something for me?"

"Aight... I guess so," Will replied. He hopped up and slid on a pair of sweats.

"You're the best," Regina preached.

"I know girl... I know. What do you need, baby?"

Regina broke the news to Will for the first time, and then told him exactly what she needed. Will thought it was a good idea to find out now, but really wasn't worried. He loved Regina and had zero fears about his future with her.

"I'll be back in sec'," he exited the bedroom, Regina heard the front door close, and he jumped in Regina's red '98 Integra. Will reached down and released the parking brake, reversed out of the parking space, and was off in the direction of the nearest grocery store.

Once in the parking lot, Will reckoned he wouldn't be long, only needed to buy one item for Regina and maybe some chocolate candy for himself – a late night craving that might spark up the energy for another round. Will steered Regina's car into a vacant handicap spot. Actually, *all* the handicap lanes were open, so he just randomly picked one. Will opened the car door and started for the store, and then remembered he'd left his wallet behind.

He scampered back to the car, reached inside for his wallet, and then heard the sound of someone screaming. The shrieking cry rapidly increased. Now, instead of one voice shouting, it was a cacophony of angry voices filling an alley around the east side of the store. Will – being the good American he was raised to be – sprinted in the direction of the voices. Without thinking, without any hesitation, Will Coleman began running faster toward the cries.

When he veered around the corner, he saw first; a young black boy cringing in the middle of the alley and holding his head while he cried and screamed, and second; three older kids, two black, one white with a bandanna, kicking the boy in the ribs and head. As Will approached them, he overheard them hollering things at the boy like,

Stop crying muthafucka' and *If you don't shut up I'm going to kill you fool* and *Shoot that nigga'!*

Will, sensing real danger for the first time, shouted at the older kids. "Hey! Y'all punks leave that kid alone!" Instead of running at the sound of his voice like he thought they would, they kicked and battered the adolescent all the more. Will Coleman continued to close in on them. And when he was within fifteen feet, one of the black boys faced him and said:

"You want sum' of dis' too, fool? 'Cause we would sure be happy to fuck you up, too."

"Oh yeah, punk? Picking on the small boy, bunch of weak ass niggas to me," Will yelled back, the blood beginning to flow through his body like venom. He felt like a cobra, ready to strike. "Why don't you leave this boy alone and take a fuckin' walk?"

"Why don't you make us, old man?" the white boy with the rag bellowed, drawing an eerie, Satanic laughter from his companions.

"Aight, aight... you want to play like that," Will took his lightweight jacket off, dropped it to the ground and said, "Come get some then."

The youngest looking one charged first. Will gave him a left jab in the jaw that sent him wheeling backwards and collapsing on the concrete. Then the white boy came. He received a similar dose of medicine. He swung at Will and missed badly. The shortstop, after ducking his punch, grabbed him by the arm and swung him into a nearby garbage can. The sound of the boy exploding into the can, constructed of tin metal, echoed throughout the dark alley.

Will rotated his body to face the oldest of the bunch. He raised his arms, motioned for the boy to *come get some, too* with his hands, and then walked towards the last one standing. The punk didn't step towards Will, nor did he step back. He simply held his ground with one fist raised and the other hand hovering by his side. Will took one final quick step, lunged at the boy, and heard the sound of a gunshot fill the air.

Will's body began to fall downwards uncontrollably. He crashed solidly into the ground with a "thud." He turned his head in time to see the older three kids running out the opposite end of the alley, and the young boy chasing behind them, seriously doubting if he was after them. The next thing he experienced was pain. His side started throbbing, and the pain was almost unbearable. He tried to get up, but crumpled back to the hard, cold concrete. He wanted to shout out for help, or holler that he had been shot, but no words came from his mouth.

The warm blood flowed out of his body and onto the litter-filled sidewalk, forming a puddle on the ground. Will Coleman's eyes blurred, his head pounded, and he faded into a state of unconsciousness.

VIII

9:42 p.m.

Jeff had fallen asleep, to Shae's disappoint but not disbelief, about halfway through the movie. The distant sound of something ringing was what aroused him from the brief snooze.

"Are you going to answer that, sweetie, or do you want me to?" Shae asked, still glued to the Lifetime channel and the love story that was playing. He shook his head back and forth, stood up and stretched his back, and finally reached for the ringing phone.

"Hello," he said in a drowsy, clogged-up voice.

"Jeff? This Gina," she replied, rushing her words and skipping the *is* between this and Gina.

"Oh hey girl, what's up?"

"It's Will. He ran to pick up something for me at the store and has been gone for over an hour. He's in *my* car and has his keys, so I don't have a way of going to see where he is. I'm worried, Jeff." The sense of urgency in her voice was now apparent.

"Don't worry Regina. I'm sure everything's fine. Maybe he saw somebody he knew and was held up talking to 'em." Jeff made a funny, disgruntled face at Shae, now realizing he was going to have to get out of bed. Truly wishing he didn't have to, Jeff automatically said, "I'll drive down there and see if I can find 'em, though. If that's what you want."

"You will? Oh, thank you so much, Jeff. And tell him to hurry up and get his ass home when you see him," she said, trying to force out a laugh... trying to smile.

"No problem. I'll call and let you know something. Umm... what store did he go to again, Sherry's Twenty-Four Hour Groceries? The one he always goes to down a few blocks?"

"Yeah that's it. You know the place... thanks again. Bye Jeff."

"Bye," he said. Jeff told Shae where he was going and why; she said she would be right there waiting for him when he got back, and he seized the truck keys. Jeff hauled ass to *Sherry's*, feeling slightly frightened at this point. More and more horror stories entered his head as he sped to the store.

What if this happened? What if that happened? What if...

When Jeff turned into the parking lot, he didn't see any sign of Will talking to someone outside. Jeff circled up and down the one-way lanes and then spotted Regina's Integra. *What's that idiot still doing in the store?* he wondered as he found a place to park the F-150. Jeff locked his truck, trotted to the store, and entered through the automatic sliding doors.

He explored every aisle from the frozen foods section to the fruits and vegetables to the dairy products to the cosmetics. Nothing. No sign of Will Coleman anywhere in the store. Jeff even ventured in the bathroom to see if he was taking a monstrous dump. If the Demons' shortstop was still in this store, "I'd lick a dog's ass," Jeff mumbled.

He asked the workers in the express lanes if they'd seen his friend. After describing Will to them, none of the employees remembered him. Jeff said thanks for nothing, now really confused, and departed the store. *This had to be some sort of mistake, didn't it?*

He went to where Regina's car was parked, on the east side and in the handicap zone. This made him laugh inside, but the fear for Will's safety wasn't saying goodbye.

Jeff's eyes searched everywhere across the parking lot and storefronts around the twenty-four hour stop. They stopped on a dark alley between some long-standing buildings and the store itself. *No way he went in there. That place gives me the creeps.* But trembling or not, he was going to give it a shot. He walked to the edge of the alley, peered in, and saw nothing due to absolute darkness.

Jeff crept down the alley, keeping to one side. When he traveled halfway through the gloomy passage, he became aware of a low, gurgling sound. The same sound that is produced when your washing machine is running and some of the water bubbles up into the kitchen sink, supposing the water lines are connected. Except this noise was slightly lower... and scarier.

Jeff took another step and saw something. A shadowy

outline of a person lying on the sidewalk just behind a set of garbage cans. "Hey buddy, you alright?" he asked, shaking at the sound of his own voice repeating off the alley's walls.

No answer. Jeff moved towards the person...

Will! His mind roared.

No, it couldn't be!

He touched the figure curled half-in and half-out of the fetal position and rolled him over.

Oh fuck me, it is Will!

Jeff's head was racing.

Is he dead?

One of Will's eyes opened and the shortstop gagged, blood leaking from the side of his mouth. Jeff panicked, "Will? Will? What happened?"

Still no response. "I'm going to get help man, hang in there!" The fear had set in, striking Jeff like a blunt object. He started to get up and race down the tunnel for help, but Will's arm squeezed his. He lifted his head and looked into Jeff's face with a set of eyes that were outright haunting.

"D-Don't go-oh. I'm d-done... 'eff." He coughed up some more blood, and then laid his head on the concrete. Jeff tilted his face closer to Will's lips, removing Will's hands from his side to see the damage that had been done.

"You're going to be alright buddy," Jeff said, and then he saw the bullet wound in Will's upper stomach. Jeff wasn't sure the Demons' starting shortstop was going to be alright, after all.

"N-n-nah bro. T-t-tell Regi... Regi... na, that-that I love huh —" his coughing commenced. Then he finished. "Love her. And..." He sat up once again with all the strength and vigor he had left. "And you k-k-cuh-no what de' 'prise was?"

"Nah man, I don't," Jeff answered, feeling tears start to

stream down his cheeks. "Don't have a clue, dawg."

"G-Gina and I-I-I 'er gaged. En-en-gaged! An' I kuh-kuh-cameto the store-ore for a t-t-test. She-She's preg." Two more coughs, more blood. "Pregnant!" he said with one final thrust of energy. Then he collapsed limply back to the ground, eyes opened and gleaming into the moonless sky. A slight smile remained behind on his face. It appeared to be saying, 'Things were too good to be true.'

"No Will... you can't!" Jeff screamed, holding his best friend with all his might. "You can't die on me motherfucker! WILL... DAMMIT... WAKE THE FUCK UP! You can make it!" But Will's heart had already stopped beating, and his pulse was gone. Jeff leaned against the alley wall with his friend dead in his arms, crying and bawling the word *No* over and over again.

This has to be one of those dreams Shae is always telling me about. He assumed it to be true to ease the suffering, but inside Jeff knew this wasn't a dream.

Will Coleman, shortstop, was dead.

IX

Although Jeff knew his middle-infield counterpart and teammate wasn't magically coming back to life, he ran inside the grocery store and told the manager to call 911. Jeff explained the situation to the manager while the clerk tried to calm Jeff down. They waited for the paramedics to arrive.

Jeff lied to himself, believing there was still a chance Will could live. It was false, but the lie assisted in coping with the things that had just happened. His new friend, his best friend, was out of his life as quickly as he came into it.

And this fact burned inside his mind, and inside his heart. The ambulance arrived exceedingly swift. Jeff now knew it didn't matter, but he directed them to his friend nonetheless. They checked his pulse, shone a light in his eyes, and informed Jeff of what he already knew. He sobbed through the police officer's questions one by one, and told him he had to call or get back to his girl before she started to worry.

X

"The rest is just too hard to think about," the old man says aloud and alone, insisting on not going any further with this part of the remembering. *It was hard enough to tell Shae. And then we had to let Regina know. Shae and I made an effort to comfort and support Regina Johnson, but she couldn't handle any more of Los Angeles without Will Coleman. She, and the child growing inside of her, moved back to her mother's in Fresno, California and passed out of our lives forever.*

Jeff Hartes sits in silence without a thought in his head. He sheds one, lonely tear, lies down on the couch, and drifts off to sleep.

Just another good guy left behind in the dust...

The next morning, he awakes fresh with sticky, dried teardrops on his cheeks. The insomnia lets up for one segment; but if he doesn't finish remembering, it will surely return with a vengeance. His eyes are heavy, with darkened bags hanging under them. He takes his morning medicine and walks outside to get the newspaper. The air is chilly, stinging his bare feet as he steps along the rock path he built over eight years ago. He brings the *Louisville*

Courier-Journal inside to read, being one of the few remaining subscribers to the physical paper, everyone else receives their news electronically, but changes his mind. In place of more news of murder and crime, Jeff thinks he will turn back to his thoughts about 1999 once again, sooner rather than later.

But this time, he wants to fast forward his memory. Not because he can't distinctly remember every last bit that has happened, but because he truly doesn't want to remember. They are his own... "missing memories."

Chapter Fourteen
Large Shoes to Fill

I

I wasn't functioning like a human being.

The death of a friendship, the death of Will Coleman, meant the end of something special and the last of our turned double plays. I knew I would miss him like a brother. The only person I've ever missed more, despite knowing Will for just a short time, would be my wife, Shae.

I remember the days that followed the death, but try not to. The terrible games — the feeling of nothingness standing beside me at second base. I barely recall playing against Washington, and losing, on the 18th. The score was two-to-one, or something very close. I barely recall the days off before hosting a two-game series with the Montana Tigers, in which we also lost both games. Getting pounded on the 20th, 13-5, and then dropping a close one on the 21st, 3-2. And I barely recall the first time I met Nathan Willis, the new shortstop. It was after the second game against the Tigers and before a much needed day off.

It had to be hard for him. The whole team felt an undeserved hatred towards him, despite the person he might have been. Granted, we would grow with him, and grow to know him for who he was, rather than the person trying his best to fill the Demons' largest shoes ever.

The thing I hate to remember worse than Will's death

is still to come. See, as much as I had trouble coping with what happened to my friend, deep down I knew there was nothing that could have been done. This was just one of those gruesomely unfortunate things that happened. Be it bad luck. Be it ill chance. Be it God's will. You choose. Either way, there wasn't any real possibility of preventing the death or saving Will from his heroic choice to help the poor kid in the alley. The kid that got away thanks to my friend.

I'm not sure if he ever went to the police as an eyewitness or what happened to the criminals. They probably spent a couple of months in a juvenile center and then were released, back out into society, ready to create some new havoc with their heinous acts.

It didn't matter now. I could care less about those troublesome boys. I had only wanted my friend back.

But regarding Shae, that could have been helped. If I wasn't so selfish and caught up with the idea that Will's death had something to do with me and was more painful to me than anyone else, I would have realized this. I would have seen that I was hurting Shae and pushing her away. I wanted pity. And I wanted to be alone.

Shae wouldn't give me either of those. She urged me to snap out of it and encouraged me to get "back in the game." She was supportive. She was perfect. She was always so much stronger and understood things with such hidden wisdom it was scary. But I pushed her away.

It was the dumbest mistake I've ever made in my life. And lucky for me... yes, I mean lucky. Shae gave me a second chance. She gave me another opportunity to share my life with her and that second time, I didn't let her down. I had promised her I would never make the same mistake again, and I didn't. We had a wonderful, near perfect marriage and relationship.

If not, speaking about her leaving me would probably not have been this tolerable—easy is just not the right word. Shae left me after Will's death. She left me within the same twenty-four hours that Nathan Willis came into my life.

She walked out because I needed my time alone. I needed my own time to heal. And she understood this, like she understood everything it seemed. I know it hurt her worse than anything that had ever happened before or after, because that's how much it hurt me. It only made me stronger, though.

It made me realize that I didn't just want her in my life and want her through some passionate love... I needed her.

I needed her in my life.

For eternity—

II

Jeff sits in his recliner. He sips on an ice-cold Diet Coke. "Still tastes like shit, after all these years one might think a diet anything wouldn't taste so bad."

The sun is going down, leaving behind a fiery-tangerine glow. The heat dances just above the Earth's horizon like gasoline fumes. A few evening clouds move with a rippled effect, looking like sliced bread. Jeff thinks of a world beyond this one. A world where all people dream, and all dreams have more truth behind them than their reality counterpart. Wake up world, smell the roses. Smell life for what it's really worth.

He stares out the window, watching a woodpecker crack away at a crabapple in the front lawn.

He simply relaxes for awhile. He finds the silence,

besides the bird's beak connecting with wood, comforting. He shifts to his side a bit, leaning over the edge of the recliner. "Brrrrmm." Jeff lets out a good rip, one that might peel the paint from the walls. The woodpecker even stops pecking, a comical coincidence. "Son of a bitch," he says, smelling the rank over coming from his back side. "I think I just shit my pants."

Painfully, sore limbs all over, Jeff rises quickly from the chair to head to the bathroom. He shuffles along and laughs to himself, wishing he had a diaper on so he wouldn't have to get up. He thinks of the time he messed his britches with Shae. Right after a nice steak dinner, on their way home, Jeff tried to sneak out a silent killer in the car. One, he hoped it was only a fart, and two, he hoped it wasn't going to be too odorous. He missed on both accounts. The damage was done. He felt a growing wetness in his underwear while driving, and the smell hit the seats and Shae's nose almost instantaneously.

She told him to pull over and find a restroom, but Jeff was laughing too hard. Being the romantic and wonderful husband he was, he drove all the way home with Shae angry but smiling, complaining but laughing, and sharing in another fine moment in hookup history.

After cleaning up in the bathroom and finishing the mess he started, Jeff heads to the bedroom for some new drawers.

He wonders what Leslie is doing this evening, but then dismisses that thought as he wants to remember some more. When he returns to 1999, it will be only for the reader. He really, really doesn't want to remember the day Shae left him. Everything had happened so fast. One second, they were in love and everything was perfect. The next second, Will's death was tearing apart their previous connection and turning it into emptiness. Jeff really doesn't want to remember that part. Or for that matter, the things that were said.

But he will, nonetheless. He will fill in what needs to be known, only skipping a few days of memories as a type of honorary silence in remembrance of Will Coleman.

Things with Shae had gotten bad. It was entirely my fault. I pushed her away, whether I intended to or not.

Chapter Fifteen
Shoe Leaves

I

May 22nd, 1999. The Demons' day off.

Jeff couldn't accept the fact that Will wasn't going to be playing shortstop beside him anymore. It was too troublesome to swallow. The Demons needed a spark, something to lift their spirits. But rallying the guys after they had been swept by Montana was the last thing he wanted to do. He had briefly met Nathan Willis, the team's replacement player, and then headed straight out the clubhouse door. Frankly, he didn't care much whether the season ended now or later. Jeff just wanted his friend alive.

With Will Coleman already gone and things appearing to be at their lowest, today would be the second time someone near and dear to Jeff would leave. He had reached rock bottom. He had reached the Nadir.

He stared at the blank television screen for what seemed like hours. Sometimes, an image would surface in his mind, and he would watch something that truly was not there. But mostly, the television screen appeared black, dusty, and still. He didn't want to play another baseball game; the three games, of which two he had played in immediately following Will's death had been like a trance. He swung the bat, he fielded the ball when it was hit to second, he threw it when it was necessary, and he sat on the bench with regularity, but neither concentrating nor aware of the situation.

He never checked the scoreboard. He only muttered 'nice job' when something happened in favor of the Demons or 'better luck next time' when something happened against the Demons, but showed no true passion. He was every bit a zombie and robot combined, stalking in and out of the dugout with the same programmed pattern.

Shae had tried to see him constantly, but he either fought with her or ignored her. Things were turning sour. It was no use, she couldn't help him, nor even begin to try. It wasn't her fault. It wasn't because of her *not* trying. Jeff simply did not want the help. He had convinced himself that he didn't want her, or anyone, anymore.

His family also called, left messages, but Jeff wasn't ready to let them in either.

He'd lost the love of his best friend, might as well add the love of his life in the mix. *Why the hell not? I don't need Shae anymore.*

Maybe I'll take a nice, long bath, he thought. *Or maybe not.*

His fascination with sitting on the sofa in the dark grew. He hadn't eaten, but a modicum of food of late and laughter was as rare as diamonds. His back ached from sitting hunched over; Jeff threw his legs onto the sofa and laid his head against one of the arms, staring up into the dim ceiling.

He remained motionless, depressed to say the least, and full of fear. Fear of what? Fear of moving on, fear of taking the next step, fear of overcoming. Lack of sleep ultimately won the battle over sadness, and he drifted off.

II

Jeff was standing on smooth, raked sand. It was night, but gleaming lights filled the sky. He turned to his right; second base. He quickly reversed his head in the other direction; first base. The area Jeff was fixated in was surrounded by bleachers—stands with seats for people to watch something from. The lights were lifted high by silver metal poles, and only shown in his direction. Bright as they were, they pierced his head and burned his eyes. Jeff tried to shield his eyes with his arms, but they wouldn't move. Next he tried closing his eyes, it worked.

He waited. His head spun. He then re-opened his eyes. The lights were turned off. Darkness engulfed him; fear followed. The ground below him wasn't the infield sand anymore; it was replaced with something cold and hard. *Why didn't I wear some shoes?* Jeff questioned as he glanced down to the ground, realizing his feet were bare. To the front and back of him, the darkness continued for what could have been miles. But to the sides of him, large shadowy objects stood tall and grew as high as the human eye could see.

Jeff heard a piano playing. He looked in the direction of the sound, and focused his attention on a window that had appeared on one of the shadowy towers. The piano player (or piano) only played the low keys, making an eerie noise—in horror films this usually meant something evil was lurking.

A rattling sound. And then a crash! The lid of a tin garbage can rolled past his feet and disappeared into the shadows. *Footsteps heading my way.* His mind insisted that he flee. But Jeff found himself immovable once again.

"Jeff," an unseen voice spoke, sending chills down his spine, "you should have got here sooner, Jeff. Maybe I'd still be playing shortstop." Despite not seeing who or what was speaking these words, Jeff understood now.

"Will? I came as fast as I could, man." The sound of his own voice frightened him, but not to as great an extant as the footsteps moving towards him did. Another step, now two more steps, and then silence. Jeff whispered as softly as was possible, "Will?" No answer, just silence now.

He felt a hand on his shoulder, his body tensed up, and Jeff screamed. Not wanting to turn around, he closed his eyes and visualized a night out with the guys. Steve, Will, Jason, the whole gang, drinking and harassing women until early morning. What an incredible time they always had; the laughter never ceased.

"How Could You Let Me Die, JEFF? DIE?" the figure behind Jeff shrieked, still holding onto his shoulder. Jeff whirled around, afraid of what he would see next, but more afraid that if he didn't act now, he might never act on anything again. When Jeff spun, he crouched low, throwing the intruder's hand off of him. What he first saw in the gloomy night was his white shirt. Well, not exactly white, the entire right side was stained red with blood. Jeff screamed again.

Finally able to move, he took a few steps back, staring into the ghost's face with absolute terror. Blood flowed from Will's eyes and nose, and streamed down his face. When he opened his mouth to speak again, there was a gurgling sound, and more blood spilled down his chin. "Don't Leave Me Here Again JEFF! PLEASE!"

Jeff turned and sprinted down the dark tunnel. His feet hurt when they pounded the concrete, but fear overcame any pain. He believed he had run a mile before he glanced back to see if Will was chasing him. Upon rotating his head, he caught his left foot in a crack, and went tumbling.

Jeff's hands, elbows, and knees stung as the solid ground ripped his skin open. He rolled over on his back; the night remained pitch black. He lay there breathing in spurts, trying to catch his breath. Jeff's breathing was the only sound that he could hear until the knocking started. The knocking repeated itself, louder this time. More knocking, and then silence all over again.

"Jeff? I know you're in there, I can see you!" the voice shouted, but the sound wasn't clear. It sounded as if the spoken words that traveled towards him in waves were being blocked by something, like a wall or window. "Jeff! Wake up and open this door!"

He shot straight up into a sitting position on the sofa. Sweat dripped down his forehead, and he knew this wasn't his familiar dream. This one he remembered. And it wasn't anything similar to his other dreams, he just knew. He felt it in his veins—in his heart. Jeff looked at the window, he was shaking. Shae was peering in through a gap in the curtains. He stood up, walked to the door, and unlocked it.

He really didn't want to talk to her right now. He didn't want to talk to her... period.

III

"Shae... what do you want?" he asked sadly; his face and palms of his hands covered with sweat. He was already irritated, and she hadn't even answered him yet.

"I-I, wanted to see how you were doing," Shae

responded. After a momentary pause, she continued, "And *how* are you doin' Jeff?"

"Who the fuck cares! It doesn't really matter anymore. Does it, Shae?" he asked.

"Yes, Jeff, it does. You can't just keep going on like this, it's not healthy. I talked to your mom and—"

"You don't know what the fuck is healthy for me or not. You don't know how I feel. You don't know shit!" Jeff proclaimed, interrupting her. He turned his back to Shae and marched into the kitchen. Deep down he knew differently, but right now he felt as if Will's death and Regina's leaving town only affected him. Somehow he didn't think it could bother everyone else just as much.

"Jeff! Don't be like that! I came over here to help, not to fight. That's all we've done, fight! I came over to give this one more chance."

"Well you're not HELPING! I don't want any more chances. So just leave," he said as he opened the refrigerator door to grab something cold to drink. Jeff reached into the fridge and pulled out a Bud Light—bottle.

He popped off the cap on the kitchen counter; Shae stood staring at him, her eyes on the verge of tearing up.

"WHAT THE FUCK ARE YOU STILL STANDING THERE FOR?" Jeff shouted at her and then gulped down a third of his beer.

Shae began to cry, wiping at her cheeks with her hands. Her mouth shook as she opened it to say something in response, but then held her voice. She only stood in the kitchen opening and cried. She knew she wanted to be with him. But she was also smart enough to know now wasn't the time. Whether there was ever going to be another time, another chance, Shae didn't know.

Jeff didn't feel sorry for her because he truly didn't care about anything right now. He felt no remorse for anything right now. The loss of his best friend hurt deep inside. He just wasn't thinking straight. He wasn't Jeff Hartes. If only he had known better how much the loss of Shae would hurt before saying what he said next.

"CRY! I don't fuckin' care! I told you to get the hell out, didn't I?" This was Jeff's last question. The saddening night could only get worse.

"Yes, Jeff. I heard you loud and clear," Shae replied. She maintained her calm demeanor and bit down on her lip, producing a tiny droplet of blood. The blood trickled down her chin. She swiped it clear with her hands.

"If... if I-I leave, I'm not 'uh coming b-back. Do you hear that loud and clear, Jeff?" Shae raised her voice to the max. "I'M NOT COMING BACK... YOU FUCKIN—" Shae caught herself at the last minute and didn't want to stoop as low as Jeff had. She didn't want to lower herself or act on anyone else's level. She felt she was better than that and that this situation was caused more by the outside world than their inner relationship. But she knew it was probably best to go.

The extreme tone her voice carried startled him at first, but fueled his anger ever more. His voice rose even louder. He stamped his feet as he moved to her. Jeff squeezed her right arm; she drew back, but he didn't release his hold.

"Don't come back! I don't care. You're just like the OTHERS, anyways!" His derogatory shouting was so thunderous that his apartment neighbors could easily have heard. Through lack of wanting to get better and through half-drunken, half-not-knowing-what-he-was-doing rage, the word 'others' slipped out. He didn't even know what he truly meant by it. He didn't want anyone's help. And everyone, all the 'others,' wouldn't leave it be.

Shae threw her body away from him, pulling free of his hold. She slapped at him, but he blocked her swing with his forearm. Then she turned and sprinted for the door, tears running down to the sides of her mouth and dripping off her chin.

When Shae reached the door, she hesitated. She turned back to face Jeff and said, "When times are hard and you lose a loved one, you are supposed to seek those you love. Be around those you love. Apparently, your love for me wasn't real, Jeff."

Before he could rebut, Shae had slammed the door and left him. He collapsed down onto the floor, spilling a few drops of beer on the tile. His back leaned against the wall as he took another sip from the bottle. *Focus Jeff. Gather your thoughts and refocus them on the remainder of the season. That's what Will would have wanted.*

"Yeah. That's what Will would have wanted," he said aloud; the first time his voice left his vocal cords in a normal tone since before Shae's arrival.

"Will would have wanted me to take over the rest of the season. To fuckin' dominate, man."

The beer went down like water. He drank until he passed out on the couch, watching *Sportscenter.*

IV

After three hours of traveling, nearly halfway to Arizona, Jeff Hartes awoke on the Demons' bus with a throbbing headache.

The new guy, shortstop Nathan Willis, was nowhere to be seen in the back. He was riding in the front of the bus, with headphones on. He understood the situation. He understood that things would be difficult because of the tragedy that befell this professional ballclub. He would later say, 'I'm not here to replace anybody or try to be like someone before, I'm only here to win.' Simple, yet it spoke volumes.

Today was the first Saturday that Jeff Hartes was going to spend this season without his friend, without Shae. But Shae's departure the day before may have been for the best. In some sordid, bizarre way, Jeff truly felt that. He was feeling alive, again. He was sad that she was gone, but one thing had happened because of it, something he truly needed, he saw the big picture once again. Not necessarily with life, or his life for that matter, in general, but winning, and winning for Will Coleman, seemed important once again. And who knows? Maybe he would cross paths with that beautiful brunette once again.

This was the last series of the regular season—a three-game match between the Los Angeles Demons and the Arizona Scorpions. *Just like it all started,* he thought. And because the Demons had lost three straight games since the passing, the Scorpions still had some life. They still had a chance to finish second in the South Division and make the playoffs. They were only two games behind L.A., and needed to win all three games in the series.

It was time to play baseball again. It was what Will would have wanted. *Snap out of it and let's focus on the task at hand. Game on.*

V

Hanging in the Arizona visitor's dugout was the lineup card. It featured an unfamiliar name penciled in by Skip Bailey. But it didn't matter now. It was time to win again.

Earlier, before the team came onto the field, Skip had

called a meeting. It was the first time he'd done this all season. He didn't even wait until the players got off the bus. They all congregated in the aisles, ready to listen. Hartes guessed it took Skip a few games and a few losses to grieve as well, before he could come out of his own shell and speak on the subject. Since the funeral, there hadn't been a handful, if any, of words spoken about what happened or why it happened? Nobody really knew why. But for some of the players, it wouldn't hurt to know what happens next. Skip told them.

"This is a winning team. We are all winners in here, every last one of us. The last thing Will would have ever fucking wanted was for you goddamn pussies to quit on him." Skip pointed his finger around the room, almost catching everyone with its zeroed-in message. He continued to wave his finger with every spoken sentence. "Now I know it's been rough. Hell... it's been absolutely heart-breaking. But the time has come to wake up. This fucking moping around and feeling sorry for one another like a bunch of fucking pansies is THROUGH!" Skip's voice increased with the word 'through,' and then he pointed both hands at the ground, saying, "FINISHED!"

He paused before starting again, letting it all soak in. "It starts right here. We are a team. We win together. We lose together. We *suffer* together. And we *succeed* together. Shit, some of us even share groupies with the ol' in, out, in, out." Some laughter followed. Even Hartes grinned, thinking, *it feels good to smile again.*

Skip closed, "We've got a new face amongst us. Granted, he hasn't been here through the trials and tribulations. But he's here to help us now. We're going to make do with what we have and win this goddamn... this motherfucking... in the words of Funk himself... this fucking turkey leg!"

364

An emotional outburst followed, players letting out what had been trapped deep inside for too long. Some tears of joy and easing the pain were shed. Some handshakes and hugs were passed around. Some long-forgotten smiles and pleasant gestures surfaced. And before the team vacated the bus to the field, the new chap with dusty brown hair, curly and shaggy, stood up. Nathan Willis was all of 5'10", 170 pounds, but was reported as backing that small frame with some hidden power. His face was like the hair on his head, rough and not very well groomed. There was a handsome fellow beneath the uncleanliness, but the middle infielder didn't seem to give a damn. He spoke for the first time since getting on the Demons' bus back in Los Angeles.

"I'm not here to replace anybody or try to be like someone before, I'm only here to win."

That was good enough.

Simple, yet it spoke volumes.

Demons' Baseballl   May 23, 1999

(1) Lewis   8
(2) Hartes   4
(3) Hicks   5
(4) Gunn   3
(5) Rutherford   7
(6) Fetters   2
(7) Goodwin   9
(8) Willis   6
(9) Perry   1

VI

The Scorpion Den, the proclaimed nickname for Arizona's Bonnard Field, was packed and rocking. The lights were crystallized before a falling sun. There was a buzz in the air. The aura was baseball at its best. And dammit, it was good to be back on track.

Darren "The Duke" Marinville, still not panicking, still one-hundred percent behind his team, called the game back home with high hopes. "Good evening sportsfans. Welcome to another day of Demon baseball. The Scorpion faithful have seen there team come from what appeared to be 'dead and gone' to 'right back in the thick of things.' They are running on all cylinders behind back-to-back wins while the Los Angeles Demons are trying to stop the spiraling slide they just can't seem to get off. The Demons have lost three straight games and haven't had much help from either the pitching or the hitting. Steve Gunn, Erric Rutherford, and Jeff Hartes are a combined eight-for-thirty-seven with only three runs driven home in those three games. That amounts to a two-seventeen batting average and not much help for a tired pitching staff. The main reason seems to be..." The Duke trailed off, holding back tears and trying to prevent his voice from cracking so badly.

"Why we're all grieving in our hearts. I would like to say, once again, how much Will Coleman meant to the Demon organization and its fans. And for him, we battle on. I'd like to send my condolences, and my deepest sympathies, to all of his family and dearest friends. We'll miss you, Will Coleman, all-star shortstop for the Los

Angeles Demons. A moment of silence if we may."

The Duke moved away from the mic via his cushioned, black rolling chair and sat with his chin touching his chest. Arms folded, Marinville closed his eyes with complete sincerity and said a silent prayer.

In the dugout, oblivious to The Duke's memoir, the missed chatter and feeling of liveliness had returned. "Let's go now D-Lew, lead us off, baby!" Gunn hollered, slapping Parks, who had the day off behind the plate, on the backside. The young catcher shook his head, smiling, and ignored the painful red hand print Steve had most likely left him under his uniform.

Jason Hicks, standing in the hole, came over to the circle next to Hartes and asked, "You feeling better?"

"Yeah, man. I'm back," Hartes replied.

"Me too," Hicks said, one of the few Demons still swinging the bat fairly well. And those were all the words that needed to be spoken. The two of them had grown to know each other, and they knew tonight would be different. Tonight would be better. Back to Demon Baseball, missing only Will Coleman in person, but not in spirit.

Marinville rolled on, "Arizona (15-16) needs to sweep these last three regular season games to pass Los Angeles (17-14) in the standings and make the playoffs as the second seed in the South Division, behind the twenty-one-and-eleven San Diego Knights.

"Damon Lewis steps in for the Demons. He's hitting three-oh-one and is second in the league with twenty-seven runs scored. The first pitch from David Compton underway—" *Crack!* "Line drive up the middle, it almost takes Compton's head off, leadoff single for Lewis to start the game. He was sitting on a first-pitch fastball and wasn't going to sit back and wait out the count. Lewis on first, the second baseman, Jeff Hartes now coming to the plate."

Hartes strolled to homeplate with a newfound swagger. The nonchalant way he moved carried the winds of a game—a passion—he'd had since he was a child. He thought that he had never felt so alive. A vibrant juice flowed in his veins, he was ready to finish what he started. For Shae, who he was missing deeply, while now understanding the reasons why she left him. For Will, his friend, his counterpart, his teammate up the middle.

Sometimes, it took a terrible twist of fate for someone to realize how they might have been truly blessed. It seemed tiresome, but it was true—people simply took things for granted. They took their fortunate lifestyles. They took the kind deeds from others around them. They forgot how easily, and how abruptly, those things could change in a heartbeat. And then sometimes, when those evil happenings arose, the strong learned from them and grew inside. They grew as people. They began to see how much the simple things meant to them once again.

Hartes watched the first pitch go by... a ball about a foot outside. His average had dropped to .292, plenty respectable, but about thirty points down from where he was. He had his first career game with two stolen bases two nights before against Montana. Once, running because he missed a sign and luckily beating out a bad throw by Billy Marbury. The other time, running because that had been what he felt like doing, since Will's death, running...

The second pitch was a little closer, but still off the outside portion of the plate. Ball two. Compton paced around the mound a few times, shaking his head. Apparently, he thought the pitch was closer than the umpire. But it seemed a bit early to be bitching about calls. *Quit crying, it's only your third pitch of the game.*

Hartes stepped out of the box to read the signs from Larry George. *Option steal.* Basically, he was relaying to

Lewis to take second if he thought he could. And for Hartes, because of his slumping and diminished confidence of late, now would be a good time to "take one" and give Lewis a chance to steal while not helping out Compton.

The pitch, a fastball, was low in the dirt. Derrick Hundly made a good block, but with the speedy Demon centerfielder running, there was no throw. "Damon Lewis steals his twelfth bag of the season," Marinville called.

Hartes was taking all the way again. This time, though, Compton finally found the strike zone with a grooved fastball right down the pipe. The count was 3-1, a perfect hitter's count.

Look fastball you bastard. Hartes thought as he rolled his bat over like a spinning tire—like Jeff Bagwell. He stepped back in the batter's box, calmly tapping his lumber against his back shoulder. *Bring it, bring it, bring it...*

David Compton peeked back at second, making sure Lewis wasn't trying to take third as well, and then came home from the stretch. *Fastball inside!* Hartes turned on the heater and drilled it to leftfield. The line drive was too hard for either Miles Hunter or Hank Hughes to get to, and dipped down just in front of a charging Jake Kimmons in left. Lewis hesitated on contact, making sure the ball got through, especially with no outs, so George held him up at third base. With runners now on first and third, Jason Hicks, having another all-star caliber season, strolled to the plate.

"Jason Hicks now up with two on, nobody out. The Demon third baseman is having another stellar year," Marinville relayed. Hicks would have been seriously considered for back-to-back MVP's if it wasn't for the phenomenal, unheard of numbers from Cal's J.L. Conrad. Conrad was sporting the Triple Crown, boasting a .369

batting average, with 16 HR's and 44 RBI's. Hicks, on the other hand and in a sarcastic tone, was hitting a measly . 355 (second in the league), with only 11 HR's (tied for second) and 25 RBI's.

But the Demons' ladies man wouldn't get a chance to showcase his skills this time. With a 2-0 count, Hartes stole second base with ease. And with first base now open, the Scorpions elected to intentionally walk Hicks in the first inning—a bold decision early in the game that could backfire.

"Bases loaded for the Demons. 'Big Daddy' Gunn standing in the batter's box with his upright stance and the bat resting on his massive shoulders." The Duke painted the picture for the listeners. "Time out says the homeplate umpire as the Arizona pitching coach, Ned Simpson, jogs to the mound to have a word with David Compton. Gunn isn't having one of his better years. A two-time homerun champ, once in the Western League, and once in the Texas-Louisiana Baseball League, is batting only two-fifty-five with nine dingers. Oh boy, now would be a nice time for his tenth."

Do it for Will, you big son-of-a-bitch! Hartes took his lead at second. He watched Nico Chavez and Hughes move into double play depth, a hair closer to home and tightening up the middle. He got a solid lead, wanting to get a good jump on a base hit and score, but cautious to not get doubled off by a hard-hit line drive.

The Demon second baseman witnessed the count turn to 2-2. Two strikes, bases loaded, and no one retired yet in the top of the first. Hartes glanced around him, bending his knees and getting ready for the next pitch. The pitch now underway, Hartes began taking his secondary lead.

The fastball, up and over the plate, was redirected by Gunn's big bat, looking like a toothpick in his hand beneath his brawny build. The ball soared past the infield, Hartes turned and picked it up somewhere over centerfield. Chadley Michael, already robbing a couple of long balls this season, darted towards the outfield wall. Hartes sprinted back to second base, ready to tag if Michael made a catch in the warning track or climbed the wall.

"This ball's way back, way—" Marinville zealously shouted in the booth.

Get the fuck outta' here! Hartes thought with an enthused voice.

Gunn must have known he got all of it, because he was still camped on homeplate, with his bat by his side and still in his left hand. Michael halfheartedly jumped up the wall, but he could only watch as Big Daddy's monster blast carried beyond the deepest part of the park.

"Thatta' baby!" Hartes shouted as he began his jog around third and towards home. He gave one Jeter-like fist pump; and, if he wasn't alive before, he felt alive now. The dugout cleared, led by newcomer Nathan Willis. Thomas Perry, tonight's starter for Los Angeles, was clapping excitedly, knowing Gunn just spotted him a four-run cushion.

Gunn was greeted at homeplate by Lewis, Hartes, Hicks, and Rutherford, who was on deck. Hicks patted his friend on the helmet, helping Gunn back to the dugout and through the slapping hands and congratulations from the rest of the Demons. Skip, who rarely showed much emotion on the field, came out of his chair and also wore a "ready... cheese" smile.

The life had been sucked out of the stadium. The Arizona fans who had come to watch their Scorpions sweep the series and backdoor their way into the playoffs were now dead quiet. The Los Angeles players, knowing they only needed one win to clinch, felt relieved, knowing the game wasn't anywhere close to being over, but happy to put the pressure back on Arizona rather than let it keep on mounting on their own backs.

Compton started to settle down, allowing only one more hit, a two-out single by Goodwin. He got Rutherford to fly out, struck out Fetters, and then with Goodwin on first, Nathan Willis stepped in.

"The new shortstop for the Demons now up to bat. Nathan Willis grew up in the Dallas-Fort Worth area and played one year of college ball at Texas Christian University before signing a minor league deal with the Colorado Rockies. He was batting three-forty-two with their single-A affiliate, the Modesto Nuts in the California League.

Goodwin gets a pretty good lead at first, the pitch from Compton... strike one. The Arizona pitcher welcomed Willis to the Western League with a first pitch curve ball. Compton from the stretch, Goodwin going... the throw to second base from Hundly! In time! The Scorpions' catcher guns down Billy Goodwin to end the top-half of the first, leaving Willis to lead off the second for his first Western League at bat. But the damage has been done, four runs on four hits. Michael, Chavez, and Kimmons due up first for Arizona when we return here with Demon baseball."

Jeff Hartes jogged to second base, feeling a little strange inside. He worked a few games with Simon Luthers at shortstop. But that was different. That was someone who had always been there and was simply a temporary replacement. Now, with Nathan Willis, this was his new, hopefully permanent, counterpart.

Willis, a year older than Hartes, seemed so much younger. He seemed so much newer to this "Big League" type of experience. Hartes had been to hell and back, he had been inside the ropes, he didn't think there was anything that could be more defining than Will's death or Shae's leaving. But man was he wrong...

The dreams weren't finished.

Chapter Sixteen
The Home Stretch

I

"High fly ball hit by Allen to centerfield. Lewis takes a few steps back, and makes the catch. That ends the fifth, Demons one, Knights nothing. Due up for Los Angeles in the sixth, Parks, Hicks, and Gunn," Darrell Marinville announces to the Demon faithful.

...

"DOUBLE PLAY!" Marinville shouts, his excited voice splitting my ears as I tumble forward, rolling in the plush, manicured grass. I hear a scream of pleasurable joy, and look up in time to see Lake raising his fist as he animatedly hops off the mound and sprints to the dugout.

Marinville's unbelievable voice in my head, followed by Lake's cheering yell, quickly turned into a disappointed hush as the Knights' field quieted. I run back to the bench, receiving pats on the back and words of praise, but never truly knowing who gave them... or understanding... because...

Because I see *her* again. Standing. Clapping. Cheering. *For me?*

Of course it's for me.

I duck my head away, under the dugout roof. I simply can't take it. Not knowing — not knowing her name. This time, I'm sure, I even recognize the person she is sitting next to. But his name, all the same. *All the same.*

"Nice fuckin' play!" Gunn taps me on top of the head and takes a seat next to me.

The words trail away in my mind… "fuckin' play…" "in' play…" "play…"

I bury my head in my hands. I see my face in my palms — reflecting like a mirror. Reflecting like a gleaming pond. I can't bear to see it. I feel shame and disappointment. *Sure, I just made a play… but it's only postponing the failure. Failure is an option, Jeff.*

Failure is an option. Failure is —

If only I could place her name… It seems like it would save much strife and stress… It would help, wouldn't it?

The bench comes to life around me. Bodies jump up and align the padded railing at the top of the dugout. I follow suit, not sure why, but because it feels like the thing to do. I hear Thomas Perry shout, "One time, one time!"

And then the air is thin again, a long sigh releases from everyone's mouths. The players, thinking that "The Vet" Brett Chambers, pinch-hitting for Lake, might have just gone yard here in the top of the eighth to break the tie, return to the bench. The nervousness, the tightness, the feeling that time is running out is all around me.

The noise returns via a burst of excitement — constant cheering by the San Diego fans following a great catch in the warning track by leftfielder Waylon Ponds. I can feel the overwhelming sense of victory beneath me. The stadium is moving; the entire place is alive with an incredible energy.

I watch Damon Lewis return to the dugout after being struck out by Jerod Wilkes. He slams his helmet down, bouncing it off the concrete floor. A few 'F' bombs follow. Parks ends the top half, grounding out to third.

I follow the rest of the team back onto the field. I stay away from the stands. I keep my head focused on the things around me. I don't know what to do. I don't know what will help more or what will hurt more. But either way, the girl in the stands remains a mystery to me.

Javier Jimenez stands on the mound now, relieving Lake Williams after a masterful game five performance. My mind wanders again. It's stuck on the girl in the stands, but my eyes are focused on the batter. I don't even know the count on the hitter. I pat my right hand into my leather glove. Reaching down, I scoop up a handful of the rich red infield sand and let it sift through my fingers. It's cool to the touch; the weather a rare treat in early June.

J.P. Garces heads back to the dugout after striking out on a Jimenez cutter. Skip comes out to get Javy, tapping his left arm, motioning for Darren Luthers to face the left-handed leadoff man, J.J. Frazier. My vision throbs like a boxer's head going into the final round. It's like a pounding drum inside my skull. Things blur, things clear, things warp, things just aren't always right.

Frazier singles up the middle, the ball closer to the... the man I now recognize. The shortstop... the new shortstop... Nathan Willis. My eyes meet his as the ball bounces between us into centerfield. He looks so scared. He looks as though he's playing in the biggest game of his life — which he is. He looks like me.

Timothy Greener, the second baseman, bunts the go-ahead run over one base. I cover first, taking the throw from Gunn. I turn away from the stands, staring up at the lighted scoreboard. The white lights are as loud as the buzzing noise in my head. They glare at me and cause everything to distort. They are a million, enlarged Christmas lights bound by strings of mass confusion. The score is tied. There are two outs with Frazier on second,

Waylon Ponds coming to bat.

Luthers hangs a 2-2 curveball that Ponds drills to rightfield. I run out just on the edge of the infield, where the beautifully plush grass meets dirt. I don't have time to line up Goodwin as he's already fielded the ball on the second hop and is firing towards the plate. I turn to home. The throw is slightly off-line and late... the Knights take the lead. The stadium has its volume at a crest. The crowd is absolutely bedlam.

Ramon Garrido flies out to Lewis to end the inning, but the damage has been done. The fans cheer and applaud, not one person sitting in the entire ballpark. I jog in, turning to see the score—San Diego 2, Los Angeles 1—avoiding the girl in the stands. The dugout is alive with optimism and hope. Hicks comes by me, saying, "Get a fucking helmet on, Hartes!"

I wasn't due up until fourth in the last inning. *Don't mess with the Karma, Hartes. Get up and get ready! It's all around you.* I move to the helmet bin like a patient drugged for surgery. Everything feels so numb. I need something to help me snap out of it. I just don't know what. *Maybe the girl in the stands?*

"Let's go Hicks, get on base, baby!" Fetters yells beside me.

I can hear The Duke once again, somehow, someway. His voice carries through the radio waves and into my mind. I look around, just checking for the millionth time if anyone else appears to hear him as well, but no one has a clue. He announces Jason Hicks, and then says that Gunn is on deck, followed by Rutherford. If anyone were to get on base, that would bring up Jeff Hartes.

Jeff Hartes? Get a fucking helmet on, Hartes!

Hicks is in the box now, facing the Knights closer, Rich Treplow. Everyone on the Demons' bench is up against the rail, sporting rally caps and clenched fists. I feel someone up against me on my right. I turn and see the bat boy, Wade Smith. He looks up at me, smiling with confidence. He appears to be the only person that isn't feeling the pressure. He appears to be —

"Hicks is going to do it," Smith says to me. "He's going to tie this game right here."

I hope so, my friend.

I truly hope so —

II

Sweating like it's over a hundred degrees, Hartes rose up from sticky pillows in an unknown bed. He searched the room. He saw a lamp, a table, some chairs, a television, but he must have slept in the only bed in the room. He was alone.

And he had been dreaming the dream. This, as always, he knew. Where he was he didn't exactly know. He didn't have Shae to wake him up from this one. Nor Will, for that matter.

The last thing he remembered was riding the bus from Bonnard Field back to the hotel. He remembered the team celebrating their playoff-clinching win over Arizona by throwing back some beers along with a few bottles of Martini & Rossi Asti. They stayed on the bus long after it parked at their nightly quarters. They shared stories of Will. They shared stories from the entire season to date. They even got to know Mr. Willis a little better. It was a blast.

The only part of the jubilant night that stuck in Jeff's mind was a humorous tale by Nathan Willis. How they got on the subject that led to this small fact, Jeff didn't recall. But that didn't matter, it was damn funny. Nate, as they now called him, said that there had been a guy on his team, Brandon... Brandon something. They called him B-Dub for short, so Jeff guessed his last name started with a 'W.'

Anyways, Nate said that this B-Dub character had the biggest set of balls he'd ever seen. In the dressing room, he would do a thing called the "Flying Squirrel," where one holds the far corners of their nut sac and pulls them up towards their belly. Imagine it if you can. For most people, their scrotum would barely reach above their pubic line. But Nate said this B-Dub fellow's balls were so big that they would stretch all the way up to his chest, covering his belly button and all. The irony of the whole story is that Nathan Willis met this baseball player while playing with the Modesto Nuts. So they were fond of saying that Brandon, whatever-his-last-name-was, was *The Modesto Nut.*

The entire back of the bus, where Willis now found a home, bellied over in laughter and hysterics. Gunn couldn't wait to emulate the "Flying Squirrel" in the clubhouse the next night, even though his wrinkled prunes wouldn't stand a chance size-wise.

Hartes got up out of the bed and headed to the restroom. And yes, he was alone on this road trip. He didn't want to dishonor Will by having a new roomy. He'd rather have an old roommate in spirit. He didn't remember any more details from the celebration party. He saw the hotel alarm-clock radio flashing 4:47 in red digits.

With a playoff spot locked up, tonight's game would be much more relaxing. For the first time in awhile, the Demons would be able to just play, and not think or worry about too much else. Arizona was eliminated from a postseason trip.

We had gone on to beat Arizona 11-6 in that first game, despite the Scorpions making a charge in the fifth, scoring three runs and tying the game at one point, 5-5. Nathan Willis struck out in his first at-bat, but finished the game 1-3 with a double and his first Western League RBI. Thomas Perry picked up the win and moved to !500 baseball at 4-4 on the season.

Gunn's grand slam gave him 27 RBI's on the season, while Ron Fetters hit his fourth homerun and also drove in four runs. All in all, it was a solid, all-around team effort. We clinched second place in the South Division and would be playing the winner of the North Division.

That was a tight race, with Carson City and Montana tied at 18-14 apiece and Cal two games back with two to go (playing Montana). If Cal were to win the last two against Montana, they would have a one-game playoff for second, pending that Carson won one of their final games. If not, it began to get rather complicated.

San Diego had already wrapped up the South Division, standing at 21-11. They were a lock for the best record in the league; they relied on solid defense and phenomenal pitching. Waylon Ponds helped carry them with timely hitting and some pop, batting .336 with 9 homers and 29 runs batted in. While Jerod Wilkes, the ace of the staff, wasn't hurting the club, either, posting a 7-0 record and a 1.54 ERA.

And those damn dreams... they kept coming, too. The one after the Arizona game left me with a throbbing headache. Or maybe that was all the Coors Light, combined with champagne, I drank the night before? Who knows? But I did feel like I had a migraine all day leading up to the next game on the twenty-forth.

We won that game. Lake threw a gem, looking primed and ready for the postseason. We turned the tables on the Scorpions; instead of being swept by them for their heroic playoff run, we pounded them all three games, winning on the 24th, 4-0 behind a Lake Williams complete-game shutout. On the 25th, the final game of the year, we scored eleven runs again, and won the game by the same margin as the first of the series, 11-6. Steve Gunn was also looking playoff ready, collecting four hits to go along with his eleventh homer of the season.

Cal completed their sweep of Montana, forcing a one-game playoff to decide who would move past the regular season. I didn't think there was any way the Gold Miners could beat the Tigers four straight. Boy was I wrong.

The only other excitement around the league besides the postseason buildup was caused by a nineteen-year-old kid from South Texas, named Justin Ray. He had been signed and pitched one game out of the bullpen, picking up a win, for the Tucson Sun Rays. On the final day of the season, Ray got his first professional start. He set a league record by striking out the first eight batters he faced, totaling twelve K's for the game. And remember, this just wasn't any team, this was against the ballclub sporting the league's best win-loss record, the San Diego Knights. Justin Ray went on to get the win, moving his record to 2-0 in just 2 professional appearances. I never saw that young phenom again. Somebody mentioned his name the next season; it caught me off guard for awhile, and then I remembered his story from the year before. I inquired about his whereabouts, and somebody, I don't quite remember who, told me that he had had Tommy John

surgery on his throwing arm along with another major
surgery to repair damaged muscle in his shoulder. I guess
he never fully recovered because I don't recall ever seeing
the name again.

The old man rises out of his favorite recliner. He scratches his nose, trying to either remove a sneeze or bring it on for God's sake. The act, causing a "God Bless You" amongst a group of people, doesn't come. Jeff doesn't give a damn either way. He stretches his back, placing both hands on the lower part like a gay person about to say 'oh my gosh.' He walks to the kitchen, needing to warm up his coffee — in his McNally Sales mug.

Lying on the table, now buried under some other mail and letters, lies the "Midnight" letter. Jeff's now completely forgotten about it, but if he ever elects to go through his mail and stop remembering for awhile, he may come across it again. What's inside? He hasn't a clue.

Jeff pushes sixty seconds on the stain-resistant and self-cleaning microwave and presses the start cooking button. He whistles and waits, making the sounds of some Beethoven piece. The timer beeps, and Jeff removes his hot coffee. He doesn't even blow on it; he simply dives right in. "Son of a bitch, that's hot!"

It scalds his lips and tongue to the touch. Jeff shakes his head like he can't believe it — like an ignorant child. He sets the mug down on the kitchen counter and stares out the kitchen window. Jeff doesn't know whether he wants to keep on remembering today, if he wants to go for a walk, or if he wants to call Leslie. He really is undecided.

I know...

I know what I should share... what I should remember.
Jeff had never cheated on Shae during their relationship before marriage, nor had he ever cheated on her after getting married. He had cheated on others, but she was

different. Frankly, he cared for her too much. He loved her more than himself. He loved her more than the world. He would never hurt her in that manner, doing something so easily avoidable and undisciplined.

I suppose I wasn't the typical big-leaguer, living the indestructible life and feeling no guilt.

But between their relationships, when Shae left him after Will's death, during the days that separated the end of the regular season and the first round of the playoffs, Jeff had a brief encounter with someone else.

Katrina was her name —

IV

I remember watching as Katrina slid down a glowing staircase with angelic features. She created an aura of sex appeal around her; a bubble that prevented the majority of men from having the cajones to say hello. Sometimes, it appeared that the pressure put on these young gentleman was just too much. And with such a stunning physique, Katrina didn't help the cause.

The days drew longer since Shae's departure. We had finished the season, and had four days off before the series with the Carson City Gamblers, winners of the North Division. Those days were full of long, dry spells of remembrance and regret. Not that I regretted how I had behaved at the time, under the given conditions, but I did feel sorry over the whole situation.

I also felt so ashamed of having met Kat that I still hadn't the urge to kiss her. I guess I didn't have the killer instinct when it came to women. Most all of the other players, including Jace, 'E', Billy, Javy, Bobby-O, and Nate, would have tried to bang Kat without any hesitation. Or without any ounce of shame. I guess I really was a good catch.

It was true. I was overwhelmingly attracted to her lengthy, brown hair and delicately petite figure. The smallness of her distinct curves only promoted how incredible her breasts and buns were. Even when I first met Katrina the day before, the glasses she wore looked sexy. They were small-framed, sharp reading/sun glasses held together by a black rim. I believed only Kat could pull it off, remaining just as beautiful with or without the bifocals. I think Hicks even compared her to Lisa Loeb, or someone like that.

It's funny the things you remember. Shae wouldn't like it if she were still alive; but for some strange reason, I remember the conversation and brief fling as if it were yesterday.

"Hey honey!" Katrina smiled and pecked me on the cheek. I flushed a light, pinkish-red, and then responded with a caressing hug.

"Hey, what's up?" I asked, not awaiting or requiring a response. I was simply initiating my part of the greeting. "Sorry I'm late. It took me forever to drop Darren off at his apartment. His car's in the shop, again."

"No prob', I've just been enjoying myself upstairs with a couple of old friends. Wanta' join us?"

"Sure, but let me get a drink first."

"Our waitress will bring you one up there."

"Okay. Sounds good."

Katrina took me by the hand and led me through the dense crowd of dancing puppets. Every hairstyle and possible attire was represented, swishing abruptly across the lighted floor as techno blared from the speakers. Kat moved through the galleries of people with much more *ease than I would have been able to due to the fact that every male cleared a path for her. She was allowed to pass as a princess; every guy got their free glance, looking Kat up and down.*

Our hands were locked as we began mounting the steps to the second floor. I thought that I should have brought Jason along, and then I remembered Hicks was already supposed to bang this other hooya named Melanie. Plus, for some peculiar reason, I didn't want anyone else around on my first encounter with another woman after Shae. And my first encounter outside of watching sports in the apartment.

Since Will's death and Shae's leaving me all alone, I had found it extremely hard to pass the time during the day. The only escape from my hell was baseball. The dreams had ceased to return since Arizona (the baseball dreams, at least). The nightmares hadn't. They filled my sleep frequently and cost me many hours of rest every night or two. Maybe the best way to ail the pain and suffering was to move on, as I was now trying to do with Kat. This would erase the memories that clouted my mind daily.

The table Katrina and I headed for was currently seating four other people. Three girls, one guy. 'Screw me,' I thought. 'The fellas would have loved me if they could've met any of these chicks.'

"Baby, this is Chloe, Heather, and Melissa. And that's my good friend, Davis." I shook all of the ladies' hands with a pleasant smile, being careful not to give one girl a more lustful glance than another. I wanted to greet them all equally, including the fruity-looking Davis.

Immediately following my predetermined assumption about Davis's sexual preference, he answered my question by saying, "Hi Yeff, nice ta' meet ya." I now knew that

Davis preferred the other sex. In baseball terms, he was a switch-hitter. He batted both ways. I almost giggled like a schoolgirl when Davis accented the 'c' in "nice" into a long, hissing sound. Also, the way he said my name came off as very funny to me..

Davis flipped his wrist with a tender move and then gently shook my hand. Kat, realizing my need to chuckle, pinched my side and glared at me. I retorted with a simple, innocent smile as we slid into the green cushioned booth.

The day before, Katrina and I had hit it off instantly despite my worrisome, unable to relax fidgeting. I was tentative in my actions, almost coming off as being bashful. Katrina watched my playful shyness and thought it was very cute and attractive. It made it much easier for her to talk to me about some of her troublesome past and dangerous habits. I listened intently, selfishly happy to hear that someone else's life was just as much of a struggle as my own.

We chatted in the park where Shae and I had walked hand-in-hand many times before. Kat and I acted as if we'd known each other for quite some time now. We rotated swapping stories, and Kat's sensitivity and warmth allowed me to spill almost everything that had occurred recently. I spoke of my best friend's murder, my girlfriend's departure, and my declining batting average. For some unexplainable reason, my lacking baseball skills stuck out the most on this day. Maybe it was the instantaneous attraction to Kat that lessened the other two dilemmas. Maybe it was just me using her as someone to share my problems with. Maybe the connection wasn't really as strong as I thought it was—as I hinted before. I might have just needed someone to let it all out on... to heal me.

She mentioned her past with drugs, and how she was

hospitalized twice for overdosing with heroine. The ODs were her fault, she said. I didn't judge her; I found it very comforting that her problems might exceed my own mishaps. I also found it comforting that as much as I wanted her to be, she wasn't Shae, and she wouldn't ever be in Shae's league.

She continued on about a night when she walked in on her fiancée and a seventeen-year-old girl having sex in her bed. How the teenager got pregnant and her ex-fiancée didn't want anything to do with the baby. And of course, Katrina wasn't going to allow him to have anything else to do with her life. She spoke of her ex with hatred that I believed I could never have for Shae. That I never did have for Shae. But of course, Shae's fleeing was mostly due to my inability to deal with my own troubles.

Katrina and I chatted with her friends and drank religiously. She sipped on daiquiris while I stayed faithful to my Coors Lights. When Kat made arm motions during her chit-chatter, I could see the faint scars left behind from years of needle use—from possibly past attempts at cutting herself. These marks didn't affect or damage her beauty. They were simply implications of a tough life she had lived, the mistakes she had made. Katrina said she had been clean for over two years, but if she ever went back she would most likely not return. In this, Kat meant that she was doomed to die if her and the needle ever reunited. She had kicked the habit both times after her friends had her committed. Both overdoses were very near death experiences.

My feelings for her increased as the night went on. They were mostly selfish feelings, though. I needed someone to help me think less and less of Shae, and I also found it much more relaxing to think of Kat without her panties on. Not only that, but the thought of Kat staying *the night, ailing my loneliness, suited me perfectly fine.*

Heather was the first to leave the club. After complaining about her on and off boyfriend treating her like shit, she left to that same guy's place around 12:30. Davis and Chloe were next to go; he was heading to another bar (not a straight bar, I was sure of that) after he dropped her off at her house. The last girl — freaky Mel, as Katrina dubbed her — was still grooving on the dance floor. She rubbed up against every guy who tried to dance with her and wasn't afraid to let everyone in the club get a handful of her backside. She touched more cocks that night than a Chicken Chaser.

I chilled with Kat as she laid her head on my chest and smoked a cigarette. Smoking was the only thing about her that bothered me. Besides her not being Shae. Deep down, I really wanted Shae back. Katrina was just a pinch-hitter in the game of life.

I didn't care about her past. I loved her personality, charm, and physical appearance. It wasn't Katrina smoking that troubled me; it was her particular style of smoking that was a nuisance.

She inhaled a long puff, turned, and cast it into the air in a freight liner stream of smoke. The smoke rose towards the roof similar to steam out of a coal stack. She lifted her head slightly to look into my eyes and said, "Kiss me, Jeff."

Without any pause in the action, I swooped in for the thrill. I slowly, and softly, allowed my lips to touch hers. Not opening my mouth, I tenderly connected with her lips. I pulled away immediately upon contact, seeing the initial disappointment in Kat's eyes. And then I followed up my quick peck with an intense, passionate kiss.

I let my hands fall through her hair as our lips locked and tongue's became entangled. Besides the first taste of smoke, I found her much to my liking. I wanted to kiss her over and over again. Maybe just make out like high school freshmen until the dance club shut down.

"Jeff, I need to ask you something," Kat said as our lips parted, and they recovered from the heat just applied to them.

"What's that, baby?" I responded without any worry or hesitation. Kat took me by the hand and kissed my cheek before beginning.

"I know I've told you a lot about my past and everything. And you've been completely awesome in understanding. But I need to know... this sounds so horrible." She paused.

I gave her a flashy smirk, raising my eyebrows. This facial signal was enough to comfort her worries and allow her to continue. "I know baseball players, I've heard at least. That some players are pretty wild and crazy, so here I go." She shifted in her seat as I thought to myself that maybe she was going to ask me something kinky. Something like, 'Would you ever have a threesome with me and another teammate? Would you ever...?'

"Go on sweetie," I said.

"Okay. Does anyone on the team, that we, if this gets serious, if we get serious... Does anyone do heroine? I mean, that we might hang out with?"

"No, babe." I responded so abruptly and sure of myself that this comforted Katrina. "Nobody does that shit in baseball. Just weed and alcohol... and Greenies in your coffee before the game and Valium to bring you back down and get a good night's rest."

Jeff chuckles at the last remark, wondering how much Valium he currently had in the medicine cabinet. He thinks that one might do him good tonight, help his mind stop remembering for awhile and catch up on some sleep. "Greenies in your coffee before the game and Valium to bring you back down and get a good night's rest," he repeats aloud. "That's funny."

My laughing at Kat's question seemed to relax her even more. Her scowl, worried look disappeared from her face and was followed by a gleam in her eyes. We embraced and kissed some more.

We both forgot about the question, but Kat knew herself incapable of refusing the drug that almost killed her. She steered clear of any party or scene that she thought she might encounter her nemesis. Avoiding the situation, she learned, was the cure of all cures.

We exited the night club without getting a chance to tell Melissa farewell. Mel was currently being entertained by a young looking man with Rico Suave hair and guinea charm. His Italian presence was more than enough to trap Melissa in his web, as she practically had all her clothes off in one of the club's side rooms. Rico was rapidly sucking her neck and chest and stomach as Melissa began exploring new regions of his body. This quick Showtime flick got me a little riled up, feeling my buddy downstairs start chirping.

I now really wanted to get Kat back to my place and get physical. I didn't care about all the shit she had shared with me. I simply wanted to fuck away all the bad memories. All night, if possible. We couldn't take our eyes off of each other in my truck. Katrina was a bit too drunk to drive her own car, so she left it at the club. This pretty much guaranteed that she was staying the night, unless something really dramatic happened. I believed I was in now.

▼

On May 26th, a Tuesday, before I had met Katrina, I left the house for the first time with a real intention to socialize. I remember it had rained the night before, but the sun had quickly dried everything up. I hadn't cared for going out or meeting anyone new. Outside of the baseball clubhouse or road bus, I just wanted to be alone watching sports and most likely getting wasted.

The alcohol that cluttered my brain left me with intense headaches. That, along with the dreams and nightmares, was becoming nearly unbearable. I knew drinking wasn't the solution, but what the hell. It helped to lessen the pain and suffering. But no drinking today. Four days had passed since Shae left, and it wasn't getting any easier to deal with. So I had put down the bottle as they say and headed outdoors for a day in the sun.

My teammates helped a lot with the healing. But as they were also trying to overcome Will's death themselves, and get ready for the playoffs, it dampened their own spirits in attempting to raise my hopes. Looking at me and my depressing customs only made the other players feel bad. The only chance for me to snap out of this spell was to do it my damn self. No help from Shae. No help from my teammates. And no help from my family.

Today, I was going to take that next step to recovery and stroll through the park. I was facing my fears (memories of Shae) head on, believing that this was the only way. I thought, 'Wish I would have done this sooner and stopped fucking around.'

"La Di Da Di, we likes to pawdy. We don't cause

trouble, we don't bother nobody." I heard the music blaring from a passing vehicle as I locked my apartment behind me. I flowed along with the rap song until the noise faded off, trying to do my best Snoop Dogg impersonation. I grabbed my shades from the F-150 and headed down the hill to the city park.

That's where I first met Katrina Page. She was also strolling through the park, but she was accompanied by a miniature cocker spaniel. The brownish-red canine darted through bushes and benches and high grass, never tiring. The dog suddenly sprinted towards me, the girl jogging, holding onto her leash. The leash became tangled around my leg when the dog raced by in a giant circle.

I was caught up in my thoughts, and I almost tumbled over. If it wasn't for the dog becoming frightened at my wavering arms and circling back to his master, I would have gone down. But luckily, I gathered my balance and undid the rope tied around my ankle. Feeling slightly awkward, I waited to see if the attractive looking girl would say anything. I gave her a common smile as she drew the leash closer to her, pulling the dog.

"Missy, come here sweetie! Don't make the nice young man fall now." She snatched a glance back at me, checking to make sure I didn't take offense to her comment. I only stood in place, beginning to watch her more interestedly. She was wearing a white tank top, partially revealing her small, but perky breasts. Her legs glistened beneath her skin-tight blue jean shorts. She had her hair held back by her sunglasses, allowing the spring sun to shine upon her pretty face.

"Hi there. I'm Katrina, but most people call me Kat." She tentatively extended her hand. She paused, awaiting my introduction.

"My name's Jeff. But most people call me... Jeff." I

smiled, doing a *Blazing Saddles* impression. She giggled. Excited that my comedic line made her laugh, I realized how attracted I really was to her.

"Sorry about Missy. My dog... She's pretty playful, ya' know. I mean, full of energy I wish I had."

"It's fine, no sweat. I was sorta' lost in my own world, anyways. Didn't see where I was goin'."

"Where are you goin'?" Katrina bluntly asked. Her snappy remark intrigued me. She was definitely interested in me.

"No place special." I used another one of my best *Blazing Saddles* lines as it fit the moment. The first one, I remembered, was said by Gene Wilder. 'But most people call me... Jim.' The last one finished off Mel Brooks' classic comedy. I then added, "Basically, just getting some fresh air."

"Oh, I see. Well, I'm gonna' let Missy play some more over there—" she pointed behind herself, "—while I rest on the bench. Care to join me?"

"Umm... sure. I'd love to." Without intending to do so, I answered her invitation with a short pause. Her facial expression changed from curiously fascinated to somewhat unsure of me. Katrina did want me to join her, but the hesitation made her think I wasn't as interested.

What I really was... was somewhat scared. It's hard to move on. It's hard to simply forget the ones we love and invite new ones into our lives. Even though nothing had even happened, yet, it felt like a big step.

I followed her to the rest area. We sat on a medium-length, green bench made of wood and steel. The wood composing the bench was damp and worn. The forest green paint coating the steel frame was peeling off, revealing a rusty, black inner layer. Despite the age of the bench, its comfort was welcomed. I was glad to get off my *feet for awhile.*

We both opened up to each other with a fondness that would have led outsiders to believe that we'd known one another for years. Katrina shared the enormity of her past life, growing more and more comfortable with me as her private counselor. I did the same, using her as my own personal psychologist. I let out everything that had happened to me recently, still not believing the words that were exiting our mouths. We had just met less than two hours ago, and already, both of us were exploring the most delicate and fragile parts of our lives. I guess it really is easier to talk to strangers... to share things that embarrass us—that we might not want people close to us to know about.

Within three hours, upon the arrival of dusk, Katrina knew about the shortstop's death, Shae, and the Demons. Probably my inner demons as well. Meanwhile, I listened and tried to understand—not really minding—Kat's past drug problems and the seriousness of her situation. We connected with a bond of trust, as we really didn't have much more to hide from one another. We set up a date for the next night, planning on meeting at Sosa's. The place was one of the swankiest and hottest clubs in West L.A.

I walked Katrina halfway home, leaving her when a split in the sidewalk diverted our paths. We embraced in a friendly, warmhearted hug and said goodnight.

VI

After Kat slept over the following night, we saw each other for two more days, making it four in a row. We indulged in each other's passionate lovemaking each of those days and usually fell asleep with our naked, sweaty bodies touching. Katrina had even planned on making it to our home playoff game, which was on June 1, game two of the three-game series against the Gamblers.

The phone rang at two-thirty in the morning — the day before the first playoff game in Carson. It was Shae. I was speechless for what seemed like several minutes but was only a few, uncomfortable seconds. I didn't know what to say. She had caught me completely off guard. I finally just told her that I was super tired and didn't feel up to talking right now. Realizing how distraught this made her, I countered by adding that I would call her later that day.

"I miss you, Shae. I'll call, I promise."

"Miss ya' too, Jeff. Night."

I dropped the cordless phone to the floor with a small thud and saw that Katrina had awakened. Her face was innocently beautiful; she smiled, puffing out her cheeks.

"Who's that baby?"

"An old friend. No big deal."

"Okay, hun." The thought of my ex calling probably entered her mind, but Kat didn't seem to be bothered by it at this time. She crawled on top of me, and we succumbed to our desires for lust.

But later that morning, Katrina showed her jealousy and insecurity. I don't know exactly when it happened, but she threw away my list of phone numbers, male and female, family and friends. This pissed me off to on end. And when I called her on it, she completely denied it and said she didn't know what I was talking about. I tried to tell her that I just saw the list earlier that day, and that we had been the only two people in the apartment. But she still denied doing it.

I mean, in my experience, people have fights. Normal people have disagreements and solve their problems.

Normal people even sometimes cheat on one another. But what normal people don't do is delete phone numbers. That's just crazy. And no matter how much she said she didn't do it and how hard I tried to forget about the incident, that's all I could think about when I talked to her.

And when I wasn't talking to her for those few days, I thought of Shae.

VII

Shae's phone call was pretty much it for Katrina. It started the final love spiral that changed my life forever. Just like that, I wanted her back. I wanted back in.

I felt bad for using the poor girl, Katrina. At least, that's what it seemed like. Besides her few acts of craziness, she facilitated my needs to spill my heartache and despair. She aided my loneliness and served as a stepping stone in my life. But what I really wanted... what I really missed the entire time, was Shae. The love of my life. My future wife.

But Shae and I didn't see each other immediately. I dropped Katrina; she never made a Demons' game. I felt somewhat sympathetic, but it was the easiest of my pains to get over. I didn't know when I was going to see Shae again. We talked on the phone, but never committed to anything. She was extremely busy with work. Both of us were taking the next step slowly.

I invited her to the game Katrina had wanted to go to, our home playoff game on the first. She politely declined but said that she would make one of them. I told her that if she didn't hurry up, the season could well be over.

Like a flash in the pan... Katrina Page was gone and

out of my life forever. I never knew what became of her. I remember saying how quickly things can change. This was another prime example of this.

This was just another buffer between the Dreams and Baseball.

The tired man wants to sleep. The Valium he snuck into his coffee a couple of hours ago is in full effect. He never got around to calling Leslie. But that's all right, Leslie was probably out on the town, eating chili at *Check's* or playing Keno at Caesar's.

"Is there anything else I should remember tonight? Before the playoffs?" Jeff asks himself, rising out his recliner and heading to the bedroom. An antique grandfather clock, with polished wood carvings lining both sides like ancient hieroglyphics, signals the hour of midnight. "There is one thing," Jeff's eyes are beginning to sink into the back of his head.

He sits on the edge of his bed. He's determined to get one last thought in before his nightly slumber. He smiles, thinking about how unimportant this last memory is, but also its humor.

Salmon, along with being quite comical, was difficult to manage in the way a child can sometimes be. You want to get mad at him and scold him, but because of his innocence or ability to act like he didn't think he did anything wrong, it's a hard thing to do.

During the last game of the season, with Arizona, the game already getting out of hand, Salmon disappeared from the dugout and the bullpen. Now Salmon and Javy both hung out in the dugout during the early parts of the game and then made their way to the bullpen around the fifth inning or so. This happened quite frequently. But leaving the bullpen as well was definitely a baseball no-no. Something Seavers had done a few times before. But this game, he got caught.

I remember Skip in the dugout, asking, "Where's Salmon?"

At first, no one answered. But then Simon Luthers said, "I think he went down to the pen, Skip."

Skip turned to Larry George, saying, "Get Salmon on the phone." George, also unaware of Salmon's frequent disappearances, called down to the bullpen. To this day, I don't know what Skip wanted. Maybe he was on to Salmon. Maybe he knew about this all season and just wanted to wait until the last game... wanted to wait until the Demons clinched the playoffs before calling Salmon out.

George phoned, asking, "Hey Freddy, where's Seavers at? Skip wants him."

Sanders, covering for his fellow relief pitcher, answered, "He just ran to the bus real quick to take a shit, why? What's up?"

George turned to Skip and told him the response. Skip then hung up the bullpen phone and told George to go get Salmon out of the bus and tell him to come to the dugout. When Larry George got on the Demon bus, there was Salmon, spread out with only his tights on watching Bull Durham.

Now this had been an ongoing occurrence. At least, all the players knew. And they didn't care. As long as Salmon Seavers kept bringing the heat and doing his job in the late innings—closing games—there wasn't any problems or complaints from his colleagues. His stats spoke for themselves; Seavers had no losses on the season, tied for the league lead with 10 saves. He also had a low, 2.12 ERA and led the league in strikeouts per nine innings, with a 13.75 ratio.

Larry George asked, "Salmon, what's going on in

here?"

Salmon responded, *"Wow! Must be nice to walk on in the bus, disturb me from my shitting ritual. Must be nice to not have a game to coach."*

Salmon said this with such an innocent, harmless tone that he could almost make the other person feel at fault or bad about bothering him. But not this time. Larry George blew up.

"Get your fuckin' uni' back on and get the fuck off the bus!"

"Alright, alright."

Larry George stormed out of the bus and came back to the dugout. I remember overhearing Skip and him shouting profanities, both against Salmon's disappearing acts.

Skip said something to George, directed at Salmon of course, like, "That's fucking ridiculous! Hiding out on the bus during the fucking game! Get your goddamn jersey back on and join your team!"

George agreed. But both of them knew that without Seavers, we wouldn't be where we were today. He was the "ace-in-the-hole." He was our stone-cold lock. He was our closer, and he was having a nearly flawless season.

"I mean, c'mon. Give the guy a break. So he doesn't feel like watching all the game. If I played like some of you, I probably wouldn't want to watch you play nine innings, either," Big Daddy had said in response to Salmon's time spent hiding on the fun bus that had now been revealed.

He was one hell of a character. That wasn't the only time Salmon and Skip had words. There was this other time, let me think... earlier in the —

The old man can't fight it anymore. His eyes grow as heavy as a bag of rocks. His body is shutting it down for the night. He leans back, trying to find a more comfortable resting position, lying with his head now touching his pillows. That—along with the Valium—was the final stage in conquering the insomnia. Sleep has finally found him.

When the morning sun comes to greet him, shining a dazzling light through his veiled window on the eastern side of the bedroom, Jeff will remember some more. It's getting harder, though. The pains... the fatigued mind... the feeling of utter helplessness within one's own body. His baseball aches and ailments from years of professional sports, that he tolerated quite well. That is something he has always been used to. But these new feelings. *These* are inside of him. They are the real tell-tale signs that Jeff Hartes isn't a young man anymore. Age has finally caught up with the second baseman.

But the memories will go on...

Chapter Seventeen
Round One

I

Carson City, Nevada.

The Demons pulled into the Holiday Inn around 11
p.m. on Friday, a little later than scheduled because of the
bus driver having to fight a hard, steady rain. It was the
29th of May, just one day before the first game against the
Gamblers.

The team had only had two practices during their four
off days. Skip wasn't worried about rust as much as he
wanted his players to be perfectly rested and healthy. In
those few days, Jeff had grown close to a new girl and then
broken away. He didn't need any extra craziness. He didn't
need any more distractions—talking to Shae again was all
he wanted.

The series with Carson would be a best-of-three,
meaning win two and you move on. The first game was set
at High Roller Ballpark in Carson, and then it was back to
Los Angeles for game two on June 1st—an off day
between. If necessary, game three would be back here in
Carson on the 2nd. Hopefully, the Demons wouldn't have
to head back to Nevada.

There wasn't nearly as much festivities on the bus as
usual. Granted, the players had a good time and laughed
plenty, but the drinking and horseplay stayed at a
minimum. Hartes and several other players even dozed off

on the short trip. There weren't any planned activities for that night, either. Hartes, along with most of the team, went straight to their hotel rooms and crashed out.

II

The following morning, Jeff awoke before 8 a.m.

He headed down to the hotel lobby, meeting up with Fetters, Gunn, and Perry for some morning grub in the breakfast room. It wasn't the usual buffet-style "Continental Breakfast," but rather a fancier, made-to-order menu. Hicks was supposed to join them, but decided to sleep in the last minute. Hartes, searching around for somewhere to get a newspaper, was tapped on the side by Perry.

"There's one already on the table," the starting pitcher said.

"Sweet," Hartes responded. They sat at a table for four, ordering a mixture of water and juice to start. Hartes opened the *Nevada Appeal* to the sports page.

The newspaper featured an entire section on the Western League's final standings and statistics, including an article previewing that night's game. Hartes read the article first...

May 30, 1999

Defending Champs Prepare to Gamble Away Title

The Carson City Gamblers (19-15), winner of the North Division, host the Los Angeles Demons (20-14) for game one of the three-game first round series.

Neither of the two teams had an edge during the regular season, splitting the series 2-2.

"It's definitely been a battle every time we've played this year," said Gambler Coach Hank Mathis. "But this time, something's gotta' give."

Pitching game one for Carson is the righty, Norwood Gibbs (5-3, 2.87 ERA). He will be up against the Demons' ace, lefty Lake Williams (5-2, 3.57 ERA).

Last season's Western League Championship Most Valuable Player, leftfielder Aaron Craig, seemed confident in the Gamblers' pursuit of a repeat.

"I never give any credit," Craig said. "When the series is over and everything's all said and done, then I'll give credit where credit's due. But right now, I'm focused on the task at hand. I like our chances to beat the other team. That's it."

There should be plenty of fireworks ahead, not only tonight in this series, but in the first round period.

Also beginning their series tonight, the Cal Gold Miners (19-16) travel to play the best team during the regular season, the San

Diego Knights (22-12).

Carson City versus Los Angeles game's first pitch is at 7:15 p.m. Bring your entire family, and get your popcorn ready.

—CR Spring

After finishing the sports article, Hartes and the others ordered their food. He momentarily set the newspaper aside, asking for a breakfast sandwich that consisted of sausage, egg, and cheese on a toasted croissant, with a side of hash browns.

The only bizarre order came from Gunn, who said he always ordered a T-Bone before big games—steak and eggs. "I suppose a lot of people do get steak for breakfast," Fetters said. "But not usually the twenty-ouncer this early in the day."

Gunn just shrugged, patting his stomach. Before Hartes returned to his paper, he heard someone calling his name. All four of them turned and saw Salmon, Javy, and 'E' walking down the corridor, separated from the dining area by a decorative pony wall.

"Y'all want to check out—" Rutherford, holding up some papers, started before being interrupted Damon Lewis calling behind them.

"You fuckers, wait up," Lewis yelled down the hallway, running to catch up. "I'm starving," he added, trying to catch his breath.

"Nice to see our star centerfielder get out of breath jogging down the hall," Gunn shouted from the table. A couple next to the foursome stared, probably wondering if all the loudness was necessary. Lewis, laughing at Gunn's remark, jumped on Javy's back as the two of them headed out of sight.

Rutherford stayed behind, trying to finish saying what

he tried to verbalize earlier. "You want deze stats, Hartes? Or n'body?"

"Sure," Jeff said, getting out of his chair. He walked over to the separating wall, taking the papers from Erric. "What are they?" He asked while looking at them and already knowing the answer.

"Our numbers," 'E' said as he sprinted off to catch the others. They were headed for breakfast elsewhere. Most likely just picking up something to go and bringing it back to their hotel rooms to simply chill.

Hartes opened the folded white papers, seeing an up-to-date, end of season, stat sheet for the Los Angeles Demons, along with the final season standings. He was still shocked over Cal's playoff berth. The Gold Miners were three games back of Montana going into the three-game series with them. They swept the series, forcing a one-game playoff to see who would play San Diego in the Western League's first round. Most fans still doubting them, Cal found a way again, scoring the winning run on a Joey Bonham single in the eleventh inning off of Montana's starter, in relief duty, Clyde Mann. *Simply unbelievable,* Jeff thought.

After reading the Demons' stats and league standings, Jeff moved back to the feature section in the *Nevada Appeal* and looked through the league's leaders across the board.

Western League Standings
(MAY 26, 1999) --End of season--

North Division	W-L	GB	WP%
Carson City	19-15	--	.559
Cal	19-16	.5	.543
Montana	18-17	1.5	.529
Washington	13-21	6	.382

South Division	W-L	GB	WP%
San Diego	22-12	--	.647
Los Angeles	20-14	2	.588
Arizona	15-19	4	.441
Tucson	11-23	11	.324

TEAM STATS HITTING   Los Angeles Demons

	AVG.	HR	More...
Chambers, Brett	.207	1	2 Runs, 3 RBI
*Coleman, Will	.313	6	23 Runs, 25 RBI, 1 SB
Fetters, Ron	.262	4	11 Runs, 10 RBI
Goodwin, Billy	.277	5	21 Runs, 12 RBI, 9 SB
Gunn, Steve	.286	11	22 Runs, 32 RBI
Hartes, Jeff	.308	4	16 Runs, 17 RBI, 4 SB
Hicks, Jason	.341	11	25 Runs, 30 RBI, 2 SB
Lewis, Damon	.319	5	32 Runs, 16 RBI, 12 SB
Luthers, Simon	.217	1	2 Runs, 2 RBI
Parks, Bobby	.241	2	7 Runs, 9 RBI, 1 SB
Rutherford, Erric	.282	8	18 Runs, 20 RBI
Willis, Nathan	.400	0	1 Run, 3 RBI

TEAM STATS PITCHING   Los Angeles Demons

	W-L	ERA	More...
Jimenez, Javier	2-1	3.23	2 Saves
Luthers, Darren	1-1	5.38	
O'Dell, Jay	4-4	6.22	
Perry, Thomas	4-4	4.52	
Sanders, Fred	0-0	6.79	
Seavers, Salmon	0-0	2.12	10 Saves
Tims, Michael	4-2	4.64	
Williams, Lake	5-2	3.57	

Western League Leaders
May 26, 1999

Batting Average (North Division)

1.	Conrad, J.L., Cal	.384
2.	Craig, Aaron, C.C.	.338
3.	Kato, Jessie, C.C.	.336
4.	Grace, Stephen, Mont.	.332
5.	McCarty, Dom, Was.	.321
6.	Falconer, David, Was.	.318
7.	Rogers, Rob, Mont.	.306
8.	Wayne, David, C.C.	.297
9.	Thomas, Alon, Cal	.297
10.	Ward, William, Cal	.290

Batting Average (South Division)

1.	**Hicks, Jason, L.A.**	**.341**
2.	Ponds, Waylon, S.D.	.339
3.	**Lewis, Damon, L.A.**	**.319**
4.	Bonham, Joey, Tuc.	.318
5.	Michael, Chadley, Ari.	.315
6.	**Coleman, Will, L.A.**	**.313**
7.	**Hartes, Jeff, L.A.**	**.308**
8.	Frazier, J.J., S.D.	.302
9.	Hughes, Hank, Ari.	.291
10.	Vargas Jr., Anthony, Tuc.	.288

Western League Leaders Cont...
May 26, 1999

Homeruns (North Division)

1.	Conrad, J.L., Cal	17
2.	Grace, Stephen, Mont.	12
3.	Rogers, Rob, Mont.	11
T4.	Falconer, David, Was.	9
T4.	Woit, Bruno, Cal	9
T6.	Craig, Aaron, C.C.	8
T6.	Lucas, Penny, Mont.	8
T8.	Spews, Martin, C.C.	7
T8.	Gnass, Moran, Mont.	7
T8.	Petty, Jeff, Mont.	7

Homeruns (South Division)

T1.	**Hicks, Jason, L.A.**	**11**
T1.	**Gunn, Steve, L.A.**	**11**
T1.	Vargas Jr., Anthony, Tuc.	11
4.	Ponds, Waylon, S.D.	9
T5.	Martin, Jacques, S.D.	8
T5.	**Rutherford, Erric, L.A.**	**8**
T7.	Degginger, Charlie, S.D.	7
T7.	Kimmons, Jake, Ari.	7
T9.	Greggs, Ken, Tuc.	6
T9.	**Coleman, Will, L.A.**	**6**

Western League Leaders Cont...
May 26, 1999

Runs Batted In (North Division)

1.	Conrad, J.L., Cal	50
2.	Grace, Stephen, Mont.	36
T3.	Craig, Aaron, C.C.	25
T3.	Falconer, David, Was.	25
T3.	Lucas, Penny, Mont.	25
6.	Rogers, Rob, Mont.	24
T7.	Spews, Martin, C.C.	22
T7.	Woit, Bruno, Cal	22
9.	Ward, William, Cal	21
10.	Bean, John, Cal	19

Runs Batted In (South Division)

1.	**Gunn, Steve, L.A.**	**32**
2.	Ponds, Waylon, S.D.	31
3.	**Hicks, Jason, L.A.**	**30**
4.	Martin, Jacques, S.D.	27
5.	Kimmons, Jake, Ari.	26
6.	**Coleman, Will, L.A.**	**25**
7.	Degginger, Charlie, S.D.	23
8.	Vargas Jr., Anthony, Tuc.	22
9.	**Rutherford, Erric, L.A.**	**20**
10.	Hundly, Derrick, Ari.	18

Western League Leaders Cont...
May 26, 1999

Runs Scored (North Division)

1.	Grace, Stephen, Mont.	33
2.	Conrad, J.L., Cal	28
T3.	Craig, Aaron, C.C.	23
T3.	McCarty, Dom, Was.	23
T3.	Rogers, Rob, Mont.	23
T3.	Lucas, Penny, Mont.	23
T3.	Thomas, Alon, Cal	23
8.	Gutierrez, Ivan, C.C.	21
T9.	Stone, Tony, Was.	19
T9.	Brown, Arthur, Mont.	19

Runs Scored (South Division)

1.	**Lewis, Damon, L.A.**	**32**
2.	Ponds, Waylon, S.D.	27
3.	Martin, Jacques, S.D.	26
4.	**Hicks, Jason, L.A.**	**25**
T5.	**Coleman, Will, L.A.**	**23**
T5.	Michael, Chadley, Ari.	23
T7.	Hunter, Miles, Ari.	22
T7.	**Gunn, Steve, L.A.**	**22**
9.	**Goodwin, Billy, L.A.**	**21**
T10.	Vargas Jr., Anthony, Tuc.	19
T10.	Bonham, Joey, Tuc.	19

<u>Western League Leaders Cont...</u>
May 26, 1999

<u>Stolen Bases (North Division)</u>

1.	McCarty, Dom, Was.	17
T2.	Brown, Arthur, Mont.	10
T2.	Kato, Jessie, C.C.	10
T2.	Gutierrez, Ivan, C.C.	10
5.	Thomas, Alon, Cal	8

<u>Stolen Bases (South Division)</u>

1.	**Lewis, Damon, L.A.**	**12**
2.	Bonham, Joey, Tuc.	10
T3.	Michael, Chadley, Ari.	9
T3.	**Goodwin, Billy, L.A.**	**9**
5.	Frazier, J.J., S.D.	7

Western League Leaders Cont...
May 26, 1999

Win-Loss Record (North Division)

1.	Mann, Clyde, Mont.	6-2
2.	LeDuc, Grant, Was.	5-0
T3.	Gibbs, Norwood, C.C.	5-3
T3.	MacKenzie, Max, Cal	5-3
T3.	Ryan, Kevin, Mont.	5-3
T6.	Cox, Lenny, C.C.	4-1
T6.	Martin, Julio, Cal	4-1
8.	Ontaro, Ramon, C.C.	4-3
T9.	Smith, Antonio, C.C.	3-1
T9.	Neubauer, Jim, Cal	3-2
T9.	Calder, Julian, Mont.	3-4
T9.	Wolinsky, Cary, Was.	3-5

Win-Loss Record (South Division)

1.	Wilkes, Jerod, S.D.	7-0
T2.	Anderson, Robert, S.D.	5-2
T2.	**Williams, Lake, L.A.**	**5-2**
T2.	Ridel, Eric, Ari.	5-2
5.	**Tims, Michael, L.A.**	**4-2**
T6.	**O'Dell, Jay, L.A.**	**4-4**
T6.	**Perry, Thomas, L.A.**	**4-4**
T8.	Heilmann, Barnes, S.D.	3-2
T8.	Sierra, Enrique, Ari.	3-2
T10.	Hammel, Erwin, S.D.	3-4
T10.	Benes, Sandy, Tuc.	3-4

Western League Leaders Cont...
May 26, 1999

Earned Run Average (North Division)

1.	Gibbs, Norwood, C.C.	2.87
2.	LeDuc, Grant, Was.	2.94
3.	MacKenzie, Max, Cal	3.19
4.	Ryan, Kevin, Mont.	3.41
5.	Martin, Julio, Cal	3.53
6.	Mann, Clyde, Mont.	4.01
7.	Ontaro, Ramon, C.C	4.16
8.	MacNelly, Ken, Mont.	4.34

Earned Run Average (South Division)

1.	Wilkes, Jerod, S.D.	1.72
2.	Anderson, Robert, S.D.	2.57
3.	Sierra, Enrique, Ari.	2.89
4.	Benes, Sandy, Tuc.	3.35
5.	**Williams, Lake, L.A.**	**3.57**
6.	Hammel, Erwin, S.D.	3.96
7.	Ridel, Eric, Ari.	4.04
8.	**Perry, Thomas, L.A.**	**4.52**

Western League Leaders Cont...
May 26, 1999

Saves (Western League)

T1.	**Seavers, Salmon, L.A.**	10
T1.	Wilson, Binner, C.C.	10
3.	Markel, Charlton, Cal	9
T5.	Smith, Mayflower, Ari.	8
T5.	York, Chuck, Mont.	8
T5.	Treplow, Rich, S.D.	8
T7.	Johnstone, Frank, Was.	7
T7.	Valentin, Eduardo, Tuc.	7

III

Hartes was so caught up with the Western League leaders page that he only picked at his hash browns and occasionally took a bite off his breakfast sandwich. The other three guys had already finished their meal; including Gunn, who murdered all of his steak.

At the end of the feature's section, there was a footer that noted the Western League All-Stars and Award Winners would be announced following the first round's opening games, in the following day's paper. *Hmm... that's something to look forward to,* Hartes thought. To be perfectly honest, the thought of being an all-star or playing in the all-star game had never even crossed his mind. He had been so focused on the "team" that the individual awards escaped his concerns. Hartes didn't even know he was up for the Western League Rookie of the Year award.

Nap time. Perry unnecessarily picked up the tab for everyone, despite each of the other three — Hartes, Gunn, and Fetters — offering him money for their own meals. They sat around and bullshitted a little longer before heading on their separate paths — most likely back to their rooms for some rest.

Hartes took the paper with him. He was staying on the fourth floor, in room 424. After sliding his key card to the single-bed room, Hartes disappeared from the Holiday Inn corridor and immediately crashed into bed. He lay there with eyes wide open, thinking about Shae. After some debating on whether or not to bother her, he decided to take the initiative and call. Using his phone card, Hartes dialed Shae's number on the old-fashioned, cream-colored phone with square, translucent gray digits.

She didn't answer.

And he didn't leave a message.

What he had really hoped to accomplish was to simply hear her say 'good luck.' Nothing more, nothing less. *Maybe even an 'I love you' as well...*

Hartes set his alarm to three-thirty. The Demons' bus was leaving at precisely 4:15 p.m. to head to High Roller Park. Skip wanted everyone to loosen back up and shake off some cobwebs by taking some pregame B.P. and fielding a couple of balls off the fungo.

Hartes fell asleep watching *Sportscenter,* not waking until the alarm sounded for him to get ready to head out.

IV

Game one, Los Angeles Demons @ Carson City Gamblers.

The rains had gone and besides a few scattered clouds, the sky had opened to a beautiful teal baseball mecca at High Roller Park. The winds were calm, but it was still a cool seventy degrees for first pitch. The field was buzzing with a packed house of over five thousand screaming Gambler fans.

"The team from the City of Angels heads into town to face the rival Gamblers," Darrell 'The Duke' Marinville called. "It's a near perfect night, and I'm here to bring you another piece of Demon baseball history." The broadcast paused for commercials; The Duke was restless in his seat. It had been a few years since his Demons last made the playoffs, missing out by one game last season. He was eager to get things rolling.

Top of the first...

Damon Lewis, leading the South Division with 32 runs scored this season, started off the game with a walk. Jeff Hartes hit the first pitch from Carson City ace, Norwood Gibbs, right at David Wayne, who turned the 4-6-3 double play. Jason Hicks, having another solid year at the plate, finished the inning, grounding out to short. Gibbs whistled through the first inning, no hits, no runs.

Bottom of the first...

Jessie Kato, the Gamblers centerfielder who batted .336 on the season, lined a fastball back up the middle for a leadoff single. Lake Williams, the crafty Demon veteran, then struck out Wayne for the first out. Last year's Western League Championship MVP, Aaron Craig, batting .338, ended the inning with a hard grounder right at Nathan Willis. The shortstop rolled the double play with Hartes smoothly. One hit, no runs.

Top of the second...

Steve "Big Daddy" Gunn, the Demons' longtime first baseman, flied out to Kato in center to start the inning. Gibbs went 2-2 with Erric Rutherford before striking him out on a wicked slider, low and away. Ron Fetters, the Los Angeles catcher, ended the inning with a ground out to James Colbrunn at first. No hits, nobody on.

Bottom of the second...

Colbrunn, not having one of his better offensive years, hitting only .238, led the second off with a high fly out to Lewis. Martin Spews, the Gambler third baseman and nicknamed the "Back Bone" for how long he'd been a part of the franchise, struck out on four pitches. Williams looked relaxed and appeared to have complete control of his stuff so far. But after getting two strikes on Ivan Gutierrez, the Gambler rightfielder singled up the middle with two outs. Gutierrez then showed off his speed, taking second and clarifying why he was amongst the league leaders in stolen bases. The catcher, Barry Hunt, who batted only .216 with 4 homers, broke open the scoring with a two-out double down the leftfield line. Gutierrez crossed the plate, making it one-to-nothing in favor of Carson. Lionel Silcy, the Gambler shortstop, kept the two-out rally going with a single past Gunn at first. Billy Goodwin charged hard, but had no throw to home as the ball wasn't hit hard enough and Hunt scored to make it now two-oh. Williams struck out his pitching opponent, Gibbs, to end the inning and strand Silcy at first. But the damage had been done, 2-0 Gamblers.

Top of the third...

Goodwin, .277 with 21 runs scored, grounded out to Colbrunn at first to begin the third. With one out and nobody on, newcomer Nathan Willis stepped to the plate. He batted .400 with 3 ribbies in his first three games with the Demons. He followed Goodwin's lead, also grounding out to first base. Gibbs ended the inning by striking out Williams. He had faced the minimum through three innings and still hadn't allowed a Demon hit.

Bottom of the third...

Kato began the inning, flying out to center. With one away, Wayne blasted a 2-1 curveball over the leftfield fence, the first homer of the game. The solo shot got the fans on their feet; the place was bedlam. Three-to-nothing now. Craig teed off on a rattled Williams, giving the crowd a reason to keep standing by doubling to right-center. And then the Gambler leftfielder moved to third on a passed ball that slid under Fetters' glove. So instead of just moving the runner ahead a base, Colbrunn's slow roller to short now scored Craig, adding another run for the Gamblers. With two outs and two runs already in, Spews struck out on a curveball low and in. Through three innings, the Gamblers led 4-0.

Top of the fourth...

Lewis tried to spark the comeback, getting the first hit of the night off of Gibbs, a lined single to right. Hartes, hitting .308 in his first professional season, kept it going with a broken bat single up the middle. With runners on first and second, last year's MVP, Jason Hicks, came up to bat. Hicks couldn't do anything to move the runners, flying out on the first pitch to shallow center for the first out. He looked a bit geared up, trying to force the issue. Gunn, with 11 homeruns that tied him for the South Division lead in homeruns with teammate Hicks and Anthony Vargas Jr. of Tucson, ended the mild rally, hitting into a 4-6-3 double play. The Demons got two runners on but couldn't score them. It was still a shutout for Gibbs.

Bottom of the fourth...

Gutierrez grounded back to the pitcher for the first out in the fourth. Hunt, who started the Gambler scoring earlier with a two-out double, grounded out to Hartes for the second out. Just when it looked like Williams was settling down in the fourth, Silcy got his second hit on a seeing-eye single up the middle. After a couple of pitchouts, making sure the Gambler shortstop wasn't trying to take second, Gibbs grounded out to second to end the inning. One hit, no runs.

Top of the fifth...

Rutherford grounded out to short. Fetters grounded out to short. And then Goodwin flied out to left. It was an eight-pitch inning for Gibbs, who appeared to be in cruise control.

When the broadcast went to commercials again, The Duke let out a few profanities. He had been so excited before the first pitch, and so far, the Demons hadn't done anything to keep that excitement going. When the light went back on, he updated the listeners, "The game between the Cal Gold Miners and the San Diego Knights is also underway, currently in the bottom of the fourth inning with San Diego winning, two-to-nothing. Jerod Wilkes, frontrunner for pitcher of the year with his unheard of one-point-seven-two earned run average, has allowed only two hits and has struck out four batters through the first four. Wilkes also won seven games on the season without any marks in the loss column. Phil Kramer, the Knights' second baseman, tallied one of the San Diego runs on a solo homerun in the second. I'll keep you updated on that game, but right now, we return to Demon baseball."

Bottom of the fifth...

Demon shortstop, Nathan Willis, made a spectacular diving play to rob Kato of a leadoff single. With one out, Wayne hit a rocket grounder right at short, and Willis made his second out of the inning, this one a little more routine. Craig couldn't get a two-out rally going this time, closing the fifth with a ground out to Hartes. Three up, three down. The score still 4-0 Carson City.

Top of the sixth...

Gibbs struck out Willis on five pitches for the first out. Pinch-hitting for Williams was backup catcher Bobby Parks, who hit .241 on the season, sharing time with Fetters. He lined out to rightfield for out number two. Gibbs had now retired eight batters in a row. Lewis broke that streak up, doubling off the leftfield wall. With a runner in scoring position, Hartes couldn't get the Demons on the board, grounding out to second to end the inning.

Bottom of the sixth...

Colbrunn lined out to Hicks at third off of the new Los Angeles pitcher, Funk Sanders. Martin Spews hit the Gamblers' second homer of the day, a deep drive over the left-center power alley, five-to-nothing the new score. Gutierrez singled, but was then gunned down at second, trying to take his second bag of the game, by Fetters. Two outs now, Hunt at the plate. Sanders struck him out on a low fastball, keeping the Gamblers from scoring any more runs.

Top of the seventh...

Jason Hicks got the few Demon faithful on the feet at High Roller Park, but it was just a deep teaser as Kato ran the long fly down in the centerfield warning track. Gunn hit the ball hard, but right at Gutierrez in right for the second putout. David Wayne answered Willis' previous diving play, making a picturesque backhand stab on a grounder up the middle, and then throwing out Rutherford from his knees. Still no runs for the visiting team.

Bottom of the seventh...

Silcy grounded out to Hicks. Gibbs, staying in the game, then lined out to Hartes at second. And Kato flied out to center, ending the seventh. Sanders rolled through the lineup that inning. But it didn't matter if Demons couldn't get on the board.

Top of the eighth...

Fetters started the eighth off with a shot to deep rightfield. Gutierrez jumped up and caught the ball that was probably going to hit the base of the wall. Goodwin hit a hard grounder between short and third; Silcy got his glove on it but couldn't make the play. It was ruled a one-out single for the Demon rightfielder. With an oh-two count, Willis fought off an outside fastball, singling through the right side. Goodwin moved from first to third. And with one out, the Demons had two runners on base. Skip Bailey went with youth when deciding to pinch-hit Simon Luthers for Sanders. Gibbs' shutout was still intact, as he got Luthers to ground into a 5-4-3 double play to end the inning. The decision to use Luthers over Brett

Chambers was probably haunting the back of Skip's mind.

Bottom of the eighth...

Simon Luthers' brother, setup man Darren Luthers, entered the game to pitch for Los Angeles. He struck out Wayne to start the inning. And then for the second out, Luthers got a little help from his defense as Lewis ran an Aaron Craig shot down in deep right-center. Colbrunn flied out to left to end the eighth, one last chance for the Demons.

Top of the ninth...

The entire stadium was standing and cheering. The book was closed on Norwood Gibbs, who threw eight shutout innings and struck out three batters. Damon Lewis broke the scoreless streak for the Demons, momentarily sending a hush through the stands by hitting a leadoff solo shot off of new Gambler pitcher, righty David Parker. That homer moved Lewis to a perfect three-for-three in the game with a walk. If there was one positive note—one positive thing—so far, it was Damon Lewis' big game performance. Hartes then grounded out for the first out of the last inning. Hicks got his first hit of the game, singling straight up the middle. Gunn flied out to center, leaving Hicks at first. The Gambler fans, with two outs, had their celebration temporarily delayed as Rutherford tripled to left-center, scoring Hicks. The score was now Carson City five, Los Angeles two. Parker sealed Gibbs' masterful performance, getting Fetters to fly out to Kato at center, ending the game.

The final score was 5-2 in favor of the Gamblers. The fans at High Roller Park were going crazy, seeing their ballclub take a huge first step in repeating as Western League Champions.

The Duke, disgusted but still confident, summed it up for the Demon faithful, "Not much excitement tonight for the fans back home. The rally came, but a little too late and a little too short. The linescore is Los Angeles, two runs on eight hits, no errors, and Carson City, five runs on nine hits, no errors. The play in the field behind Lake was solid, he just simply didn't have his best tonight. He made a few mistakes with pitches that are usually down, and give the Gamblers some credit, they made him pay."

After going through some more game stats and review, The Duke announced the other game's score, "The final score back in San Diego, Knights three, Gold Miners one. San Diego ace, Jerod Wilkes, picked up the win by starting the postseason just like he left the regular season. Eight innings, no runs, six K's, and only one walk. Rich Treplow gave up one run in the ninth on an R.B.I. single by Cal shortstop, Alan Gardner, but held on for the save. Max MacKenzie got the loss, allowing two runs through six innings. Waylon Ponds and Phil Kramer both went yard, and each had two hits, while Timothy Greener scored the third run and finished two-for-three with a double and a walk. That pretty much wraps up tonight's action. San Diego travels to Oakland to play the Gold Miners tomorrow night at seven-thirty. The Demons have a day off before hosting Carson City on the first of June. This is Darrell 'The Duke' Marinville signing off, I'll see you in a couple of days."

V

The bus ride back to Los Angeles was long. And quiet.

The team's spirits had been dampened, but not destroyed. The Demons weren't *that* upset over the loss to Carson; but instead, over the way it had happened. They felt that their offense was peaking just at the right time, exploding for two eleven-run games against Arizona.

But Norwood Gibbs found a way—a way to keep the big bats in the lineup silent. There was a brief spark in the ninth, possibly something to build on for game two. Being down oh-one in a best-of-three wasn't the best case scenario, but the Demons have had their backs against the wall before, and sometimes it seemed they'd already overcome bigger obstacles.

Rolling into the Demon Stadium parking lot around seven the following morning, sleepy heads all around, the Demons had their mojo lifted. Skip greeted each and every one of them at the base of the bus's door steps. Whether the tired athlete—Hicks, for instance, stammered off the bus with closed eyes—appeared lively or not, Skip patted them on the back and said:

"No worries, we'll get 'em 'morrow night. Light practice this evenin' at three. Go home and get some rest."

That's exactly what Jeff Hartes did. He went home, crashed out, and didn't wake until one-thirty that afternoon. He may have heard the phone ring a few times, or maybe it was just his dreams or noises in his sleep. But that's the only sound he remembered before getting up. He phoned Shae before getting ready to head to the field.

"Hello," she answered.

"Hey!" Jeff said, excited to hear her voice.

"Hey yourself!" Shae bemusedly yelled back at him. "What's up?"

"I was just calling to see if you knew we lost last night," Jeff responded. "It was—"

"Yeah... I listened to it on the radio," Shae cut in.

"But we play tomorrow night at home, if you think you can make it?"

Shae got quiet for a few seconds. And then she said, "I

don't know if I'm ready, yet. I know deep down I want to see you. I want *us* to work out. But it's just... I dunno'... taking me time. I was hurt, Jeff. I want to make sure I've thought everything out a hundred percent before jumping right back in."

Jeff's initial response was to get pissy. Not mad. Not upset. But just simply irritated. He tossed that "sadface" out the window and put on a more mature, more understanding expression. He said, "I couldn't agree with you more. My only argument... baby—" Jeff tossed in a 'baby,' trying to get that comforting, relaxing feeling back in their relationship, "—is that this might be final game. This might be your last chance to watch me play."

And then Shae said something so perfect—so right. "There will be plenty more years to watch you play baseball, Jeff."

I couldn't have said it better, myself. It couldn't have been more true. The conversation turned to Shae's work. And then, some family updates. 'How's so and so doing?' or 'What have they been up to?' Jeff said for her to call if she thought she might make it. She said she would. They exchanged "I miss you's" and "I love you's" and then said goodbye.

Jeff stopped at *Taco Hut* to grab a couple of fajita tacos and a newspaper. He had completely forgotten the all-star voting and selections were finished yesterday, at least until he opened the paper. On the backburner of *L.A. Times'* Sports section, were the Western League All-Stars and Award Winners.

North Division All-Stars

STARTERS

1B – Falconer, David, Was.
2B – Grace, Stephen, Mont.
3B – Rogers, Rob, Mont.
SS – McCarty, Dom, Was.
OF – Conrad, J.L., Cal
OF – Kato, Jessie, C.C.
OF – Craig, Aaron, C.C.
C – Higgins, Marc, Was.
SP – Gibbs, Norwood, C.C.

BENCH

2B – Wayne, David, C.C.
3B – Spews, Martin, C.C.
OF – Lucas, Penny, Mont.
OF – Ward, William, Cal
SP – LeDuc, Grant, Was.
SP – MacKenzie, Max, Cal
SP – Mann, Clyde, Mont.
RP – Cox, Lenny, C.C.
RP – Westen, Theo, Cal
RP – Wilson, Binner, C.C.

South Division All-Stars

STARTERS

1B – Gunn, Steve, L.A.
2B – Hartes, Jeff, L.A.
3B – Hicks, Jason, L.A.
SS – Bonham, Joey, Tuc.
OF – Ponds, Waylon, S.D.
OF – Lewis, Damon, L.A.
OF – Michael, Chadley, Ari.
C – Degginger, Charlie, S.D.
SP – Wilkes, Jerod, S.D.

BENCH

SS – Coleman, Will, L.A.
3B – Hunter, Miles, Ari.
OF – Vargas Jr., Anthony, Tuc.
OF – Martin, Jacques, S.D.
SP – Anderson, Robert, S.D.
SP – Sierra, Enrique, Ari.
SP – Williams, Lake, L.A.
RP – Seavers, Salmon, L.A.
RP – Treplow, Rich, S.D.
RP – McCall, R.C., S.D.

Western League Awards

Western League MVP –
Conrad, J.L., Cal
.384 AVG, 17 HR, 50 RBI, 28 Runs

Western League Pitcher of the Year –
Wilkes, Jerod, S.D.
7-0 Record, 1.72 ERA, 63 K's

Western League Rookie of the Year –
Kato, Jessie, C.C.
.336 AVG, 3 HR, 18 Runs, 10 SB

This time, seeing his name in the paper, as an all-star, was a million times better than ever before. He had been in the transactions' section before the season started. And then, he had been in a dozen or more write-ups and even one small feature. As an all-star, not only had he accomplished a dream of playing professional baseball on any level; but now, after only his first season, he was considered amongst the Western League elites.

He shed a few tears on the drive to the stadium, not because he was proud of what *he* had achieved, but because he read the first name on the South Division's bench. *Shortstop, Will Coleman, L.A.* He wouldn't ever get to play in an all-star game with his friend, but knowing they made the team together was enough. *I'll miss you buddy.* Another tear rolled down his cheek. These were the good tears. He was happy inside, once again.

VI

"How in the hell did Ron Fetters get snubbed again? Missing another all-star game," Gunn hollered from first base, shagging grounders hit by Salmon Seavers. It was just past four in the afternoon. The Demons were taking a light batting and fielding practice. "I mean, give the guy a break. Let's see, Degginger hit what? Like two-seventy with seven homers and twenty-plus batted in. That's garbage! Ron, motherfucking, Fetters hit like two-sixty, with four big-game dingers and like nine ribbies. All... game winning runs!"

"That's ten ribbies, you cocksucker!" Fetters had heard enough. He was waiting for his turn to hack in the Hartes, Lewis, and Goodwin group. The same four had taken B.P. together since opening day—one of Skip's milder superstitions.

Fetters stepped in, last in the group on this day, driving some balls from Larry George to deep right. Every time he would swing, Salmon would pause hitting grounders to the infielders and grunt as loud as he could, continuing to bust Fetters' balls.

"Ahh... ahh... kuhh... ahh... kuhh!" Seavers didn't miss a beat. The left-handed catcher just shook his head, smiling, and finished with his session.

"Now that's some serious pop," Hicks joined in the fun from third.

"Don't you start in, too, asshole," Fetters said, jogging by Hicks on his way to participate in the *Great Fly Ball*

Shagging by Catchers and Pitchers of 1999.

Of all the uncoordinated and out of shape pitchers, Javy, despite being young and athletic, was by far the worst fielder. He butchered fly balls left and right. Skip even made him sit down one day because he was afraid he might take one a la Jose Canseco, right off the dome.

The best pitching fielder was Michael Tims. Only because of his speed and youth did he have an edge over Funk Sanders. Sanders didn't miss too many balls. He just had trouble getting to a lot of them.

Parks, hitting in the last group with S. Luthers, Chambers, and Willis, was driving some balls into deep left-center. Tims ran one of those balls down, catching it over his shoulder in the warning track. He gently collided with the wall, spun, and lobbed the ball back in near second base.

"Nigga' just made a play," Rutherford said, eyes wide. Skip, who had been talking with tomorrow night's starter, Thomas Perry, near the Demon dugout, saw the catch. Nobody in the outfield could understand his yelling verbatim, but they all managed to hear the word "idiot" in there.

Skip shouted something like, 'Tell that IDIOT to get the fuck outta' the outfield!'

Huddled in a group was Tims, Rutherford, Lewis, and Goodwin, and they all started laughing. They could see Skip shaking his head, not angry at Tims, but questioning his decision-making. *Why risk getting hurt chasing down fly balls when you were the next game's starter if the Demons won game two.*

"Fuckin' idiot," Lewis said, grinning from ear to ear, agreeing with coach.

"What?" Tims asked, laughing as well. But one thing was for sure, the Demon starter didn't sprint for any more spectacular catches. He only caught those in his near vicinity.

Lake Williams, the game one loser, now joined the party. He did a little long toss and fielded the batting practice balls in shallow left with veteran pitcher, Funk Sanders.

After a couple of players took their swings, Lake and Funk walked back down to the dugout, chatting. Lake began ranting about the defense and pitching in the Western League, and how overall, he'd seen better.

"You know what, Funk," Lake started once they reached the dugout steps. He paused as he reached into his duffel bag, grabbed a pack of cigarettes, and lit one. "I mean just look at the shit in this league. Look at these fuckin' guys. Hell... I could hit two-ninety in this league." Lake took a long drag from his cigarette, shook his head, and then said, "Nope... nope. Not giving myself enough credit. I could hit three-hundred."

Lake then patted Funk on the back as the fellow pitcher smiled. He took one last drag of his heater before tossing it on the concrete and squashing it with his cleat. "Shit, Freddy, you could even hit two-twenty."

Funk Sanders laughed as the Demons' ace headed for a shower. He knew Lake still needed to vent, and Funk was happy to oblige. The middle reliever knew this story would be an instant classic amongst the team.

Back in the infield, Hartes and Willis were still fielding hard-hit fungos from Seavers. They were rolling two with style, imitating some Omar Vizquel to Robbie Alomar turns, or vice versa. Willis fielded one ball to his left side, heading up the middle, and then he flipped it from behind his back and out of his glove as he was passing the second-base bag. Hartes bare-handed the baseball, turned, and threw a laser to Gunn at first. A few grounders later, Hartes back-handed a tough one heading between the middle infielders and shuffled it to Willis between his legs, falling down in the process. Willis let the ball hit his chest, like a hacky-sack at second base, before scooping it out of the air with his throwing hand and rocketing the ball to Gunn.

"What's going on tonight, Jeff?" Willis asked. He fielded another ground ball, but threw this one directly to first base.

"Nuthin' I know of. Hadn't really thought much on it," Jeff answered.

"Well... I think Simon said something about going out and grabbing a few cold ones. Nothing too crazy, just a beer or two. Parks said he might even go, too, but the only place that will serve his underage ass is the Hardball."

Hartes thought about it while waving Salmon off, signaling that he'd had enough fielding for today. "That sounds good to me. Hardball's fine, then I don't have to worry 'bout going home and changing."

"Nigga' please," Rutherford said, not really knowing what was being talked about, just interrupting for amusement while Lewis and him jogged in from the outfield. Hartes didn't respond to him.

He turned to Nate and said, "I'll see who else wants to go." And then all smiles. "We'll have a team meeting."

Skip stopped Hartes on the way into the clubhouse, saying, "Hey Hartes, ya' know I called you this morning, a couple of times, to let you know you made the all-star team, right?"

"Nah, coach, I missed those. I saw it in the paper, though."

"Just making sure you know we didn't leave you hanging." Skip put his arm on Jeff's back as they both went through the locker room door. "By the way, congrats."

"Thanks, coach."

VII

Hartes woke up the next morning around noon. He wasn't hung over. He was just tired. The group of Hicks, Fetters, Willis, S. Luthers, Parks, and himself stayed past midnight at the Hardball, all but Ron switching from beer to either soda or water after a couple of alcoholic beverages.

Fetters, meanwhile, got smashed. Jeff didn't know if it was because Carson had a lefty throwing and that Parks would be getting the start or if it was because Fetters just wanted to toss more than a few back. It probably totaled to around a dozen tall glasses of tapped brew before they had left the joint.

The funniest stage of the night came when Fetters—hammered—began rambling on about his world-famous gumbo. "Shit," he had said. "Back in da' swamp, when I'ze yunger, we make some good eatin' boy. I would cook up sum' of my irresistible gumbo, you know, Hicks, like the shit I made last season. With chicken, with sausage, with shrimp, throw in some dove or tree rat if you got 'em, man, it's out of this world. Even some hard-boiled eggs to top it off."

Fetters' chattered trailed off as he got up and headed for the pisser. That's when the real laughter had begun, as Hicks added. "Fuckin' boiled eggs. Ron served me a bowl of his world-famous gumbo and then dropped one of those eggs right on top. As soon as he turned his head, I spooned that egg over my shoulder. He turned back around and said, 'whaddya' do with your egg, Hicks?' I said, 'I ate it, man, delicious,' trying to hold back my smile."

The table had laughed until the Demons' catcher

returned. He had asked what was so funny. But in his drunken state, he had forgotten his original question before anyone answered.

Hartes passed on a late breakfast with Hicks and Willis, who were now shacked up in the same ritzy hotel Jason had been staying at all season in Los Angeles. They were going to some restaurant called *Gardenia*, where the eggs – not hard-boiled in gumbo – had some super protein and fuel for a needing body. Hicks promised a big game two. Instead, Hartes warmed up three hot pockets for a breakfast lunch combo – the meal of a true champion. One was chicken with broccoli and cheese, the other two were ham and cheese.

After eating, he jogged a few blocks to the Valero to pick up a Gatorade and the Monday morning newspaper. He wasn't a routine paper guy, he usually only read the sports page whenever it suited him or he wanted to find something specific. In this instance, he was checking the game two score between San Diego and Cal.

He opened the paper outside the store, flipping immediately to the Western League section of the sports pages. *Wow, Cal got pounded. Shit, they led two-nothing after four and then the shit hit the fan.* The final was San Diego 8, Cal 2. The Knights produced runs with only two extra-base hits – both doubles – one by Timothy Greener and one by Jacques Martin. Martin finished the game three-for-five with two runs scored and one run batted in. The catcher, all-star Charlie Degginger, also collected three hits with a run scored and a RBI. It was an all-around offensive explosion, one-through-nine all getting at least one hit in the game. For Cal, their entire offense came from Alon Thomas, leading the game off with a solo shot and then delivering a two-out single to score Thomas Brentile in the second. That was it. Western League MVP and triple crown winner, J.L. Conrad, was held one-for-seven with no runs scored and no runs batted in by the San Diego pitching. The winner was Robert Anderson, another all-star, who threw eight innings allowing only the early two runs, striking out five. The loser was relief pitcher Joey Gonzalez, who gave up five earned runs in just an inning pitched.

The series was over. San Diego's sweep meant healthy arms and a rested team going into the Western League Championship, especially if L.A. could win game two and force the do-or-die game. The championship series would start on Wednesday, June 3rd, if the Gamblers swept the Demons. But if Los Angeles won and the series had to go three games, the championship wouldn't start until the fourth of June.

With their backs against the wall, the Los Angeles Demons would be playing for their season tonight.

VIII

Game two, Carson City Gamblers @ Los Angeles Demons.

Back in sunny California, the sky was clear, the winds were breezy, and it was a cool seventy-seven degrees for the first pitch at 6:30 p.m. in Demon Stadium. The Duke had a day off to forget the game one loss and was ready to get things back on track. "A crystal clear glass sky with slight, western winds from the Pacific, it's a terrific night to be a Demons fan. It's a terrific night for Demon baseball." He paused, letting the listeners soak in the scene, and then rolled on, "Pitching for the Los Angeles Demons tonight is experience rather than raw youth. Skip has elected to go with veteran Thomas Perry over the rookie firearm Micheal

Tims. Tims is projected as the game three starter back in Carson, if necessary. Perry finished the year four-and-four with a four-point-five-two ERA. His run support was the lowest of the Demons' staff. Throwing for the Gamblers, the lefty, Antonio Smith. Smith closed the season at three-and-one with a four-point-five-zero earned run average, and just missed being an all-star for the first time in his career."

On the field, Kyle Queen announced the Demons by batting order and position, and the players sprinted out of the dugout accordingly. They were accompanied by two little-leaguers from the best area teams. Hicks, usually loving those pregame 'F' bombs, managed to contain himself for the youth of American baseball. He barked into his glove at third, getting a couple of giggles from a freckled, red-headed kid and a shaggy-haired Hispanic boy.

Some local celebrity, an up and coming pop star, sang the National Anthem. She had the longest golden hair, which was probably only an inch or two from her crack. She was a beautiful girl, and the fact that Jason hadn't made any derogatory remarks across the infield meant only one thing, he wasn't fucking around tonight.

As soon as the word 'brave' exited her mouth— Demons fans applauded and going bananas—Jeff pounded his right fist into his glove. He reached down, scooped some sand, and then blew it out of his hand. This was his new superstition... his new pregame routine. He started it sometime after Will's death. He truly didn't know why he did it, but something felt comfortable, relaxing in the silly method. It was a tribute to his friend. It meant something more to Jeff, and sometimes that's all that really mattered.

"Let's go T.P.!" Gunn shouted from first base, tossing the between-inning practice ball to Chambers, who was standing on the Demons' dugout step. And with that, the game was on.

Top of the first...

Jessie Kato, who went 1-4 in the first game, was first pitch swinging. He hit the Perry fastball right at Hicks, who fielded and fired it to first for out number one. David Wayne (1-4, 1 HR) drilled an 0-2 fastball right at Hartes. The second baseman fielded the hard grounder and threw to first. With two down, leftfielder Aaron Craig battled Perry to a full count before connecting on the game's first hit, a single right back up the middle. Perry threw to first a couple of times, and then fell behind in the count, 3-0, to James Colbrunn. The Gambler first baseman had the green light, swinging on the "take" pitch and driving it off the rightfield wall. Goodwin fielded it and relayed it quickly to Hartes, forcing Craig, who had stumbled a bit turning second, to hold at third. With two outs, Carson City had runners on second and third with Martin Spews (1-3, 1 HR) coming up. On another full count, Perry got Spews to pop up to first on a wicked slider. Two outs, no runs, with two runners left on base.

Bottom of the first...

The Damon Lewis magic continued, starting off where he left last night's game, a perfect three-for-three. Lewis hit a 2-0 bouncing ball through the left side of the infield, and then caught all-star Aaron Craig napping. The speedy centerfielder sprinted from the time he made contact and slid into second base underneath Wayne's tag for a lead-off double. The dugout was alive and excited about the hustle and aggressive, yet smart baserunning. Hartes, hitting .250 in the series, made a productive first out, hitting the ball to the right side and moving Lewis to third. Arguably the best player in the South Division, Jason Hicks stepped into the batter's box. On a one-and-two pitch count, the Demon third baseman fought off a low and away fast baseball, hitting a chopper to second base. Wayne had only one play — to first. Another productive out as Lewis crossed home, one-to-nothing Los Angeles. All-star first baseman, Steve Gunn, ended the inning, popping up to the catcher, Barry Hunt. One run on one hit.

Top of the second...

Ivan Gutierrez, who had two hits in the first game, grounded out to Hartes for the first out. The new shortstop for tonight's game, Everett Gorley, struck out on a high heater for his first plate appearance of the series. With two down, Hunt (1-3, 1 RBI) also struck out on a fastball, ending the second. No hits, no runs. 1-0 Los Angeles.

Bottom of the second...

Erric Rutherford, who had a triple in game one, led off the second with a smashed line-drive single to rightfield. Billy Goodwin, the Demons' rightfielder, tried to lay down a bunt and move the runner. Smith hopped off the mound like a cat, fielding the ball that was bunted too hard, and got the lead runner at second. With Goodwin now on first and one out, the right-handed hitting catcher, Bobby Parks, flied out to deep left-center. Nathan Willis (1-3) stepped up and tattooed a 2-1 fastball that was out over the plate. The ball traveled between Craig in left and Kato in center, scoring Goodwin. Willis then moved to third on an errand throw back into the infield. Two-to-nothing Los Angeles. Perry was trying to help his own cause out by knocking in Willis; but instead, the Demon starter struck out to end the second inning. The Demons scored once on two hits.

Top of the third...

Pitcher, Smith, struck out on four pitches to start the inning. That was the third strikeout in a row for Perry. Kato hit a pretty solid grounder towards the middle, but Hartes showed his defensive range, back-handing the ball and throwing to Gunn for the second out. With two down, the Gamblers got a man aboard. Wayne singled up the middle. His single was followed by a Craig single to right, the leftfielder's second hit of the game. Runners on first and second now, with lefthander Colbrunn (a double already tonight) up to bat. He hit a soft liner that Hicks pulled out of the air easily. Two hits, no runs.

Bottom of the third...

Smith and the Gamblers finally found a way to get Damon Lewis out. On a 2-2 changeup, the Demon centerfielder hit a hanging, shallow fly to center. Kato made the catch for the first out. Hartes hit a hard shot between short and third, but backup shortstop Everett Gorley made a diving stab. He jumped up and fired to first just in time, beating Hartes by a half-step or less. Skip had a few words to say about that "out" call from the dugout, but it wasn't crucial enough to get him on his feet. Hicks grounded out to first to end the inning, Colbrunn fielding the ball and gently tossing it to Smith, running to cover the bag. Three up, three down.

Top of the fourth...

Spews flied out to Lewis for out number one. Gutierrez, batting right at .500, hit a liner right by Perry's glove, almost taking the pitcher's head off. With one out and a runner on first, Gorley flied out to leftfield. Rutherford fired the ball in to Willis, two outs now. Gutierrez got his second stolen base of the series, moving on a 1-1 count on Hunt. Parks' throw was online, just simply not in time. Perry's next pitch, a two-two fastball, got away from him high and inside, hitting a turning Barry Hunt in the backside, near the shoulder. Smith didn't get a chance to bat. The Gamblers had on some sort of hit-and-run or double steal; and it turned out to be a costly decision by the coaching staff as Smith swung and missed and Parks gunned down Gutierrez at third base for the last out. Once again, the Gamblers stranded two runners. The opportunities had been there, but Carson just wasn't capitalizing.

Bottom of the fourth...

Gunn, still hitless in the series, led off the fourth with a fly out to center. Smith then struck out Rutherford on a low and in slider. With two outs, Goodwin couldn't get a rally going, striking out on another good slider from Antonio Smith. Through four full innings, the score was Los Angeles 2, Carson City 0.

Top of the fifth...

Perry got his fourth 'K' of the game, striking out Smith to start the inning. Kato hit a swinging bunt in front of homeplate, Parks fielded it and got the Gambler centerfielder easy for the second out. Perry blew a high fastball by Wayne for the final out, a relatively simple inning for the Demons' starter.

Bottom of the fifth...

Parks flied out to shallow left. Willis popped up to Spews at third. That was now nine straight retired by Antonio Smith. He appeared to have found his groove since allowing the early two runs. With the count 0-2, Perry swung and missed at a slider in the dirt. A one, two, three, fifth inning for Smith.

Top of the sixth...

Craig, two-for-two with two singles in the game, hit a solid grounder right at Willis. The Demon shortstop fielded the ball and gunned out Craig for the first out. So far, the Demons were doing exactly what Carson City did the night before. They were scoring on their few chances, while the Gamblers hadn't been able to get any runs across. With that said, Colbrunn blasted a deep shot to leftfield. Rutherford raced back and leaped up, catching the shot at the top of the wall, and robbing the Gamblers' first baseman of at least a two-bagger. With two down, Spews struck out to end the top half of the inning. The Demons had quite a pitching performance going by Perry. So far, Skip was loving his decision to go with the veteran.

Bottom of the sixth...

Lewis grounded out to second for the first out, dropping his average to a mere six-sixty-seven. Hartes hit the ball hard, but Craig ran it down in deep left-center for the second out of the inning. Hicks then grounded out to short on a full count. It was an eleven pitch inning for Smith, who now only needed some run support. 2-0 Demons.

Top of the seventh...

Gutierrez grounded out to second on a 2-2 count. Gorley followed suit, making Hartes a busy camper so far in the seventh. And with two outs, Hunt grounded out to Gunn at first. Perry was cruising with seven shutout innings and five strikeouts.

Bottom of the seventh...

After the glorious "seventh-inning stretch," Gunn got his first hit of the series, a line drive single to leftfield. Carson City coach Hank Mathis got Alvin Snider (1-0) up and throwing in the Gamblers' bullpen. With Gunn on first, not likely to be running, Rutherford struck out on another solid slider, low and in, from Smith. Goodwin then hit into a 6-4-3 double play to end the seventh. The score was still 2-0 L.A.

Top of the eighth...

Lionel Silcy, two hits in the first game, pinch-hit for the Gamblers' pitcher and grounded out to short. The numbers on Antonio Smith were seven innings pitched, allowing only two earned runs, five strikeouts and no walks. That was it for Demon starter Thomas Perry as well. He threw seven and one-third innings of solid shutout baseball, striking out six along the way. After getting the first out of the eighth, Skip Bailey came and got him. The new pitcher was the crafty righty, Funk Sanders. Sanders threw two innings in the first game and allowed one run. The reason Skip went with the middle-reliever instead of the setup man, Javier Jimenez, was probably Kato's lifetime numbers against Sanders. The Gamblers' centerfielder was hitless in eight at-bats in his career against the Demons' pitcher. But Kato proved the numbers wrong, singling through the right side for his first hit of the game. Skip came back out, calling for the right-handed Jimenez to now get the Demons out of a small jam and get the ball to their all-star closer, Salmon Seavers. Wayne stepped in and drove the ball to deep center. The slight breeze might have helped Lewis run this one down for the second out. With two down and a runner on first, and Seavers now throwing in the Demon bullpen, Craig lined out on a 2-2 fastball from Jimenez, keeping the Gamblers scoreless through eight.

Bottom of the eighth...

Parks grounded out to first off of Snider, the new pitcher for Carson City. Willis then hit a soft chopper back to the mound, Snider fielded it cleanly and threw out the Demons' shortstop for out number two. Brett Chambers pinch-hit for Jimenez, and in his first at-bat of the playoffs, he grounded out to Gorley for the last out. With eight innings in the books, it was still 2-0 Los Angeles, one more chance for the Gamblers.

Top of the ninth...

Salmon Seavers (0-0, 2.12 ERA during the regular season), tied for Western League lead with ten saves, got Colbrunn to ground out softly to second for the first out of the ninth. On a 1-2 count, Seavers got Spews to ground out to first with a ninety-eight-mile-an-hour fastball, one out away from evening the series. The Demon fans on their feet, screaming, clapping hands, and stomping the bleachers. Marinville called the final pitch, "One-two count on rightfielder, Ivan Gutierrez. Seavers, from the stretch, sets and comes homes... STRIKE THREE! He got 'em on the high heat! The Demons have tied the series and will travel back to Carson for the closing game!"

The game was over. Los Angeles Demons 2, Carson City Gamblers 0. Thomas Perry picked up the win while Antonio Smith, despite an outstanding effort, got the loss. Salmon Seavers snatched his first save of the playoffs, striking out the last hitter in the process.

The Demon players were all high-fives and fist bumps near the Demon Stadium mound. Gunn gave Perry a big hug, wrapping his arms around the pitcher's head and patting Perry hard enough to remove his cap. There wasn't much time to celebrate, though. The Demons' bus was fueled up and ready to roll back to Nevada. The players had a chance to briefly chat with wives, friends, and family before showering and jumping on the bus, which was leaving as soon as it was loaded. Jeff wished he could give Shae a celebratory hug, but knew that day would come soon enough. Tomorrow's game was set for a 7:15 p.m. start. The pitching matchup would be nineteen-year-old Michael Tims (4-2, 4.64 ERA) versus Ramon Ontaro (4-3, 4.16 ERA).

Jeff was excited to win his first playoff game. He was excited to head back to Carson City for a chance to move to the Western League Championship. He only wished he could share this with Shae—in person. Or even with his family. His mom's sister—a different aunt than the one with the gambling addiction, who lived in Oxford, Mississippi—had been really sick in critical care. His family, all but his brother Eric, had flown to spend time with the family and grieve. Eric had been staying at a friend's house, keeping the family's baseball tradition alive by playing in the Desert Shores All-Star's Tournament. Jeff's dad had really hoped the Demons would win against Carson, not only with supportive intentions, but because he really wanted to catch as many championship games as possible in Los Angeles—or in San Diego, for that matter.

The bus trip back to Carson was a blur. So was the next morning. Jeff slept and watched *Sportscenter* reruns throughout the morning. He called Shae to tell her they'd won, but she already knew. The same with his father. He had gotten the number to his ill aunt's house through information; and luckily, a cousin Derek answered the ringing phone. Neither his dad nor mom was at the house; they were visiting and giving their support at the hospital. But Jeff left a message, saying for his dad to call him at the Carson City Holiday Inn, room 404. Around one that afternoon, Jeff's dad phoned.

He told Jeff that he knew they'd won. He said that he had called the Demon Stadium directory and gotten through to the pressbox. Mr. Hartes didn't know if he talked directly to Darrell Marinville or with whom he'd spoken to the night before, but got the final score either way. Jeff told his dad that he was hitless on the night, but winning was all that mattered now. His father agreed, telling him that if the Demons could only win one more, he promised that the family, including Eric, would try their damnest to stay for the entire Western League Championship series.

Jeff was secretly pumped. He *did* have someone in his corner. Even though he knew his family's support was always there, it would just be nice to see them in person. Jeff's father, and mother, both said the normal 'good luck' and 'I love you' before saying goodbye.

The rest of the day was uneventful. Everybody was anxious, eagerly waiting to strap it on for game three. It would be that time soon enough...

IX

Game three, Los Angeles Demons @ Carson City Gamblers.

High Roller Park was ecstatic. The Gambler fans, more than fifty-five hundred and filling every standing-room-only vacancy, were waving black and red towels with all four suits of aces imprinted on them. They were a free handout to the first thousand Gambler extremists. And they enhanced the magnificent visual of a wild and crazy sports venue during playoff time.

"Tonight's game is the rubber game," The Duke called back to the Los Angeles listeners. "But only this time, unlike the regular season... somebody's going home. The rivalry stood two games apiece going into the postseason. It now stands three games apiece. Tonight... something's gotta' give. This is Darrell 'The Duke' Marinville, and I'm here to bring you another piece of Demon baseball history."

Hartes remembered stepping out of the dugout and onto the field for the first time, about forty minutes before first pitch. The aura was surreal. The smells of cotton candy and ballpark dogs and large cokes filled the air. If he died today, this was where he'd want to spend eternity — on a baseball diamond, with thousands of rooting fans. Occasionally, it seemed even more fun when ninety-percent of them were rooting against you. He now understood what Reggie Miller felt like at Madison Square Garden.

The tightness that usually filled in the pit of an athlete's stomach, in their legs, had seemed to steer clear of the Demons' dugout so far. Most of the veterans appeared loose. Just another day at the office — at the ballpark.

"Goddammit Ontaro, I'm gonna' get you!" Goodwin shouted, pulling his long hair that he had just drenched with cold water. He shook his head like a wet dog, spraying droplets of water on his teammates.

"Let's go, c'mon!" Simon Luthers answered Billy's fire, walking over and chest-bumping the rightfielder.

Hartes, Hicks, and Willis huddled near the end of the dugout closest to homeplate. Nate said, "Boy, I'm dead red tonight."

"What if you got to move the runners over, put the team before the big swing?" Hicks asked.

"Fuck that shit," the new shortstop responded. "Like I said, I'm dead red. If you throw me that breaking stuff, I'll look silly. But if you throw me the heater, Jesus Pete."

Fetters, back in the lineup versus the Gamblers' righty, joined the pregame conversation. "If I hadn't put the team first all season, I would have been top five in the league in homers. But that's just the way it goes."

If any of the players in that section of the dugout had been tight before, listening in on Fetters comment loosened them up. They laughed until Skip walked by and said, "Ron, you wouldn't have led my nephew's little league team in homeruns, with the centerfield wall as deep as two-ninety." And then they laughed some more.

The Demons were ready. They watched as the Carson City Gamblers took the field, hearing the loud cheers and rambunctious fans rooting on their home team.

Top of the first...

Los Angeles' hottest hitter, Damon Lewis (.667 AVG in the series, with the only homer for the visiting team), got the do-or-die game underway. He swung at a first pitch fastball from Ramon Ontaro, flying out to left for out number one. Lewis wasn't the traditional, work-the-count, leadoff. But who could argue with his production all season? The Demons lived with it. With the count 1-2 on Jeff Hartes, the Demon second baseman grounded out to David Wayne at second base. Two outs, nobody on. Last season's MVP, Jason Hicks, came to the plate hitting only .143 with no extra-base hits. On a hitter's 3-1 count, Hicks drilled a hard grounder right to Lionel Silcy as short, the smooth-fielding Gambler came up with the ball cleanly and threw to first for the final out. Three up, three down.

Bottom of the first...

Rookie Michael Tims made his postseason debut, throwing an electric 94-mph fastball for a first-pitch strike on Gambler centerfielder, Jessie Kato (.250 AVG). Veteran catcher, Ron Fetters, was behind the plate for the Demons. On a 1-1 count, Kato flied out to Erric Rutherford in left for the first out. David Wayne, a solo shot in game one, struck out on an outside heater, not able to catch up with Tims' healthy fastball. Bases empty, two down. All-star Aaron Craig (currently hitting .375 for the series) followed with a swinging bunt single. Hicks was playing too far off the infield at third base, and Craig got a lucky break, as none of the Demons' players could field the ball and throw him out in time. Craig then showcased some of his all-around abilities, stealing second on a one-and-one count. With two away and a runner in scoring position, left-handed first baseman James Colbrunn lined one to the opposite field. With Rutherford playing more shallow than normal against the lefty, and with the ball being hit so hard, Carson City's third base coach held Craig from trying to score on Colbrunn's single. The Gamblers would need a big two-out hit from Martin Spews. Fetters jogged out to chat with

Tims, trying to calm him down and stress that he needed to keep his pitches down. But Tims got a fastball up, Spews caught up with the pitch and drove it over Goodwin's head in right. The two-out double would score only Craig, as Colbrunn wasn't the fastest runner. One-to-nothing in favor of the home team. Runners on second and third now, rightfielder Ivan Gutierrez tried to blow this game wide open. Instead, he hit a sharp grounder to third for out number three. Heading to the top of the second, the home team had struck first. Gamblers 1, Demons 0.

Top of the second...

"Big Daddy" Steve Gunn tried to get the middle of the order going for Los Angeles, but failed, striking out a nasty splitter from Ontaro. Rutherford followed, grounding out to second. Fetters, hitless in the series, ended the quick half of the inning by grounding out to Silcy on a 3-1 fastball. Three up, three down, for the second time.

Bottom of the second...

Barry Hunt singled through the left side on the first pitch from Tims. Silcy, batting .500, kept the rally going, doubling to left-center. With nobody out, Hunt was held up at third. The pitcher, Ontaro, couldn't get a run home, striking out on three pitches. The Demon infield were playing in at the corners, and very near the grass at second and short. Kato, 0-1 on the game, hit a hard grounder to Hartes. The slick-fielding second baseman quickly fired home, gunning out a charging Hunt. Fetters applied the tag as the runner barreled him over, holding on to the ball for the second out. With two away and no runs home yet in the second, Tims couldn't get out of the inning unscathed. Wayne blooped a single to rightfield, driving home Silcy. The score was now 2-0 Carson, runners on the corners for Craig, who had already singled and scored in the first. The fans were on their feet, making all the noise they could muster. Craig, on a 1-1 slider, popped up to the catcher to end another rough inning for Tims, even though the damage was light. Two-to-nothing Gamblers after two.

Top of the third...

The Demons' dugout seemed to still be alive, realizing things could have gotten much uglier. Ontaro remained perfect to begin the third, striking out Goodwin looking. Nathan Willis, two-for-six in the series, flied out to Craig for the second out. Tims, one of the better hitting pitchers in the Western League, couldn't get the Demons a much-needed spark, flying out to rightfield on a full count. The Demons went down quietly again.

Bottom of the third...

Colbrunn grounded out to Hartes for the first out. Spews, with an RBI double on the game, then flied out to deep center, just shy of the wall. With two quick outs, Gutierrez kept Tims from having an easy inning by singling up the middle. The super-speedy rightfielder then stole second, already his third stolen base of the short series. Gamblers catcher Barry Hunt was hit by an inside fastball. Once again, Tims would have to try and dodge another bullet. Two runners on for Silcy, who scored the second run of the game. The Gambler shortstop flied out to right, ending the third and keeping Tims on the mound. The score remained, 2-0 Carson City.

Top of the fourth...

After sailing through the first three innings, Ontaro allowed his first base runner. Lewis fought off several full-count pitches before drawing a leadoff walk. He then stole second base, Wayne not able to come up with Hunt's throw cleanly. It was his first SB of the series. Hartes, with only one hit in the first two games, lined a single to the opposite field, driving in Lewis for the Demons first run of the game. The Los Angeles bench were on their feet and truly alive for the first time. Ontaro kicked some dirt around on the mound, appearing as though he was trying to delay pitching to Jason Hicks, even though the Demons' third baseman was slumping. But on a full-count fastball, one that the hard-throwing Gambler pitcher left over the heart of the plate, Hicks finally got solid wood on the ball. He sent a rocket-shot down the leftfield line, clearing the fence without any doubt and disappearing beyond a collection of exotic palm trees. Los Angeles had their first lead of the game, three-to-two.

"You really knocked the shit outta' that one!" Gunn congratulated his teammate as Hicks crossed home. The team had funneled out of the dugout and were giving Hartes and Hicks their props.

"Too high!" Fetters said, holding his right hand above his eyes, pretending to look far into the sky beyond the High Roller Park's green-padded wall.

"Too far!" Goodwin added, doing the same gesture. They exchanged excited laughs before prancing back into the bench area with the rest of the fired-up ballclub.

"Dead red?" Nate asked.

"Dead red," Hicks answered.

With three in and nobody out, Gunn hit a hard liner right to Silcy at short. A bit of bad luck on a well-struck ball. Rutherford then walked. This brought Gambler pitching coach, Bruce Hopkins, out to the mind for a brief visit. Ontaro kept shaking his head, signaling that he was still okay and wanted to keep pitching. Hopkins went back to the dugout, leaving the starter to do his thing. The Gamblers had a lefty, all-star, Lenny Cox, and a righty, their fourth starter, Ricky Martinez, now throwing in the bullpen. On a first-pitch fastball, Fetters hit a hard grounder to second, which Wayne fielded easily, flipping to second to Silcy, who then fired to first for the easy, 4-6-3, double play. That ended the top of the fourth, but the damage had been done.

Bottom of the fourth...

Many times in baseball, a team has several opportunities to get to a star pitcher early. When they don't capitalize, scoring only a few runs or none when they could have blown the game open, good pitchers typically find their groove, knowing they had been let off the hook, and then it was time for them to close the door. Tims began this process in the fourth. Ontaro, remaining in the game as the starter, struck out to start the inning. Kato followed, flying out to shallow right on a 2-2 slider. And then, on a one-two fastball, the Gambler second baseman, Wayne, swung and miss. It was by far the easiest inning for Tims, as he appeared to be in cruise control. 3-2 lead for Los Angeles.

Top of the fifth...

Goodwin, hitting under .150 for the series, walked on five pitches. Ontaro's third walk brought Hopkins out to the mound for the second time, the Carson City bullpen picking up its pace. Nathan Willis, collecting a hit in both of the first two games, kept his playoff streak alive, drilling a 2-0 fastball over the leftfield fence. The Demons lead was now three, ending Ontaro's night. As the Demon shortstop stepped into the dugout, surrounded by cheering players, Hicks asked:

"Dead red?"

"Dead fuckin' red," Nate replied, giving his teammate a hard fist bump, followed by a helmet-to-helmet clash.

Ramon Ontaro, who threw 4 innings, allowing 5 earned runs, was replaced by righthander Ricky Martinez. Martinez (1-4) struggled early in the year as a rookie starter for the Gamblers, but began showing signs of consistency towards the tail end of the season. He now had a big job before him, trying to keep this game close and not let the Demons pull away, tallying any more runs. He got the first batter he faced out, as the Demons' pitcher, Michael Tims, lined out to second base. Lewis, who stole a base and scored in the fourth, flied out to Craig in left. Hartes collected his second single of the night, fighting off a 2-2 changeup and punching it over Wayne's head for an opposite-field hit. With a runner on first, Hicks struck out looking, arguing an outside fastball that had been called strike three. Moving to the bottom half of the fifth, the Demons now led five-to-two.

Bottom of the fifth...

Tims looked rock solid again. The Gamblers' leftfield all-star, Aaron Craig, waved at a one-two, low-and-away slider for the first out of the inning. Colbrunn struck out right behind him, frozen in place on an 0-2 curveball, a rare strikeout pitch for Tims, but a perfect call by Fetters behind the plate, keeping the Gamblers guessing. Spews followed with two outs, getting wood on the ball. He hit a towering fly to center, which was a can of corn for Damon Lewis. Another one-two-three inning for the Demon rookie, the score remained the same.

Top of the sixth...

Martinez kept the Gamblers at a kicking distance, getting through the sixth without any damage done. After a leadoff double by Gunn, his first extra-base hit of the series, Rutherford, Fetters, and Goodwin went down in order. Nobody was able to drive the stranded duck from the pond.

Bottom of the sixth...

"Since the Demons' escape artist, Michael Tims, came out of the early innings allowing only two runs, he has been simply amazing," The Duke announced.

Gutierrez grounded out. Hunt singled on a full-count

fastball, the eighth pitch of the at-bat, battling all the way through. Silcy then flied out to shallow center, leaving Hunt at first. And pinch-hitting for Martinez, the local fan favorite, Mickey Larsen, got this first hack of the series. He hit a crowd-pleasing shot that Goodwin ran down just short of the rightfield warning track for the final out. The score at the end of six: Los Angeles 5, Carson City 2.

Top of the seventh...

Lefty, Lenny Cox (4-1, 2.14 ERA), entered the game to pitch for Carson. This was his first appearance of the series, and the all-star didn't waste it. He made "Dead Red" Nathan Willis look silly, diving for breaking balls in the dirt. He got Tims to ground out for the second out. And after walking Lewis on nine pitches, Hartes flied out to leftfield. The Gamblers' bullpen had now done their job for three innings, keeping the Demons' lead from increasing.

Bottom of the seventh...

After a seventh-inning stretch that featured an United States Air Force flyby and some fireworks, the traditional "Take Me Out to the Ballgame" sung by the proclaimed guitar master, Gregory, Tims returned to the rubber. He showed his first sign of fatigue, walking Jessie Kato to lead-off the inning and then stretching his throwing arm. Larry George jogged out to the mound, met by the infield, including Ron Fetters. Simultaneously, Skip got the Demons' pen going—righty starter, Jay O'Dell, and lefty reliever, Darren Luthers. After a brief chat, the pitching mound cleared, leaving Tims to hopefully do what he did best, get batters out. But Wayne followed Kato's walk with an off-the-wall double to left-center, driving in the first Gambler run since the second inning. The gap was closing, five-to-three in favor of the visitors. With an open base, Tims didn't give Craig anything to hit, walking him on five pitches. With runners on first and second, the bulky lefty,

James Colbrunn, strolled to the batter's box. Meanwhile, Skip Bailey walked to the mound, motioning for his lefthander, D. Luthers. The night was over for Michael Tims, leaving with the tying run on first base and the lead. He pitched 6 innings, allowing 3 earned runs thus far; he was responsible for both baserunners, and struck out 6 batters. This was Luthers' second relief appearance, as he pitched the eighth in game one, striking out one batter and allowing zero runs. Javy Jimenez now joined O'Dell in the Los Angeles bullpen, getting his arm loose.

High Roller Park was a steady roar, the bleachers shaking beneath stomping feet and the thousands of voices echoing through the plush outfield. Colbrunn, hitting .200 in the series, took a big swing and missed at a first-pitch slurve—Luthers' signature out pitch. Luthers then came in on the lefty, throwing a low fastball that Colbrunn jumped all over. He hit a screamer to the right side, but Big Daddy made one hell of a play. Gunn backhanded the hard shot, snagging it out of the air after its first hop. He stepped on the first-base bag, trading the ball from his glove hand to his bare left hand, and then fired it to Willis at second. Craig, a smart base runner, didn't give up the easy double play, knowing there wasn't a force at second after Gunn retired the hitter. The Gamblers' leftfielder got in a rundown, forcing a couple of throws back and forth between first and second. Kato, while Craig tried to divert the Demons' attention his way, passed third and turned towards home. Hartes, who had taken the next role in the rundown, saw the runner moving towards home out of the corner of his eye, now hearing Fetters call for the ball as well. The Demon all-star second baseman fired home, Fetters applying the tag just in time. It was the second runner that Hartes had thrown out at home on the game. And it was a huge second out for the Demons. Craig moved up to second base, but the Gamblers' rally, along with their hopes, had been demoralized. Jimenez entered the game to pitch to the right-handed batter, Martin Spews. It was Jimenez's second playoff appearance as well. He got the third baseman to fly out, ending the seventh and holding the Demons' lead at two runs.

Top of the eighth...

Cox showcased his abilities, keeping the Demons from scoring on the Carson City bullpen yet again. He walked Hicks to leadoff the inning, but then struck out Gunn for the first out. Rutherford grounded out to third. Fetters then got his first hit of the series, drilling a mistake pitch to right-center for a two-out double. Goodwin couldn't make the Gamblers pay, though, grounding out to Silcy to end the mild threat. With six more outs needed for the Demons to advance to the Western League Championship, the score remained 5-3.

Bottom of the eighth...

Gutierrez, on a 2-2 count, grounded to Willis for the first out. Jimenez then dealt Barry Hunt (two hits and a walk on the night) a barrage of cutters, sawing off his handle on a broken-bat dribbler to the mound. Jimenez fielded the ball cleanly, and tossed it to Gunn for the second putout. Silcy lined out to Hicks, ending the eighth, and setting the stage for an exciting last inning.

Top of the ninth...

The Carson City closer, Binner Wilson, who tied for the league-lead in saves with L.A.'s own Salmon Seavers, 10 saves apiece, entered the game. He didn't pitch in game one, feeling a slight tightening in his throwing arm while warming up in the bullpen. And he hadn't been needed. But tonight, well-rested, Wilson was asked to come in and not close the game, but rather keep the Gamblers within striking distance. He first faced Nathan Willis, who had a two-run homer back in the fifth. The shortstop grounded out on the third pitch, an outside heater. Pinch-hitting for the Demons, as Salmon Seavers was warming up for the bottom half of the inning, was Bobby Parks, 0-4 in the series. The backup catcher singled through the left side, a bouncing grounder just out of Spews' and Silcy's reach. With a runner on, Lewis hit a 1-1 fastball by the pitcher's mound. The ball didn't have enough steam to make it through the infield, as Wayne fielded it, tossing it to Silcy at second for the force, who then fired to Colbrunn. The throw to first wasn't in time to get out the speedy centerfielder. Wilson, with two down, now faced Jeff Hartes. He proceeded to strike out the second baseman, ending the top of the inning and doing his job— maintaining scoreless performance for the Carson City relievers. Heading to a possible last inning for the Gamblers and their season, the Demons led by two.

Bottom of the ninth...

Due up for the Carson City Gamblers: pinch-hitter Everett Gorley, and then Kato and Wayne. If anyone got aboard, the dangerous Aaron Craig would get a chance. Seavers sprinted to the mound, drawing harsh boos and profane chants from his previous team's fans. The lefty closer, coming off a save in game two, lived for this moment. He lived for this opportunity to eliminate the defending Western League Champions; and at the same time, take his team to the championship against the waiting San Diego Knights.

"Seavers is all focus, pacing around the pitching mound with fierce eyes and a balled fury inside him. The Demons closer digs a suitable hole in front of the rubber and then sets himself. He stares in, I'm not sure if he's locked in on the catcher's mitt or the pinch-hitter, Gorley." The Duke was more nervous than any of the Los Angeles players on the field. If he wasn't responsible for calling the game back to the Demon faithful, he might not have watched the last inning. He wanted to put his head in his hands and ball up, waiting for someone else to come by and tell him, 'The Demons won.'

Gorley waved his bat over the plate, slightly bending his wrists back and forth. Seavers took the ball from his glove and rolled it around in his magical throwing hand. After watching two inside fastballs pass by, both called strikes that caused Gorley to shake his head in disagreement; the Gamblers' sub choked up on his lumber and dug in a little deeper. Seavers came a little more in, and a little higher up, driving the opposing batter out of the box and stumbling backwards. Another deafening sound of boos filled the ballpark. A second ball on the outside corner, and then with a 2-2 count, Gorley put the pitch in play. He fought off another heater and hit a dying chopper towards short. Willis fielded the ball with his bare hand and threw on the move, beating the hustling runner by a step for the first out. One away. Kato, 0-3 on the night, followed in a similar fashion. But this time, the weak grounder was right to Gunn, who took it to the bag himself for the second putout. The Carson City all-star centerfielder had a disappointing series, now hitting .167 with only one run scored. The Demons were one out away from the championship.

"The Los Angeles Demons are on the brim of their first Western League Championship appearance. David Wayne steps in to face Seavers, the last ray of hope for the fans here at High Roller Park," The Duke announced.

The count was one ball, one strike. Wayne, two-for-four on the night with a double, appeared to fear no one. He had played with Seavers. He had seen his electric stuff time and time again. He believed he knew the pitcher's tendencies quite well. And with a 1-1 count, he guessed fastball in. Wayne turned on the 95+ mph pitch and drilled it towards third. Hicks fielded the ball perfectly, snagging it on the ball's last hop from the infield grass. He fired towards first. The throw was high, sailing over Gunn's head and into the rightfield bleachers. Wayne moved to second on the error, and the game continued. While Hicks cursed himself, Aaron Craig moved from the on-deck area to homeplate. The crowd was rambunctious — a solid, piercing roar — cheering their superstar, who played the part of the tying run, at the plate. The Demons were at the dugout steps, praying for Seavers to do what he'd done all year, close this mother out. They were eager to sprint onto the field and let their inner youth release, not worrying about what other people thought or how one was perceived in a certain setting, this was time to let it all out. Craig jumped on the first pitch — an outside fastball — and drove it down the rightfield line. The ball hung in the air, seeming to hover in an area where gravity didn't exist. That extra hang time was just long enough for Goodwin to close the distance between the moving object he was suppose to catch and his outfielder's glove. Letting it all hang out, Goodwin fully extended, diving without fear for the fly ball. He made a sensational catch, skidding on his belly, bumping his chin on the spongy grass, and then holding the ball — trapped in his glove — above his head. The ump bellowed, "He's out!"

The Demons dugout, players and coaches alike, stormed the visitor's field. Hugs, high-fives, fist bumps, dog-piling, and more spread through the entire team like a frenzy. They hadn't yet reached their ultimate goal, but they had achieved another stepping stone along the way. Something to be very proud of.

Jeff Hartes remembered turning around, after he was one-hundred percent positive that Goodwin made the spectacular grab and the series was truly over, and sprinting towards the rightfielder. He felt Gunn on his right, and Nathan Willis behind him. Hartes ran towards Big Daddy, jumping into him with a chest bump. He missed the attempt at a high-five, and then Gunn wrapped his head in his arms and tackled Hartes to the ground. They never reached Goodwin. The rightfielder, along with Damon and Nate, joined their own, smaller dog-pile, in the outfield. The rest of the Demons gathered around the pitching mound, celebrating and hollering cheers of an unexplainable joy.

The Los Angeles Demons were moving on to play the San Diego Knights for the Western League Championship. The series would begin on June 4th at Diego Field, allowing one day of travel and rest for the hungry underdogs.

That night, the Demons traveled straight from Carson City to San Diego. The players knew their celebrating wouldn't last long, because once the morning of the fourth rolled around, it was all business yet again. They sprayed champagne in their visitors clubhouse, dousing the room and each other with the sparkling wine. They poured and wasted more than they drank, but saved a few bottles for the bus ride.

There was laughter and smiles during the road trip, but the heavy drinking — besides the bubbly — and the long night of cards or some other form of gambling ceased to exist. Sleep overtook many of the players before the fancy travel bus even crossed the Nevada state line. Hartes, curled up in his bunk in the back of the bus, shivering beneath the AC's chilling blast with only a light blanket, finally allowed the exciting moment to calm... and he finally found some rest.

Chapter Eighteen
Storytime

I

"High fly ball hit by Allen to centerfield. Lewis takes a few steps back, and makes the catch. That ends the fifth, Demons one, Knights nothing. Due up for Los Angeles in the sixth, Parks, Hicks, and Gunn," Darrell Marinville announces to the Demon faithful.

...

Luthers hangs a 2-2 curveball that Ponds drills to rightfield. I run out just on the edge of the infield, where the beautifully plush grass meets dirt. I don't have time to line up Goodwin as he's already fielded the ball on the second hop and is firing towards the plate. I turn to home. The throw is slightly off-line and late... the Knights take the lead. The stadium has its volume at a crest. The crowd is absolutely bedlam.

Ramon Garrido flies out to Lewis to end the inning, but the damage has been done. The fans cheer and applaud, not one person sitting in the entire ballpark. I jog in, turning to see the score — San Diego 2, Los Angeles 1 — avoiding the girl in the stands. The dugout is alive with optimism and hope. Hicks comes by me, saying, "Get a fucking helmet on, Hartes!"

I wasn't due up until fourth in the last inning. *Don't*

mess with the Karma, Hartes. Get up and get ready! It's all around you. I move to the helmet bin like a patient drugged for surgery. Everything feels so numb. I need something to help me snap out of it. I just don't know what. *Maybe the girl in the stands?*

"Let's go Hicks, get on base, baby!" Fetters yells beside me.

I can hear The Duke once again, somehow, someway. His voice carries through the radio waves and into my mind. I look around, just checking for the millionth time if anyone else appears to hear him as well, but no one has a clue. He announces Jason Hicks, and then says that Gunn is on deck, followed by Rutherford. If anyone were to get on base, that would bring up Jeff Hartes.

Jeff Hartes? Get a fucking helmet on, Hartes!

Hicks is in the box now, facing the Knights' closer, Rich Treplow, a South Division all-star with eight saves on the season. Everyone on the Demons' bench is up against the rail, sporting rally caps and clenched fists. I feel someone up against me on my right. I turn and see the bat boy, Wade Smith. He looks up at me, smiling with confidence. He appears to be the only person that isn't feeling the pressure. He appears to be —

"Hicks is going to do it," Smith says to me. "He's going to tie this game right here."

I hope so, my friend.

I truly hope so —

I watch the last strike go by, Hicks swinging and dropping to his knees. A seemingly valiant effort from the hero... the role model... the Demon all-star with the weight of an entire season on his shoulders. I turn back to Wade Smith. But the bat boy is gone. I see Gunn standing in the batter's box. I see Rutherford standing in the on-deck circle. My instincts guide me off the pine; they pull me to the helmet bin. The #9 beckons, dirt and Pine Tar soften the edges. I grab the head protector, standing on the dugout's steps.

I watch a puddle—of Gatorade, of water, I don't know—as it reflects the immense stadium lighting from the concrete below. *It must be cold.* It speaks to me from another world. The gills of a dying fish, breathing... searching for its final breath of cruel air. It says so much more. It understands that this situation isn't for me. *This isn't my time to shine...*

This isn't my place. This is definitely somewhere else. This *is* someone else's time to shine. I stare into space. My wandering mind and phallic eyes gleam deep. My reserved thoughts are interrupted by screams of joy—screams of ecstasy. I look down from other worlds to see Steve Gunn rounding first base. The burly infielder returns to the bag with a one-out single. I realize it's now my time to move out into the dreaded circle—mocking me with white-painted guidelines. Walking, I follow Rutherford's movements. He does the cross thing, lets out a casting breath of nervous air, and then digs in.

The fans are at an unexplainable high; their noise carries through one's mind and into the realms of a front row seat near the orchestra pit. My eyes water. An unseen, imaginary smoke glazes the lens, coating them with a cut onion's insensitivity. I swing the bat like I'm supposed to. I'm getting loose. Unless some unforeseen... some catastrophic mishap occurs, I will get my shot. I wasn't thrilled with it. *I am thrilled with it. I am.* But the doubt fights harder. The lies, the convincing attempts, can't win tonight.

A hush clears my distractions. Rutherford walks by me. "Muthafuckin'... muthafuckin'... godda—" he stops next to me, meeting eyes like locking lasers. He tells me,

"It's all you, nigga'."

I close my eyes. I feel my feet move towards homeplate — the internal pattern guiding as though I were blind with a recollected memory.

I see my father sitting in the dinner chair, back to the wall of an empty room. *Failure is an option...* But he doesn't speak. I put the words, the thoughts, in his mouth for him. I force the dialogue. But only in my mind. No lips move. He places his hands, fist on top of fist, acting as a readied batter. He rises from the chair, still grasping the imaginary lumber. He imitates the immortal swing of Henry Aaron. He smiles. I shake my head. *I just don't know if I have it in me.*

Will appears in a window that wasn't there before. The paned glass is dirty with streaks of dusty film, cobwebs hang from the corners. Will peers through the translucent barrier and nods. "Everyone's got *it* in them," he says. "Some just don't know where to look for it. Some just don't know how to bring it to the surface."

My mom and Eric replace my father in the simple room. The chair is gone as well. They stand side by side, Eric one-arm hugging her and saying an eyes-closed prayer. His lips move, soft sounds leaving his mouth, but they aren't clear. His prayer seems to be for his brother's success. His mother squeezes Eric harder, forcing good things to happen in the future.

They are all gone. I spin in circles, staring at one blank wall and then another and then another and then the fourth of the squared room. The dizziness overcomes me. I sit on the floor, pulling my knees towards my chest. I shake my head, saying 'no' over and over again. I stare at the floor, the hardwood below opens up. I've literally burned a hole in the floor with my eyes.

Down into the deep black, way down, out of reach and

willingly out of mind, Shae's face appears. She's laughing and tossing her gentle, brown hair from side to side. "It's in you, Jeff Anthony Hartes. I've known it from the beginning. I knew it when we were apart. I knew things would work out in the end."

What end? The question repeats itself in my head. *What end is she talking about?*

But she continues, ignoring my thoughts. I try to teleport into her own. "Search deep, you've come up big plenty of times before now. You've overcome and delivered. Block out the negative thoughts. Block out the San Diego crowd. Forget everything you've ever learned or ever practiced for... and simply trust the swing. Don't think, just—"

"STEEE-RIKE ONE!" the homeplate umpire stirs me from my out-of-body visions. I turn to see him laughing on the inside. *He must know, too.* The San Diego catcher throws the ball back to the mound. I see Gunn leading off of first base, clapping his hands and hoping for me to do something—something to tie this damn game.

The stands are empty. *The noise, the overwhelming noise that enters my mind from ever opening, from ever direction, ceases to exist.* Everyone has left the field, players and all, except for me, the pitcher, the catcher, and the head ump. The dugouts have evacuated. The booth is silent. The world, everything besides this tiny mound-to-home peninsula, jutting out from the outfield walls like the tip of an anchor, has disappeared. I can't imagine why the San Diego pitcher starts his wind up. Doesn't he know? Doesn't he realize that something is terribly wrong? But the pitch comes anyway. Unprepared, I watch a fast one slide by. I turn to the umpire, thinking, *this can't be happening. There's no way he's going to make the call.*

"STEEE-RIKE TWO!" he bellows. Simultaneously, the

fans, the players, the coaches, the front office personnel, everyone and every last thing, returns like a crashing wave. *The noise* is back, blaring in my ears like a king's trumpet. 'Your majesty is here,' *but is he really?*

I step out of the batter's box. *The game has gotten out of hand. They can't allow it to go on this way. This isn't how it ends, is it?*

The pitcher nods. Cold, dead eyes stare into the mitt — trying to intimidate, trying to win this game mentally. *I gotta' swing the bat.* His arms were jello. Rubbery. Weak. The weight of the world had moved onto Hartes' shoulders, and the load was impossible to bear. *There is no end... there is no end...*

The ball's coming, Jeff! Swing the fucking —

Wood clashes with rawhide. My hands sting as I had tried to get the bat head through, but was jammed. I start to run to first, my instincts guide me down the base path. Sawed off, I toss the bat handle aside full sprint now. I find the ball floating in the air, a magical dancing sphere orbiting towards the left-side of the plush diamond. A fielder races from third base. A fielder races from short.

Get through you son of a bitch!

"Get through —"

II

One minute sound asleep, dreaming the dream.

The next...

Hartes was wide awake with a shielded heat lighting the back of the bus. The tinted blinds had been tugged down, doing their best to block the morning from waking the drowsy passengers. He knew he had had another you know what. But in his mind, he heard three words repeating... *the last one.*

What they meant? He didn't really know. He didn't understand what was happening during his restless nights, but he did understand that *something* was happening. He knew the dreams were there. He just didn't know what was inside them. Inside the core. Inside his own confused body.

"Let me get through," Lake said, disturbing the quiet and gently kicking at someone sleeping in the bus' back aisle. The words, 'get through,' struck a chord in Jeff's mind. They hit a confused nerve, just as lost as the rest of his body was. Nonetheless, the words rang with a larger-than-life aspect. Something greater. Something that lay ahead. "I've got to take a dump," Lake added.

"Oh hell," Fetters said, rolling over in his bunk across the aisle from Jeff's. "Take that smelly black ass somewhere else."

Lake chuckled and ignored his catcher. The player on the floor moaned, but rolled to one side, allowing passage. Lake tiptoed the rest of the way, disappearing inside the bathroom. Hartes dozed off again, not waking until the team had traveled inside San Diego's city limits.

III

After arriving at the fancy 32-story Omni San Diego Hotel, nestled in the heart of the historic Gaslamp Quarter, and checking into the rooms, Skip Bailey called a rare "meeting."

It was held in the hotel's banquet room, which served dinner buffets upon special request, and the Demons' owner, Greg Viselli, was going to pick up the tab. Once the entire team had arrived, serving themselves to an assortment of food possibilities—there was top sirloin, fried chicken, hot wings, meatballs, grilled Italian chicken, mashed potatoes, fries, steamed broccoli, red cabbage, fried okra, and not to mention the desserts, carrot cake, German chocolate cake, apple and cherry cobbler, and more—Skip rose from his chair and tapped the side of his glass of tea with a spoon. The noise died down, and the remaining players returning to their seats found them.

Skip asked, "Can I have everyone's attention, please?"

The room hushed. The only sounds were ice rattling in a glass that was being drank from, or forks, spoons, and knives colliding gently with the porcelain dishes. Skip began, "I've been thinking of a way to make this special night enjoyable and entertaining, and all the while, educational and relaxing towards your baseball knowledge. I know I've shared some of these stories with the veterans, a couple of years back at the least, and I feel you younger players deserve to hear them as well. I believe it will serve you well in understanding who you are playing for tomorrow, not just yourself, the Demons, your fans, but also me, your coach, French Bailey.

"I didn't play college ball. I went straight to the pros, signing a contract to play in the rookie-league straight out of high school. My high school team made it to the state finals, where we lost in the bottom of the ninth, on my fielding error. It was the first error I had made since our district, and playoff, games had started. After that, I played several seasons in the minors, making it to one more championship, and losing that one as well.

"I then played five seasons in the 'Bigs.' Three with the Reds between '70 and '72, and two with the Mets in '73 and '74. I made it to the World Series three times, never winning a single one of them. That brought my personal total in my baseball life to oh-and-five in championships. I hung up my cleats, my knees couldn't take anymore behind the plate, watching baseball as a spectator for almost a decade. Then I took the head coaching job at the single-A level with the Stockton Ports. As a head coach, both in single-A and double-A, before coaching the Demons, I lost two more championships. I really thought that lucky number seven would be the one I finally got over the hump with, but it wasn't the case.

"So for all of you who hadn't yet known, your trusted coach, whom you love so dearly and worship—" Skip paused while laughter filled the banquet room. He waited for the noise to lessen, and then proceeded, "—Now you know. You are going to face a good San Diego team, with an oh-for-life coach. The gambling odds aren't the only ones against you. Fate, as well, stands in your way."

The room was silent.

Big Daddy stood. "There's always time for a first time!" he shouted, bringing the Demons to life. Some cheering, applauding, and players discussing things amongst themselves followed. Skip, smiling, patted Larry George on the back and waited for the commotion to die back down. He waved a hand, motioning in a polite manner that he wasn't yet finished.

And then Skip continued his speaking. "I've got a few stories, from my days of baseball, to share with you. Some that I've personally experienced and been involved with. Others I've been told, something worth passing to you now. I think it will take your mind off the series ahead and hopefully replace any tension with some humorous baseball tales.

"The first... boy, it's a humdinger. A friend of mine, a guy I shared a room with in the minors during my playing days in the southeast, Davey Phillips was his name, we were both fond of late-night fishing. Anytime we were on the road, playing in Louisiana, Georgia, Florida, we were always seeking out the perfect fishing hole to wet our lures. It just so happened, the two of us ended up in the swamp one night, fishing after dark. We knew the waters were infested with gators, so we cast from the shore, sometimes sitting on the back of Davey's Ford's tailgate to rest our feet.

"I don't know how these other idiots found us, but they did. Two of our relief pitchers, and our drunken first baseman, a fella missing a few brain cells that we called, 'Deuce.' They came from one of the local bars, where Deuce had drank one too many. I've never seen a grownup so shit-faced. He was staggering around the water's edge, mouthing about this and that, carrying on and on, never making any sense. I kept telling Massen, *his* roommate, to get a hold of him and keep him away from the damn water. We finally got Deuce to calm down and sit on the tailgate.

"Just when things got quiet, and we thought he might be passing out in the back of the truck, I heard this stomping noise. It was like dunt-dunt-dunt, and then here came Deuce full-speed, staggering like a madman right between us and our rods, falling face-first into the alligators' den. With his arms flailing and his legs kicking, the idiot stayed afloat in the two-foot deep area near the bank. But with all the panicky splashing, we thought for sure he would arouse a gator and make a nice meal. Me, Davey, Massen, and the other pitcher, a reliever who didn't last long, and I forget his name anyways, all helped in pulling that idiot from the water. Soaking wet, Deuce stripped out of his clothes, down to his tighty-whites and put them in the back of the truck. He sat on the tailgate again, one might think the cold, muddy water with gators lurking, might sober one up. But not Deuce... not on this night.

"He sat on the tailgate, looking as drunk as ever. Shaking. Shivering. Damn fool. And you won't believe this. Not ten minutes later, as we kept on fishing and swapping our own stories, that stupid S.O.B. did the same damn thing. Here came Deuce again, stumbling forward full steam ahead, flying face-first into the water once again. This time... we left him to splash around a little longer. Shaking our head half the time, because the idiot had ruined our fishing, laughing the other half of the time. When we finally decided to yank him back out, Massen and the other pitcher said they were leaving. Me and Davey had none of that. Bullshit if we were going to babysit our teammate. We weren't the ones who brought him out of the hotel. So we packed up his clothes and sent him with the pitchers back to the hotel. Deuce riding with only his undies on, no shoes, no socks, nothing else.

"This is where my part in the story, until the next day, ends. But this isn't where Deuce's wild ride finished. No. That dumb S.O.B. found more trouble. So I'll tell it as best as it was told to me."

Skip paused to take a drink of water from his table. Hartes and the rest of the Demons had already laughed plenty, enjoying their coach's past, and were eager for more. After wetting his beak, Skip cleared his throat and proceeded.

"Somewhere along the line, Massen and the other pitcher ditched Deuce. It was either just outside the hotel. Or somewhere inside. But either way, the drunken first baseman got locked outside in the parking lot. Wearing nothing but his whites, no one really knows where all he wandered, walking around barefoot through the asphalt and gravel and broken glass. He banged on the locked hotel entry door, sometime between four and five in the morning, and one of our outfielders, wandering around the hotel's hall, let him in. Deuce found his room, no telling how many doors or people he frightened along the way. Massen let him in and told him to take a shower, seeing that there was dirt and grass on his knees and shit all over him. Plus, his feet were cut up and bleeding everywhere. Massen put his idiot roommate in the bathroom, pushing him onto the floor and turning the shower on, and then going back to his own bed for some sleep.

"After Massen couldn't fall asleep, he said he heard the shower running for at least an hour, he went back to the bathroom. There, still sitting on the floor was Deuce. He hadn't even made it into the running water. Massen picked him up and pushed him into the shower. He then dragged him out of the shower and had had enough. He left Deuce's cold, wet ass lying in the bathroom and went back to bed.

"He awoke again, soon after, this time to the sound of Deuce taking a piss in the room's trashcan, which was between their two beds. Massen couldn't believe his eyes. He knew there was only one thing left to do. The relief pitcher got out of bed, grabbed Deuce by the shoulder with one hand, and then belted him in the face with a straight-on punch right in the eye. Deuce dropped to the ground. Finally, some peace and quiet.

"The next—"

Before Skip could continue, Fred Sanders interrupted. "Did Massen hit him with his pitching hand?"

Skip scratched his head, and then shrugged his shoulders. "Hell if I know," the Demons' coach replied, "This was before Tim Robbins and Kevin Costner movies."

Larry George hopped up and said, "This was before anyone gave a damn which hand was hurt. Pitchers in those days just pitched. We didn't cry about sore arms and pitch counts."

There was laughter from the position players and amusing boos from the pitching staff. Once the room calmed yet again, Skip finished his first story.

"The next day, the first time I saw Deuce, I couldn't stop laughing. He had the biggest, swollen, black eye I'd ever seen. He walked with a profound limp, hobbling along to keep up with us as me and some of the other players got a ride in the hotel's bus to grab a late lunch before we headed to the visiting ballpark. Before we even pulled completely out of the parking lot, Deuce hollered at the driver to stop. The goofy bastard jumped out of the van and disappeared into some nearby bushes. When he came back, there in his arms were his clothes and boots from the night before. I guess it's true what they say about returning to the scene of the crime. He remembered hardly nothing. But he did remember where he stashed his clothes after being abandoned the night before. It was a riot in the hotel van. All the players laughing their balls off. The only other funny thing was when we got to the park and began getting ready for the game. That's when I first saw Deuce's feet. They looked horrible. They had puss-filled blisters and cuts all over them. But you've got to hand it to 'em, he played the game. Got two hits as well."

The Demons stood and applauded as though their coach had just received an award and finished his "celebratory speech." They wanted more. They wanted to Skip to keep them coming. So he did.

Skip drank some more water and then started, "This one's a little shorter. It's just a quick story that I always found quite amusing and one that has stuck in my mind for a good while now. This was a few years after Deuce's wild night. I was catching in the minors in Pennsylvania. I had this teammate we called R.C. He had just been sent down from the Twins on a rehab stint.

"Well... we went out to this hot new club where all the 'big-leaguers' were supposed to go. After a couple of hours of drinking with about a dozen teammates, it was my turn to go to the bar counter, along with R.C., to buy the next round. When we finally pushed our way through the packed crowd and got to the actual bar, I remember looking over and seeing R.C. reaching in his pants. The ex-Twin's pitcher, in the darkness and with all the loud music, pulled his dick out and started peeing underneath the bar top and began ordering the drinks at the same time. I smiled, doing my best to keep from laughing like a fool and also trying not to forget the drink orders.

"When we got back to our seats, I told the story to the rest of the players. R.C. laughed and said, 'That's how the big-leaguers do it, just so you minor-league hacks know.' The rest of the fellas shrugged off R.C.'s comments and kept on chatting and drinking the night away. Another hour of drinking passed, and R.C. was now quite hammered. I took my turn again, with him behind me, and headed for the bar. I stood at the counter, R.C. on my left, and started to order the next round. I glanced over, seeing him doing it again. I shook my head and laughed. 'Big-league, right?' I asked. He nodded, started to release a stream of urine, and said, 'Right.'

"Just then, this beautiful blonde bombshell, wearing a gold cocktail dress and showing the finest pair of legs I've ever seen, walked up on R.C.'s left. I watched her lean against the bar and holler for a Vodka Martini, straight. She turned to her right, seeing the pitcher, and shouted, 'Hey! Don't I know you?' R.C., beyond drunk, didn't miss a beat. He turned to face the girl, saying, 'Hell yeah, you know me.'

"All the while, that constant stream of pee kept flowing. It sprayed her pretty dress, her legs, her shoes. It was a water hose turned on high that had gone array. Piss was everywhere. I don't know if she screamed first at it getting on her or at the sight of R.C.'s dick, but she screamed loud. It's safe to say that the ex-big-leaguer was tossed from the nightclub that night. But his approach at the bar makes one hell of an amusing memory."

For the second time, the Demons all stood from their white-clothed tables and cheered. They clapped their hands and whistled at their coach. The chant started, "More, more, more, more..."

And Skip had no choice, but to keep feeding his little warriors. *Keep the Indians happy, they will fight for the Chief.*

"This last story is one I'm sure most of you have already heard. This isn't from my glory days, but from your's. It's probably my most recent favorite; at least, the best that you yay-hoos have actually felt it necessary to share with me. It involves three of your teammates, Mr. Hicks—"

"Of course," Thomas Perry added, sitting near the front of the room. Skip nodded and continued.

"Mr. Hicks, Mr. Goodwin, and Mr. Fetters. Now this was a few years back, when Ron drank a little too much and got in a bit of trouble now and then. Nowadays—"

This time, Skip was interrupted by Lake Williams, who dropped the bomb on his favorite catcher. "What the fuck's changed?" he asked of Ron Fetters in comparison to his past and present.

Skip turned to face Lake and said, "Well... now that you mention it, not much."

Fetters now stood, saying, "Why don't you sons-a-bitches sit down and let Coach tell the damn story."

And everyone laughed. Larry George slapped his table hard enough to rattle the silverware and knock Jay O'Dell's drink over. Fetters shook his head, his cheeks full of a post-meal wad of tobacco, and sat back down. Skip, also chuckling, tried a third time to get the final story underway.

"Like I was saying, this was in Fetters' prime—" the Demons' coach smiled and waited for another remark, but none came this time. The players were ready for another tale. "So these goofballs head out for a night on the town, in... in... Oakland. And they find them a real hottie.

"I believe Billy was a rookie, but I'm not sure—" the Demon outfielder nodded from his seat, "—him and Hicks and Ron over there, went to this bar and hit on some of the California girls. As Jason said it, he took Billy under his wing, and the two of them landed a couple of hot brunettes. Some dancing, some chatting, and then the girls introduced their darker-haired friend to Fetters. Ron tried to be extra smooth with this smokin' olive-skinned, black-haired firecracker. She was way out of the catcher's league. Hell, she might have been..."

As Skip trailed off in thought, Hicks said, "Shiiit, Coach, she really wasn't that hot!"

Laughter in the room followed, and then Skip smiled and continued, "I know, Jason. I was just trying to build up Ron some more. Add a little flavor to the story because everyone knows the quality of ass he usually gets... *not very.*"

Fetters interrupted again, "Can we just tell the damn story?"

Skip Bailey motioned for the catcher to calm down. He scratched at his rough-skin cheek and proceeded, "Anyways, this girl wouldn't dance with Ron. She said she was tired and didn't feel like shakin' it that night. Her friends went along with her story. So Ron sat with her at her table, sharing some drinks, getting a little too drunk, while Jason and Billy danced with her friends. And then somehow, maybe roofies, maybe not, he convinced her to let him take her back home, where she roomed with the other two girls. The catcher and the bar-girl snuck out of the bar, leaving Jason, Billy, and her friends behind, and they rode in Ron's ride back to her place. Somewhere along the way, they started kissing and loving and getting all fired up. Oh Ronnie, oh black-hair. He must have been pretty drunk or carried her inside to miss that limp. But either way, they went to the bedroom, and she dropped down on the bed back first. Ron started to tug her tight jeans off and lo and behold, he pulled her freakin' prosthetic leg right off, right out of the socket. So there stood this idiot, holding onto her fake leg.

"At that time, Jason and Billy arrived with her roommates. Jason said he remembered staggering to the front door, hearing someone scream like a little bitch, and then the front door blew open, with Ron Fetters running out of it faster than he would trying to turn a gapper into a double. He carried the poor girl's leg under his arm, still screaming and running for his car. Ron was slow and all, but he was just a bit faster than the one-legged girl after him. The catcher yelled for Jason and Billy, who didn't know what the hell was going on, to get the hell out of Dodge. Following Jason's lead, a veteran in matters of the heart, Billy and the third baseman darted for their own vehicle. The three idiots left the scene, driving separate vehicles away from there and back to the Demons' hotels as fast as they could go. All the while, Ron Fetters still had that poor girl's prosthetic leg with him."

Skip raised both hands as the room applauded and cheered. Jay O'Dell asked, "What happened to the leg?"

And Skip responded, "Hell, we put that good-luck charm front and center, hanging in the clubhouse showers for the rest of the season. Didn't work too well, though. We didn't win shit."

Jeff and Nate and some of the other youngsters thought that Skip's recollections were perfect. The fascinating accounts distracted the Demons' players from being nervous, from dwelling on the future, and from getting antsy.

Some of the players snacked some more, eating the splendid variety of foods on the buffet line. Others allowed their full bellies to relax, continuing with their own table of conversation and reminiscing over past ventures.

After a couple of hours, tired baseball stars began to funnel out, heading for their exquisite Omni rooms, eager to lie down and attempt sleep. But for the majority, a good night's rest was one series away.

Jeff Hartes didn't sleep much that night, either. He rested in bed, eyes closed, but still awake, thinking. Thinking of Shae. Thinking of his current situation and how proud he was to be here. Thinking about Demon baseball.

IV

The Los Angeles Demons were less than five hours away from their first championship series, against the San Diego Knights.

And for rookie Jeff Hartes, it was his first shot at a ring on any level. It was an opportunity that the veterans would tell you, 'Don't ever take it for granted, when you make it early in your career to any championship, don't take it for granted. You think, man, this is how it's gonna' be every year. And then... you've played a decade of professional sports and haven't even sniffed another opportunity. Sometimes they come in spurts. Sometimes they come early and then late. And sometimes they don't come at all. But if they do, don't take it for granted that there will ever be another. Give it everything you've got.'

With Pantera's *Walk* blasting out of the speakers in the back of the bus, the Demons headed to Diego Field for game one.

Chapter Nineteen
Western League
Championship

I

A long, harsh coughing spell disrupts the old man from his memories. He feels like he is choking... gasping... searching for a release so that he can take in one full breath of air.

The moment comes. A painful blast surges his thirsty lungs. Lightheaded and dizzy, Jeff unfolds his favorite chair to its reclining position. He shoots one burst of wind from his mouth, and then another, up towards the ceiling, taking in fulfilling breaths of oxygen in between.

I'm running out of time...

The ninth inning is here and the baseball game that is my life is almost over. It's night coming in the early ages of the game, before there were lights — during the Golden Era of Baseball. The stands are emptying. The people you've shared your life with are all going home. You're on your own, Hartes. There's no pitcher. There's no catcher. There's just a lonely hitter, standing in an eternal batter's box that carries with it no immortality, just the inevitable fate we all face... death.

With his breathing finally returning to a steady rate, Jeff drops the recliner down and sits up straight. He drops his chin to his chest, closes his eyes, a momentary check that everything is working properly, before attempting to stand. "I think I've got one more game in me. One more. A good game, that one, without holding back."

Jeff returns to the scrapbook, lying amidst a pile of stacked mail and unread magazines on his coffee table. He picks up the book of memories, its weight feeling heavier this time around. He hasn't needed the aid in memory for some time now. *Remember, the beginning and end are always perfectly retained, it's the middle that gets lost in the shadows.*

He knows, and fully understands, that age, along with his sickness, is catching up with him. The news from his last doctor's visit was far from good. And it spelled only one result, if he continued refusing treatment... death. He is scared of what lies ahead, beyond this existence, but he's not afraid of the rest of the 1999 season with the Demons. Jeff worries that he might not have the time to accurately remember each game against the Knights; so instead, he cheats his story one more time. In this thought, he promises to give the last game everything he's got. Every piece of him, no matter how tired, how fatigued, how exhausted, no matter the cost. Similar to his playing days, he will leave it all on the field.

He carries the scrapbook to his recliner, plopping down. Jeff flips through pages of boxscores and images, coming to a stop nearer the end of the book. The pages reveal four distinct box scores, those belonging to the games played in the 1999 Western League Championship.

Jeff grins at the players he sees, fingering their names and game summaries on the pages. He nods, acknowledging the box scores and their assistance with his remembering in admiration—without jealousy. He dives back into the past.

Western League Championship - Game one
Los Angeles Demons @ San Diego Knights, June 4th, 1999

1	2 3 4 5 6 7 8 9	R	H	E
L.A.	0 0 0 0 5 0 0 0 0	5	9	1
S.D.	0 0 0 0 0 0 1 2 0	3	5	0

DEMONS	H	AB	R	RBI	AVG
cf Lewis	2	4	1	0	.500
c Parks (HR-1)	2	5	1	2	.400
3b Hicks	0	1	1	0	.000
1b Gunn	2	4	1	0	.500
lf Rutherford	1	4	1	1	.250
2b Hartes	1	4	0	2	.250
rf Goodwin	1	4	0	0	.250
ss Willis	0	4	0	0	.000
p Williams	0	3	0	0	.000
ph Chambers	0	1	0	0	.000

KNIGHTS	H	AB	R	RBI	AVG
cf Frazier	1	3	1	0	.333
2b Greener	1	3	1	0	.333
lf Ponds	1	4	0	2	.250
rf Martin	0	2	1	0	.000
1b Garrido	0	3	0	0	.000
3b Kramer	1	4	0	0	.250
c Degginger	1	4	0	1	.250
ss Winslow	0	4	0	0	.000
p Wilkes	0	1	0	0	.000
p Broderick	0	1	0	0	.000
ph Allen	0	1	0	0	.000

WP – Lake Williams (1-0, 0.00)
LP – Jerod Wilkes (0-1, 9.00)
Save – Salmon Seavers (1 save, 0.00)

Western League Championship - Game two
Los Angeles Demons @ San Diego Knights, June 5th, 1999

```
      123456789  R  H  E
L.A.  100100000  2  6  0
S.D.  41000130x  9 11  1
```

DEMONS	H	AB	R	RBI	AVG
cf Lewis	1	4	0	0	.375
2b Hartes	1	4	1	0	.250
3b Hicks (HR-1)	2	4	1	1	.400
1b Gunn	1	4	0	1	.375
lf Rutherford	0	4	0	0	.125
rf Goodwin	1	4	0	2	.250
c Fetters	0	3	0	0	.000
ss Willis	0	3	0	0	.000
p Perry	0	2	0	0	.000
ph Parks	0	1	0	0	.333

KNIGHTS	H	AB	R	RBI	AVG
cf Frazier	3	5	2	1	.500
2b Greener	1	3	0	1	.286
lf Ponds	2	4	1	1	.429
rf Martin	0	2	2	0	.000
3b Kramer (HR-1)	2	4	1	3	.375
1b Garrido	1	3	1	0	.167
c Degginger (HR-1)	2	4	2	3	.375
ss Harden	0	3	0	0	.000
p Anderson	0	3	0	0	.000
ph Allen	0	1	0	0	.000

WP – Robert Anderson (1-0, 2.57)
LP – Thomas Perry (0-1, 10.80)

Western League Championship - Game three
San Diego Knights @ Los Angeles Demons, June 7th, 1999

```
      123456789  R H E
S.D.  030000000  3 4 1
L.A.  000000000  0 4 0
```

KNIGHTS	H	AB	R	RBI	AVG
cf Frazier	1	4	0	0	.417
2b Greener	1	4	0	0	.273
lf Ponds	0	3	0	0	.300
rf Martin	1	4	1	0	.125
3b Kramer	0	3	1	0	.273
1b Garrido	0	3	0	0	.111
c Degginger (HR-2)	1	4	1	3	.333
ss Winslow	0	3	0	0	.000
p Hammel	0	3	0	0	.000

DEMONS	H	AB	R	RBI	AVG
cf Lewis	1	4	0	0	.333
2b Hartes	0	4	0	0	.167
3b Hicks	1	3	0	0	.375
1b Gunn	0	4	0	0	.250
lf Rutherford	1	4	0	0	.167
rf Goodwin	0	4	0	0	.167
c Parks	1	3	0	0	.333
ss S. Luthers	0	3	0	0	.000
p Tims	0	3	0	0	.000

WP – Erwin Hammel (1-0, 0.00)
LP – Michael Tims (0-1, 3.00)
Save – Rich Treplow (1 Save, 0.00)

Western League Championship - Game four
San Diego Knights @ Los Angeles Demons, June 8th, 1999

```
       123456789  R  H  E
S.D.   020002000  4  9  1
L.A.   101100 30x  6  9  0
```

KNIGHTS	H	AB	R	RBI	AVG
cf Frazier	1	4	0	0	.375
2b Greener	1	4	0	0	.267
lf Ponds	1	4	1	0	.286
rf Martin (HR-1)	2	2	1	1	.300
rf Allen	1	2	1	0	.250
3b Kramer	0	4	0	1	.200
c Degginger	1	3	1	0	.333
1b Garrido	1	4	0	1	.154
ss Winslow	1	4	0	1	.091
p Heilman	0	3	0	0	.000
ph Garces	0	1	0	0	.000

DEMONS	H	AB	R	RBI	AVG
cf Lewis	1	4	1	0	.313
2b Hartes	1	3	0	0	.200
3b Hicks (HR-2)	2	4	1	2	.417
1b Gunn	0	4	0	0	.188
c Parks (HR -2)	1	4	1	1	.308
lf Rutherford	1	4	1	0	.188
rf Goodwin	0	2	1	0	.143
ss Willis	2	3	1	3	.200
p O'Dell	0	2	0	0	.000
ph Fetters	1	1	0	0	.250

WP – Jay O'Dell (1-0, 5.14)
LP – Barnes Heilman (0-1, 9.00)
Save – Salmon Seavers (2 saves, 0.00)

II

And with the series tied at two games apiece, Jeff Hartes remembers, with every last ounce of draining energy, trying to recount the events with an unmatched precision, the final game of 1999.

III

"Well..." Skip said in the visitor's clubhouse. Part of the Demon squad were putting on the final pieces of their uniforms while others waited to head to the dugout, trying to stay relaxed. "This is it, boys. Probably the last chance for me to go out a winner. And a chance for y'all to stand on top of the Western League world. You know what I expect out there, and goddammit, who needs a pep-talk before game five of the title game." Skip bowed his head and turned toward the door exiting out into Diego Field's leftfield. Without turning back to his players, he spoke just loud enough for them to hear, "I'll see you on the field."

Hartes nodded in approval and then finished pulling his Demon-blue socks up just below his knees. He put on his left shoe first, and then his right, and laced his cleats to a nice snug fit. The clubhouse was silent. The field door opened, letting in the evening light, and a couple of the bullpen pitchers, Darren Luthers and Javy Jimenez, headed out to the sounds and smells of the last game of the season, victory or defeat, one way or another.

Hartes felt like he was in a daze. He sat in front of his

locker in a confused state. He kept thinking that something familiar was approaching... in his mind... on the field. He couldn't quite put his finger on the thought, though. Hicks tapped him on the shoulder with his black and dark red Mizuno bat, disrupting him from his daydream. "You ready, kid?"

"Yep," Hartes answered. He put on his ballcap and glove, grabbed his bat bag, and hopped up.

Hick said randomly, possibly attempting to help Hartes relax, "When I was a rookie playing ball with the Tyler Wildcatters, I was traded midseason to a team in Lafayette. Their coach was Feldin Mathews, big power hitter with a swing like Gary Sheffield. My first batting practice with the team, I got in the cage, dropped a couple of bunts down, and then took a couple to rightfield. Feldin started waving his arms and hollered at me and the pitcher, 'Hold on! Hold on! What the hell are you doing?' I said, 'You know, coach, just working on driving the ball to all parts of the field.' Feldin shook his head and said this shit, Hartes, 'Down here, we don't spray the ball Hicks, we backleg everything.'"

Hicks smiled, and Jeff laughed. And without another spoken word, Hartes and the rest of the players funneled out onto Diego Field before a crowd that would end up with nearly ten thousand baseball fans by first pitch.

The weather was perfect, currently about seventy-degrees, and expected to drop into the mid-sixties once the game was underway. The sun was still shining, warming, yet descending for the day. Hartes carried his bag, walking along the leftfield foul wall to the visiting dugout on the third-base side. Willis said something about one of the early fans, drawing a courtesy laugh from Gunn and Parks, but Hartes remained speechless. He was letting it all soak in, and hoping that whatever he felt inside — *the dreams...*

*the dreams... the dreams—*wasn't real. *There was no way any of those dreams had anything to do with this game, was there?*

Hartes dropped his bag on the dugout floor and kicked it under the bench. He set his fielding glove on the bench seat and placed his batting gloves in his back pockets. He then proceeded to lightly jog down the leftfield line back toward the foul pole. He ran a few sprints with Nate and Hicks in the outfield, getting good and loose.

He then ran back to the dugout, grabbed his glove and a ball from the shag bag, and returned to the field to warm up with the Demons' shortstop. There was only a light chatter during the team's pregame warmup and throwing, and the most relaxing idea started with Goodwin, Hicks, and Parks, who got a game of *Pepper* going. A few other players joined in, laughing and trying to deke the batter or the next guy in the fielding line. Hartes was just about to jump in when he heard his name being shouted from the leftfield bleachers.

"Jeff! Hey Jeff!"

Hartes shielded the sun's glare with his glove and saw his brother, Eric, and then the rest of his family leaning over the wall. He jogged over and hugged everyone but his brother, who wanted a fist bump instead. His family wished him good luck and then headed to their designated seats. Hartes, as ready as one could get before the biggest game of their career, walked back down to the dugout and plopped down on the padded metal bench.

Hartes reached for a bag of sunflower seeds, leaving the Hawken's to the veterans on this night. Last thing he wanted was to feel nauseous, as he wasn't the most experienced tobacco-user. The stadium public announcer, Kyle Queen, who was considered a traitor amongst Los Angeles fans as he started the season as the Demon P.A.

but then moved with his family to San Diego and took advantage of an opening they had after their stadium guy retired due to his health, spoke for the first time.

"Welcome to sunny San Diego, a beautiful night here at Diego Field for game five of the Western League Championship between your home team—" the stadium crowd, about half-full and growing, cheered, "—the San Diego Knights, and the visiting team—" followed by boos, "—the Los Angeles Demons.

"Please be aware of all your emergency exits and also follow baseball etiquette as the opportunity arises. Please also..."

Hartes blocked out Kyle Queen as he continued over the P.A. He glanced at the lineup sheet hanging in the end of the dugout closest to homeplate—*six hole*—and then grabbed one of his bats to take a few practice swings just atop the dugout steps.

On the radio, Darrel "The Duke" Marinville relayed the Demons' starting lineup back to Los Angeles after his signature introduction, "Hello sportsfans, this is Darrel 'The Duke' Marinville, and I'm here to bring you another piece of Demon baseball history. The final piece of this season, and hopefully, one of a delightful tune.

"And now for the lineups... leading off for the visiting team, playing centerfield and batting three-thirteen in the Western League Championship, Damon Lewis. Batting second and swinging a hot bat, the catcher, Bobby Parks. He's already hit two homeruns in the series. Batting third, your third baseman, hitting four-seventeen with two homers, Jason Hicks. In the cleanup spot, looking to come up with some big knocks tonight, Steve Gunn. In the five hole, the leftfielder, Erric Rutherford. Hitting only a buck-eighty-eight thus far. Second baseman, Jeff Hartes, is your sixth hitter, also struggling a little against the solid San

Diego pitching. Batting seventh and playing rightfield, looking to get on and use his legs and aggressive baserunning, Billy Goodwin. In the eighth spot, coming up with a huge three-run homer in the bottom of the seventh in game four, your shortstop, Nathan Willis. And pitching and batting last, big-game veteran and Demon ace, Lake Williams. He is one-and-oh in the championship series, and has not yet allowed a run to the Knights."

The Duke continued with the San Diego starting lineup while back on the field, Kyle Queen announced the Knights' players as they took their respected positions. The singer for the National Anthem, a tall blond-haired fellow with a small mouth, residing from Austin, Texas, then walked to the microphone behind homeplate. Kyle Queen announced the game-five guest, "Ladies and gentlemen, please rise for your National Anthem. Now performing... Chase."

The Demon team stood on either the top step of the dugout or just on the field, removing their caps. Before the man started singing, Javy, who would make his way to the bullpen after the anthem, said, "Como se dice, Chase?"

Tims and Fetters did their best to try and tell the reliever that "Chase" must be the singer's name. Before they could get everything clarified, Chase began.

Butterflies filled Hartes' stomach while he stood as still as he could, his hat and hand across his chest. The anthem seemed to carry on forever; it was hard to appear courteous and polite when your insides were churning and your legs were electric with anxious nerves. Chase finished and received an enthusiastic applause, one more act to go before the game was underway.

Throwing out the first pitch was the mayor of San Diego. Gunn started the bets, "Twenty bucks says he at least one-hops it to Degginger."

"No bet, here," Lewis responded. "No way this guy reaches home."

"I'll get some of that action," Hicks joined in. "This fucker pitched college ball for the Bruins."

"Seriously?" Gunn asked, turning his head.

"Fuck if I know," Hicks said and smiled. "Either way, bet's on."

Right on cue, the mayor wound up and threw to the plate. The throw not only came up short, two-hopping the catcher, but it was also a couple of feet outside. The San Diego catcher Charlie Degginger looked game-ready as he made a nice backhand stab with his mitt.

"Just a bit outside," Parks said, mimicking Harry Doyle.

"You can owe me," Gunn said.

"Let's win this bitch and I'll pay you my bonus." Hicks stepped back into the dugout and grabbed his bat.

It was gametime.

IV

"Damon Lewis strides to homeplate to lead off the game against the Western League Pitcher of the Year, Jerod Wilkes," The Duke called. "The San Diego lefty finished the season seven-and-oh with a one-point-seven-two E.R.A.; however, the Demons really got to him in the fifth inning of game one, scoring five runs with the help of a Bobby Parks two-run dinger and a big double by Jeff Hartes, also driving in a pair."

Lewis stepped into the perfectly-manicured batter's box and began rooting around with his spikes. He found the comfortable spot and dug in, crouching low while taking a couple of half swings. Wilkes also found his own locale on the mound and came set.

Parks squatted and stood a couple of times in the on-deck circle, waving his bat, with a weighted donut wrapped around it, behind his head. The catcher watched as the first pitch flew from the lefty's hand...

"Ball one," called the homeplate umpire, A.B. Cartwright. This was the ump's fourth season in the Western League; and amongst his peers, he was considered one of the best—amongst the coaches, one of the most consistent.

Wilkes didn't waste any time. Once his catcher, Charlie Degginger, tossed the ball back to the mind, he was ready to deliver again. He threw another fastball, this one a bit high, and the count was now two-and-oh on the Demon centerfielder.

"Come on D. Lewis," Goodwin shouted from the dugout. "Gonna' get something to hit now."

Lewis stepped out momentarily and then stepped back in. When the count was in his favor, he tended to close his stance and crouch just a bit more, lessening the strike zone. But he was an aggressive leadoff hitter, and he wouldn't be taking the 2-0 pitch if it was something he could drive.

Wilkes, though, had many out pitches, and when you are arguably the best pitcher in the league, you aren't afraid to throw them on any count. He came home with a solid slider, low and away. Lewis must have been looking straight heater because he was way out in front, rolling over the baseball and pulling a chopper to third base. Phil Kramer, playing closer to the grass than usual because of the Demons' leadoff man's speed, fielded the ball quickly and cleanly, firing to Ramon Garrido on first base for out number one.

The crowd, completely into the game-five atmosphere,

cheered raucously. "One away, one away," the Knights' second baseman yelled, holding up his pinkie.

"Now batting for the Los Angeles Demons, catcher Bobby Parks," Kyle Queen announced in a monotone, sounding disgusted that he had to even relay the opposing team's hitters over the P.A.

"Parks is hitting three-oh-eight with two homeruns in the series, a part of the reasoning behind Skip Bailey batting him in the two-hole," The Duke called to the Demon listeners. "Another factor, he is a better hitter against lefties than veteran catcher Ron Fetters."

Wilkes was ready, Parks was in the box, and umpire A.B. Cartwright was set to make the call. The pitch...

"Strike one," the umpire bellowed.

Parks watched a fastball go by on the outside edge. He then laid off two straight balls, both good pitches just missing low, and the count was 2-1 in his favor. Wilkes then threw his first cutter of the night, a little softer than his four-seam fastball but with lots of movement toward the right-handed hitters. Parks got jammed and fouled the pitch off his foot.

The Demons' bench could hear him yell 'shit' as he hopped around in circles. One of the trainers jogged out, but Parks waved them back to the dugout. Slightly limping, he hobbled back into the batter's box and awaited the fifth pitch of his at-bat.

Wilkes missed high with a hard fastball, bringing the count to full. The Duke picked up the action, "Wilkes is going to have the challenge the Demons' catcher with this next. He comes set and delivers... ball four. A one-out walk for Bobby Parks."

"Good eye there, kid," Larry George shouted from the third-base coaching area.

"Thatta' baby, Parks," his fellow catcher shouted from

the dugout.

Parks jogged down to first, still showing a bit of discomfort in his foot.

Jason Hicks strolled to the plate, feeling very confident and in his own words, "The baseball looks like a beach ball right now."

Wilkes threw to first base a couple of times—Parks wasn't as slow as Fetters, but he still wasn't going anywhere. Wilkes continued to fall behind the Demon hitters, missing on a 2-1 slider to Hicks. With a hitter's count, Hicks looked fastball.

Wilkes fired the heater toward the outside portion of the plate, and Hicks drilled it. *Crack!*

The liner never got more than five-feet off the ground, screaming into rightfield. Parks didn't get a good jump on the hit, pausing to make sure it got through. He picked up Coach George rounding second and headed for third. The San Diego rightfielder, Chance Allen, fielded the ball cleanly coming forward and threw a laser to Kramer on third. The ball one-hopped into the third baseman's glove, right on line. Kramer slapped the tag across the head-first-sliding Parks' wrists for the second out.

The stadium roared with early excitement. Instead of two runners and one away for Steve Gunn, there was now only a runner on first and two outs. Gunn proceeded to fly out to shallow left on the first pitch from Wilkes, a changeup that had the burly first baseman swinging early.

Gunn shook his head at Hartes, standing near first base as the middle infielder brought Gunn his glove for the bottom of the first.

"Wilkes didn't look untouchable in the first, sportsfans, but the Demons sure did find a way to get him off the hook. After the top-half of the first, the score, zero-to-zero." Marinville flipped the "on-air" switch off and then, in disgust, slid away from the microphone in his rolling chair.

The Demon infielders took rolled balls from Gunn and threw back to first, loosening up for the bottom-half of the inning while the outfielders tossed a little long ball.

Lake Williams was on the mound, and without a doubt, the Demon players were elated to have their ace pitching the final game of the season. Kyle Queen's demeanor lifted a notch when he announced the San Diego players.

"Now batting for the home team, centerfielder, J.J. Frazier."

The Duke also relayed the Knights' first batter. "Frazier is hitting a solid three-seventy-five for the series, leading the Knights with six hits. Frazier doubled off Lake in game one for his only hit against the Demons' lefty. He is the spark in the lineup; and usually, where he goes, the Knights go. Williams is on the mound, he picks up the sign from catcher, Bobby Parks, and he delivers... strike one. A fastball over the outer edge. I believe Frazier was taking the whole way there."

"Thatta' baby, Lake," Gunn called from first. The Demon defense was alive and ready to leave it all on the field. Hartes kicked some dirt at second, slapped his knee with his glove, and then prepared for the second pitch. He watched Lake throw an early, but really filthy changeup that Frazier swung over for the second strike.

And with an 0-2 count, the lefty wasted no time. He fired a chest-high fastball that the Knight centerfielder swung through—a little late—for the first out of the inning.

"Three pitches, three strikes, one away for the Los Angeles Demons," The Duke called over the air.

On his way to the dugout, Frazier mouthed something in the vicinity of, "Damn shadows. Hard to pick up the ball," to the on-deck hitter, second baseman, Timothy Greener. Greener nodded his head and stepped in to take his hacks.

Sometimes, just before darkness arrives, when the pitcher's mound is still in the sun and the batter's box is shaded, the change of lighting can make it difficult on a hitter. Possibly, the same effect took place against Greener, as Lake Williams, with a 1-2 count, locked up the righty with a backdoor slider for the second out.

"Two down, two down!" Hicks shouted toward the outfield, holding up his index and pinkie fielder.

"Now batting for the San Diego Knights, the third hitter–" the already rambunctious crowd buzzed even heavier, " –leftfielder, Waylon Ponds."

Ponds had three doubles in the series and was batting . 286, respectable and still very much feared. During the regular season, the all-star hit .339, second only in the south division to Jason Hicks, and also had 31 RBI's.

Lake tossed the rosin bag in his left hand, drying the sweat and keeping the blisters away. He found his comfortable side of the rubber, and glared in. He nodded at the first sign Parks put down, and wound up. The first pitch fastball was a little in, and a little high. Ponds backpedaled out of the batter's box, overreacting a bit as the pitch really wasn't that close.

The San Diego outfielder gave Lake a quick glance, but said nothing. He dug back in, preparing for the second pitch of the at-bat. Lake threw an offspeed pitch, and got Ponds to make contact off balance and out in front of the plate. *Whack.*

"Ponds hits a dying quail to the shallow center. Willis and Hartes are sprinting out, Lewis is charging hard, calls 'em off, and makes a nice grab on the run to end the first!" The Duke announced with some extra enthusiasm.

After one inning in the Western League Championship, the score was zero-to-zero.

V

"The sun is quickly descending, which should favor the hitters again as the shadows escape and night comes forth," The Duke called. "It's nothing-to-nothing here in San Diego. The Demons have one hit, the Knights are hitless."

Erric Rutherford swung a couple of bats between innings, tossed one back to Wade Smith, the batboy, and then strolled to the plate with a confident stride. He was hitting only a buck-eighty-eight, yet to produce the big hit or spark the Demons needed during the postseason.

Jerod Wilkes wasted no time firing a ninety-five-mile-per-hour fastball over the heart for strike one. Rutherford took a second strike, a wicked change piece over the outside corner. With two strikes, the Demons' leftfielder swung at the third pitch, chopping a weak grounder to the right side. Greener fielded the ball coming forward and sidearmed it Garrido at first for the first out of the inning.

"The struggles continue for Rutherford, his timing seems to be off, and he has not been able to get bat on ball solidly," The Duke followed. "One out, with Jeff Hartes coming to the plate."

Hartes flexed the muscles in his arms and back, gripping the pine tightly, then relaxed in the batter's box. He held the bat in his left hand, rolling it towards the mound, and then letting it drop to his side. He repeated this motion a couple of more times, then got ready as Wilkes glared in from the rubber and had his sign.

The first pitch was a fastball on the outer edge, which Cartwright enthusiastically beckoned. "Strike one!"

Hartes grimaced and shook his head, thinking that the San Diego pitcher got the benefit on that call. The Demon second baseman was hitting .200 in the series thus far, and appeared less comfortable at the plate than during the regular season. Playoff jitters, of course. It was a bigger stage, and this was the biggest game the Western League had to offer. Hartes' struggles were a deciding factor in Skip Bailey moving him down to the six-hole, trying to free that good aggressive swing up.

Hartes then watched Wilkes drop a big curve over for strike two, digging himself a possible early grave against the veteran lefty. Jerod Wilkes wasted a fastball high, and then a slider in the dirt before throwing the fifth pitch of the at-bat.

"Two-two count on Hartes. Wilkes shakes once and then quickly nods, he and Degginger have worked more than a few games together and now seem to be on the same page, comes home... a swing and a miss for strike three," The Duke called to the Demon faithful.

Hartes slowly marched back to the visiting dugout, head down. With two outs, Wilkes pitched to the switch-hitting rightfielder, Billy Goodwin. Goodwin was also struggling against the solid San Diego pitching, collecting only two hits in fourteen at-bats in the series. He did have some pop, and swung large at times, and this kept Wilkes cautious.

After fouling off two straight full-count pitches from the lefty, Goodwin worked a hard two-out walk. This brought up the Demons shortstop, Nathan Willis.

"Willis steps in the box from the right side with Goodwin leading off first base," Marinville announced. "Big shoes to fill, a tragic day in Demon baseball history, when our beloved shortstop, Will Coleman, passed. I can only imagine, myself feeling a part of this team on the outer edge, what the players in the clubhouse went through, the emotions they had to play through, the anger and sadness and the difficulty to jump back in the saddle again; except the next time, it would be with someone new. First, Simon Luthers, and then Nate Willis, who stepped in and has performed admirably, not only at the plate and on the field, but with his teammates, the press, and the fans.

"Willis had a big night in game four, helping the Demons even the series with two hits and three runs batted in. He raised his championship series average to two-hundred, and now looks to get a two-out rally started."

Goodwin took a huge lead off first, most likely leaning back towards the first-base bag, urging a throw from Wilkes. Instead, the lefty went home, a fastball just low.

"Good eye, Nate," Lake said from the on-deck circle. "Let's go now."

Jerod Wilkes would bare down against the eight-hitter for Los Angeles, not wanting the opposing pitcher to come up this inning, but rather lead off the third.

Goodwin, with a smaller lead now, stared at the pitcher. Wilkes came set, glanced to first, back to home, then to first, and then to home again, starting his windup. Goodwin got a pretty good jump, digging for second base. The pitch—fastball—came in right over the heart of the plate.

Willis let the bat fly— *whack*—ripping a hard grounder back up the middle. It wasn't a designed hit and run, but a straight steal from Goodwin instead. Willis, though, got a good pitch to drive and took a chance.

The Duke's voice rose, "That ball is hit hard towards center, past Wilkes, backhand stop by Greener, and he steps on second base for the force and final out. If you're counting the breaks, mark down bad break number one for the Demons. That ball would have been an easy single up the middle as the only player that should have had a shot was Wilkes, who made a stabbing gesture to his right. But Greener, who was covering second base on the steal, happened to run right into the ball on his way pass the bag. Well, tough luck. Nothing yet here, zero-to-zero heading to the bottom half of the second."

Gunn brought Willis his glove and hat, patting him on the back as the Demon shortstop rolled his helmet towards the dugout. "Bad beat."

Lake Williams, receiving plenty of crude and profane remarks from the San Diego fans, threw his warmup pitches and was ready to go. He had no problem with San Diego's first baseman, Ramon Garrido, who was batting cleanup in place of the injured all-star, Jacques Martin, who drove in 27 runs during the regular season and had also homered in this series. Garrido, who struck out on four pitches from Lake, did not only big shoes to fill batting cleanup, but also needed to show some signs of getting his bat going to help protect Ponds. Garrido was hitting a dismal .154 before his first appearance in game five, only to drop his average some more.

San Diego third baseman, Phil Kramer, came up to bat next. He spat a large wad of tobacco in the sand near the box, and then dug in. On a first pitch fastball, Williams jammed him. Kramer hit a weak grounder towards the right side. Hartes charged forward, barehanded the ball, and slung it to first.

Two away.

"Nice play, Hartes," Willis yelled from short. Lake pointed his glove-hand at Jeff and nodded in acknowledgment. He received the ball from Gunn, and prepared to work to the next batter with two outs in the bottom of the second.

The San Diego catcher, Charlie Degginger, who homered in game two and was hitting .333 for the series, stepped to the plate. Degginger was a coach's dream, a starting all-star for the South Division that not only called a great game and could stop anything thrown his way, but Degginger could also swing the lumber.

"Williams comes set and delivers the first pitch... ball one. He misses with something offspeed. I believe it was a changeup to start of the catcher," The Duke announced. "One-oh the count, the sun now completely saying farewell for today, the stadium lights bright and mecca-like for baseball fans, the weather perfect, what a night for a do or die game.

"Lake fires... strike one. Degginger takes a fastball over the outside corner to even the count. I see a lot of younger fans and kids in the seats tonight, and that always brings a big smile to my face. Our future fans, our future stories, America's pastime. Williams from the windup, two outs, nobody on, the pitch—" *Crack!* "—hard liner towards the left si-, caught by Willis! Who left his feet and made a nice snow-cone grab for the last out! We have completed two innings of baseball, and it's shaping up to be a fine pitcher's duel between Lake Williams and Jerod Wilkes. Nothing to nothing."

VI

"Back here at Diego Field, a scoreless game heading into the top of the third, due up for L.A., the pitcher, Williams, followed by Damon Lewis and Bobby Parks." The Duke sipped from his tall blue coffee mug, personalized with the

Demon logo, a gift from the organization for calling games a few years back.

"Now batting, the starting pitcher, Lake Williams," Queen announced to the excited crowd. They hissed, they booed. They were on the edge of their seat, ready for their Knights to cross home and get on the board. But first, Jerod Wilkes had to work his magic.

"The San Diego lefty has allowed zero runs through the first two," The Duke informed. "He has walked one, and also struck out one batter."

There wasn't a lot of chatter in the Demons' dugout. Focus, yes. Passion, yes. Everyone seemed to be caught up thinking, grinding, pushing their brain to the limits to solve the Wilkes' puzzle before the late innings. Lewis rolled two bats behind his head in the on-deck circle, waiting for his second time around. The centerfielder watched Lake take a first-pitch fastball for strike one. The San Diego infield encouraged their starter with robotic words, and the home fans made as much noise as possible.

Williams swung and missed the second pitch, a nasty breaking ball, showing that Wilkes wasn't giving an inch to the opposing pitcher. By any length, a hitter's a hitter in game five, and a hit's a hit, regardless of the opposition. Wilkes was taking no chances.

Lewis dropped the second bat in his hand and simultaneously strode towards the plate as homeplate umpired A.B. Cartwright shouted, "Steee-rike Three!" on a fastball swing and a miss. Williams headed back to the dugout to put on his pitching jacket and keep his golden left arm warm and ready.

Damon Lewis ignored the fans' banter behind him and crouched in the batter's box in his compacted stance. He liked to look fastball early, a leadoff hitter with some Rickey Henderson or Derek Jeter pop, but then switch gears to an average contact hitter once down a strike or two. He took his job as a leadoff man seriously, wanting to set the table for the big boys in the lineup.

Wilkes missed with the first two, both pitches just a bit high for Cartwright, crossing home around Lewis' elbows. The San Diego starter didn't like the first call; and then on the second called ball, he and Degginger both let the ump know they weren't pleased.

"Come on now, A.B., fuck," Degginger mouthed without turning to face the umpire, his face hidden inside the catcher's mask. He was just communicating on a veteran level, and he didn't want to turn around and show 'blue' up this early in a game. "Those are both good pitches."

Wilkes, meanwhile, glared in, shrugged with arms slightly open, and muttered beneath his breath, "Goddammit. Let's go now." He returned to the mound. Wilkes cleared the mechanism, looked in for the next sign from his catcher—fastball—and fired the 2-0 pitch.

"The pitch underway, Lewis swings—" *Smack.* "— Screamer to the left side and through!" The Duke enthusiastically called. "The ball is fielded in left by Ponds coming forward, a one-out single for Damon Lewis. Winslow made a valiant effort at short, diving to his backhand side, as he's now knocking some of the infield off his uniform. A true sign of hustle and tough play, that is, a uniform stained with sand and dirt and sweat. Lewis took a small turn around first but never looked to be thinking two as the ball was hit too hard and Ponds wasn't very deep in left. The Demon centerfielder has been aggressive this year, and has caught more than one lazy outfielder fielding a ball nonchalantly, turning singles into two-baggers."

"Ooh, Dolly, I'm hot today," Hicks said, exiting the

dugout and heading to take his warmup hacks in the on-deck area. Bobby Parks, who worked a solid walk in the first inning, was at the plate. George relayed signs from third, no bunt, no steal, but Parks knew Lewis would do his best to get a good jump and run if he could.

Lewis held his batting gloves in his hands, took his lead off first, and then reached down and knuckled some dirt. He measured his lead strategically while never taking his eyes off the pitcher. A sliver of a smile crossed Damon's face as he often thought of Clu Haywood telling Willie Mays Hayes, "Real hard to steal second with your shoe untied."

Wilkes came set, his left hand on the ball in his glove, and then he fired a snap throw to first. Lewis got back easily, diving headfirst into the bag, wary to keep his palms and hands up, sliding over the base and not getting his wrists rolled downward. Garrido took the throw and slapped Lewis' back with a gentle tag, no chance. He tossed the ball back to Wilkes, who prepared to work the hitter again. Wilkes came set a second time, and this time threw to first with an effortless move over. Lewis was back standing up; this was Wilkes 'bad move.' Sometimes a lefty likes to show you a mixture of an okay move and a bad move, and then when they think you aren't expecting it, they give you their Andy Pettitte. And it's game over. The runner is caught leaning towards second, and they have no chance getting back in time.

Wilkes didn't have as good a move to first as Pettitte did, not many lefties ever have. And Wilkes was also slower to home, so if a base stealer did get a decent jump, they had a pretty good chance of taking one.

On the first pitch to Parks, Lewis guessed first move on Wilkes and guessed right. "Wilkes comes home, the runner's going, fastball in there and the throw from

Degginger!" The Duke's voice grew. "SAFE! A stolen base for Damon Lewis, sliding on the outside of the bag and beating the strong throw easily. He just got too good of a jump and stole that one off the pitcher."

With a runner in scoring position, Parks worked the count full, seeing an assortment of Wilkes' pitches again and getting his money's worth in game five. Wilkes then threw a slider that missed on the outer edge, walking the catcher for the second time.

"Now batting for the Demons, Jason Hicks," Queen announced, followed by a cacophony of boos and ill wishes.

The Duke summed up the seven-pitch at bat. "Parks trots down to first for the second time tonight, putting runners on first and second. Boy, it sure looked like Wilkes was pitching around him, or at least, not wanting to give in, throwing Parks a full-count slider. Why anyone would want to face Mr. Hicks? Your guess is as good as mine; but here he is, Demon fans, your all-star third baseman, striding towards home to try and inflict the first damage of the game."

"C'mon Hicks, make it hurt!" Gunn shouted. Parks slapped his hands together at first, smelling a possible rally. Hartes sat next to Goodwin in the dugout, both quietly pulling for their teammate while trying to get mentally out of their funks and spark some inner confidence of their own. The batboy methodically tapped the concrete steps with a cracked bat, given to him by Will Coleman during the regular season. He was willing Hicks to get a big knock here, something to drive in Lewis and get his team on the scoreboard.

A dirty slider from Wilkes, better than the ball four to Parks, got Hicks way out in front, swinging over the top for strike one. The Los Angeles third baseman was looking for the heater and thought he had it. Wilkes wasted no time. He quickly got back on the rubber, got his sign, and delivered.

"The oh-one pitch to Jason Hicks, a swing and contact. Ball hit to right side, jam-job, fielded cleanly by Greener, who flips to Winslow for one back to first... double play." The air out of the sails for The Duke. "Hicks busted it down the line and Parks with a hard slide at second, but the San Diego defense turned that four-six-three double play with ease, ending the brief rally. Heading to the bottom of third, the scoreboard remains zeroes in the runs column."

"Fuck!" Hicks hollered into his helmet, tossing the headgear aside. A look of disgust and a head-shake followed.

"No worries, bra, get 'em next time." Goodwin tapped his teammate on the butt with his glove, heading to rightfield.

Lake Williams appeared to have his full command and arsenal of pitches now. Sometimes, if an offense didn't get to a great starter early, they might not ever get to him. Lake looked that way now.

He worked the San Diego shortstop, Arod Winslow, hitting only .091 for the series, to a 2-2 count before getting the Knights' leadoff man to ground out to Hicks on a weakly hit ball. Hicks had to show off that strong arm, throwing a belt-high screamer over to Gunn at first.

With one out, San Diego rightfielder, Chance Allen, who was starting in place of Jacques Martin, came up to the plate, lefty on lefty. Allen fell behind in the count 1-2, and then Lake buried him a filthy curveball that had Allen bailing early, locking up the hitter's knees. Allen began walking back to the Knights' dugout before Cartwright could even ring him up on the called strike three.

Pitcher on pitcher, Wilkes came up hacking. On a first-pitch fastball, Wilkes got wood. Just barely. He hit a straight up pop-up, called by Parks just out in front of home and secured for the final out of the third.

The Western League Championship headed to the fourth inning, scoreless.

VII

"Before we head to the fourth inning, we would like to take a second to congratulate the Washington Thunder first baseman, David Falconer, who is the recipient of the Albert L. Sportsman of the Year Award for the Western League, presented by Eerie Sports, 'Where you can get eerie good, or wicked better.' We've seen Falconer and his abilities on the field, I can only imagine how satisfying it is for one to achieve off-the-field success as well. My congrats and applause to him and his hard work.

"Due up here in the fourth for Los Angeles, the cleanup hitter, Steve Gunn, followed by Rutherford, Hartes, and Goodwin if anyone reaches."

Gunn took his practice swings and readied. Wilkes had thrown three scoreless thus far, and started the first baseman off with a fastball inside. A.B. Cartwright punched the air, and the count was 0-1. Wilkes then delivered a slider low and in on the righty, Gunn swung, fouling the pitch off inner bone in his left ankle. The big man hopped up and down a few times, swearing, and then limped out of the box. He checked his bat and hobbled toward the Demon dugout.

"Grab me another bat," he told Wade Smith. The batboy disappeared in the dugout momentarily.

Rutherford, waiting to bat next, said, "You are the toughest sum-bitch I know, Big Daddy."

Gunn didn't respond, he simply held up the number two with his fingers. Rutherford shook his head, smiling. "The second? Nah, who's the toughest then?"

Wade Smith hustled back up the dugout steps, bat in hand. He handed the lumber to Steve, who smiled at Erric and said before turning around, "John Wayne."

That brought a good chuckle and some much needed relaxation from the players near enough to hear. The word spread quickly along the bench.

Gunn stepped back in and took two straight balls before flying out to shallow centerfield.

"Frazier makes the easy catch at his side for the first out of the inning," The Duke announced. "This brings up the fifth hitter, Erric Rutherford. Hitless today and struggling like so many of the Demons' batters against this top tier staff San Diego puts on the mound night after night.

"Rutherford hit lefties just over fifty points higher than he hit righties this year. The score still zero-to-zero, Wilkes comes home... ball one. He just missed with a breaking ball to start the leftfielder. Wilkes readies, Rutherford looking to get something going... ball two. The lefty misses with another breaking ball, a little low."

The Demons' chatter picked up with the 2-0 count. The fans and players alike were waiting for something to happen in this game, whether to cheer or hang their head.

The Duke continued, "Rutherford appears to be trying to get in Wilkes' head, thinking, and then he steps back in the box, possibly solving his own equation. Wilkes comes set... and fires home—" *Crack!* "This ball is hammered to deep left center. Both Frazier and Ponds give chase, going back, IT CLEARS THE FENCE!"

Rutherford fist pumped going around first base. The Los Angeles players had all left their seats, standing on the rail or just out of the dugout, waiting anxiously to congratulate their teammate, who had just broken the tie, and took Wilkes' yard.

"IT'S ONE-TO-NOTHING DEMONS! The visitors strike first here in game five on a solo blast from Erric Rutherford," The Duke exclaimed.

Hartes greeted Rutherford first with a double forearm bump and then slapped his helmet. He was swarmed as he jogged closer to the visitor's bench, a fresh excitement filling the air. Diego Field, however, had drawn as quiet as it had been since the gates first opened.

Jeff Hartes got Jerod Wilkes' best stuff, and continued to look flustered at the plate, striking out on four pitches. Goodwin, who walked in the second, ground out to short on the first pitch to end the top of the fourth.

J.J. Frazier led off against Lake, dropping a peach of a bunt down the third-base line. Hicks was playing on the grass and gathered the ball cleanly, showcasing his cannon for an arm and gunning down the runner by half a step.

"No way!" Frazier shouted as he ran it out past the first base bag, hearing the call from the first-base umpire, Daniel Gamm. Frazier didn't offer any more rebuttal, shaking his head and heading back to the home dugout.

"Nice play, Jason," Lake said, nodding. He got ready to face the next batter. Timothy Greener battled Lake to a full count, but went down swinging on a beautiful changeup that had the Knights' second baseman out in front. With two outs, Waylon Ponds headed to the plate.

"Ponds steps in. He flew out in the first on a ball that he didn't seem to miss by much. He, at least, reacted that way, realizing he got a rare good pitch to hit from Lake, but didn't quite catch it as good as he wanted." The Duke paused, flipping through some of his notes.

"Ponds has been aggressive of late, not going deep in the counts. Lake is ready, two down, and the Demon starter fires—" *Whack!* "—Ponds hits this ball hard, on a line to leftfield, looks like it's gonna clear the feh... NO! It hits off the very top of the wall and caroms along the fence towards center. Rutherford tracks it down and slings it to the cutoff, Willis, standing a few yards out in the outfield grass. Ponds stands up at second with a double, holding up his arms in disbelief and wondering if the call on the field is the correct one. The umpires are getting together, meeting near the third base line to talk this one over." The Duke waited for his televised version of the game to replay the shot from Ponds on the 25-inch television in the booth. "Okay, here it is fans, in slow motion. Yes, the umpires got the call right. The ball never left the field, and Ponds just missed tying the game by a matter of inches."

Lake Williams didn't waste the gift from the baseball Gods. He jammed Ramon Garrido and fielded a weak grounder near the mound, tossed it to Gunn, and left a San Diego runner in scoring position. Close the books on the fourth.

Los Angeles Demons 1, San Diego Knights 0.

VIII

The fifth inning offered no rallies. Jerod Wilkes and Lake Williams continued to baffle hitters and use their combination of good stuff and great command to their advantage. A true pitcher's duel in the final game of the season. Win or lose for either side, their aces were giving them all they had.

Nathan Willis lined out an a bleeder to second. Lake Williams grounded out an a softly hit ground ball to opposite field. And Damon Lewis fanned on a 2-2 cutter in on his hands for the third out.

After a leadoff single by Phil Kramer, who found a gap in the right side, Lake struck out Charlie Degginger and then got Winslow to pop up in the infield — infield-fly rule called by homeplate umpire A.B. Cartwright.

Kyle Queen announced over the stadium speakers, "Now batting, number seven, and playing rightfield, Chance Allen."

Lake threw a curve for strike one, another curve low for a ball, a fastball just a little up for a ball, bringing the count to two-and-one. He delivered.

"High fly ball hit by Allen to centerfield. Lewis takes a few steps back, and makes the catch. That ends the fifth, Demons one, Knights nothing. Due up for Los Angeles in the sixth, Parks, Hicks, and Gunn," Darrell Marinville announced to the Demon faithful.

IX

Jeff Hartes jogged in from second, his head buzzing with sounds that couldn't be accurate, couldn't be real. *Get outta your own head, kid,* Hartes told himself, entering the dugout amidst a few high fives and praise for another solid half-inning for Lake Williams.

The Demons' second baseman sat in the left side corner of the dugout bench. He smelled sweat in the air, tasted the cool, once-refreshing breeze turn sour. He thought of going to Dodgers games with his dad. He thought of Tommy Lasorda and Pedro Guerrero and reflected on some guy who sat near him and his father, who seemed to be a magnet for homerun balls from the Dodger rightfielder.

Hartes leaned against the back wall, befuddled. He heard sounds in his head; he heard noises that weren't his own voice and noises that spoke with a familiar voice but not his voice, and in an unfamiliar manner. *Am I just replaying the series in my mind?*

"Here's a recap for the fans who may have missed one of the earlier games in this dazzling series. The Demons took game one in San Diego five-to-three, but San Diego's offense came alive in game two to get the split. The final was San Diego nine, L.A. two. They headed to Los Angeles for games three and four, where the Knights got a great performance from Erwin Hammel, who threw eight shutout innings and helped San Diego blank L.A. Three-to-nothing.

"Once again, though, like the Demons have done all year long, they battled back. This L.A. team left the yard three times, with homers from Jason Hicks, Bobby Parks, and Nathan Willis (hearing the name stings my side; it aches my heart for reasons unknown), leading the home team to a six-four victory and a trip back to San Diego. Jacques Martin injured his knee in that game on a bang-bang play at first, and it sure looks as though San Diego is missing his bat in the lineup right now."

The sounds grew unbearable. Hartes struggled with the crowd's constant chatter, diving into his brain through one ear, while he swore he could hear The Duke in the other. The dugout talk now entered through God knows where. Hartes couldn't take it anymore. *What the hell is going on?*

Hartes settled his nerves momentarily and focused his attention elsewhere. He gazed into the sky, witnessing the full moon, which appeared to be smiling back at him in a devilish way. Stars shone bright behind the stadium lights, but the noise, blaring from every direction, remained.

Hartes turned his attention southward into the stands. People visited, yelled, kids ate popcorn, hotdogs, drank sodas. As he roamed the San Diego crowd, one girl caught his eye while making her way down the stairs. He felt tightness in his throat and stomach, rising and squeezing and twisting. He stared at the girl with recognition... *her name, I know her damn name, why can't I just say it. Why can't I—*

The girl threw her hair back and took another step down the stairs. She then hesitated, adjusted her bra strap, and then took another long step down towards the field. Hartes' heart was pounding; his mind raced.

The noise of the crowd, of the dugout, of the game, of The Duke's broadcast, all came forward full force and drowned out any other rational thoughts. Hartes was not able to think clearly. He wanted to hop off the bench, run across the field, and exit the stadium.

The girl slid down another flight of stairs and then stopped to say 'hi' to someone in the stands, someone that looked familiar to her. She knew them, Jeff Hartes knew them, and he could tell by the gestures and familiarity in her motions. Hartes watched her without the capability of looking away. His eyes were glued to her movements, without any chance of rest.

She looked directly at Hartes, straight in his direction, right into the Los Angeles dugout—*Shae*.

"Holy shit," Jeff Hartes muttered, receiving a look of inquiry from Simon Luthers next to him.

"Time Out!" the umpire shouted as a big bouncing ball, full of air, flew out of the stands and onto the field. This turned Hartes' attention from Shae and back on the game. He had to clear his mind. He felt like something was happening to him that had happened before. He had to return to the game. The Demons needed him. Will needed him. His folks rooted for him. This was his job.

Bobby Parks batted to start off the sixth inning. Hartes watched as he flew out to leftfield; Ponds needed to take only a couple of steps to catch that one. Hartes, dazed, then watched Hicks double to center, crushing a ball over Frazier's head in the centerfield warning track. Degginger came out to talk to Wilkes, checking on the San Diego ace. The Demons dugout was alive, rooting for a rally, but Hartes remained in his alter state. He felt drugged. He felt numbed. He felt as if he didn't exist... didn't belong.

He watched Gunn strike out and Rutherford ground out, ending the top half of the inning and killing the Los Angeles faith.

Hartes jogged back out to second base like a zombie, replaying what was happening to him, not understanding, but trying to figure out a clue. He steered clear of looking into the stands while playing second; he was distracted enough, without adding Shae into the mix. Hartes turned to glance at the scoreboard in center. It read 1-0 in the Demons favor. The San Diego pitcher, Jerod Wilkes, led off the bottom of the sixth with a grounder down the first base line that Gunn dove for, caught, and hurried to the base for the out number one. The next batter, Frazier, walked and then stole second. Hartes caught the throw from Parks, slapped the tag, but it was just a bit late.

His body played the part, but in that same numbed fashion. Dreamlike. Surreal. *Wake up, Hartes!* The problem was that this time—whether he knew it or not, remembered the dreams or not—this time, Hartes was awake.

Lake made his first mistake. Hartes watched as he

delivered a chest-high fastball that Timothy Greener, who was 0-2 with two punchouts, belted to right. Frazier scored the tying run, while Greener wound up on second. Jeff Hartes clapped his glove, keeping the runner on second on his toes, but it wasn't necessary. Williams got through the meat of their order as he struck out Ponds and Garrido to end the sixth.

Los Angeles Demons 1, San Diego Knights 1.

X

Hartes came up to bat in the seventh, leading off—the *noise* returned inside his head. It returned with a vengeance—full throttle. It infected his mind, buzzing, disturbing, distracting, anything it could do to take Hartes off his game. *What is going on?*

Get your mind on the game, you're batting in the biggest game of your life.

Before Hartes gathered his thoughts, and himself for that matter, Wilkes had two strikes on him. Hartes heard Marinville calling his at-bat over the radio.

It's just not possible.

"Two strikes now on Jeff Hartes. He's oh-for-two tonight, having struck out twice already. Hartes has been a leader down the stretch here for the Demons, but struggling to get the ball on the bat so far tonight." The San Diego pitcher Jerod Wilkes wound and fired. Hartes swung... and missed. "Strike three. Hartes has the hat-trick, and it's only the seventh inning."

The Los Angeles second baseman felt like quitting. It was as simple as that. His mind was racing and his heart felt shattered. It wasn't like being dumped by your high school fling, but shattered as in pierced with a bronze-tipped spear. He looked down and saw blood on his uniform. *The spear must have penetrated my skin and hit a major organ... The Heart.* Hartes closed his eyes. He wished the blood away. He opened them. It was gone, but his heart still ached – along with his head. *And that noise!*

The noise wasn't getting any easier to deal with. Hartes not only wanted to quit, but to run, just run away. Scared? One could definitely say that. Nothing made sense at the moment. There was this *noise* echoing in his brain; Shae, who he hadn't seen in quite some time, now showing up for game five; and he was failing his team. Hartes was letting them down after all the hard work and dedication they had committed themselves to. After a gut-wrenching and emotional roller coaster of a season, what more did Hartes need on top of that? He rooted for Chambers to pinch hit for him next time.

Jeff's pops once said, 'There are some people who believe they are going to fail, Jeff. And then there are those who believe that failure isn't an option. Sorry to tell you Jeff, but failure is. And it is easier to fail than succeed.' *No shit pops.* Failure seemed to be the only option he was being dealt.

– Failure is an option –

Hicks said, "It's okay Hartes, you'll get 'em next time."

Hartes plopped down on the bench. He felt hands upon him, grabbing the sides of his face. Nathan Willis' hands did not touch Hartes in a fierce or jerking movement, but rather a soft, gentle placing of the shortstop's hands on Jeff's face.

Willis moved his hands to Hartes' shoulders. Hartes placed his head in his own hands, burying it and somewhat ignoring the kind gesture. Willis removed his hands from Hartes and whispered, "Will's watching you, bro."

He then jogged to the end of the dugout, grabbing his bat and helmet and joining the on-deck circle. Hartes tried to silence his mind, but nothing appeared to be working properly. This was hell. And Jeff Hartes was in it.

The shapes moved on the field in a blur. It was an abstract painting with unclear colors. The creamy-white ball — fuzzy — traveled to the area of second base. It then disappeared in a hazy brown. It reappeared in the air this time, flying towards first base. Garrido snagged it out of the air, and the shaded blue man signaled the second out, Goodwin. The blurriness continued as Hartes watched the Demons' next batter, Nate Willis, swing his tanned lumber, looking like a darkened mirage, and drive the creamy-white fuzz to leftfield. It disappeared again in the brown. Ponds began his jog in, his movements appeared like someone looking through distorted, warped glass. The top of the inning was over. Jeff Hartes prayed for his vision to clear — to return.

The second baseman shook his head, closed his eyes, and rose from the pine. A slang term, as San Diego's benches were a padded, metal bleacher. His prayer was answered.

He headed back out to second base, immediately making a play on Kramer as he hit a rocket grounder right at Hartes. Tossing it to Gunn at first; if it didn't happen with such instinct, such habit, such ease, Hartes probably wouldn't have been able to make the play. But his body was still a seasoned machine. It was a weapon of past repetitions, and it is still working... at least, working better than his twisted mind.

"One out in the seventh," Hartes heard Marinville call back to the Demon faithful; the radio listeners who weren't fortunate enough to make the inner-state drive. Jeff hardly saw the next two at-bats; his mind wandered. *Failure is an option, Jeff. All this, everything you've fought for all season, sliding away...* And then, a different voice, one full of warmth, sincerity, and "truth." *You have to snap out of it, Jeff. I believe in you. Will believes in you. Everyone is rooting for you.* Hartes looked around to see runners on the corners. Lake had given up back-to-back singles to Degginger and Winslow. The voice continued... *Jeff? Jeff? You have to believe, Jeff. You must—*

And then like a shot of pure adrenaline, the sound of wood colliding with rawhide alerted Hartes. He saw the ball headed up the middle. Lake tried to make the play but couldn't get his glove down quick enough. Hartes darted to his right, towards the second base bag. Cutting the ball off on the edge of the infield grass, he turned to flip it to Willis, covering. Never pulling the ball out of his glove with his hands, using his padded leather as the initiator, Hartes quickly tossed the ball to the shortstop covering second. He took the perfect pass and fired it to first.

"DOUBLE PLAY!" Marinville shouted, his excited voice split Hartes' ears as he tumbled forward, rolling in the plush, manicured grass. Hartes heard a scream of pleasurable joy, and looked up just in time to see Lake raising his fist as he animatedly hopped off the mound and sprinted to the dugout.

XI

Marinville's unbelievable voice was still in Hartes' head, followed by Lake's cheering yell, quickly turned into a disappointed hush as the Knights' field quieted. Hartes ran back to the bench, receiving pats on the back and words of praise, but never truly knowing who gave them... or understanding... because...

Because he saw *her* again. *Shae.* Standing. Clapping. Cheering. *For me?*

Of course it was for Jeff Hartes.

He ducked his head away, under the dugout roof. He simply could not take it. Not at this moment.

"Nice fuckin' play!" Gunn tapped the second baseman on top of the head and took a seat next to him.

The words trailed away in his mind... "fuckin' play"... "in' play"... "play"...

Hartes buried his head in his hands again. He saw his face in his own palms—reflecting like a mirror. Reflecting like a gleaming pond. He couldn't bear to see it. He still felt shame and disappointment. *Sure, I just made a play... but it's only postponing the failure. Failure is an option, Jeff.*

Failure was an option. *Failure is—*

The bench came to life around Hartes. Bodies jumped up and aligned the padded railing at the top of the dugout. Hartes followed suit, not sure why, but because it felt like the thing to do. He heard Thomas Perry shout, "One time, one time!"

And then the air was thin again, a long sigh released from everyone's mouths. The players, thinking that "The Vet" Brett Chambers, pinch-hitting for Lake, might had just gone yard here in the top of the eighth to break the tie, returned to the bench. The nervousness, the tightness, the feeling that time was running out was all around Hartes.

The noise returned via a burst of excitement—constant cheering by the San Diego fans following a great catch in the warning track by leftfielder Waylon Ponds. Hartes felt the overwhelming sense of victory beneath him. The stadium was moving; the entire place was alive with an incredible energy.

Hartes watched Damon Lewis return to the dugout after being struck out by Jerod Wilkes. He slammed his helmet down, bouncing it off the concrete floor. A few 'F' bombs followed. Parks ended the top half, grounding out to third.

The Demon second baseman followed the rest of the team back onto the field. He stayed away from the stands. He kept his head focused on the things around him. He didn't know what to do. He didn't know what would help more or what would hurt more. But either way, Shae needed to stay out of his current thoughts.

Javier Jimenez, who had thrown two and two-thirds of scoreless relief thus far in the series, stood on the mound, relieving Lake Williams after a masterful game five performance (7 innings pitched, 8 K's, allowing only 1 earned run). Hartes' mind wandered again. It was stuck on the beautiful girl in the stands, but his eyes focused on the batter. Hartes didn't even know the count on the hitter. He patted his right hand into his leather glove. Reaching down, Hartes scooped up a handful of the rich red infield sand and let it sift through his fingers. It was cool to the touch; the weather a rare treat in early June.

J.P. Garces, pinch-hitting for Wilkes, whose night was now complete (8 innings pitched, 8 strikeouts, and also allowing only 1 earning run), headed back to the dugout after striking out on a Jimenez cutter. Skip came out to get Javy, tapped his left arm, motioning for Darren Luthers to face the left-handed leadoff man, J.J. Frazier, who scored the Knights only run. Hartes' vision throbbed like a boxer's head going into the final round. It was a pounding drum inside his skull. Things blurred, things cleared, things warped, things just weren't always right.

Frazier singled up the middle, the ball closer to Nathan Willis than to Jeff Hartes. Willis looked scared, which momentarily masked Hartes' own feelings of confusion and disappointment. Willis looked as though he was playing in the biggest game of his life—which, he was. He looked like Jeff Hartes felt.

Timothy Greener, the second baseman, bunted the go-ahead run over one base. Hartes covered first, taking the throw from Gunn. He turned away from the stands, staring up at the lighted scoreboard. The white lights were as loud as the buzzing noise in his head. They glared at him and caused everything to distort. They are a million enlarged Christmas lights bounded by strings of mass confusion. The score was tied. There were two outs with Frazier on second, Waylon Ponds coming to bat.

Luthers hung a 2-2 curveball that Ponds drilled to rightfield. Hartes ran out just on the edge of the infield, where the beautifully plush grass met dirt. Hartes didn't have time to line up Goodwin as he had already fielded the ball on the second hop and was firing towards the plate. Jeff Hartes turned to home. The throw was slightly off-line and late... the Knights took the lead. The stadium had its volume at a crest. The crowd was absolutely bedlam.

Ramon Garrido flied out to Lewis to end the inning, but the damage had been done. The fans cheered and applauded, not one person sitting in the entire ballpark. Hartes jogged in, turning to see the score—San Diego 2, Los Angeles 1. The dugout was alive with optimism and hope. Hicks came by him and said, "Get a fucking helmet on, Hartes!"

XII

Hartes wasn't due up until fourth in the last inning. *Don't mess with the Karma, Hartes. Get up and get ready! It's all around you.* He moved to the helmet bin like a patient drugged for surgery. Everything felt so numb. He needed something to help him snap out of it. He just didn't know what. *Maybe Shae?*

"Let's go Hicks, get on base, baby!" Fetters yelled.

Hartes heard The Duke once again, somehow, someway. Marinville's voice carried through the radio waves and into his mind. Hartes looked around, just checking for the millionth time if anyone else appeared to hear what he was hearing as well, but no one had a clue. The Duke announced Jason Hicks, and then Kyle Queen did as well, and then The Duke said that Gunn was on deck, followed by Rutherford. If anyone was to get on base, that would bring up Jeff Hartes.

Jeff Hartes? Get a fucking helmet on, Hartes!

Hicks was in the box now, facing the Knights closer, Rich Treplow, a South Division all-star with eight saves on the season. Everyone on the Demons' bench is up against the rail, sporting rally caps and clenched fists. Hartes felt someone up against him on the right. He turned and saw the bat boy, Wade Smith. He looked up at Hartes, smiling with confidence. He appeared to be the only person that wasn't feeling the pressure, ignorant to the size of the situation. He appeared to be—

"Hicks is going to do it," Smith said to the Los Angeles second baseman. "He's going to tie this game right here."

I hope so, my friend.

I truly hope so —

Hartes watched the last strike go by, Hicks swinging and dropping to his knees. A seemingly valiant effort from the hero... the role model... the Demon all-star with the weight of an entire season on his shoulders. Hartes turned back to Wade Smith. But the bat boy was gone. He saw Gunn standing in the batter's box. He saw Rutherford standing in the on-deck circle. His instincts guided him off the pine; they pulled him to the helmet bin. The #9 beckoned, dirt and Pine Tar softened the edges. Hartes grabbed the head protector, standing on the dugout's steps.

Hartes watched a puddle — of Gatorade, of water, he didn't know — as it reflected the immense stadium lighting from the concrete below. *It must be cold.* It spoke to him from another world. The gills of a dying fish, breathing... searching for its final breath of cruel air. It said so much more. It understood that this situation wasn't for Hartes. *This isn't my time to shine...*

This wasn't his place. This was definitely somewhere else. This *was* someone else's time to shine. Hartes stared into space. His wandering mind and phallic eyes gleamed deep. His reserved thoughts were interrupted by screams of joy — screams of ecstasy. Hartes looked down from other worlds to see Steve Gunn rounding first base. The burly infielder returned to the bag with a one-out single. Hartes realized it was now his time to move out into the dreaded circle — mocking him with white-painted guidelines. Walking, he followed Rutherford's movements. He did the cross thing, let out a casting breath of nervous air, and then dug in.

The fans were at an unexplainable high; their noise carried through one's mind and into the realms of a front row seat near the orchestra pit. Hartes' eyes watered. An unseen, imaginary smoke glazed the lens, coating them with a cut onion's insensitivity. He swung the bat like he was supposed to. He was getting loose. Unless some unforeseen... some catastrophic mishap occurred, he would get his shot. Hartes wasn't thrilled with it. *I am thrilled with it. I am.* But the doubt fought harder. The lies, the convincing attempts, couldn't win tonight.

A hush cleared Jeff's distractions. Rutherford walked by him. "Muthafuckin'... muthafuckin'... godda—" he stopped next to Hartes, meeting eyes like locking lasers. Rutherford told him, "It's all you, nigga'."

Hartes closed his eyes. He felt his feet move towards homeplate—the internal pattern guiding as though he were blind with a recollected memory.

He saw his father sitting in the dinner chair, back to the wall of an empty room. *Failure is an option...* But he doesn't speak. Hartes put the words, the thoughts, in his mouth for him. Hartes forced the dialogue. But only in his mind. No lips moved. Hartes' father placed his hands, fist on top of fist, acting as a readied batter. He rose from the chair, still grasping the imaginary lumber. He imitated the immortal swing of Henry Aaron. He smiled. Hartes shook his head. *I just don't know if I have it in me.*

Will appeared in a window that wasn't there before. The paned glass was dirty with streaks of dusty film, cobwebs hung from the corners. Will peered through the translucent barrier and nodded. "Everyone's got *it* in them," he said. "Some just don't know where to look for it. Some just don't know how to bring it to the surface."

Hartes' mom and Eric replaced his father in the simple room. The chair was gone as well. They stood side by side, Eric one-arm hugging her and saying an eyes-closed prayer. His lips moved, soft sounds leaving his mouth, but they weren't clear. His prayer seemed to be for his brother's success. His mother squeezed Eric harder, forcing good things to happen in the future.

They were all gone. Hartes spun in circles, staring at one blank wall and then another and then another and then the fourth of the squared room. The dizziness overcame him. He sat on the floor, pulling his knees towards his chest. He shook his head, saying 'no' over and over again. He stared at the floor, the hardwood below opened up. He literally burned a hole in the floor with his eyes.

Down into the deep black, way down, out of reach and willingly out of mind, Shae's face appeared. She was laughing and tossing her gentle, brown hair from side to side. "It's in you, Jeff Anthony Hartes. I've known it from the beginning. I knew it when we were apart. I knew things would work out in the end."

What end? The question repeated itself in his head. *What end is she talking about?*

But she continued, ignoring his thoughts. Hartes tried to teleport into her own. "Search deep, you've come up big plenty of times before now. You've overcome and delivered. Block out the negative thoughts. Block out the San Diego crowd. Forget everything you've ever learned or ever practiced for... and simply trust the swing. Don't think, just—"

"STEEE-RIKE ONE!" the homeplate umpire stirred Hartes from his out-of-body visions. Hartes turned to see Cartwright laughing on the inside. *He must know, too.* The San Diego catcher, Degginger, threw the ball back to the mound where Treplow was trying to finish the game. Hartes saw Gunn leading off of first base, clapping his hands and hoping for him to do something—something to tie this damn game.

The stands were empty. *The noise, the overwhelming noise that enters my mind from every opening, from every direction, ceases to exist.* Everyone had left the field, players and all, except for Jeff Hartes, the pitcher, the catcher, and the head ump. The dugouts had evacuated. The booth was silent. The world, everything besides this tiny mound-to-home peninsula, jutting out from the outfield walls like the tip of an anchor, had disappeared. Hartes couldn't imagine why the San Diego pitcher started his wind up. Didn't he know? Didn't he realize that something was terribly wrong? But the pitch came anyway. Unprepared, Hartes watched a fast one slide by. He turned to the umpire, thinking, *this can't be happening. There's no way he's going to make the call.*

"STEEE-RIKE TWO!" A.B. bellowed. Simultaneously, the fans, the players, the coaches, the front office personnel, everyone and every last thing, returned like a crashing wave. *The noise* was back, blaring in his ears like a king's trumpet. 'Your majesty is here,' *but is he really?*

Hartes stepped out of the batter's box. *The game has gotten out of hand. They can't allow it to go on this way. This isn't how it ends, is it?*

The pitcher nodded. Cold, dead eyes stared into the mitt—trying to intimidate, trying to win this game mentally. *I gotta' swing the bat.* My arms were jello. Rubbery. Weak. The weight of the world had moved onto Hartes' shoulders and the load was impossible to bear. *There is no end... there is no end...*

The ball's coming, Jeff! Swing the fucking —

Wood clashed with rawhide. Hartes' hands stung as he had tried to get the bat head through, but was jammed. He started to run to first, his instincts guiding him down the base path. Sawed off, he tossed the bat handle aside full sprint now. He found the ball floating in the air, a magical dancing sphere orbiting towards the left-side of the plush diamond. A fielder raced from third base. A fielder raced from short.

Get through you son of a bitch!

"Get through—"

XIII

It did.

That little ball, featuring a cork center, wrapped in yarn and covered in leather, roughly nine to nine and a quarter inches in circumference, got through.

Well... enough, I suppose. It was perfectly placed on the left side, exactly between third and short, where Winslow had to field it very deep moving to his left. He then made a terrible decision, trying to throw me out at first, and the ball skipped by Garrido. Gunn moved to third, and I ended up on second base. I didn't win the game myself, no one ever does. The media may show the winning hit, over and over and over, but the guy who worked a walk, or got a broken-bat single before the winning hit, well, that guy came up just as big.

He is hardly remembered many times throughout history. Which was fine with me then, and fine with me now.

Rich Treplow intentionally walked Billy Goodwin to load the bases with two outs. And that brought up Nathan Willis, Will Coleman's replacement, and a chance to be a hero, an ironic opportunity to make all right in the baseball world from my perspective.

Nate ripped a double down the leftfield line, and the rest is history. Gunn scored, and then I followed, scoring the run that broke the tie, 3-2 in favor of Los Angeles.

Ron Fetters, hitting for the pitcher, ground out to end

the inning, setting up a game-five save opportunity for the best closer I ever played with, Salmon Seavers.

Seavers would have the chance to record three saves in our three Western League Championship victories if he could keep San Diego off the scoreboard. He did it in exciting fashion, ripping the life from the Knights' fans right before their hopeful eyes.

After allowing a leadoff walk, a clutch at-bat by Phil Kramer, San Diego catcher Charlie Degginger sacrifice bunted the runner over, and the game-tying run was now in scoring position with only one away.

Seavers never wavered as he struck out Winslow and Allen to end the game... end the series... and put a championship ring on my finger.

The final line for Los Angeles was 3 runs, 7 hits, no errors. And for San Diego, 2 runs, 7 hits, and 1 error.

The dog-pile happened just behind the pitcher's mound, with Parks and Seavers on the bottom. I celebrated like a madman, newly awakened from the final dream of dreams, the real dream, the childhood dream, the there-aren't-words-for-it feeling of being a champion.

I celebrated and celebrated. And then I celebrated with Shae, like nothing had ever happened. We embraced and lost each other's cruelness and harsh words in the eyes of love. Of course, we talked later, and we had our trials and tribulations, but as they say, the rest is history...

Chapter Twenty
An Unexpected Visitor

I

The old man sleeps.

He sleeps like a child. He sleeps like a man that wasn't recently diagnosed as terminally ill. And he sleeps without dreams. Jeff Hartes won a Western League Championship with the Demons while beating his own... *demons.* And now he's beaten the insomnia that allows only sleep to come when dire fatigue sets in. He sleeps for over half a day.

The doctor said a month or two, that was all he'd have left to live. Jeff Hartes says, *fuck that, I'll beat that, too. One way or another.*

He opens his eyes and stares up at the ceiling. His body is warm; it's the first time he's actually slept under the covers in his own bed in a long time. He kicks the bedspread off, and then the sheets. He wipes his brow, removing the moisture from his forehead. He rolls over and looks at the time — 2:47 p.m.

Time to make the call, he thinks.

Jeff removes the wireless phone from its stand and presses the number three, holding it until Leslie's name appears on the screen. He holds the phone to his right ear and listens to the music, Beethoven or Mozart or Bach, or something else composed by a classical genius. A clicking sound soon follows.

"What the hell do you want, Hartes?" Leslie's voice replaces the music.

"How did you know it was me?" Jeff asks in response.

"Goddammit, I've had caller I.D. since you played pro baseball. You know, your name pops up on my phone."

Jeff chuckles and says, "Sometimes I forget." And then sarcastically, "I'm not caught up with all this new technology like you are."

"Huh?" Leslie speaks louder into the phone. "You got to speak up. I've got the phone up against my not-so-good ear."

"Well switch sides then, dumbass."

"Fine." Jeff hears a banging sound followed by a short silence. Leslie then returns to the line, saying, "Sorry, dropped my phone."

Jeff nods on his end of the line and diverts the conversation back to the main reason for the call. "Anyway, Leslie, I just called to tell you that you have been a most wonderful, true friend, and that I'll never forget it. I'll miss you dearly. And I just wanted to wish you a heartfelt farewell."

Silence.

And then Leslie says, "Are you going on one of those space shuttle cruises to the moon?"

Jeff grins and laughs. "No Leslie, I'm afraid not."

"Then what the hell are you talking about, you old fart?"

"Nothing, Leslie. Nothing really. I just wanted you to know how much you mean to me and how good a friend you've been, just in case something happens. You know, old bastards like us can drop any minute."

"Well... shit. You're a good friend as well," Leslie says.

"Thanks. That means everything." Tears swell in Jeff Hartes' eyes, and he wraps up the courtesy call. "I guess

I'm gonna' run. That pretty much sums it up."

"Alright, Jeff. You sure everything is okay?"

"Never better. I'll see you soon enough."

"Alright. Let me know if you are seriously going on one of those space shuttle cruises... I'll go with you."

"Okay, my friend." Jeff laughs and sniffles. "Goodbye now."

"Bye bye," Leslie Paxton says, ending the call.

Jeff sets the wireless phone down on his nightstand, away from its charger. He sits with his butt on the bed, and his bare feet touching the cool floor. He stands, aching, and walks to the bathroom. He looks in the mirror, staring at the tired old man before him. His eyes are reddening against the tears he tries so hardly to hold back. Behind the mirror, in a different plane, he sees Shae's face. He smiles and thinks, *I'll see you soon, my love.*

Jeff walks back into the bedroom and makes his bed, placing all of Shae's handpicked pillows, from different parts of the globe, each symbolizing something special — even if it was just for her — in their designated resting places. He then goes to the walk-in closet, stripping away his old boxers and tee. He replaces them with a hand-sewn pair of briefs, followed by a specially-tailored pair of black suit pants, silk black socks, polished dark dress shoes; and underneath his finest sports jacket, Jeff Hartes wears a now skin-tight Los Angeles Demons' undershirt.

He heads back to his favorite recliner, stopping only once along the way to open a dresser drawer and remove a small, but heavy object. He sits in the chair with the reclining legs down. He sits in silence and thinks for a moment.

He doesn't think about what he is going to do. He doesn't second guess. Second guessing is for pansies or individuals who are unsure. One thing he is certain... he is sure. He only thinks of his friends, his family, and his wife, all of those who have passed away, and the few who remain on this Earth. He closes his eyes tightly, squeezing until his head begins to ache. He places both of his hands against his face, setting the small object in his lap. He cries into the palms of his hands, releasing a lifetime of tears and emotions and love and the pains of one's past. He drops his hands, crossing his fingers together like someone praying, but he doesn't pray. He allows his right hand to fall to his lap, and he wraps his fingers around the object's cold handle.

He raises his right hand to his face, and then without any more hesitation, he places the barrel of the small-caliber gun into his mouth. He feels his index finger shakily touching the trigger, readying the final act of his life. He takes a deep breath, tasting the metal in his mouth. And then—

A knock on his door.

Many thoughts pass through his mind. *Shae, how crazy is that? Leslie, how did he get here so fast? Who the hell is it? Just finish the job.* But he doesn't. He waits.

And another knock follows.

Jeff Hartes rises from the chair and sets the gun down on the coffee table. He turns to the door, stops, and then turns back. He then covers the revolver with old mail, newspapers, and yes, the forgotten "letter."

He walks to the door, trying to control his rapid breathing and appear somewhat normal in the peculiar situation. He pats at his face with his Demon baseball tee. *Trapped in a horrible world where everyone's ending is same... we all die.* Jeff pulls the side window's curtain back a bit and takes a peek. He sees a black man in his forties or fifties, standing on his doorstep and looking more nervous than the man inside.

Jeff unlocks the door and cracks it open. He peers through the reveal, looking at the stranger wearing a dark button-down shirt and ironed slacks.

"Mr. Hartes," he speaks. Jeff doesn't respond. He is still trying to figure out if he recognizes the man or not... which he doesn't. "Did you receive my letter?"

The word "letter" strikes a chord. Jeff raises his eyes and then blurts out, "That goddamn thing. That peckerhead little shit disturbed me in the middle of the night to give me that letter. Hold on."

He shuts the door on the unknown man, leaving him waiting on the porch. Jeff stumbles over to the coffee table, moving the old mail and newspapers again. He sees the butt of the pistol and shakes his head, ignoring that demon. He finds what he is looking for, "A-ha!" And then tears the envelope open, marked only with the name, *Jeff Hartes*.

He pulls the single sheet of paper from inside and unfolds it. He reads...

To Mr. Hartes—

On my mother's deathbed, Regina Johnson, she told me to find a man named Jeff Hartes. She told me that you played baseball with my father, and that you were the last person to speak to him... alive. I will be in Louisville this week, and I plan to stop by your home. I hope you will allow me the opportunity to speak with you. I would be delighted to take you out for some coffee or lunch, your preference?

Will Coleman's son,
William Johnson

"Well... sonofabitch," the old man says, all in one word. He puckers his lips tightly together and scratches his head. Jeff walks to the bedroom, collecting his wallet and his keys, which had been placed neatly beside each other on his nightstand.

He returns to the front door and opens it, wider this time. William Johnson remains, standing in the same spot. Jeff sticks out his hand and says, "It's very nice to meet you, Mr. Johnson."

After shaking the fellow's hand, Jeff adds, "And yes... I would be delighted to have lunch with you, Will."

"That's just great!" Will Johnson exclaims, taking Jeff by the elbow and leading him to his rented car parked along the street, for a bite to eat, for old memories — many new memories for Will's son, fresh on the old man's mind. A chance, perhaps, for Jeff Hartes to remember the good parts again.

He can only smile at the hands of fate as they drive away from his Kentucky home.

II

"What the hell are you wearing?" Leslie Paxton asks the chirpy old man, appearing on his porch later that evening in the same fancy shoes, suit pants, and sports jacket he fashioned earlier that day.

"My funeral clothes," Jeff responds with a grin, opening his unbuttoned top and revealing his Los Angeles Demons' shirt underneath.

"Looks like it," Leslie says. "And what's all this I love you and goodbye shit you were spillin' me over the phone?"

"Oh... that?" Jeff plays the role. "I told you I was going to die soon, the doctor said so. I just wanted to make my peace with a good friend."

"Well hell, I knew that. But you're not going to die today, are you?" Leslie asks, seeming more worried about what comes next in their daily adventures rather than the real answer.

"Nope."

"Then what are you doing still standing outside?" Leslie reaches behind his back with his left hand and scratches vigorously.

"Waiting for you to invite me inside."

"You stubborn old bastard, I'm trying to watch the Yankees-Red Sox game, are you coming in or not?"

"Of course," Jeff Hartes replies. They enter Leslie's home together, and the door closes, ending one more inning in Jeff's life, yet beginning another.

THE END

LAST GAME BOX   DATE — Jun 10   R H E

```
LA 000100002 - 3 10 0
SD 000001010 - 2 7 1
```

LA vis SD			4	AB	R	RBI
Lewis cf	SB,K2		1	1111		
Parks c	W2			11		
Hicks 3b	K2,2B		11	1111		
Gunn 1b	1L,🔲		1	1111	1	
Rutherford lf	HR,1K		1	1111	1	1
Hartes 2b	K2		1	1111	1	
Goodwin rf	W2		⊘	⊘11	⊘	
Willis,N. ss	2B		1	1111		11
L.Williams p	K			11		
Chambers ph / Feters ph				1/1		
Williams p			‖‖‖11	‖‖‖111	1	1
Jimenez rp			1/3	1		
Luthers rp			1/3 1m	1K	1 ER	w
Frazier cf	1L,W,SB		1	111	11	
Greener 2b	1L2,Sac		1	111		1
Ponds lf	2B,K		11	1111		1
Garrido 1b	K2			1111		
Kramer 3b	W		1	111		
Degginger c	1K,Sac		1	⊘⊘⊘111		
Winslow ss	1L		1	1111		
Allen rf	K2			1111		
Willces p				11		
Garces ph	K			1		
Wilkes p			‖‖‖111	‖‖‖111	1	111
Treelow rp	Loss		1	11	11	1

🖎 Martin injured game four

LA Tims						
~~Brad~~ rp	Win		1/3			
Seavers rp	Save		1	11	·	1

May 1, 1999   GAMES

S.D. ^{s} 2 @ Wash. ^{s} 1 — W- Wilkes (4-0)
L- Johnstone (0-1)
HR- Allen (1).

Ariz. ^{s} 7 @ C.City ^{s} 2 — W- Ridel (3-0)
L- Gibbs (2-2)
HR- Kimmons ^{2} (5), Kato (2).

Cal ^{4} 4 @ Tuc. ^{4} 3 — W- Westen (1-1)
L- D. Gonzalez (0-1) S- Markel (4)
HR- Conrad (8), Greggs (3).

L.A. ^{4} 2 @ Mont. ^{4} 4 — W- Herrmann (3-1)
L- Perry (2-1) S- York (5)
HR- Rogers (5), Rutherford (3).

May 2

Cal ^{s} 5 @ Tuc. ^{s} 0 — W- Mackenzie (4-1)
L- S. Benes (3-2)
HR- Camp (2), Gardner (2)

L.A ^{s} 10 @ Mont. ^{s} 4 — W- Williams (3-2)
L- MacNelly (1-3)
HR- Gunn ^{2} (6), Brown (3).

May 3

Cal ^{2} 3 @ C.City ^{2} 5 — W- A. Smith (3-0)
L- Gonzalez, J. (1-4) S- Wilson (2) x
HR- Craig (5), Conrad (9).

L.A ^{2} 6 @ Wash ^{2} 5 — W- Jimenez (2-0)
L- Johnstone (0-2)   x
HR- Higgins (2), Hartes (2), Coleman (2).

@ Tuc. ^{2} 5 @ Ariz ^{2} 2 — W- Wilton (1-3) S- Valentin
L- Morlas (1-4)   (3) x
HR- Greggs (4), Maldonado (3),

S.D. ^{2} 5 @ Mont ^{2} 11 — W- Ryan (3-1)
L- Anderson (3-1)   x
HR- Frerck (2). Lucas (4).

M/S

Demon's Roster

		Name		#		Race	B-T
	SP	Lake Williams "Lefty"	CF	28		Bleck	L-L
M	SP	Jay O'Dell		28		White	R-R
M	SP	Thomas Perry		30		White	R-R
	SP	Michael Tims "21"		19 R		Black	L-R
M	RP	Fred "Funk" Sanders		38		White	L-R
	RP	Darren Luthers		25		White	
	RP	Javier Jimenez	o	22 R		Dom.Rep.	R-R
	Cl	Salmon Seavers	o	27		Black	L-L
M o	1B	Steve Gunn "Big Daddy"		30		White	R-L
	2B	Jeff Hartes	o	21 R		White	R-R
	3B	Jason Hicks	o	25		White	R-R
	SS	Will Coleman	o	26		Black	R-R
	CF	Damon Lewis	o	22		Black	
	LF	Eumic Rutherford	o	23		Black	R-R
	RF	Billy Goodwin	p	27		White	S-L
M	OF	Brett Chambers "Vet"		34		White	R-R
M	C	Ron Fetters	o	29		White	L-R
	C	Bobby Parks	o	20 R		White	R-R
	2B	Simon Luthers	o	23		White	R-R
	Clubby	Wade Smith		Clubby 14		White	

~~IF Nathan Willis o 22 W R-R~~
~~IF Charles _____ 21 R W R-R~~

"Western League"
Standings

NORTH	W	L
Wash.	卌 III	卌 卌 IIII
Carson City	卌 卌 IIII	卌 IIII
Montana	卌 卌 III	卌 卌 I
Cal	卌 卌 I	卌 卌 III

SOUTH	W	L
S.D.	卌 卌 卌	卌 IIII
Tucson	卌 II	卌 卌 卌 II
Arizona	卌 卌 II	卌 卌 II
L.A.	卌 卌 III	卌 III